First
RESPONSE
to love

JESSICA POWELL

For everyone still searching,
May you stumble upon love in the most unexpected way or places
and recognize it when it finds you

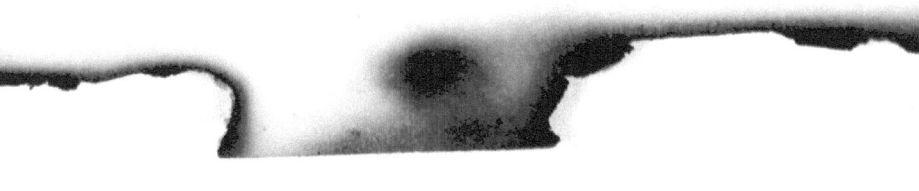

Playlist

Skyscraper – **Demi Lovato**

Rise Up – **Andra Day**

Versace on the Floor – **Bruno Mars**

Boy With Luv – **BTS ft. Halsey**

Corazón Sin Cara – **Prince Royce**

Beautiful Soul – **Jesse McCartney**

PILLOWTALK – **ZAYN**

a thousand years – **Christina Perri**

爱, 存在 (Love, exists) – 魏奇奇 **(Wèi QíQí)**

pov – **Ariana Grande**

Danza Kuduro – **Don Omar ft. Lucenzo**

Hold On – **Wilson Phillips**

I Love You Boy – **Suzy**

Promise – **Ciara**

Falling in Love – 林檀雨 **(Lín Tán Yǔ)**

Bonus Song
I'm Broke – **Nobody Sausage**

CHAPTER ONE

Vulcan

I'm hot and sweaty in all this gear, despite the fact that the "fire" is only burning fake wood. I'm right in the middle of the chaos of the training drill, my heart pounding with the intensity of it all. I search the smoky room for the pretend victims who need saving. I know this is practice, but we always have to work as if it's real.

"Jackson, keep that area secure! Stop it from spreading," I say firmly. I turn to watch my team fall into step like a well-oiled machine.

Ramirez holds on to the hose, eyes locked on her target as she feigns putting out a fire. "Keep it steady." I give a nod as she adjusts her stance. I didn't think Ramirez was going to cut it the first time I saw her. She was too dolled up on her first day—full face of makeup and long nails too, but it's been five years, and she is still one of the best damn firefighters in my fire station.

I scan the room, my sights landing on another firefighter. "Nice work, Thompson!"

Then there's Chen, climbing up the ladder with ease despite all his gear. As our tech expert, he's accustomed to heights and challenging situations. His hands move fast over the controls. Even though my station is short-staffed, they are fucking great at what they do.

"Listen up!" I say, and everyone stops what they're doing and turns to me. "You're all doing great, but remember, it's not just speed; it's doing it right. Lives are on the line. We train hard so we can handle anything. Stay sharp, stay safe, and let's make this city proud!" It's a saying my father instilled in me, so it's only right that I share it with my team.

A chorus of agreement follows.

Twenty minutes later, the exercise ends, the pretend flames are gone, and alarms are quiet. Each successful drill is a promise that we'll be ready when real danger hits. Their sweaty faces turn to me, waiting for instructions.

"Great job, everyone. Debrief in twenty," I announce as they disperse, but I catch their appreciative glances. Station 112 thrives off constructive feedback as much as they do positive reinforcement. Another reason why I believe ours is the best station in the city. Even though it needs a little TLC.

Our red bricks aren't as shiny as they used to be, the paint is peeling, and every day I do an assessment of what needs fixing, making mental notes of what we can handle ourselves and what needs professional help. Besides the bricks, the ceilings are starting to get water damage from the leaky roof, the lockers are from the '80s, and the kitchen has appliances older than most of the rookies. But what this place lacks in modern aesthetics, it makes up for in heart.

I head to my office, pushing open the door with my shoulder. The hinges squeak—another thing to add to my repair list. My desk is cluttered with paperwork, budget reports that never seem to have enough zeros to fix everything we need, and a framed photo of my father in his chief's uniform from twenty years ago. His stern face stares back at me, a constant reminder of the legacy I'm trying to uphold.

A knock at the door jolts me from my thoughts. "Cap, you in there?"

I recognize Harry's voice. He's always been perceptive and able to read me like an open book. A blessing and curse, if you ask me. The fucker struggles to take the temperature of a room at times.

"Yeah, come in," I say.

Harry enters, his blue eyes scanning my office. Probably looking for the jar of peppermints. I haven't had time to refill them. "Quite the drill today, huh? You really put us through the wringer." He eyes me like he has more to say before settling on, "Anything you wanna talk about?"

He's always sniffing for information. If becoming a firefighter hadn't worked out for him, he would have done great as a journalist. "Someone's gotta keep you on your toes, Harry. Can't have you getting complacent on me." I'm deliberately ignoring his question and he knows it.

"Me? Complacent? Never." He grins. "But seriously... you doing okay, Vulcan? You seem a little... *off*."

I wave away his concern. "Just tired. Nothing a strong cup of coffee can't fix."

Harry raises an eyebrow, unconvinced. "If you say so. But you know I'm here if you need to talk, right? We're more than just coworkers. We're brothers from another mother."

"I know, man. And I appreciate it. I just have a lot on my mind. We're understaffed and I need to hire some new recruits and this place is—never mind. I'm rambling." I scrape a hand along my jaw. "I got this handled."

In all honesty, lately, it's a little more than work stress. This station is my life, and I'm content for the most part, but when I get home, I want more. I need more. The problem is time, and that's running in short supply.

He nods. "I've heard that the new candidates are more promising than last year's. Don't stress yourself over something out of your control, Vul."

He's right; I can't control what the new candidates are like, but I can manage the ones under my watch. And that means shaping them into the best damn firefighters in NYC.

My drive home is plagued with the memory of Harry's words earlier. It's becoming harder to ignore the gnawing gaps in my social life. As I pull up to my building and take the elevator to my empty penthouse, I think about how my life compares to that of my younger coworkers. Most of the crew have partners waiting up for them after a tough day on the job; if anything, I'm the outlier. Perpetually single and constantly subjected to blind-date fixups.

Don't get me wrong, I'm devoted to my career, and I know it's a calling that demands sacrifice. But sometimes I wonder if there's more out there for me. More connection, more meaning. Maybe even love. Not that I have time for romance in my position. I'm the captain—lives depend on my single-minded focus. A relationship could be a reckless distraction.

Still, as I fall onto my cold, rumpled sheets alone, *again*, I can't deny the longing that wells up within me. The part of me that craves the tender understanding of a partner, of someone who sees beyond the badge to the flesh-and-blood man beneath. Someone whose soft sigh in the darkness tells me I'm not alone.

But even as I try to resign myself to solitude, a wry voice in my head pipes up. *Keep telling yourself that, Vulcan. Maybe one day you'll actually believe it.*

My phone rings out in time to save me from my spiral, and I lean over to grab it from the nightstand, squinting at the too-bright screen. It's Harry. Fucking hell, I can never get a moment of peace. He's like the annoying little brother I'm happy I never had growing up. My baby sister, Valkyrie, is enough. Though with how busy she's been with her own career, we don't see each other as much—which explains how Harry has taken her place, come to think of it.

"I think I know why you seem a bit off. When was the last time you got laid?" he asks by way of greeting, and I roll my eyes.

"Jesus," I grumble into the phone, my free hand massaging the bridge of my nose. "You know damn well my sex life is none of your business."

"Oh, come on, Vulcan. I'm just looking out for you. All work and no horizontal cardio makes Vulcan a dull boy. You're one scowl away from turning into that statue at the station entrance. I'm trying to keep you young here."

I sink back against the headboard. "Thanks for the concern, Dr. Phil, but I'm perfectly fine."

"Sure you are. That's why you were moping around the station after the briefing, is it?"

"I'm not moping," I protest, but even I can hear the lack of conviction in my voice. "Everyone has off days."

"Right. And I'm Keanu Reeves." Harry's eye roll is practically audible through the phone. "Listen, all I'm saying is maybe it's time to dust off the dating skills. I know people. Non-terrible people who might tolerate your charming personality. Just to get your equipment serviced, if nothing else."

I snort. "Because between fourteen-hour shifts and budget reports, I've got so much time to wine and dine strangers."

"Hey, you never know. Maybe your dream girl will walk out of a burning building and sweep you off your feet."

"You've been watching too many Hallmark movies, my friend. And if she *did* walk out a burning building unscathed, I would be more concerned if she was human rather than my dream woman." I feel a smile tugging at the corners of my mouth.

"Nah, I just have a sixth sense for these things. Mark my words, Vulcan. Your luck's about to change. I can feel it in my bones. Your love drought is about to get a flash flood warning. Your future Mrs. or Ms. Right-For-Now is closer than you think."

"Sometimes I think you missed your calling as a fortune teller," I shoot back, trying to keep it light. "I'm touched you're so emotionally invested in my love life. But you don't need to be worried about it."

He lets out a dramatic sigh. "Someone has to be. You act like abstinence is a badge of honor. I'm just saying you might want to take a break from celibacy before it qualifies as a lifestyle."

This fucker is relentless.

I give Harry a hard time about his gossiping, but it's a goddamn relief to let him in on the parts of my life I can't always say out loud. He's the only one at the station who knows me well enough to call me out. He's also the only one who'd get away with it.

"I think you should focus on your own love life. Riley's is running out of women you haven't slept with," I tease. The last time we got beers there, he was propositioned *twice* before finally leaving with one of the bartenders.

"I resent that. I've slept with maybe… forty percent of the women there. Tops."

"That's still disturbing," I say, shaking my head. "You're like a sexual pandemic."

"I prefer the term *romantic enthusiast*. But seriously, think about it. The next woman who looks your way, throw caution to the wind and talk to her. See where it goes."

"Whatever you say, Casanova. Now, get some sleep. We've got an early shift tomorrow."

"Aye aye, Captain." He chuckles. "Night, Vul."

"Night, Harry." I hang up, tossing the phone back on the nightstand.

As much as I hate to admit it, he has a point. Maybe I need to start putting myself out there. It's been a long time since I was in a relationship. Not that I'm jumping ahead to thoughts of anything serious—that's just wishful thinking. Few people understand the demands of my job or the ghosts that haunt me from losses I couldn't prevent.

Yeah, nope. Maybe it's better not to hope for the impossible. Far easier to keep things simple.

CHAPTER TWO

Karina

My pulse quickens as the sirens grow closer and louder, not with fear but with readiness. The double doors fly open with a crash, and paramedics rush in with an air of absolute urgency, wheeling in a man whose life is precariously balanced on the edge.

"Multiple contusions, suspected internal bleeding," one of the medics reports briskly as I step forward to meet the incoming gurney.

"Let's move, people!" I command as the team of nurses gathers around the stretcher. Each member is aware of their role, yet all eyes turn to me for direction.

"Let's get him intubated, stat. We need a full panel…" My orders flow like rapid fire as I take in the man's ashen complexion, the erratic, labored rise and fall of his chest—an undeniable cry for immediate intervention. The patient's skin is clammy beneath my gloved fingers as I examine the extent of his injuries. His face is a roadmap of lacerations, and his blood-matted dark hair sparks memories of my father's accident years ago. I blink and push them away. I can't afford to go there right now, not when this stranger's life depends on my focus.

"Blood pressure's eighty over fifty, dropping!" a nurse shouts.

"Start him on norepinephrine. Keep those numbers up," I instruct without missing a beat, my hands steady as I slide a laryngoscope into the patient's mouth, exposing his vocal cords. "Hang in there," I murmur, the words as much a mantra for myself as for the unconscious man before me.

"Karina, we need you to make the call on surgery," another voice interjects, heavy with the gravity of the situation.

I nod, my mind already racing through protocols and possibilities. "Push another unit of O-neg and prep for emergency surgery. I need an ultrasound to confirm internal bleeding."

This is the paradox of emergency medicine, the exhilarating rush of saving lives contrasted with the crushing weight of knowing sometimes it's not enough. I've lost patients before, and it's not a good feeling. Their faces haunt my dreams on the nights I manage to sleep at all.

The ultrasound confirms what I suspected: his abdomen is filling with blood, fast. The spleen is likely ruptured, maybe the liver too.

"Call upstairs. Tell them we're coming with a priority trauma. Have an OR ready."

We're rushing him toward the elevator when my phone vibrates in my pocket. I know without looking it's my mother. Third time today. She needs money again; it's always money.

"Doctor Reyes? Are you coming?" The elevator doors are open, waiting. I silence my phone and step inside, watching the numbers climb as we ascend to surgery.

"Stay with us," I whisper to the patient as his vitals continue to fluctuate. I don't know if he can hear me, but I say it anyway.

The surgical team awaits us, gowned and ready. As I transfer care, giving them the information they need, I feel that familiar tug of reluctance. Letting go is always the hardest part—relinquishing control, trusting others to finish what I started.

"Good work, Dr. Reyes," the chief surgeon says, but I barely hear the compliment. My thoughts are already splintering between the patient I'm leaving behind, the inevitable next emergency downstairs, and the unanswered calls from my mother that will end in yet another argument. "Go get some rest," he adds, and little does he know rest is a stranger I seldom entertain.

I take one last look at the patient. "Will do," I lie smoothly, already thinking of the patient charts in need of review. I head to the break room for some quiet before diving back into the madness I call life.

My back finds solace against the cool wall as I slide down, pulling my knees up. My breath slows, giving me a moment of peace. But then the break room door swings open and Cassie strides in, her red curls bouncing with each determined step. She spots me on the floor. "Rough one, huh?" She sits down beside me, brushing her shoulder against mine. "Wanna talk about it?"

I shake my head, a wry smile forming on my lips. "You know me, Cass. I'd rather stitch myself up than spill my guts."

"Ain't that the truth. But hey, I'm here if you change your mind. Lord knows you've been my sounding board more times than I can count."

"Thanks. I just need a minute, you know? To process. To breathe."

Cassie nods. "Take all the time you need, girl. I'll hold down the fort. Well, as much as a nurse can." She pushes herself up, dusting off her scrubs. "But don't think you're off the hook. Drinks tonight. *Non-negotiable.*"

"Yes, ma'am." I chuckle.

With a final salute, Cassie disappears, leaving me alone with my thoughts once more. I close my eyes, letting my head fall back against the wall. In the stillness, I can almost hear the whispers of the lives I've touched; the ones I've saved and those I've lost. Each one is a reminder of the weight I carry. The responsibility. The privilege. But it's a weight I bear willingly because this is my calling. My purpose. I'll keep fighting. Keep pushing. Keep reaching for the light.

Because, in the end, that's all we can do. We rise, time and again, no matter the odds.

We enter the bar, and Cassie guides us to two empty stools, waving to the bartender as we sit. "Two Long Islands, and make them strong," she calls out. The bartender nods. Cassie turns to me, eyebrows raised. "It's busy tonight."

"It sure is. You would think it's a Saturday, not Thursday." I look around at all the people packed inside Riley's. I didn't see a sign about half-price drinks. So I'll assume everyone had a rough day, like me.

"All right, spill. What's going on in that head of yours? You've been all over the place lately."

A glass appears before me and I wrap my fingers around it, taking a slow sip to gather my thoughts. I don't like to talk about my problems because no one can help. And at the end of the day, it's still *my* problem. But knowing Cassie, she isn't going to let up. "It's my mom," I finally say. "Her calls are becoming increasingly demanding."

She frowns, propping her elbow on the sticky bar top. "What did Hurricane Gabby want this time?" Cassie has always seen my mother for who she truly is: manipulative, demanding, larger-than-life.

"The usual," I reply wryly. "Money for the twins' college fund that she refuses to contribute to. Guilt trips about how I don't visit enough. As if *visit* doesn't equal dishing out more money than I have." I shake my head, anger and hurt churning in my gut. "She doesn't care about me. I'm just a resource to be tapped."

At times, I wonder how I ended up with her as a mother. We couldn't be more different. The amount of love and care she has for the twins is noticeable from a mile away. When I reflect on my childhood, I don't think she ever showed me that type of motherly affection.

Correction, there were moments of motherly love... until the twins were born. For eight years, I was an only child. And my mother doted on me, as if I were the apple of her eye. Then the boys came, and her source of love for me diminished. Nothing I did was ever good enough. I'm unsure I would have coped without my father's love to make up for it.

Cassie reaches out and squeezes my hand. "Hey, look at me," she says gently. "You're so much more than that. You're talented, caring, one hell of a doctor, and the best bestie anyone can ever have." She pauses, holding my gaze. "Don't let your mother's words or actions tear you down. You're amazing, Rina."

I squeeze her hand back, offering a small smile. She always knows exactly what to say. "Thank you. I don't know what I would do without you."

She grins. "Crash and burn, obviously." She takes a sip of her drink and glances around. "This is super random, but have you ever noticed how many firefighter photos they've got in this place?"

I angle away from the bar and follow her gaze. It doesn't take me long to understand her curiosity. The walls are lined with them, each frame capturing vivid moments of bravery and teamwork. There's an entire section dedicated to candid shots of fire crews in action, with some black-and-white images of fire engines that give the place a historic and almost sacred feel.

It has character, I'll give it that.

With its dim lighting casting a warm glow over the worn-out booths, Riley's is what we New Yorkers call a hidden gem. A place that never changes, regardless of gentrification or trends. The leather booths are torn and patched up with duct tape, adding charm more than diminishing it. The floors are scuffed and usually filthy, and the DJ booth hasn't worked in years, but looking around, none of the regulars care. If anything, the throwback '90s to early-2000s music playing from the bartender's laptop is a hit with this weekday crowd.

"Yeah, these are stations 112 and 118. Also…" I point to one of the photos with a firefighter and Mr. Riley. "That's Thomas Montgomery, station 112's old captain. Saved this place from burning down," I tell her.

"How do you know all this?" Cassie's eyebrows come together.

I shrug and take a sip of my cocktail. "A few months ago, one of their firefighters tried to flirt with me." I pause to chuckle at the *And I'm just hearing about this now?* look she's giving me. "The way he was talking about it, you would have thought *he* saved the building." I grab a handful of nuts from the bowl on the bar, avoiding her curious gaze. "Anyway, moving on, how have you been? Anything new? Love life? I feel like we haven't spoken in weeks."

Between picking up shifts and helping at nearby care centers on my days off, I barely have time to impress a man, much less let a man impress me. My mother's constant demands and my profession as an emergency medicine doctor would likely be a deal breaker for any man, with the former being more of a concern than the latter.

Since my love life is nonexistent, I like to live vicariously through Cassie. If her love life were televised, it would be the number one dating show.

She rolls her eyes playfully. "Because we haven't really. Those doubles are *killing* me. I'm just an RN, and I'm ready to crash out. I don't know how you do it. But you do it well!" She winks at me. "As for my love life, there's nothing serious on the horizon. You know me, miss *fuck 'em and leave 'em.*"

"Well, miss fuck 'em and leave 'em, you're going to have to settle down soon. Maybe you should let one of those firefighters take you out sometime. They seem to have a thing for medical professionals."

"Ha! I don't think I could handle the constant worry. Dating a firefighter? No thanks." Cassie pauses, and a thoughtful look blooms on her face. "Although I must admit, there's something about a man in uniform. Just imagine all the role-playing in the bedroom. Like, *come here and take out my hose.*"

"Cass, oh my god." I toss my head back, laughing.

"Seriously! And they are all so strong. Imagine them picking you up and fucking you against the wall. Ugh, the sex probably goes crazy with firefighters. Maybe I *should* give one a go." She sighs, looking dreamily across the bar.

I follow her gaze, spotting a group of men by the pool tables. One person in particular catches my eye. Captain Montgomery—the living, breathing one, not to be confused with the hero in the framed photo. He's not in uniform, but he still manages to stand out. Tall, dark, and handsome, he's the classic trifecta. I feel a flutter in my stomach as I watch him, but I quickly push it aside. A man like him would never be interested in someone like me.

I've seen the women who fight for his attention. Older blondes and brunettes who appear to have their lives together. Me, not so much. For starters my hair is black, and my life is truly a shitshow that I sprinkle glitter on to sell the lie that I've got it together. The only time I feel some semblance of normalcy is when I'm sleeping, because at that point, it's out of my hands.

"Earth to Karina!" Cassie's voice snaps me back to reality. "You were totally checking out the Cap, weren't you?"

I feel my cheeks heat. "What? No! I was just... admiring the decor."

Cassie snorts. "Sure you were." She leans closer, lowering her voice. "I heard he's single, you know. Has been single, for a while now. That's what some of the nurses have been saying. And rumor has it, he's great in bed. A real *pleaser,* if you know what I mean."

"Then I definitely don't want to talk to him." I'd rather not get involved with someone who's done the rounds at my hospital, so to speak. "If he's been with the nurses—"

"It's just a rumor. Who knows if it's true," she adds. "Besides, no one even knows his first name, so that's a sure sign the rumors are just that, rumors. I refuse to fuck a man and call him by his title."

"I'm not interested. I've got enough on my plate. The last thing I need is a complicated relationship. And look at him, there's obviously a massive age gap. Men his age probably want something serious or at least someone with their shit together. I'm a far fucking cry from the latter."

"Who said anything about a relationship? Sometimes, a girl needs a little fun." Cassie wiggles her eyebrows suggestively. "Besides, he's the walking definition of a silver fox. The man is massive, and the dick must be too."

I groan, my cheeks on fire now. "Really, Cass?"

"Come on. The dick is huge. *It has to be.* How about you fuck him and let me know."

"Can you imagine the gossip at the nurses' station if I were to hook up with him?" I sigh, my gaze drifting back to where he stands, his broad shoulders and chiseled features drawing me in like a moth to a flame. "I don't have time for casual sex anyway. I barely have time to *breathe.*"

Cassie leans back in her chair, studying me with a knowing look. "You know what I think? I think you're scared. Afraid of letting yourself feel something real, something that might actually bring you happiness for once. Even if it's for an hour or so and might be the best orgasm you will ever receive in your entire life."

Her words hit a little too close to home, and I feel my defenses rising. "I'm not scared. I'm practical. Getting involved with someone like him would only complicate my life further. And let's not forget the age difference, he's probably looking—"

"You're thinking too much into this." Cassie's voice softens. "Come on, Rina, what do you have to lose? Oh, I know."

"What?"

"Your voice, from screaming his name."

"You're ridiculous. But..." I bite down on my lip. "God, I don't know. I don't think I have the mental capacity to go through heartache again. Even if it's casual, like you're suggesting."

"But isn't that what life's all about? Taking risks, embracing the unknown? You never know what might happen if you just let yourself go for it. Also, not everyone you meet and get to know more intimately will take advantage of you." Her hand tightens around the glass.

"You're right. I'll take a risk, just not with him."

Cassie grins, raising her Long Island in a toast. "Here's to taking risks!"

I laugh, clinking my glass against hers. "Cheers to that."

"Oh wait."

"What now?" I eye her suspiciously.

"Have you heard back from that lady... about the date?"

I shake my head. "They probably went with someone else, or it could have been a scam. Because who the hell is *paying* for someone to date them in this economy?"

A month or two ago, Cassie told me she had heard from a friend about someone willing to pay a substantial amount to find a date. The details were vague, but I imagine it was some sort of upscale escort service for professionals—though there was never any mention of solicitation, which was the only reason I entertained the idea. I'm still stuck on why someone would be so desperate, but at the time, I jokingly told her to pass my information along. I never thought she would do it until I got a call from a lawyer. We spoke for almost two hours, and she asked me more questions than I've ever been asked on an SAT. After that, I didn't hear from her again. Maybe my answers weren't up to scratch for what her mysterious client was looking for.

It would have been an easy way to make some money, but I wasn't desperate enough to follow up. I bet the woman who was picked never has to work again, even though the amount was never disclosed. If the client retained a lawyer to do his bidding, he has to be loaded, right?

"True. But damn, that could have been some good money." Cass nods slowly.

"Yeah, and then my body would be floating in the Hudson River," I say, only half joking.

As we carry on goofing around, I find my gaze drawing back to the captain. There's something about him that intrigues me despite my better judgment. A part of me can't help wondering what it would be like to lose myself in him for just one night.

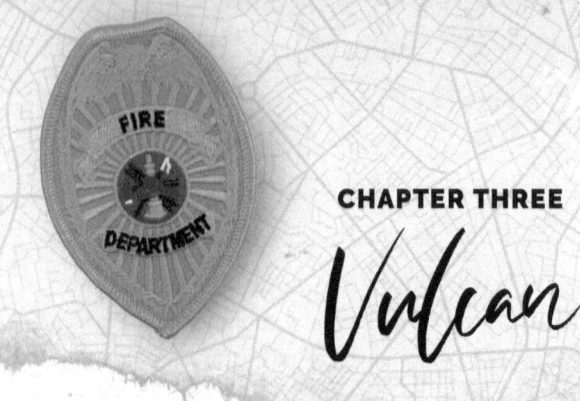

CHAPTER THREE

Vulcan

The moment the door swings open, the pulse of the bar hits me like a wave. I breathe it in, that scent of aged whiskey and lowered inhibitions, and for just a second, the weight on my shoulders eases.

"Looks like it's buzzing," Harry says, his eyes scanning the room as if he's casing the place. Or, more likely, he's looking for someone he wants to take home tonight. "Pretty women everywhere, too." Right, the latter. It's *always* the latter with Harry.

We sidestep a couple locked in a dance that's more about passion than rhythm, heading to our usual spot at the end of the bar. A few others are already sipping beers and letting loose.

"Two scotches, neat," Harry orders before I even have a chance to signal the bartender. He knows me well—knows that after a day shadowed by smoke and sirens, I want the fire in my glass instead of at my back. "Make it the good stuff, Danny!"

Not a minute later, our drinks arrive, the amber liquid promising a burn strong enough to chase away my worries for a while. "Here's to tonight, Vulcan," Harry says, raising his glass.

"Tonight," I repeat. My eyes linger on the photos peppering the walls, a silent tribute to those who have served before us. Their faces, including my father's stern one, represent legacies etched in black and white.

"Hey," Harry probes, "remember this one?" He nods toward a

picture where a much younger Thomas Montgomery stands proudly beside a fire engine, the same one I'd polish until my fingers ached.

"Hard to forget," I say. His image, with those discerning eyes, serves as a constant reminder of the man whose shoes I'm still trying to fill. And lately I've been having a hard time. I'm three firefighters short since last month, and we're feeling it on every call.

Harry raises his glass, the ice clinking over the din of the crowd. "To Thomas Montgomery," he begins. "A man who not only fought flames but who raised the best damn fire captain this city has ever seen."

I chuckle but lift my glass. "To my father," I say. The scotch burns a trail down, igniting memories and reminding me of the honor and burden that comes with the Montgomery name. People assume I have everything together or *should* have everything together.

"May we never forget the fires he put out or the ones he started in you," Harry adds, bringing a half smile to my lips.

"Thanks, man." I swirl the remnants of my drink before knocking back a generous gulp.

"Remember that summer when the whole West End lit up?" I start, the scotch working fast to loosen an old valve. "Dad was first on the scene, and he didn't even have his gear on right. He charged in like some fire-wielding titan."

Harry leans back, a grin lifting the corners of his mouth as he nods for me to go on. He's heard the story but listens anyway, because that's what you do when it counts.

"Everyone made it out because of him," I continue, feeling that familiar swell of pride. "He used to say *'We're not just saving buildings; we're guarding hearts and protecting dreams.'*" I didn't get it then. I thought it was just one of his cheesy lines. But man, was he right.

I pause, tilting my head back to scan the room again. My gaze catches a young woman with long, wavy black hair, and all the air feels like it's been sucked out of the bar. She meets my gaze, her dark eyes warm yet curious. She holds it for a beat, a hint of a smile playing on her lips as she turns back to her friend.

"Well, *hello there*," Harry says, following my eyeline. "Wanna go over there?"

"Just admiring the view."

"I'm sure she's admiring it too. I did tell you your dream woman was coming."

"She looks young. My 'dream woman,' as you put it, is more likely looking for a good time than a long time." Not that there's anything wrong with that, which is what I'm about to add when the woman glances my way once more, tucking a lock of hair behind her ear. I hold her gaze and lift my glass in greeting.

"What do you say we find out her name?" Harry suggests, clapping me on the back. "*She* obviously doesn't think age is a problem. And hey, if she wants to have a roll around in the sheets, who's to judge. Sex is great when it's done right. Now come on."

I hesitate, but the look on his face tells me he won't take no for an answer. "All right, *one* drink," I concede, getting up from my seat. He grins triumphantly, and we make our way across the bar as though answering a siren's call.

As we approach, I can't help but admire the way the red dress hugs her curves, and it complements her warm chestnut complexion. She's a vision, no doubt. But there's something else there, a depth that I see reflected back at me every time I look in a mirror. Her eyes have seen a lot of shit.

"Hello there," my friend says smoothly, flashing his trademark grin. "I'm Harry, and this tall drink of water here is Vulcan. Mind if we join you?" Leave it to him to be a fucking idiot—a *tall drink of water*?

Shithead.

She looks up at us, her gaze lingering on me for a second before turning to Harry. She doesn't say anything, and I wonder if I read the signals wrong.

The woman next to her leans in to speak over the noise. "I suppose we could use some company. I'm Cassie, and this is my best friend, Karina."

Karina smiles shyly. "It's nice to meet you both," she says, then glances at me, curiosity shining in her eyes. "Vulcan? That's an unusual name."

"Yeah, it's kind of a family tradition. My Dad was really into mythology." I rub the back of my neck, suddenly feeling self-conscious.

"Well, I like it. Suits you." Her voice does something to my chest that makes me feel like I'm twenty again instead of pushing forty. I slide onto the stool next to her, and before I know it, we've got fresh drinks in hand and are talking like old friends.

"So, *Karina*, what keeps you busy when you're not at the city's best bar?" I ask.

"I patch people up at St. Mary's," she says, running a delicate finger around the rim of her class. "Just survived back-to-back shifts. Cassie decided I needed tequila more than sleep."

Speaking of her friend, looks like she and Harry have already moved to the pool table, leaving us in an intimate bubble despite Riley's growing crowd. I cross an ankle over my knee and shift on my stool, turning to give her my full attention.

"A doctor," I say, sipping my whiskey. "So we're both in the business of saving lives."

"I try." She pauses. "I'd ask what you do, but…" Her smile changes her whole face. "I already know." She isn't slurring her words, but I can tell she has had a few drinks; she has that bright-eyed glow about her.

I raise an eyebrow. "Been keeping tabs on me?"

"Hard to miss a six-foot-something firefighter when he barrels through the ER."

"Six four and fire *captain*," I correct with a wink.

"Oh, excuse me. Fire captain." She bows of her head in mock reverence, but I manage to catch her playful smile.

"Gotta make sure you've got all the facts, you know?" I say, leaning in slightly.

She laughs. "So, you're one of those guys who likes his title."

"Only when I'm trying to impress beautiful doctors," I admit, surprising myself with my forwardness. Maybe it's the scotch, or maybe it's just her.

"You know, I have to admit"—I scratch at the stubble on my jaw, wondering how to word this—"I didn't think you would be interested in me." *Direct it is.*

She tilts her head, curiosity flashing across her face like she's working out a puzzle. "Why wouldn't I be? I mean…" Her face flushes and she pauses, the words tripping over themselves. "I'm not saying I am. Wait—that came out wrong." She cringes a little, and it could be the most charming thing I've ever seen. "I think you're handsome, so, of course I would be attracted to you. But are you meaning like romantically?"

I chuckle, her response catching me off guard and pulling me in even more. I've been around enough women to know when one's being genuine, and Karina is as real as they come. Most women I meet either throw themselves at the uniform or keep their distance entirely, unsure of the man behind the job. Karina seems caught somewhere in between, and it's refreshing.

"Let's just say I'm interested in getting to know you," I reply, holding her gaze and hoping I'm not coming off too strong. "Whatever that might lead to."

She shifts toward the bar, knocking back another shot of tequila. Her eyes drift toward the billiards table, lingering there for a moment on her friend. She's wearing a look I've seen before, and I know I've spooked her.

"I didn't mean to make you feel uncomfortable." I press away slightly, deciding to break the awkward silence. "If you want to go back to your friend, I understand."

She glances at me. "No, it's not that." She clears her throat. "I'm just not very good at this. The whole flirting thing."

"And here I thought doctors were good at everything," I tease gently.

"God, no. I can suture a wound blindfolded, but put me in a social situation with an attractive man and I turn into a complete disaster."

The music changes to something slower, its pulsing beat syncing with the way my blood is rushing through my veins. And just like that, I want to know everything about her. What keeps her going during those grueling shifts in the pit, what makes her laugh when she's not saving lives. Hell, I want to know her middle name.

"So, Karina," I say, "when you get home after a double at St. Mary's, what's the first thing you do?" I want to see where she goes in her mind, if it's the same place I go after a bad call: the shower, the silence, the need for something—anything—to mark the return to normal.

"Umm…" She bites her bottom lip. "Honestly, I take a hot shower and try to wash off the day." She tucks a strand of hair behind her ear, meeting my eyes. "Sometimes I just stand there until the water runs cold. Is that weird?"

I shake my head. "Not weird at all. After a rough call, I do the same thing."

"And then?" she prompts, leaning slightly closer.

"Then I usually grab a beer, put on some music—old stuff,

Springsteen, The Stones—and try to remember I'm still human." I find myself admitting things I don't usually share. "Some nights are harder than others."

She nods, understanding in her eyes. "I get that. Some days I lose patients I shouldn't have. Days when I did everything right, but it still wasn't enough."

"Those are the worst," I agree. "When you replay it over and over, looking for what you could've done differently."

"Exact—"

"What's your middle name?"

She blinks at my sudden change of topic, then breaks into laughter— real laughter that cuts through the bar's noise and makes my chest feel lighter than it has in weeks. I can't help but laugh, too, and it's been so damn long since I heard that sound from myself that it feels almost foreign.

"Marie," she says, still grinning, tucking an imaginary strand behind her ear even though her hair's already perfectly in place. "Karina Marie Reyes. My parents wanted something classic and Catholic."

"Karina Marie," I repeat, liking how it sounds. "Has a good ring to it. Almost poetic. Mine's James. Vulcan James Montgomery, which sounds like I should be commanding a starship somewhere, or like I'm a Bond villain."

She laughs again, and I realize I'm getting addicted to that sound. "I think Vulcan James Montgomery sounds distinguished, actually. Like you should have a leather-bound office and drink expensive whiskey."

"Well, I've got the expensive whiskey part down," I say, raising my glass. "Still working on the leather-bound office." I realize I'm grinning like an idiot. When's the last time a woman made me feel this relaxed?

"So, Vulcan James." She clears her throat. "What inspired you to become a firefighter? Was it the allure of the uniform? The chance to be a real-life hero?"

"Nah, nothing that noble. I just figured if I was going to spend my days running into burning buildings, I might as well get paid for it." I swivel to face her again, enjoying the way the bar light's amber glow throws shadows off her long eyelashes. "More than that, though, my father was a firefighter, and his father was before him, and so on. It's become somewhat of a family thing."

"Ah yes, Thomas Montgomery. I've heard of his legacy as a firefighter and station captain. Well, I'm glad you did become a firefighter; the world needs more people like you." She pauses, searching my eyes. "But if you *hadn't* joined in the family tradition, what would you have wanted to become?"

"A chef."

"So you love to cook?"

"I do." I smile. "Maybe I could cook for you sometime."

"Maybe…" She lifts up her shot glass before setting it back down when she notices it's empty.

"And you? Why did you decide to become a doctor?" I ask, then signal the bartender for a couple of waters. I'm not sure if she works tomorrow, but she'll be regretting the lack of hydration after the three shots of tequila and Long Island she's put away since I joined her.

"I always knew I wanted to help people," Karina says, her voice taking on a more serious tone. "My papà was in a fatal car accident when I was sixteen. The doctors who tried to save him were amazing, but what stuck with me was how they explained everything to us. My parents are from the Dominican Republic and moved to the States three years before I was born, so for the doctors to be as thorough and patient as they were with mother, who still barely spoke English at the time… it meant everything to our family." She drags her shot glass through the pool of condensation on the bar. "I wanted to be that person for someone else. To be that doctor who doesn't make people feel small or stupid for not understanding."

I don't interrupt as she talks and instead unscrew the top of the water bottle, handing it to her.

"Thank you." She smiles, her cheeks tinting as she accepts it.

"That's a hell of a calling," I say. "Beats following the family way."

"I don't know about that," she replies, then takes a long sip of water before continuing. "There's something beautiful about carrying on a legacy. Your father must've been proud when you became captain."

"He died before he could witness it happen, but I like to think he would have approved."

"I'm sorry," she says softly, her hand moving tentatively toward mine. When her fingers brush against my knuckles, I feel a jolt of electricity that has nothing to do with the alcohol I've consumed.

"It was a while ago," I manage, suddenly very aware of how close we're sitting. "But thank you."

Past Karina's shoulder, on the other side of the bar, I see Harry giving me an overly enthusiastic thumbs-up. I send him a warning look, though I can't stop the smile that's forming on my face. As the evening progresses, I find myself hoping it will last forever. It's been ages since I connected with someone so easily. Karina is like a breath of fresh air, and I think about how many times I must have passed her in the halls of St. Mary's and never noticed. However, the crowd begins to thin out as the bar empties for the night. Before long, our friends rejoin us, and Cassie's barely suppressing her yawns.

"I should probably get going," Karina says reluctantly, glancing at her watch. "Early shift tomorrow and Cass looks like she's about to pass out at any moment."

I find myself desperate to see Karina again, worried this chance encounter won't be repeated. As they gather their things, I gently grasp her arm.

"Can I take you out sometime?"

She looks surprised, then smiles. Not a smile that conveys a yes, but a smile like she's going to let me down gently. "I'd like that, but my schedule—"

"How about we exchange numbers? Let's start there first." I already have my phone out, not giving her a chance to come up with an excuse. She nods and we say our goodbyes, then I watch her walk away, her dark hair swaying down her back.

"So, what did you think of her?" Harry asks, nudging my arm.

I take a sip of my drink to buy myself a moment. *I think she's the most captivating woman I've ever met.*

"She seems great," I say finally, aiming for a nonchalant tone.

"Just great? It looked to me like you two hit it off. Do I hear wedding bells in the future?"

"You're pushing it. She's easy to talk to and nice to look at." Her beauty is just a bonus.

"Come on, Vul, you looked like you were ready to devour her."

I shake my head, but a smile tugs at the corners of my lips. "What would you like to hear me say? That she's… amazing?"

"I mean, that's a start. Only, don't go falling in love with her just because she's the first woman you've talked to in months. You're just getting your feet wet."

"There's this connection despite the age difference, and fucking hell is it a difference." She told me she's twenty-seven, a solid *twelve years* younger than me. That alone should be enough not to want to see her again; she's even younger than my little sister.

He scoffs, looking completely unfazed. "Did she say it bothered her?" he asks.

"Well, I didn't ask. I didn't want to ruin the mood."

"*I didn't want to ruin the mood,*" he mocks. "I think you're fine."

"Maybe you're right." I shouldn't overthink this.

"I know I am." Harry grins, taking a swig of his beer. "And I saw the way she looked at you. That woman was not thinking about your birth certificate."

"We'll see. She's busy, I'm busy. Life's complicated."

"Life's always complicated, Vulcan. That's why you gotta grab the good stuff when it shows up. And you've got her number. You deserve to be happy, don't stress."

"Enough about me." I changed the subject. "Any chance you'll be seeing Cassie again?"

Harry rolls his eyes like I've just asked the most laughable question in the world. "Not my type," he declares.

"Since when do you have a type?" I tease, knowing full well that Harry's not exactly *picky* when it comes to women.

He leans back, crossing his arms. "Since I found out she lives in Brooklyn. I'm not trying to take the L train in this heat, and it's going to be crowded. It's the last week of June, and we all know the tourists are gearing up to flock here despite how suffocating the weather's about to get," he says with a dramatic sigh. "I'll pass."

I chuckle, shaking my head. It's always some excuse with him when he makes a real connection. "You're going to let the subway kill your game?"

He spreads his hands as if to say, *What can you do?* "Hey, a guy's gotta have his limits. Other than that, she's cool." He shrugs.

I toss my head back, laughing. Harry will always be Harry, but his commitment to laziness when it comes to romantic partners never fails to amuse me. I try to convince myself I'm not the least bit disappointed, though. With those two out of the question, it'll be harder to tee something up with Karina again.

She's already got a hold on me, and I hardly know the woman.

Harry and I stick around for another half hour after the girls leave, long enough to catch highlights from the Knicks game and talk more shit over another drink. Once we step back outside, the cool night air slaps my face and the city's pulse surrounds us with honking taxis and the distant rumble of a subway. I've always loved the urban heartbeat— it's alive in a way no other place is, always moving, as if the whole city's hyped up on caffeine.

"So, you gonna text her?" Harry pushes, elbowing me as we start down the sidewalk. The streetlamps illuminate the wet pavement, and I can only hope it's water and not piss.

"I don't want to seem too eager."

He lets out a low whistle. "I haven't seen you show interest in someone like this whose life you weren't saving," he remarks, slapping me on the back as if that'll knock some sense into me. "It's just *fucking*, not rocket science. Don't make it weird." He's got this way of cutting through my bullshit, and although I'd never say it to his face, I kind of need that nudge right now.

My last relationship fizzled out over a decade ago and was mostly due to a lack of effort on both sides. It was like we were both waiting for something better to come along. But something about Karina makes me feel hopeful in a way I haven't in a long time. She's got me scared, in a good way. Like if I don't jump now, I'll spend the rest of my life wondering what might have been.

"All right, all right. I'll text her tomorrow."

"That's what I like to hear. Don't fuck this up, Cap."

By the time we step off the curb, heading in opposite directions, I'm already second-guessing every detail and wondering if I imagined the connection.

Back at my place, I unlock my door, and the familiar creak snaps me into a new line of thinking. One where I resolve to stop self-sabotaging. I toss my keys on the kitchen counter, watching them slide to a stop. I'm a man who runs into burning buildings for a living. I should not be this scared to text a woman.

Tomorrow morning, I'll text her.

CHAPTER FOUR

Vulcan

My desk is a skyscraper of incident reports and training schedules that looms over everything, including my sanity. The phone rings, a reminder that chaos isn't limited to the field. I snatch it up, my jaw setting as the FDNY Superintendent, Brandon, beats out its favorite tune: budget constraints, red tape, and, my personal favorite, staff shortages. I counter each point with a steady voice.

"Cutting my budget isn't in the best interest of my crew's safety, nor will it have the effect you think," I say, leaning back in my chair. I focus on the ceiling's neat rows of recessed lights, a perfect grid mocking the disorder of my day. "It'll cut lives, though."

"Your firehouse is going to have to learn to make do, Montgomery," he says on the other end, his voice slick as ice and about as warm. "Just like everyone else."

"Making do isn't gonna save this city," I reply. "My crew's still running three short, and with the construction schedule slipping, we might as well be working out of tents. Something needs to give."

He's unmoved. Probably sitting in a plush office where urgency is measured in caffeine intake. "Then you'll have to reprioritize. We're *all* under pressure."

I tap my pen against a stack of overtime requests. "You want me to reprioritize safety?"

"We've done what we can on our end," he says, the words so

practiced that I'm sure he's reading from a script. "I suggest you manage expectations accordingly."

I'm managing expectations all right, just not in the way he's hoping. "If the ladder falls on some senator's car, I bet the funds appear real quick."

"We're not unsympathetic, Vulcan," he says, still cruising in his lane of empty reassurances. "But there are protocols to follow."

"Tell that to the families who'll need more than protocol if we don't get our equipment up to speed," I shoot back, my voice rising before I take a breath and calm my heart rate.

The line goes silent for a second, and I imagine him flipping through a mental Rolodex of more bullshit answers. "We'll revisit staffing next quarter and look into reallocating some resources. In the meantime, please exercise patience and continue to lead your team through this transition."

"Patiently leading a ghost crew with broken gear?" I ask. "What am I, a magician?"

"There's nothing more we can offer at this time," he replies, all business and no give. "We'll be in touch."

The line goes dead before I can unleash another volley. I throw the phone down, running a hand through my hair. For a minute, I sit there, simmering like a pot about to boil over. They've pushed everything back on me, but hell if I'll let the station crumble because some suit thinks cutting corners is the new American pastime. I pace the length of my office, five steps across, five back, bumping against the limits of my resolve. We've done a lot with a little before, but this time feels different.

I grab a binder labeled *Desperation*, which is what I've started calling my Hail Mary plans. The mess of figures and feasibility studies blur together on the pages. My chair spins as I sit back down. Maybe it's time to hit up some allies and lean on old connections. I clear a spot on the desk, dumping stacks onto the floor, and start scribbling out an action plan the board can't say no to.

I'm plotting my next move when there's a knock at the door, soft but insistent. I look up to see my lieutenant. His sprained ankle isn't slowing him down, but it's clear from the way he's moving that his ego's taken a limp, too.

"Mike," I say, waving him in. "Thought you were supposed to be taking it easy."

"Yeah, yeah," he grumbles, hobbling in with all the dignity of a three-legged dog. "Did a tornado take a crap in here? You look like shit."

"Funny, I was about to ask you the same," I shoot back, nodding to his foot.

He flops into a chair, wincing a little. "Gonna take more than this to knock me out, Cap."

"If you don't rest it, you'll never heal."

Mike shrugs. "So what's the damage?" he asks, steering away from himself to more familiar ground.

"Same song, new verse," I say. "Can't budget what you can't see. Told them I'm two guys away from working solo."

"Cold bastards," he says, shaking his head. "What now?"

I'm about to answer when he interrupts, gesturing to the desk.

"I plan on cloning myself," I reply.

His smile's as crooked as his foot, but I can tell he's just as pissed about the board's stonewalling. "Think we could get the local news in on it?"

"Only if you're the one hobbling to the press room," I say, flipping through the sea of paper. "I was thinking more along the lines of calling up some old friends, playing the sympathy card?"

Mike raises an eyebrow. "Thought that was the last resort."

"It is," I admit. "But I'm not waiting for the next accident to happen." I glance pointedly down at his ankle.

"Let's do it," he says. "My wife loves a project. She can rally the rest of the station partners."

He's more serious than his sarcasm lets on. That makes two of us. I feel a little of the morning's gloom lift, but I still hate the thought of dragging families into it. Mike catches my hesitation.

"Don't get soft now," he says.

"I think I should just front it all," I say, eyeing the overflowing desk.

Mike pushes himself up, biting back a grimace. "No, your money is your money. You shouldn't have to go digging in your own coffers to take care of something the city's responsible for," he says.

I run a hand through my hair, exhaustion crawling up my spine. "It's not about the money, Mike. It's about principle. This department is supposed to take care of its own. *I* have to take care of us."

"And you're part of this department," he reasons, bracing his palms on the desk. "Look, I get it. Everything falls on your shoulders. But sometimes even the toughest of soldiers needs to share the weight."

He's right, and I hate that he's right. "Fine. Let's get the families involved. Just… keep it tasteful."

"As opposed to what? Bikini car washes?" Mike snorts. "Give Amaya some credit, Vulcan."

I wave him off, but I'm swallowing down a chuckle. "Get out of here before I change my mind. And ice that ankle. You still have a week of LOA, and I need you back in shape. Especially if I'm the next one to go out."

"And we know that will never happen. You're immortal or something," he finishes, giving me a mock salute as he ambles toward the door. "I'll get Amaya on it. She'll have the whole community baking cookies and writing checks come dinnertime."

"Well, in that case, we'll be funded in no time," I joke. Amaya's baking skills are good but not great. A few Christmases ago she left eggshells in the cake Mike brought to the station party.

I check my watch as the door clicks shut. Still three hours before I need to head to the commissioner's office. Plenty of time to obsess over every possible outcome of that meeting. The budget cuts have been coming down hard, but I never thought they'd hit essential equipment. If it boils down to it, I will pull from my savings once more to keep things afloat around here.

I lean back in my chair, closing my eyes to take a moment of peace before my phone buzzes on the desk. I don't even need to look at the caller ID to know who it is.

"Vulcan Montgomery," I answer, my voice deliberately neutral.

"Vulcan." Commissioner Harding's crisp tone cuts through the line. "I thought we could touch base before our meeting. Also, have you spoken to Brandon?"

In other words, he wants to ambush me with his decisions before I can prepare my arguments.

"Of course, I just got off the phone with him, and before you ask, it's the same old song and dance." I sigh, rubbing the bridge of my nose. "What can I do for you?"

"I've been reviewing your requests," he says, and I can picture him on the other end of the line, not a speck of soot or sweat ever daring to touch that pristine suit. "The numbers are concerning, I'll give you that. But I'm busy, and yours isn't the only department under my jurisdiction. Your father was a close friend of mine... which is why I'm giving you my time today."

"I know. I know." I press my fist to my lips to keep from cussing him out. "The numbers reflect what we need to keep my firefighters safe, sir."

"And the city's budget *reflects* what we can afford." His voice has that practiced regret that politicians love to flex. "I'll be blunt, Vulcan. The council is pushing back. Hard."

My jaw tightens. "People's lives are at stake."

"People's lives are always at stake," he counters smoothly. "That's why we need to be strategic about our resource allocation."

Right, "strategy." A new, fancy word for *no*, then.

"I'll see you at two, Commissioner," I say instead of what I really want to say. "I'm looking forward to discussing our strategic resource allocation in detail."

He chuckles, recognizing my sarcasm but choosing to ignore it. "Looking forward to it."

The line goes dead, and I consider throwing my phone across the room. I pull out the folder of incident reports related to faulty equipment I've been compiling. Every near miss. Every time we got lucky.

Luck runs out eventually.

Harry shows up at my office twenty minutes later, holding two cups of coffee.

"You look like you need this more than I do," he says, placing one cup on my desk. "Commissioner or Chief?"

"Both." I take a grateful sip, the bitter liquid burning away some of my frustration. "They aren't budging."

"While I love to hear all about spreadsheets and old men in suits, I came here about something far more important."

"And what could that be?"

"Have you called Karina yet?" he asks. His grin is as smug as I expect it to be. "I know with all this stress you could use a great reliever." He cocks an eyebrow, ensuring I catch every innuendo he throws my way.

It's been almost two weeks since she gave me her number at Riley's, and I've been too cowardly to do anything with it. I roll my eyes like

Harry's suggestions are ridiculous, but there's a sharp twinge of guilt in my chest. The truth I won't admit out loud is that I've pulled up her number at least a dozen times. I've even hovered my thumb over the call button, before bailing like a rookie. With everything going on here, I'd drop the ball and disappoint her. And I wouldn't be able to live with myself if I did.

"I've been busy," I mutter, trying to sound indifferent while shuffling papers around my desk.

"Busy? Aren't we all." He drops into the chair across from me. "Come on, it's July and you still haven't reached out. How are you going to let this one slip away?"

It's hard to tell him to shove it when he's right. Karina and I clicked at the bar. It was like the whole world quieted to just the two of us.

"Shouldn't you be doing something productive?" I try to change the subject, but Harry just crosses his arms and smirks. "Like, I don't know, your actual job?"

"This is productive. I'm saving my boss and best friend from a lifetime of loneliness and sexual frustration."

I shoot him a warning glare, a silent threat that I'm not above putting him on meal shift for a month for being a pain in the ass. "Thin ice, Harry."

"Fine, fine." He holds up his hands in surrender, but his grin tells me he's far from backing down. "But seriously, what's holding you back? She's gorgeous, smart, great body..."

... *The way she tucked her hair behind her ear whenever she laughed, the spark in her eyes that rivaled any fire I ever marched into*. It's almost embarrassing how much I think about her.

"It's complicated," I settle on.

He leans forward like he's about to tell me the secret to life. "It's really not. You call her, ask her out, maybe get dinner, have mind-blowing sex—"

"Harry." I cut him off before he gets even more graphic.

"Right, sorry. Too far." He sighs dramatically, acting like I'm killing him by not taking his advice. "But if you don't want her, I hear Richard over at Station 118 has been trying to get... cozy."

"What?"

"Yeah, I went to the bar the other night and saw them."

I lean forward in my chair. "And you didn't think to call me?"

"I tried, and you didn't answer." He smiles.

"You should've tried harder," I say, feeling a flare of something unpleasant in my chest. It takes me a moment to recognize it as jealousy.

Harry gapes at me. "Wow. You should see your face right now. You've got it bad, Cap."

"Shut up." I run a hand through my hair, trying to appear unbothered even though my mind is racing. Richard from Station 118 has that whole mysterious bachelor thing going... successful, confident, and just enough gray at the temples to look distinguished. "Were they... together *together*?"

"They were just talking," he admits, and my shoulders relax. "But he was definitely putting the moves on. You know how he gets, all 'let me tell you about the time I rescued triplets from a burning building while simultaneously disarming a bomb.'"

I snort. "That never happened."

"The ladies don't know that." Harry settles back in his chair, crossing his legs at the ankles. "Look, I'm not trying to pressure you—"

"Yes, you are."

"Okay, I am. But only because I haven't seen you like this since I've known you."

I sigh and rub at my temples. "I've got enough complications in my life right now."

"Okay, and when she's off the market… I'll be here to tell you I told you so…?"

"I will call her, just not now. It's not the right time," I admit.

"When exactly is the 'right time' going to magically appear in your busy schedule?" He sets his coffee down to make air quotes, and I roll my eyes.

Suddenly, the station alarm blares, and I'm effectively saved from the conversation. Harry jumps to his feet but keeps his eyes on me as we head out of the office to retrieve our gear.

"This isn't over," he calls over the noise.

"Yes, it is," I shout back, but we both know he's right. As I suit up, my mind drifts to Karina again. I need to make this right before she falls into the arms of another man.

CHAPTER FIVE

Karina

Cassie and I slip away from the chaos of the ER, swiftly rounding a corner to find our familiar hideaway: the supply closet. This faintly lit room, with its shelves crammed full of bandages, gauze, and antiseptics, is our sanctuary. The smell of disinfectant still hangs in the air, but it mingles with the scent of fresh linens, turning it into a much-needed refuge. This supply closet has borne witness to countless whispered secrets and snippets of hospital gossip, rivaling even the bustling nurses' station's fodder.

"Okay, what's the tea?" Cassie prompts, leaning against the wall. "Has the silver fox called or texted you?"

It's been two weeks since Vulcan pulled me into a conversation at Riley's and we exchanged numbers, yet he has not contacted me. I'm not nearly as bothered as I probably should be—my stress levels have not dropped a degree—but I'd thought he was interested in me. Had been expecting to at *least* receive a good-morning text.

But I think I know why he's gone silent. When you're staring down a twelve-year age gap, it's hard to ignore. However, after getting to know him and realizing how much we had in common, it'd meant very little to me.

I shake my head. "No, he hasn't. But it's okay, really. I know we're both busy."

"Girl, that man was drooling over you. He can't be *that* fucking busy."

I feel my cheeks flush at the memory. The smoldering look in Vulcan's gaze, the graze of his fingers against mine as we exchanged phones. There *had* been an undeniable spark, a magnetic pull that threw me off-kilter. But you never know with men nowadays.

"He's playing games, which we've established he is far too old for. We don't have time for little boys who waste our time."

"Please," I say. "He is decidedly *not* a little boy. He takes his job as seriously as I take mine. I'm sure he's just busy. Besides, I'm not *actively* looking to hook up with anyone at the moment."

Lies.

I definitely could've been swayed. Something about him made me want to throw caution to the wind and invite him back to my place that night. Whether it was his muscular arms, those huge hands, his beard, or the conversation, I'll likely never know.

"Girl, you are a terrible liar," Cassie says, crossing her arms over her chest. "I can see it in your eyes. You're into him. And why wouldn't you be? He's a total smoke show. Pun absolutely intended."

"Terrible. Your puns are getting worse."

"My puns are the least of your concern right now. Hear me out," she starts. "Maybe he's waiting for the right moment to sweep you off your feet. You know, like in those old bodice-rippers where the rugged hero rides in on his trusty steed to save the damsel in distress? But he would be riding in his fire truck with his hose in his hand. And *not* the hose that releases water."

I choke out a laugh. *This girl.* "We're not in some fairy tale."

She shrugs, a playful smile on her lips. "Hey, we can dream, right? Besides, you deserve a little romance in your life. You work too hard, always putting everyone else first."

"You might be right." I push off the wall and straighten my white coat. "But for now, I need to focus on my patients. Romance can wait."

Cassie shakes her head. "Just don't wait too long. As the saying goes: you're not getting any younger, so now is the time to grab life by the horns. Or, in your case, by the fire hose." She taps her chin in thought. "*Any* hose, for that matter."

"Yeah, yeah." I open the supply closet and walk out. "We'll talk later."

"Let me grab these bandages to make it seem like I was doing something productive." She nods at me as I slip out.

As I make my way down the hallway, Cassie's words play in my mind. I've spent so long building up walls to protect myself. Between my mother and all the failed "talking stage" with men, it's been years since I let someone new get close. It's better that way in the end. Love always seems to come at a price, and it's one I'm no longer willing to pay.

When my phone vibrates in my scrubs, I assume the worst and slip into an empty room.

"Hello, Mother," I say when I pick up the call, bracing myself for whatever demands or criticisms she has in store for me today.

"Karina, it's about time you answered," she responds sharply. "I've been trying to reach you for days. Too busy to spare a thought for your widowed mother?"

You called me three days ago and you've been a widow for nearly a decade now, I think. "Of course I care, Mother," I say, clenching my jaw. "Now, what is it you need? I'm at work."

She launches into a list of demands. First, like clockwork, it's money for Miguel and Luis. And then her voice grows louder and more aggressive as she launches into how I've failed her as a daughter. As she continues, my mind begins to drift away from her words. I've heard it all before. As much as I want to help her, I know from experience that it will never be enough.

"Karina, are you even listening to me?"

"Yes, Mother, I am." I sigh, digging the heels of my running shoes into the linoleum.

Her tone turns cold as she makes her standard monetary requests. "Send me over two grand. Your brothers need it."

I take a deep breath before responding. "I can't send you any more money right now. I'm stretched thin as it is."

Her voice turns cold. "You *ungrateful* child. After everything I've sacrificed for you, this is how you repay me? Your brothers understand family duty, but you—you've forgotten where you came from."

When she uses the boys in situations like this, it doesn't help her case. They're both at Ohio State University and neither one has a job. Something she forced me to do at their age to help contribute to the household.

"I know you struggled, and I appreciate all that you've done for me, but I have my own expenses. I can send a small amount to help, but not two thousand."

"A small amount?" She scoffs. "Just admit you don't care about your mother's well-being. I knew I couldn't rely on you. After your father passed away and you decided to become this big-shot doctor, you—"

"Mother. I'll transfer the money as soon as I can." Tears sting my eyes. I want to plead with her and make her understand, but I know it's pointless. She won't be satisfied until she has torn me down completely, and she's close to doing so. I'm just about ready to throw in the towel and move to another country.

"Good. Don't forget to call me more often, too. The phone works both ways," she says before abruptly hanging up.

I lean my head against the wall, taking deep breaths as the tears fall. She's wrong, I *know* she's wrong. But her words always seem to expose the scared, lonely little girl I've bundled away inside my heart. The one who could never be good enough. I take a few moments to collect myself and then wipe at my cheeks. How can one person manage to make me feel worthless in mere minutes?

"Hey, Karina, you okay in there?" Cassie's voice filters through the door.

I open it with an attempt at a smile. "Yeah, I'm all right. Just my mom, that's all." I wave my phone at her, trying for some levity.

"Was it a rough one?" I nod, and the tightness in my throat threatens more tears. Cassie gestures to the bed, and we move to sit down. "Do you want to talk about it?" she asks.

I hesitate, old habits telling me to brush it off, keep it hidden. But Cassie's compassionate gaze holds mine, and I feel my resolve weakening. I take a breath. I don't like to overshare, not even with her, but talking about it might help.

"It's just… she has this way of making me feel so small," I confess. "No matter what I do or how hard I try, it's never *enough* for her. I've given her almost a hundred thousand dollars this year alone, and I'm *still* the ungrateful daughter."

The look of pity shines in her eyes. A look I hate. I don't want anyone to pity me. "I'm so sorry. But you have to know her words aren't true. You are the worthiest person I know. Worthy of a lot more love and gratitude than she ever shows you."

"I know, *logically*. But in the moment, it's as if I'm transported back to the ten-year-old version of me, desperate for her approval." I shake my head, angry at myself. "I hate that she has this power over me."

"Hey, it makes complete sense," Cassie says gently. "Of course you want her validation. She's your mother. However, the problem lies with her, *not* with you. You've done all you can do, and you're still doing *soooo* much for her *and* your brothers. You can't beat yourself up over people who don't deserve you."

"Thank you." I don't know what else to say. This is why I don't tend to share. Words are only soothing and helpful for a short time, but actions speak louder than words.

She pulls me into a hug. "Don't forget, you're pretty *amazing*, and I'm the luckiest girl in this entire *galaxy* to have a bestie like you. You are the fucking best, Rina! Even if your mom can't see it."

I hug her back tightly, feeling a little more of my inner light return. I open my mouth to thank her once more, but the sound of my pager stops me. We both glance down, our expressions morphing. "Shoot, incoming trauma. Multi vehicle accident."

The sky is dark when I finally head home, feeling like I'm moving through quicksand. The day stretched into a fifteen-hour shift and exhaustion drags at my limbs. All I can focus on is the sweet release of a hot shower and collapsing into bed, where I plan to shut out the world until morning. Cassie was right when she said I work too hard, but I don't know any other way to stay afloat.

I reach the door of my apartment, a small but cozy sanctuary from the chaos of the outside world. Once inside, I drop my bag and kick off my shoes, savoring the moment my feet hit the bare floor. I run a hand through my hair, breathing in the familiar scent of coffee and my favorite sun-drenched linen candle from Bath and Body Works.

The stack of medical journals on the coffee table, the soft throw draped over the couch, and the canister of my chamomile tea on the counter are all evidence that this space is *mine*. Sure, it paints the picture of a life lived on the edge of exhaustion, but it's a testament to another day survived.

I pad toward the bathroom, eager to shed my scrubs and wash away the day's grime, when a blinking red light catches my attention. It's the answering machine, signaling yet another demand on my already limited time. I pause, torn between wanting to ignore it and the nagging obligation to respond to whatever crisis might be waiting in digital form. With a tired sigh, I shuffle over and hit play, bracing for the worst.

"Karina Reyes, this is Sarah Fletcher reaching out regarding the Heroes Gala this Friday. We have yet to get an RSVP from you. Could you please call me back at your earliest convenience? Thank you. Oh, I tried your cell phone multiple times, but the voicemail was full." The machine beeps, indicating the end of the message.

I pause, scrubs half off, as the message sinks in—the Heroes Gala, the annual event honoring first responders. I've attended the last few years with Cassie, mingling awkwardly and posing for photos. It's not really my scene. But this year, I have been requested to attend because I was the recipient of the Med Honors Clinician Award.

Part of me wants to decline to avoid the spotlight and scrutiny that come with being honored publicly. But I know Cassie and the others at the hospital would be disappointed, and the hospital administration emphasized how important it is we attend. In other words: we can't technically mandate attendance, but the higher-ups are making note of who skips out.

With a deep breath, I pick up the phone and dial. Sarah answers on the second ring, her voice bright and enthusiastic. We exchange pleasantries before I confirm my attendance. As I hang up, my stomach twists into a knot.

Shit, is it too late to back out?

The soft patter of the shower fills the apartment as I step beneath the hot spray, embracing the welcoming blast. It stings at first, then gradually starts to soothe my aching, overworked muscles. My body relaxes under the steady stream, but my mind refuses to relent, spinning with thoughts of the upcoming gala. I'll have to find a dress that isn't lingering in a long-forgotten section of my closet. And where am I supposed to find the time to write my acceptance speech? I drop my chin to my chest and try to steady my breathing, then do as I'm used to: carry on.

Clean and slightly more human, I slip into pajamas that feel soft and worn against my skin, sighing as I sink into the mattress. It's a relief so profound it almost makes me forget the pressure of obligation forming between my temples. *Almost.*

The pillow is like a welcoming cloud, and I burrow deep, craving the escape that only sleep can bring. The idea of a moment's peace calls out to me like an oasis I desperately need. I close my eyes, hoping to shut out the world and silence the mental stream of worries and to-dos.

"Finding a dress and writing my acceptance speech," I mutter as I drift off, the last coherent thoughts before sleep claims me.

CHAPTER SIX

Vulcan

The beat of the music pulses through my chest as I step into The Beaufort's grand ballroom. The Heroes Gala is the kind of event I generally avoid like cat memes on the internet. Charity functions have a way of making me feel like a monkey in a suit, and I figure my presence is usually neither required nor missed. But this year is different. This year, I'm one of the honorees. So here I am, swallowing my reluctance like a bitter pill. The ballroom is packed with firefighters, police officers, paramedics, doctors, and hospital staff all dressed to the nines.

It's clear that no expense has been spared in putting this event together. Crystal chandeliers hover like upside-down ice castles from the high-vaulted ceilings, casting a dazzling light over the packed room. The black-and-white marble floors gleam beneath my feet, adding to the opulence. A five-piece band plays from a corner, putting a jazzy spin to the decade's hottest music. They're currently belting out "Beautiful Soul" on the sax while the vocalist loops in some soft effects. Waitstaff in crisp uniforms weave skillfully through the mass of partygoers, balancing trays laden with frothy flutes of champagne and intricately garnished hors d'oeuvres.

I swipe a glass from a passing waiter, thanking him with a nod as I take a sip. The bubbly liquid slides down my throat as I scan the crowd, searching for any familiar faces. It's like being lost in a sea of people, wondering how I ended up shipwrecked on this particular social island.

"Captain Montgomery." A man in a tux nods my way, and I return the gesture, briefly recognizing him as the fire captain from station 37. I busy myself greeting others while trying to find a corner to hide for the rest of the night. I move away from a group of ladies who are less than subtle with their advances and spot a solitary table tucked away from the commotion. I make a beeline for it and take a seat, drumming my fingers against the linen as I scope the ballroom for Harry.

"Mind if I join you?" A soft voice pulls me from my thoughts, and when I look up, there she is—Karina. Her black hair cascading down her shoulders like a raven's waterfall, her warm, brown skin complementing the emerald green of her dress.

"Please," I rush out, motioning to the chair opposite mine. "You look..." I start, leaning in once she sits down. "Breathtaking."

Karina gives a small, humble smile. "Thank you, and you look handsome."

"Thank you." I clear my throat. "Look, Karina, I need to apologize for not reaching out. Work was—"

"Work. I get it," she finishes. "I've been busy with other plans anyway."

I arch an eyebrow. *Other plans?* I think back to Harry's mention of her chatting up a guy from 118 at Riley's...

"I also know better than to sit around pining for a man who's married to his job," she adds. "Besides, I've got plenty to keep me busy at the hospital."

"Touché." I grin, appreciating her quick wit. "I don't want to come across as intrusive, but are you seeing anyone? Any, um, firefighters?" I internally cringe. *What is* wrong *with you, Vulcan?*

"It's very intrusive," she says, though I catch her smile. "But no, I'm not. I'm barely seeing a fire captain and I actually gave *him* my number."

A relief, but I still feel like shit. The days have zipped by with me barely sleeping in between shifts, eating stale donuts for breakfast, and pushing through endless paperwork. I know I should have made the time and effort, but between the madness at the station and my plans for the commissioner, I've been swamped. Now, seeing her again, I realize just how much I screwed things up.

"Well," I say, my voice hesitant. "What do you say we grab a coffee sometime next week?"

Karina tilts her head, considering my offer with a bemused expression that makes my chest tighten. She hesitates, and the pause is long enough for me to think she's going to blow me off completely.

"Hmmm," she finally says. "I don't know. You said something similar three weeks ago, and my phone was dry like the Sahara Desert." Her words are teasing but pointed, and I can't say I blame her.

"I promise not to keep you waiting too long this time. One of my crew was injured, and I had to take care of things. I'll be putting your number to good use this time." I hope she can hear the sincerity in my voice, because I sure as hell don't trust myself to express it any better. Karina's smile softens, and for a fleeting moment, I catch a glimpse of longing in her gaze, as if she's considering taking a chance on me again. It's gone as quickly as it appeared.

"I'll let *you* know when I'm free."

"Understandable," I say, swallowing my pride with a grin. "I suppose I'll just have to wait patiently."

"I guess so." She laughs. I realize that beneath her playful exterior, she's giving me another chance, and damn if I'm not going to jump at it.

The song shifts, and it's as if the melody tugs at something deep inside me. Without really knowing why or how, I'm on my feet, the motion fueled by a raw impulse. I extend my hand to Karina. "May I have this dance?" I ask, holding my breath and wondering if she'll turn me down.

Her eyes flicker, a quick dart from my extended hand up to my face, revealing the conflict stirring beneath her calm facade. Her fingers slip into mine, a gentle webbing of warmth that sends a shock straight to my chest. My whole body reacts, alive to the contact of her skin against my own calloused palm.

I lead her toward the dance floor, aware of every eye that might be on us. The captain and the doctor. But all that fades away as she rests her palm lightly on my shoulder, like she's testing the waters, and I savor the sensation. As I slide my other hand to the curve of her waist, a jolt of electricity rushes through me. We move together as if we've danced a thousand times before, our bodies attuned to the faintest shifts in rhythm, in step, in breath. The music wraps around us, a melody that knows exactly what we need.

I take the lead, careful and steady, making sure she knows she can trust me. It's more than just dancing. It's as if I'm trying to prove that I won't let her fall, won't let her down again. Karina follows, an effortless grace in her every movement. She's like water flowing over rocks, smooth and naturally elegant, a force of nature.

"So, Captain, tell me something. Why is a man like you still single?"

"The short answer?" I begin. "The job takes over. You blink and suddenly it's been nearly a decade since your last real date. And now it feels like my bedroom's been collecting more dust than my firetrucks."

"Hmm, I see." Karina's lips curve into a playful smile. "Or maybe you're just afraid of commitment."

I chuckle, shaking my head. "Afraid? No, I wouldn't say that. Cautious, perhaps. When you've seen the things I have, you learn not to take anything for granted. Also, my understaffed station makes me more committed to my job than I think a potential partner would like."

"Understaffed seems to be the word of the century. I totally get it." She tilts her head, her eyes searching mine. "And what about now?" she asks. "Are you still being cautious? Or…"

"With you," I say, feeling something shift as I pull her closer, "I'm officially off the clock."

"You're a smooth talker, Vulcan. One more burning question, though. Does my age bother you?" There's something vulnerable in her voice, even as she laughs to cover it up.

"Age is just the world's most annoying number." I pause. "The connection between us? That's what I care about. And I haven't felt this in a long time."

Karina's eyes widen slightly, a faint blush spreading across her cheeks. She leans closer, her voice dropping. "Is that Captain Montgomery's roundabout way of saying he likes me?"

"I thought asking for your number made that pretty clear." I let my hand slide lower on her back, fingers grazing the exposed skin where her dress dips. "But if you need it spelled out, I've got all night."

She shivers under my touch, her breath catching. "A number ghosted faster than a horror movie victim, but who's keeping track?"

I wince, then lean in, letting my mouth hover close enough to her ear that I can feel the heat radiating off her. She smells like fresh linen and vanilla, and for a second, I'm tempted to just press my lips to her neck and see what she tastes like. Instead, I whisper, "I deserved that."

Her lips twitch, as if she's fighting a smile. "You definitely did."

"So, what exactly are you proposing now?"

"How about you tell me what you want, Vulcan?"

And there it is—the opening. I don't hesitate. "How about we start with a kiss and see where the night takes us? Hopefully, back to my penthouse for a nightcap."

"You're nothing if not honest." She laughs, a breathy exhale that stirs the hair at my temple.

"You wouldn't want me any other way." I dip my head, my lips grazing the shell of her ear—just enough contact to make her breath stutter out again. "So what do you say?"

Karina pulls back slightly, her eyes searching mine. There's a pause, a moment of uncertainty, and I wonder if I've pushed too far, too fast. I'm not used to feeling this wound up about someone, but damn, there is no denying how much I want her.

"I think we should take it slow," she says after a moment. "I'm not looking for just a nightcap."

I nod, swallowing hard. "Slow is good. Slow is... fine." It's not what I want—I want to take her hand and lead her out of here right now—but I'll go at whatever pace she sets.

"Hey, Cap," Harry says, appearing like a ghost at my elbow. His timing, as usual, is impeccable—and by that I mean terrible. I shoot him a look that could melt steel, but he just grins, completely oblivious to the moment he's interrupted.

"Karina, you remember Harry?" I ask, still holding her close.

"Of course," she says. "Lovely to see you again."

"Likewise." Harry's eyes dart between us, and I can see the exact moment when realization dawns on him. "Oh, shit. I'm interrupting something, aren't I?" He looks genuinely apologetic, which is the only thing saving him from my wrath right now.

"You are," I tell him with a dry smile.

"Sorry. I'll make myself scarce." Harry starts to back away, but then pauses. "You two look great together." He winks and disappears back into the crowd.

"He's right, you know. We do look good to—"

"Dr. Reyes, Captain Montgomery. I'm so happy you two could make it." Sarah Fletcher, the brains behind the Heroes Gala and many more prestigious events that I try my best to avoid, is suddenly at our side, her eyes bright. At some point, we migrated toward the outer boundary of the dance floor. I plaster on a polite smile, trying to mask my annoyance at the interruption. Karina steps back, putting some distance between us, and I immediately miss her warmth.

"Sarah, always a pleasure," I say, shaking her hand. "You've outdone yourself with this event."

"Oh, stop." She laughs, waving off the compliment. "I'm just thrilled to see two of our city's finest here *together*. You know, I've been trying to get the hospital and the fire department to collaborate for ages."

Karina raises an eyebrow. "Is that so? I wasn't aware of any new projects. Usually, the hospital keeps us informed about these things."

"Oh, just a passion project I've been working on. I've been wanting to dip into philanthropy. But seeing you two here and looking *so cozy* on the dance floor gives me ideas."

"I think you might be reading a bit too much into things," I chime in.

"Am I?" She glances between us. "Because from where I'm standing, it looks like the start of a beautiful partnership. Both professionally *and* personally."

Karina clears her throat. "I appreciate the thought, but I think we're getting ahead of ourselves. Vulcan and I are just acquaintan—"

"*Friends*," I say, cutting her off.

She looks up at me, her eyes searching mine. I'd never dream of bulldozing my way over a woman, but with Karina I want to stake some claim even as a friend.

"I-I wouldn't go that far."

"And why not? I thought we were making a connection?" I smirk, giving her my full attention now.

"We are, but it's too soon to call this a friendship." She widens her eyes in silent, amused warning, and takes a step back. I step forward.

"How about we—"

"*Vulcan.*" She pushes at my chest, and I freeze. "I'm going to go mingle with other people. We can catch up later." Her eyes move to Sarah. "It is lovely to see you again."

"Likewise. I'll catch up with you shortly." Sarah winks at her before turning to me. "You'll go further if you dial it back a bit. Dr. Reyes seems like the type to have a man wine and dine her first. But enough of my meddling, I've been meaning to ask about the progress on that new training program you mentioned? I'm open to hosting an event to drum up some investors?"

As Sarah draws me into a discussion about work, I keep Karina within my field of vision. I nod along politely as she details her ideas, but my eyes keep drifting, searching for emerald green and silky black in the sea of elegant dresses and tailored suits.

If I ask her out for a late bite after the gala, would she say yes?

Sarah's moved on to new initiatives and communication strategies when I notice Karina standing by the bar with a man. She leans forward, laughing at something he says, and he touches her arm with an intimacy that smarts.

I have no right to be jealous. She's not mine and is very much single. I don't know how much longer I can stand here listening to Sarah talk about funding and resources, so I offer a weak excuse, something about getting back to her with more details later. Before she even responds, I'm across the room, unable to stop myself.

When I'm just a few feet away from Karina and the mystery man she's so cozy with, my phone buzzes insistently in my pocket. I pull it out, glancing at the screen. It's a message from one of my guys at the firehouse, telling me I'm needed back ASAP.

Part of me feels like running out would leave things with Karina hanging by a thread. Is she going to think I'm bailing *again*? Worse yet, will the guy at the bar swoop in? The thought gnaws at me as I shove my phone back into my pocket and head for the exit.

The instant my phone vibrates again, I know I need to leave, but I stand, paralyzed, for a split second. Caught between the pull of Karina and the weight of obligation clanging in my pocket. I pull out my phone again and scroll frantically through my contacts, hitting Karina's name. I type quickly, my thumb fumbling over the screen as I try to craft something that doesn't make me sound like a complete asshole.

> Me: Emergency at the station. Have to leave, but I don't want you to think I'm ghosting you again. Can we talk tomorrow?

I hit send before I can second-guess myself, then immediately regret the wording. Too desperate? Not desperate enough? Christ, when did I become this pathetic?

As I stride away from the dance floor, I catch one last glimpse of Karina through the shifting crowd. She doesn't notice me. She's focused on her companion, her hand wrapped around a slim glass of champagne, her posture poised but not rigid. For a moment, I wonder if she'll even care that I've vanished, or if she'll just chalk it up to my legendary commitment to the job and move on.

With one last look, I sigh, pushing through the ballroom doors and into the warm night air, feeling like I'm abandoning something important. Something that might not be there when I get back.

CHAPTER SEVEN

Vulcan

The firehouse doors slam shut behind me. "Captain Montgomery!" someone calls out. I lift a hand in acknowledgment without breaking stride. I make it to my office and slip inside, only to find a woman I never thought I'd see again sitting on the edge of my desk. *Minji Lee.* What the hell is she doing here after all these years?

My father passed away five years ago, and Minji handled everything with his estate. She was cold and efficient, the kind of woman who could make cutting you out of a will feel like a professional courtesy call. The memories of that day unfold with startling clarity: the sterile conference room, the crisp sound of paper rustling as she went down the list, each item a precise bullet wound. My mom got the old house, my sister the precious heirlooms my father had sworn he'd never part with, and me sitting there in stunned silence, empty-handed. Minji's voice was steady and impersonal, her eyes barely lifting from the document to gauge my reaction.

My father, a man I looked up to, even when he prioritized his job over his family, had left me nothing. Not even a letter. I remember leaving that room, every expectation upended, feeling like he was a total a stranger. It didn't change how I felt about him as a father; I never wanted for anything and was showered with love my whole life. But it had thrown me for a loop.

As far as I knew, Minji's involvement wrapped up back then, every loose end tied with the kind of precision only she could manage. I haven't heard a word since, not even a whisper about anything left of his estate.

Yet, here she is.

Her very presence in this firehouse rips open the past, making the air crackle with a tension I've worked hard to forget. I can't help but wonder what else she could possibly need from me.

"Minji." I take a seat on the sofa. "To what do I owe the pleasure of this late-night visit?" My voice comes out more sarcastic than I intend, masking the anxiety that churns beneath the surface.

"Vulcan." She greets me with the same calm detachment as all those years ago. But this time, I detect a slight annoyance in her tone. What the hell is going on? "I'll get straight to the point: You've been ignoring me. I'm here about the inheritance your father left you."

Ignoring her? I have no clue what she's talking about. My mind struggles to catch up with her accusation, twisting through memories and possibilities. And—did she just say *inheritance*?

"You haven't contacted me in five years. And if I remember correctly, my old man left me nothing."

"Well, that was the case during the will hearing," Minji replies. "However, there was more I couldn't share until the beginning of this year. And you would have known, if you answered my calls or emails." Her demeanor, though professional, reveals a tangible exasperation. It's clear she's not impressed with my communication habits—or, rather, the lack thereof.

I'm always on the move in my line of work, barely processing anything that isn't an emergency. The world outside often blurs into background noise. I rake a hand through my hair, trying to make sense of how I let this slip by.

"Firefighting isn't exactly conducive to diligent communication," I admit. If her correspondence didn't have *FDNY* in the subject or email address, I likely bypassed them.

"So, back to why I'm here," Minji continues. "There is an inheritance, one whose conditions you must be aware of."

"Conditions?" I repeat. I almost hear Dad's voice, gruff and certain, outlining the terms from beyond the grave. I would not put it past the old man to have some elaborate scheme cooked up, waiting to spring it on me. Whatever this is, it's bound to bring complications.

"Indeed," she confirms, her lips curving into what might pass for a smile on anyone less formidable. "Let's just say Thomas Montgomery wanted to ensure his legacy went beyond firefighting. And he has set a challenge for you, Vulcan. A test of sorts."

"A test?" Fucking hell.

He couldn't just do things the simple way? I feel a mix of anticipation and dread curling in my gut.

The whole situation makes a weird kind of sense. The old man's passion for the department was boundless, but he always believed I should reach for more beyond its constraints.

I can almost imagine him smirking, having the last laugh at the way my life turned out—or didn't turn out. To Dad, everything was a lesson, a chance to prove myself in ways that went beyond a helmet and hose. The sheer unpredictability of it gnaws at me, and maybe that's the point.

If nothing else, he's certainly succeeded in getting my attention. I stroke my beard in frustration. Minji watches me, and behind her detached professionalism, I sense she knows exactly how I'm reacting, how little I understand this sudden shift.

"Yes, a test." She clasps her hands. "But it's not without its... prerequisites."

"Prerequisites?" I frown.

"Mr. Montgomery stipulated that you must be married to claim the inheritance," she says, and I swear my heart skips a beat. Married? I can't even manage a coffee date.

"I don't remember him being particularly sentimental about matrimony." Don't get me wrong, he never cheated on my mom. He was just rarely home to make the marriage work.

"Sentiment had little to do with it," Minji remarks, her dark eyes scrutinizing me. "It's about stability, lineage... perhaps control." She pauses, letting her words sink in. That sounds like my old man for sure.

"Control doesn't die with the man, huh?" I mutter, rubbing the back of my neck. What the hell was my father thinking?

"Apparently not," she replies. "You have two months to meet this condition."

"Two months?!" My pulse hammers in my throat. "Why so damn soon?"

"Your fortieth birthday is the cut-off," Minji explains. "That's why I've been trying to get in touch with you. I even reached out to your mother, who told me she would pass on my message, but I can see that didn't happen either."

Damn it. I've been dodging the sticky notes around my office. I swore I would call her back, but the station needed me. If it was something serious Val would have reached out.

"So, if I don't find someone willing to tie the knot by October, what then?"

"The inheritance reverts to a trust fund for firefighters' widows and orphans," she states, and my eyes widen. "A noble cause, undoubtedly, but one that would leave you without the benefits your father intended specifically for *you*."

"Benefits?" I ask, my mind racing. What could be so important that Dad set up a marital obstacle course? "What are we talking about here?

His collection of antique helmets?"

"Far from it," Minji says, tapping a file on the desk. "The inheritance is substantial enough to change lives, fund projects, secure futures. I don't know how Thomas Montgomery was able to keep this a secret, but it's over fifty million dollars."

"It's *what*?" Sure, we were well off growing up, but this? I'm stunned. The number ricochets around in my skull, and I feel like I've been thrown into one of those cheesy game shows, only this is dead serious. I can't fathom how this slipped under my radar. "Are you sure?"

I remember Dad's tendency to play things close to the chest, always the strategist, but fifty *million* dollars?

My mind races as I try to connect the pieces, the magnitude of it all threatening to flatten me. We certainly never struggled, not after he became chief, and Mom used to make offhanded comments about how he'd come from old money, but as far as we knew, he didn't have a relationship with his family. Not after he married our mother and they cut him off, but that's a different, messier story than I have space for right now.

It crossed my mind once more when he transferred over the deed to my penthouse after I became a firefighter, two years after graduating from college. And *any* penthouse in this city is fucking expensive. Thankfully, I own it, but the upkeep is costly too. If it weren't for the trust my mom set up when I was younger, I wouldn't be able to afford the utilities, even with my salary.

But this kind of money? Holy shit.

"Yes," she continues. "I was even surprised by the amount. I mean, it was less significant back then, but over time and with interest, well… it's substantial."

I stare at her for a long moment, my brain refusing to process this bombshell. *Substantial* doesn't begin to cover it. It's universe-altering.

Identity-shattering.

"Did he obtain this money through shady business dealings? I don't want to inherit money if—"

"It's all above-board. He had *a lot* of investments, Vulcan." Minji's voice softens just a fraction. "Your father may have been... complicated. Maybe even a tiny bit of an asshole to have set up this whole thing. And while I can't make assumptions about his reasoning, his intentions were clear. He believed in you, in your capacity to lead and to love."

"Lead, I can do," I concede, my chest tight. "Love? That's a battlefield I'm not sure I'm equipped to navigate, especially not under a deadline."

"Nevertheless, the choice is yours," she says. "I will assist you in any way I can, should you decide to accept this... challenge."

I rub the bridge of my nose, tension knotting between my brows.

"I wouldn't even know where to begin. To find a woman while still trying to get everything under control here?" I gesture around my office. "I don't think—"

"Which is why *I'm* here." Minji leans forward. "To offer guidance, resources... perhaps even candidates, if you're open to such suggestions."

"Are we talking about matchmaking now?" The corner of my mouth twitches, humor a feeble shield against the rising tide of desperation. She wouldn't have brought it up if she didn't already have something in place.

"Consider it part of the comprehensive legal services I provide. I've spent the past few months collating potential candidates in the event you might need it, and while I've been waiting for you to return my calls"—she pauses, long enough to drive home her point—"I managed to narrow it down some. Time is of the essence. Are you dating someone? That would help expedite this process. After all, millions are on the line."

"Two months..." My voice trails off. The reality hits me like a four-alarm blaze—hot, fast, and unyielding. "I honestly don't think I can do this. At least not by October." I don't think any woman in her right mind would want to do this. *Shit.*

"Your father knew you'd be shaken," she says softly. "But he also knew the *strength* of your character, Vulcan. You've dedicated your life to bearing others' burdens. This is one you shouldn't carry alone."

"Strength of character doesn't put a ring on my finger, Minji." I pause, thinking over my next words. "And it doesn't change the fact that I'm being strong-armed into matrimony by a man who couldn't make his own marriage work." My parents divorced when I was eighteen. My mom went on to remarry, moved to England, and took my baby sister with her. Valkyrie eventually returned to New York, but my mother stayed in the UK and Father never remarried. He dedicated his life to the fire department. So, the question once again is, why the fuck is he doing this to me?

"True," she concedes, "but it does give you the opportunity to redefine what marriage means to you. And as for support..." She rises. "You have mine, unequivocally. Whether you choose to pursue this inheritance or not, I'll be there to assist you and advise you of the next steps if it reverts to a trust."

"Thanks, Minji. I guess I need to figure out my next move."

"Take your time," she advises, then tilts her head in consideration. "But not too much. Remember, two months can pass in the blink of an eye."

"Right." A wry chuckle slips out. Two months. Sixty days to find a bride and claim an inheritance I didn't even know existed. Minji strides confidently toward the door. Right then and there, something within me shifts from dread to determination. My father may have set the board, but it's my game to play.

"Minji," I call out before she can leave. "One more thing, make sure those candidates you mentioned are thoroughly vetted, will you?"

"Of course," she confirms, a sly smile playing on her lips. "You'll have them by morning."

As the door shuts behind her, I lean against the sofa. My hands find their way to my temples, fingers massaging in a vain attempt to stave off the headache building. Two fucking months. A marriage of convenience? The very idea seems ludicrous. Yet there it sits, an uninvited guest at the table of my future, demanding attention.

Find a bride.

Then there's Karina.

This marriage stipulation changes everything. As much as it annoys me, I know I need to keep my distance from her now. The last thing I want to do is string someone along.

My phone lights up with a text. It's from Karina, asking if I'm free to have coffee tomorrow before her shift at the hospital. I sigh heavily, the weight of this decision dragging me down. She is far too good, too pure, to get tangled up in this mess. I can't ask her to stick beside me through it. That'll make me the biggest asshole of the century.

And an asshole is something I'm not—well, I try not to be.

As I type out the message I know I need to send, a feeling of loss settles over me. Even the fleeting moments we've shared have filled me with more joy and comfort than I've felt in years.

I hit send before I can change my mind. The decision has been made, and there's no going back.

CHAPTER EIGHT

Vulcan

As I scrub away at the fire truck, lost in thought, the station door swings open with a rush of hot summer air. I look up to see Minji, dressed in a pink sundress that stops just above her knees. Not only are her clothes a distraction, but it's her presence—like a bomb ready to disrupt my routine and bring uncertainty and change—that has me standing at attention.

"Got the list," she announces. Her bob swings as she thrusts a manila envelope at me. Slowly, I slide the paper out and stop.

"You never told me last night how you found these women."

"They're all single and meet the criteria. There are ways to secure these types of relationships discreetly, you know. You're not the first to have run into this type of dilemma, as absurd and foreign as it might feel to you now." She leans against the gleaming truck. "So, does it matter where they came from?"

"It does. I don't want to marry a psychopath."

"And you won't. Just look at the list, Vulcan."

I let out a deep breath, staring at the folder.

"This isn't just about picking a dinner date," she reminds me.

"Haven't forgotten," I mutter, though the truth is, forgetting would be a hell of a lot easier. The magnitude of all this hits me like a tidal wave: I have to get fucking *married*. I slide my thumb under the seal and open the envelope, trying to think of this as a tactical decision rather than a personal one.

I pull out the paper. Names leap out at me, a jumble of possibilities. Some are actually familiar, I realize, while some I've never come across. I can practically see their résumés floating in front of me, detailing not just their occupations, but how they might fit or clash with mine.

My eyes scan down the list, heart pounding like a drum. Allison Chang. I remember her from an event last year—she'd spoken passionately about her nonprofit. She was all money and social influence, groomed to perfection, but maybe *too* perfectly groomed? I'm not sure I could live up to that image for more than three days.

Emma Bowers. I'm pretty sure she's the physical therapist I keep running into when I visit Val at her clinic. Huh. Small world. From what I've gathered, Emma's got a cheerful energy that's hard to resist, but she's also got a wild streak that could burn me out quickly.

As I work my way further down the sheet, I try to see myself through their eyes and can't help but wonder what they each think they're signing up for. Do they know the real stakes here, or do they just see dollar signs? Maybe they think I'm the one who's desperate. I pause at a name that makes my skin prickle with a mix of confusion and intrigue.

Karina Reyes.

My heart skips a beat, then two. The image of her from the gala yesterday pops into my head, that emerald dress clinging to her in ways that had made it hard to think of anything else. What's she doing on this list? No way she'd willingly put herself in this type of situation. Not the career-focused doctor who needled me for wasting her time.

Unless Minji has kept the subject of the charade from these women, the same way she dropped the inheritance bomb on me…

I can't shake the feeling that there's more going on, something I'm not seeing. I stare at her name, the bold ink practically burning into the page.

"Karina?"

"Mmm, Karina Reyes," Minji says. "Emergency medicine doctor. Impressive résumé. And she's got a spirit that could keep up with yours. She's busy, so this could be a great match."

"Go on," I say, leaning back against the cool metal of the nearest truck.

"She was at the top of her class at NYU, dedicated to her work. Lives to make a difference." Minji ticks off Karina's qualities as if she's listing features on a luxury car. Part of me feels deceptive for learning this information from a third party, but I'm guessing Minji dotted her i's and crossed her t's, legally speaking. These women have offered up this information, and I'm aware it is above board... but it still doesn't sit totally right.

"Her father passed away when she was sixteen. She has two brothers in college, and her mother is a homemaker."

"Only catch," Minji adds, raising an eyebrow. "She's twelve years younger than you."

"Age is just a number," I counter, remembering our conversation. "*If* I go with her."

She gives a nonchalant shrug, but I know better. Her eyes are anything but casual. They're locked on to me, as sharp and calculating as ever, dissecting my reaction like it's spelled out in neon lights.

"Nothing I can't handle," I say.

"Think it over. Hard." She doesn't let up, her gaze drilling into me, making sure I understand the implication. "She's young."

"You wouldn't have put her on the list if you thought it would be an issue." I lift a brow slightly. "Or was her name not supposed to be here?"

"She's a great candidate. However, there are others on that list. I want you to make the best choice for you. You haven't even looked at the other names."

"I did."

"And?"

"And what?"

"Vulcan, you don't have the luxury of time. You've got one day."

"Twenty-four hours? That's it?" I choke out in disbelief. "I thought I had two months to get married."

My heart hammers against my ribs, as if it's the last alarm I'll ever hear. One day to pick a woman who'll be my wife—a week, tops. I'd thought I had at least a month, some luxury of time to consider, to flinch, to change my mind. Instead, I'm left with one lousy day to sort through names and faces, to picture a future out of this chaos. How am I supposed to build a life with a stranger in just twenty-four hours? This whole arrangement suddenly feels less like a cruel joke, the punchline aimed squarely at my sanity.

"Deadlines wait for no man," she says, the corner of her mouth twitching as though she's aware of just how absurd it sounds. "And I can't trust you to do this alone. If I let you dictate how this process goes, that money will be funneled into a trust and you'll lose autonomy."

She's right.

The list in my hand is a grenade without a pin. I'm not just choosing a date for some high-society gala; I'm picking the other half of a contract that will legally bind us. Everything in me wants to hurl the papers into the nearest fire and watch them burn, but before I can spiral further, Minji drops another bombshell.

"Three years, Vulcan. That's the minimum requirement to secure your inheritance. Three years married."

"Three…"

"Years," she confirms. "You will get twenty million up front."

Three years is a lifetime. A lot can happen—fires extinguished, lives saved, the slow burn of a marriage turning to ash.

This is insane. I swear a child is going to be the next bomb she drops on me.

"Three years." I glance at the list again. Karina's name seems to leap off the page.

"Exactly. Think about what you stand to gain. Or lose."

Gain. Lose. Two sides of the same coin flipping over and over in my head.

Her gaze softens, but only by a fraction. "It's about securing the future. You do have a sister who can also benefit from this. I'm sure."

"Right. Tomorrow, then," I finally say. My decision is already made, but I don't want to seem too eager. "I'll have an answer for you."

"Or do you already have an answer?" She knows and wants me to say it aloud.

My gaze drifts back to Karina's name. I can't shake the memory of her at the Heroes Gala, the way her laughter seemed to light up the room. I remember the instant spark of attraction toward her even before that run-in, the way it caught me by surprise and lingered long after she'd left Riley's. What would life with Karina be like? Would she be happy to find out that her "marriage of convenience" husband is me?

"Damn it." I grip the pages. Maybe I should just go with Emma the physical therapist.

"So, you don't have a choice as of now?"

I close my eyes, choosing to ignore Minji's prodding. I search for solace, for some kind of sign from the man whose expectations shaped me as much as the flames I've battled. He thought this was some grand fucking adventure, tying up my future with all the guarantees of a blind jump from a burning rooftop. He thought it'd test me, break me, mold me into something else. I wonder if he knew I'd end up here, tangled in choices that feel more like shackles than freedom.

"I can't believe my old man thought this was a great idea."

"Oh, come on, Vulcan, you know better than anyone why these stipulations are in place," she says. "Our parents think they know us better than we know ourselves. From what I gather, he watched you pour everything into this job until there was nothing left for you." Her voice softens slightly. "I can only assume he wanted you to have something real. A connection, a future that wasn't just about the next fire."

"By blackmailing me into it?"

"By giving you a push." She sighs. "This isn't punishment. It's an opportunity."

I scoff, but the truth in her words sting.

"Fine. I have my wife-to-be," I finally say. It's a gamble, all of it. But sometimes, the greatest risks forge the strongest bonds. My gaze drifts from the list to Minji's expectant face, and then back again. "I want…" I start, feeling the weight of a thousand eyes on me.

"Karina?"

"Karina," I confirm.

"Okay." She nods, her professionalism masking the curiosity in her eyes. "I'll reach out to her."

"Does she know who she's marrying if she agrees?" I ask.

"Sort of." Minji clears her throat. "I kept your identity hidden from all the candidates. It seemed… *prudent.*"

"Good." Anonymity provides a layer of comfort, a small buffer against immediate judgment. However, this can go two ways. When she sees me, she'll either run for the hills or accept this weird agreement. I'm hoping for the latter, but I told her just last night, in no uncertain terms, that I didn't have time to give to a relationship. And now, I'm looking for a wife—*fucking hell.*

"Let's get down to what you're willing to offer for this arrangement."

Hell if I know. What do I even want out of this whole thing? "She should be well compensated. I'm thinking a million at the minimum, but I'm willing to go up to five. If she wants more than that she and I will have to discuss it in person."

"So, you want to meet her? I mean, of course you do, but before she signs the contract? I will have an NDA in place for both of you." Minji makes it sound like a business transaction, which it is, but when it comes to Karina, for some strange reason, I want this to be real.

Actually, it's best if I meet her after. My gut tells me not to make this more complicated than it already is. I still don't know how she will react to learning it's me behind the veil. Would it make her laugh at the fucked-up irony of it all?

"Have her sign first and let her know I would want her to move in with me after the wedding." I'm pushing it, but if this is going to work, it's got to be all in. No halfway measures.

Minji raises her eyebrows, almost like she wasn't expecting me to come out swinging like this. "You don't have to move in together. But if you want that... are you sure?"

I huff out a breath, steeling myself for the road ahead. "Sure as I'll ever be." I'm betting on this plan, on everything. I'm betting on Karina, on the spark between us that I hope will ignite instead of fizzling out.

"I'll reach out to her and schedule a meeting time for you two. In the meantime, try not to get yourself killed," she jokes.

"No promises. Danger's part of the job description."

She rolls her eyes, a gesture that feels more like camaraderie than exasperation. "Just try not to get barbecued before you meet the bride, Vulcan. It would be a shame to waste that pretty face of yours."

"I'll do my best."

I watch as she leaves, leaning against the truck again and feeling the cool metal press into my back like a lifeline. I'm about to marry a woman who doesn't even know she's engaged to me. Hell, she might bail the second she finds out. Maybe I'm an idiot. No, I'm *definitely* an idiot. I blew her off not once but twice, and now my grand plan is to make her my wife?

I run a hand through my hair, frustration growing as my mind spins out of control. It could get messy. Real fucking messy.

She's a smart woman. The thought of her rejecting this crazy proposition, rejecting me, ties my guts into tighter knots. My palms begin to sweat, and my heart hammers a frantic beat like I'm battling a blaze I can't control. What if she never wants to speak to me again? I almost feel the ground shifting beneath me.

The alarm blares through the station, jolting me from my spiral of doubt, followed by the voice over the intercom. *"Engine 37, residential fire on 106th and 3rd Ave. Four-story complex with possible rescue situation."*

I'm moving on autopilot. This is what I know. This is what makes sense. The weight of my turnout gear settles on my shoulders, familiar and grounding. The helmet clicks into place, and suddenly, Karina, Minji, and the inheritance all fade to background noise.

"Let's move!" I call out, climbing into the rig as the siren wails to life.

CHAPTER NINE

Karina

I settle into the uncomfortable chair at my cluttered desk. My apartment is more claustrophobic and oppressive than ever. I glance around and shake my head, disgusted by its state. Furniture purchased at Goodwill years ago, stained from coffee spills and takeout mishaps. Dishes piled in the sink from three days ago, clothes draped over every available surface, and the thin curtains barely blocking out the harsh streetlights. This is not the life I imagined for myself at twenty-seven.

My life is a mess, and this apartment is just the physical manifestation of it. I drop my head into my hands, and a long, unsteady sigh escapes me. The bills. They pile higher with each new envelope my mother sends my way. Tuition. Rent. Credit card repayments. My mother's name is on so much of it, I hardly know where her mess ends and my life begins.

I want to rip up every page from that stack, scatter the pieces, watch them flutter like confetti, but the suffocating sense of duty keeps my hand still. Instead, I restlessly push them around my desk, as if reorganizing the chaos will somehow make it disappear. I drop my head back against the chair, defeated and desperate, lost in a whirlwind of obligations.

I have to do something.

I let out another deep sigh and clutch the phone in my hand. My fingers tremble slightly as I scroll through the contacts, hovering over her name. I try to imagine her reaction this time. Will she be pleading? Manipulative? Will she threaten me with tears, silence, or worse, insults? Feeling like her biggest regret all over again, the one who always disappoints, no matter how much I put my best foot forward. I take a moment, drawing in a breath for courage, and reluctantly press call.

"Karina?" My mother's voice is sharp and impatient. "Finally. I was starting to think you'd forgotten about your responsibilities."

"Hi, *Mother*," I start, "I was just going over the bills and—"

"Which you should have paid already." Like always, she doesn't let me continue. "Your brothers need their tuition settled for next semester."

I can almost see her there, her dark hair streaked with gray, those eyes that never quite warmed when they landed on me. My chest constricts with a familiar ache.

"Mother, it's not my job to—" I begin, but the words catch in my throat.

"Of course it is," she snaps, the edge in her voice like a slap. "You owe us, Karina. You owe *me*. After everything I've done for you."

Which is nothing, I want to say, but I don't. It won't do me any good.

Ever the black sheep. If my father were alive, she would be singing a different tune. Gosh, I miss him more than I could have ever imagined. "Mother, please," I say, my voice softer now, pleading for understanding I know won't come. "I'm doing the best I can."

"Then do better." The line goes dead. I drop the phone onto the desk, onto her unpaid debts. How much more of myself can I give before there's nothing left?

I open up my laptop, scouring job listings, anything that pays more than what I'm already earning, working endless shifts at the hospital. "Come on," I mutter, scrolling past another unrealistic offer. "There has to be something."

God, please send me something. Anything.

I almost miss my phone vibrating and have to shuffle documents around to find where it disappeared. My heart stutters, hope and dread warring within me as I close my eyes and think, *Please don't be her again.*

But when I flip it over in my hand, I see that it's an unknown number. I slide my finger across the screen, answering the call.

"Hello?"

"Karina Reyes?" The voice on the other end is a woman.

"Speaking." I straighten in my chair and brush a strand of hair behind my ear.

"Good evening. This is Minji Lee from Lee-Singleton Law. We spoke a few months ago." There's a pause. "You've been selected by our client, and he would like to have dinner this Saturday."

"Huh?"

"This *is* Karina Reyes?" she asks.

"Yes, but—"

"I'm the lawyer you spoke to regarding my client who is looking for a, er, date. I'm calling back to inform you that you've been selected," she repeats, but this time with an underlying tone of annoyance. *Well, excuse me, it's been months.*

"Sorry, I was just getting caught up. It's been a while, as you mentioned."

She barrels forward. "My client wishes to discuss the details of your arrangement personally."

"Arrangement?" My mind spins, reeling with possibilities, and my heart is a wild drum in my chest. Why would anyone need to discuss details for a date?

"Do you accept the invitation?" Minji's voice is precise, demanding an answer. A million thoughts crowd my consciousness, and I feel lightheaded, as if opportunity and desperation have suddenly traded places. This is crazy. Absolutely crazy. I try to think back on the details from when we spoke in March. There was mention of a sizeable fee, though no specifics were offered up.

Play it cool, Rina. What do you have to lose other than your mountain of debt? "Yes."

"Excellent. I would like to meet with you first. There are a few things we will need to discuss," she continues.

"Discuss?" I repeat, trying to keep the tremor from my voice.

"Before you meet my client. Saturday morning, ten o'clock. I will text you the information shortly. Have a good evening, Karina."

"Thank you, Minji. I'll see you then."

The call ends, and I'm left staring at my reflection on the darkened screen. A dinner. An arrangement. With him. Who is *him*? I told myself I'd forget about this whole thing, that it wasn't real. And now, months later, I learn I've been "selected"?

I set the phone down, letting out a deep sigh. What if this man doesn't like what he sees? What if I'm not enough? I have to be enough. There's too much at stake. My mom's constant harassment, my brothers' college tuition. This cramped excuse for an apartment? I've worked too hard to be living like I was back in the Johns Hopkins dorms.

I will be the best damn date this guy's ever had.

I have less than forty-eight hours to prepare, to transform myself into the kind of woman a man like him would want. He's undoubtedly well off, so I should be confident, poised, and alluring. A far cry from the sleep-deprived, scrubs-wearing doctor I am now.

My phone vibrates again, and I snatch it up. Minji's text lights up the screen—an address.

On Saturday, I arrive at the designated meeting place: a law office in downtown Manhattan. "Okay, Karina. This is it," I whisper to myself, pressing a palm to my chest in an attempt to still the rapid beat of my heart. With a deep breath, I step forward, my heels clicking against the polished stone as I approach the entrance. I straighten my spine and square my shoulders. *I can do this.* The doors glide open silently. I'm ready to walk through the fire, to face whatever strange twist of fate this mysterious client of Minji's has in store.

"Karina Reyes?" One of the receptionists greets me with a smile, her eyes glancing at the appointment book on her desk. "Ms. Lee is expecting you. Please follow me."

As I step into the elevator, my mind races with anticipation.

"Here we are," the receptionist says as she leads me down a hallway lined with polished wood and gleaming glass. "Ms. Lee will be with you shortly." She gestures for me to take a seat in the waiting area.

"Thank you."

She nods and turns on her heels. Not a minute goes by before Minji approaches with a confident stride, sporting a black bob that frames her face perfectly. Her eyes look me over. "Karina, it's great to see you," she says warmly, extending her hand.

"Thank you for the invitation," I reply, shaking her hand firmly.

"Right this way." She guides me toward a private conference room. We enter a space adorned with elegant furnishings and a sleek mahogany table. I pull out a chair and sit, my palms slick with sweat.

I cannot believe I'm about to do this.

"Give me one moment to gather the documents," she says before leaving the room. As I wait, I glance around. Everything screams of wealth, from the intricate patterns on the rug, the gleaming silver pitcher of water in the center of the table, the high ceilings. At least I can rest easy knowing I'm in capable, professional-seeming hands, right?

When Minji reenters the room, she's cradling a thick paper-filled folder in her arms. She places it on the table with a soft thud. "Let's dive in, shall we?" she suggests, sitting across from me. She opens the folder and begins explaining the arrangement's details. "My client is offering you a marriage of convenience."

I blink at her, taken aback by her bluntness. "A... a marriage?" I stammer, trying to wrap my head around what the hell she just said. "I thought this was for a date."

"Allow me to explain," she continues. "You'll be compensated handsomely, as stipulated by my client." I shift in my seat, glance around in search of, what? Hidden cameras? Surely this is some elaborate prank. "However," Minji adds, her expression turning serious. "You must understand that this is *strictly* a marriage of convenience. There will be no romantic involvement between you and my client. What he wants is a wife in name only."

I mean, that's good. I'm certainly not down to fuck a stranger.

"Who is your client?" I ask, curiosity getting the better of me.

"Unfortunately, I cannot disclose that information just yet," she replies. "But rest assured, he is a well-respected individual in his field. He has never been arrested and is not a violent man. The only downfall is that he is married to his career. So, he is not looking for someone to have babies with or go out on dates and live in the land of make-believe. If you don't think you can be that person, I'll let him know and we will find someone else."

My thoughts drift to my mother's demands, and I clench my fists in determination. No, I can do this. I have to do this. "And this arrangement won't affect my career?" I clarify.

"Your professional reputation will not be compromised," she assures me. "In fact, it may even benefit from this marriage." This woman sure knows how to speak in riddles.

With a deep breath, I weigh my options. As much as I want to find love and happiness on my own terms, I haven't had much luck in either department, if my abysmal dating history is anything to go by. And that's without even considering Vulcan's dismissal last week.

"Let's say I agree," I blurt before I can change my mind. "What happens next?"

"First, we'll finalize all the legal documentation. Tonight, you'll have dinner with my client. And then, in due time, you two will say 'I do.'"

"Right," I say slowly, my voice wavering. "And no one will know of this arrangement, correct?"

"No one but you, him, and myself, of course. There will be an NDA to sign."

Okay, knowing this will be hush-hush, I feel a bit more at ease. "Do I have to live with him?"

"He does prefer you two to live under the same roof after the wedding," Minji answers smoothly. "There will be separate bedrooms. He is also more than willing to answer any questions you may have later on tonight. So, any more questions, or shall we—?"

Just do it, Karina. "I agree."

"Are you sure?" she asks gently, her voice tinged with unexpected kindness. She regards me with a look that suggests she's giving me one last opportunity to reconsider. "The marriage timeline is three years," she continues, watching for any flicker of doubt, any hint that I might change my mind and bolt.

"Yes," I affirm, though I know that my feeble word doesn't begin to capture the magnitude of what I'm committing to, the reality of what I'm about to do. Three fucking years.

"Excellent," she replies, sliding the documents across the table for me to sign. "Now, I'm sure you are unfamiliar with most legal jargon, so I'll keep it simple." Her voice is so neutral and professional it's soothing, offering me a sense of stability in a chaotic storm.

She flips open the folder and points to the first page, a simple outline of the agreement, but I can barely focus. My mind keeps pivoting between possibilities, the wild fantasy of a new life, and the crushing reality of the one I'm trying to escape. She's saying something about financial disbursements and time commitments, breaking it down into digestible pieces for my non-lawyer brain. Her explanations are as clear-cut as her appearance. *You can do this*, I tell myself like a mantra. *Just think of it as a job.*

Minji turns a page, then stops to look at me, asking without words if I'm still in. Without hesitation, I nod.

"Here's where you sign," Minji instructs, tapping her finger on the dotted line. Her efficiency leaves no room for doubt, nor time for reconsideration. Maybe that's what I need. A push. An immediate dive into the unknown.

I pause, hovering over the paper and meeting her eyes. She's steady, and that steadiness helps me breathe a little easier. This is only temporary. Three years. That's it.

"Wait," I say, time stretching out endlessly as doubt seizes my resolve. How could I have overlooked something so basic? Visions of a white-haired man with beady, leering eyes flash before me. "How old is he?" I look up from the paper. "Age shouldn't matter," I rush out, hoping she understands what I'm not saying. "But, well. Three years is a long time…"

Minji's expression remains neutral, her calm demeanor unaffected by my outburst of panic. "He's thirty-nine," she states.

"Does he know my age?" My hands tremble slightly as I reach for the pitcher of water, and I barely manage to pour myself a cup without spilling it everywhere.

"He does, and he stated age is nothing but a number. Will this be a problem?"

I scramble, feeling about five seconds from a meltdown, and try to discern as much information while my brain is still sharp. "Can I know what he looks like before I answer that?"

"If you agree, you will be able to see him tonight," she reminds me.

There it is again, her refusal to give me anything until I've signed my soul away. "But you said earlier…" I sputter, trying to piece together the fragments of our conversation like a puzzle that refuses to fit. "What I mean to say is—"

"I see looks and the age difference is a problem for you," she interrupts, a note of finality in her voice. She stands abruptly, reaching for the folder and picking it up in a single motion, as if to close the chapter before it's even begun. What just happened? "I will talk to my client, advising him you are no longer interested."

"No!" The word escapes me like a plea, raw and unrestrained. "I want to do this, but—"

"No buts. You're either in or out." She eyes me, and I can tell she's deciding on how much to reveal. "I can assure you he is very handsome and very much in shape."

What's with this added secrecy then?

"Look…" Minji sits back down. "My client doesn't want to reveal his identity until these documents are signed. You're young, and maybe going this route is not one you should be taking. It's scary, I know, but as much as I want you to feel at ease, my client comes first. So, I thank you for coming down here, but you will no longer be—"

"I'll sign."

She dips her chin and flips open the folder. "Once this is complete, you will be transferred one million dollars."

A frenzied relief washes over me at the vision of escaping the crushing weight of bills and obligations, the demands of family that gnaw at my soul like hungry wolves. For the first time, I envision a life where I'm not constantly on edge, clawing my way toward a freedom that seems almost mythical.

But as quickly as it comes, doubt slides in like a cold shadow, a shiver running down my spine. This isn't just money for nothing; it's trading one burden for another. I can't shake the feeling that I'm selling a piece of myself, exchanging the dream of love for a practical but barren arrangement. This mysterious guy is willing to pay me a million dollars for a three-year marriage, and he's not even expecting intimacy?

"What if he falls in love. What if *I* do?" I blurt.

"Love is outside of the contractual obligation," Minji responds without missing a beat, her eyes fixed on mine. "His career keeps him occupied, as I'm sure yours does. It's unlikely that 'love' will have a chance to blossom between you two."

I chew on my lip, considering what my life has been and what it could be. It's a leap into the unknown, but isn't that where faith finds its wings? Minji slides the folder toward me. My hand hesitates, hovering over the documents.

"One more thing. I don't need that much money. Just three hundred thousand." The words spill out in a rush. I'm reclaiming some small piece of myself amidst the chaos. Minji's eyebrows arch slightly, the first real sign of surprise she's shown, but she doesn't question me. Maybe she sees I'm not as desperate as I look, respects the move, even. I flip to the page with the amount, striking a confident line through the *$1,000,000*. I write down *three hundred thousand* instead.

Then, with a breath that feels like surrender and a tremor in my fingers, I sign on the dotted line.

"Congratulations, Karina. You've just taken the first step toward a new life."

"Thank you," I reply. "I appreciate everything you've done to help me."

"Of course. If you have any questions or concerns, don't hesitate to contact me. And remember," she adds, her voice taking on a reassuring tone, "you're not alone in this journey. Your future husband is just as committed to making this arrangement work. If not more, in my opinion."

I rise to my feet and clasp Minji's hand, finalizing the agreement that will alter my life permanently. As I exit the law office, emotion swirls within me. This may not be the fairy-tale ending I once dreamed of, but it's a decision bound to give me peace of mind.

CHAPTER TEN

Karina

The moment I push through the glass doors of the upscale restaurant, a fluttering sensation takes up residence in my stomach. It's like a swarm of butterflies are having a rave in there. The restaurant's decor is gorgeous; the kind of fancy place I only ever see on TV or in my dreams. Ornate light fixtures, plush velvet booths, and what appear to be linen napkins. I realize I'm way underdressed in my simple black dress, and the feeling in my stomach doubles in intensity, turning into a full-on circus act.

I approach the hostess stand hesitantly, smoothing my hands over the fabric as I try to manage both my appearance and my nerves at once. I look around, taking stock of the crowd. Couples leaning in close over candlelit tables. Servers gliding past with trays of delicate plates. There's a hum of muted conversation underscored by gentle jazz music, and the aroma of fresh bread and delicate tomato sauce overwhelms me. I feel like an outsider, like everyone here can tell I don't belong. I give the hostess Minji's name, feeling my voice quiver just a bit, and she smiles knowingly. She gestures toward a table near the back, where a man sits alone, his face obscured by the menu he's reading.

"Your date is already here, ma'am," she says politely.

I take a deep breath and walk toward the man who will be my husband for the next three years. As I draw closer, the man lowers his menu, and my steps falter.

"*Vulcan?*" I question in disbelief.

I don't—I... He can't be. But there he sits, ruggedly handsome, the very picture of strength and poise. His salt-and-pepper hair and smoldering brown eyes are unmistakable even from this distance. He looks like he's casually stepped out of one of those cologne commercials where the guy is somehow both a mountain climber and a CEO.

My shock quickly turns to anger. This is *definitely* a prank, I'm sure of it now. I spin on my heel to storm out, but Vulcan is already on his feet, his large hand gently grasping my arm.

"Wait, please hear me out," he pleads. "Give me five minutes, Karina. Please."

"Why should I?" I try to snatch my arm from his grasp, but he holds tight. Conscious of our surroundings, I don't resist any further, desperate to escape this scene with some dignity.

"Because I'm a fucking idiot."

"Not the word I would use, but I'll hear you out." I allow him to guide me into the chair across from his.

The candlelight flickers between us, casting warm shadows over the table and illuminating the sparkling silver cutlery. I take a deep breath and muster the courage to ask the question that's burning inside me. "So, you text me that you don't have time because of work, and all along you're out scouting women to marry in a pinch?" I scoff. "If you didn't want to see me, that's all you had to say."

Vulcan sighs, his shoulders folding in as he meets my gaze. "I'm sorry I lied," he begins. "I never thought I'd find myself in this kind of situation. But when Minji presented the proposal, it seemed like the best way to, well—Jesus. Where do I even start?"

"How about with the truth."

Vulcan takes a sip of his drink before continuing. "It appears my father left me a significant inheritance. But it came with stipulations, one of which being that I get married. Apparently he thought it would help me find stability and settle down. I honestly don't know, because he died five years ago and I only just learned of it."

"But why me? You *clearly* wanted to ghost me. You lied to me. And, fine. It wasn't not a big deal, seeing as you didn't owe me anything, but you could have told me you didn't want to see me. I'm a big girl."

Vulcan sighs and runs a hand through his hair. "If I didn't want to see you, you wouldn't be sitting across from me. And to your point: yes. I agree. It was a dickhead move on my part." He scrubs a hand down his face, lowering his voice. "I *am* attracted to you. Very fucking attracted to you. But I found all this out on the night of the gala, and I thought it was best just to cut ties. I didn't want to string you along knowing what I had to do." He pauses, holding my gaze. "But then I saw your name as one of the candidates Minji vetted. I saw this as a second chance, so to speak. I mean, what *are* the chances?" He pauses, stroking his beard. "I should have been upfront with you. It was wrong to freeze you out with a text."

"Yeah, that would have been nice." I sigh. "But I still think you're lying to me. Minji reached out to me months ago about this. Yet, you're saying you just found out."

The math ain't mathing.

"I'm not lying about that. I've not been checking my emails from her office, so she came looking for me, and now I'm glad she did. She's been doing work in the background since before I even knew." He leans toward me, resting his forearms on the table. His shirt sleeves are rolled up, revealing his toned, muscular arms and tattoos on his right arm. I can't help but stare, my mouth going dry. I force myself to look back up at his face, trying to focus on the conversation at hand.

"First of all, I didn't know it was a marriage. I thought it was a *date*, and then, I don't know, curiosity, maybe?"

"Bullshit." He raises an eyebrow.

"Fine. The financial incentive was a draw." I know what he's about to ask, and I'd rather beat him to it. "You already know what I do, and I get paid well, but I have to help my family *a lot*. My mother—my money is really spread thin." I stop myself from rambling. He doesn't need to know my problems.

"I see." He nods, saying nothing more.

I pick up the menu, letting the list of gourmet dishes serve as a temporary barrier between us.

"Let's see if they have anything that pairs well with awkwardness," I quip, trying to lighten the mood.

Vulcan chuckles, and I catch myself smiling—for real this time. Maybe this won't be so bad after all. This might be the most world's most unconventional beginning to a relationship—not that it can be qualified as a *relationship*—but as I look into Vulcan's eyes, I can't shake the sense that maybe, just maybe, there's a spark there worth exploring.

"Tell me, how do you see the next three years unfolding?" I ask.

Vulcan leans back in his chair, his eyes sparkling with amusement. "Well, I imagine it will be a whirlwind of passion, banter, and the occasional disagreement over cuddling."

I nearly choked on my water, taken aback by his playful response. "Is that so? I was told you'd be more of a 'separate bedrooms' kind of guy."

"I'm not opposed to sharing a room with you." He smirks, and I can feel the tips of my ears heating up. "But in all seriousness, I think we'll need to navigate this together, one day at a time. It's not like either of us has a manual for how it's supposed to unfold."

"You mean you didn't get the memo? I hear sham marriages are all the rage these days." I can't help but match his teasing tone, finding myself drawn into the easy flow of our conversation, just like that night at the bar.

As the waiter approaches to take our order, I realize I've been so caught up in our exchange that I haven't even thought about what to eat or drink. Vulcan seems to sense my predicament and smoothly takes the lead, ordering with a confidence that I find both irritating and oddly attractive.

Once the waiter departs, I fix Vulcan with a curious gaze. "You really want to share a room?"

"Isn't the whole point of this arrangement to make it look like a real marriage?"

"We don't have to put on a show for anyone. We're grown, and I don't see my family coming to visit your place. They don't visit me as it is. Separate rooms will be fine." I take a sip of my water.

Vulcan leans back in his chair, an amused glint in his eyes.

"Understandable. So, separate rooms. Anything else?"

I lean forward, resting my elbows on the table as I meet his gaze head-on. "Nope."

Dinner goes smoothly, and somewhere along the way, I seem to have relaxed into this new reality. I'm no longer counting the minutes until I can escape. Instead, I realize I don't *want* this date to end.

We transition from dessert to sipping coffee, and the world outside the restaurant's windows fades into a blur. It's just the two of us, caught up in a strange dance of fate and choice.

The night may be founded on a contract, but the connection? That's all ours.

"I'm surprised you haven't asked the big question."

"Which is?"

"When is the wedding?"

I wave him off. "A courthouse wedding is fine with me. I already signed my NDA. We can settle on a date that works for us both, and then I'll move in."

Vulcan leans forward, his eyes locked on mine. "Eager to get hitched and shack up, are we? I thought you'd want to revel in the anticipation a bit longer."

I scoff, rolling my eyes. "Please, I'm not some starry-eyed bride. The sooner we get this over with, the sooner I can focus on my career and pay off my family's debts."

"Ah, she's pragmatic. I can respect that." A smirk plays at the corners of his mouth. "But don't you think a little celebration is in order? We are tying the knot, after all."

I raise an eyebrow, refusing to let him chip away my resolve. "What did you have in mind? A quick toast at the courthouse steps?"

"Do you not like crowds? Are you on the run from someone? Is there a warrant out for your arrest?" he jokes.

"No! Nothing like that." I laugh, but it comes out strained. "I just… I didn't think a big ceremony would be necessary. It's not like we're in love." What I really want to tell him is I don't want my mother to find out I'm getting married.

"Love or not, appearances matter in this world," he says, swirling the remaining wine in his glass. "And I would like to honor the terms of this arrangement while maintaining my reputation. And yours, by extension."

I feel a flush creep up my neck. He's right, of course. A courthouse wedding would look suspicious, especially for someone of his status. And despite my protests, I can't deny that a small part of me—the part that once dreamed of white dresses and flower arrangements before life's harsh realities set in—is curious about what a wedding to someone like him would entail.

"I'll think about it," I concede. "But what else do you have in mind?"

"I was thinking more along the lines of—"

He stands up abruptly and moves around to my side of the table, taking a seat next to me. My eyes widen, but I quickly recover. The heat of his body radiates through the thin fabric of my dress, and I have to resist the urge to lean into him.

"We could have a proper engagement party." His voice low and intimate, and it's disrupting those butterflies that have finally settled. "Nothing too flashy, but enough to make it believable. We need to sell this marriage, don't we?"

His fingers brush against mine on the table, and I feel a jolt of electricity at the contact. I swallow hard. Sweet fucking heavens, this man here. "No to the engagement party. So what else do you propose we do to sell this?"

"Okay, no engagement party. So in that case, we could practice being a bit more... *affectionate* in public."

Before I can react, he leans in and presses a soft kiss to my cheek. His lips linger for a moment, and his beard tickles my skin, sending shivers down my spine. I inhale quickly, caught off guard by the sudden intimacy. My heart races and I silently curse my body's betrayal.

"See?" he whispers against my skin. "Not so bad, is it?"

I turn to face him, our faces mere inches apart. "Vulcan," I breathe. The wine in my system is not helping me keep my thoughts pure. Hell, my thoughts have been in the gutter since our dance at the gala. I would be a liar if I said I didn't pray we'd make it back to his place for a nightcap. But the opportunity never arose.

"Karina." His eyes darken as they flick down to my lips. I can feel the heat of his breath on my skin, and it takes every ounce of willpower I possess not to close the distance between us. But my willpower is rapidly crumbling as I find myself leaning in, as if drawn by an invisible force.

Just as our lips are about to meet, my phone buzzes loudly on the table. I pull back, and just like that, the spell is broken. I grab my phone, grateful for the distraction.

> **Cassie: I'm at your house, where are you?**
> **This is the first time in months you've been**
> **out... so please tell me you're fucking?**

"Tell her yes," Vulcan says over my shoulder, placing his hand on my bare thigh. His touch sends sparks through my body, and I struggle to form a coherent thought.

My cheeks burn. "I... I can't tell her that."

Vulcan's breath is hot against my ear. "Why not? It could be true soon enough." He nips at my earlobe. I have had plenty of men hit on me, but this... from him. My God! My heart pounds in my chest as I turn to face him. His eyes are full of desire, and I find myself drowning in them. I should push his hand away; tell him this is inappropriate. But I don't want to.

So, I take a shaky breath and type out a reply.

> **Me: Out for dinner. Talk later.**

Vulcan's fingers trace lazy circles on my thigh, inching higher with each pass.

"Where were we?" he murmurs.

"I don't know." I lick my lips.

A slow grin spreads across his face. "I do."

This time when he leans in, I meet him halfway. Our lips crash together, and suddenly, I'm lost in a storm of sensation. His beard scratches my jaw as his tongue teases mine, and I can't get enough. I thread my fingers through his hair, pulling him closer and deepening the kiss.

I hope no one is paying attention to our table.

I moan into his mouth as his hand grips me tighter. Heat pools low in my belly. I lean into his touch, craving more. *Sweet fucking Heavens, Karina, you are in a restaurant.*

I pull away from Vulcan, gasping for air. My lips tingle from his kiss, and my body aches for more. Needing to douse myself in cold water, I check my phone again, finding a missed call.

"Ignore it," Vulcan growls, trying to pull me back.

I shake my head, forcing myself to focus. "I can't. It might be the hospital." I grab the phone—it's Cassie. "Sorry, I need to take this."

"You know I try not to check your location, but you left me no choice." She starts up the second I hit accept. *"And you are having dinner at Jean-Georges. Bitch, that means he got money. Who is he?"*

I look over at Vulcan and tell her, "A friend."

"A friend? A friend you will be fucking tonight or a friend you will be kissing on the cheek and saying 'we should do this again,' knowing you won't be doing it again?" Cassie questions.

I feel my cheeks pink at her blunt question. Vulcan raises an eyebrow, clearly intrigued by my flustered state.

"I can't talk about this right now," I hiss into the phone.

"Oh my god, he's right there, isn't he?" Cassie squeals. *"You have to tell me everything later!"*

"Goodbye," I say firmly, ending the call.

I set the phone down, avoiding Vulcan's gaze.

"So," he drawls, "am I the friend you'll be fucking tonight or the one getting a chaste kiss on the cheek?"

My eyes snap to his, and I see nothing but pure, raw desire. He heard. *Of course* he heard. Cass doesn't have an inside voice.

"I... I don't know," I stammer. I don't remember him being this direct at the bar. I love a man who takes charge, but I don't want him to become overbearing. *That* is a turn off.

Vulcan leans close, his breath hot against my ear. "I vote for option one."

A shiver runs down my spine, and I can't stop the small gasp that escapes my lips as his hand slides higher. I clench my thighs together, trapping his hand this time. I can*not* allow him to finger me in a restaurant. I'm not that kind of woman.

"What do you say, Karina?" he murmurs. "Want to get out of here?"

"I-I have work in the morning. Raincheck?"

For a moment, I think he might push the issue. But then he leans back. "Raincheck it is," he says. "Let me pay the bill, and I'll drop you off at home."

"No, that's fine. I can take a cab."

"I wouldn't be a gentleman if I allowed that. Nor a great husband-to-be."

I hesitate, torn between my desire to maintain some distance and the undeniable pull I feel toward him. His intense gaze doesn't waver, and I find myself nodding reluctantly.

"All right," I concede, "but just a ride home."

Vulcan's smile widens as he signals for the check. "Of course, Dr. Reyes. Just a ride home."

The way he says it, though, makes it clear this is far from over. As we walk out of the restaurant, his hand finds the small of my back, guiding me gently. The touch sends sparks through my body, and I have to remind myself to breathe.

CHAPTER ELEVEN

Karina

The ride to my apartment is quiet but filled with tension. Each time we stop at a red light, I feel Vulcan's eyes on me, and it's an effort not to meet his gaze. My skin feels too tight, my body too warm, and I'm acutely aware of how close he is in the confined space of his Audi.

Every inch is electrified by his presence, and I have to clench my hands in my lap to keep from reaching out to him. It's a battle of wills, one that I'm terrified of losing.

I've wanted Vulcan since we met nearly a month ago, and even though he bailed on me twice, my attraction to him has never waned. My heart races like I've just run a marathon, and it doesn't help that his nearness is intoxicating.

The city blurs past in a kaleidoscope of lights and darkened windows, but I barely notice. Everything in me is attuned to the man at my side. I bite my lip, trying to anchor myself to reality even as my mind spins with the possibilities of what could happen if I gave in, if I let go of all the reasons I shouldn't. I want him, but I'm about to be his wife; having sex with him now would change things, complicate them.

"You can breathe, you know that?" he teases. "I won't bite."

"I am breathing," I insist with probably a bit too much fervor.

He flashes a wicked grin, and I know he's fully aware of his effect on me. I look away, but not before the smolder in his eyes sends another wave of heat straight through me. My building is just a block away, and part of me wants to jump out of the car as soon as we pull up to escape the tension and collect myself in the safety of my apartment. The other part wants to drag him upstairs and give in to the wild night of passion he's offering.

When we stop in front of my building, I expect him to simply drop me off, but he puts the car in park and turns off the engine.

"I'll walk you up," he says.

"That's really not necessary," I protest weakly, but he's already getting out of the car. He's decisive, leaving no room for argument, and I realize I'm not sure if I want to argue at all. My defenses have been crumbling since we left the restaurant together, and no amount of logic or reason seems capable of holding them up. As I watch him stride around to my side of the car, I feel my last stand against his persistence faltering.

He opens my door with the same calm confidence he's had all evening, but now there's a gleam in his eyes, a glint of triumph that makes my breath hitch. I take his offered hand, and a jolt of electricity shoots through me at the contact. There's no point pretending anymore. With each step toward the building, my reluctance fades, dissolving into anticipation and a gnawing need that erases anything other than here and now.

The lobby is silent, but my heart isn't—it's a wild beat in my ears, in my bones, the pulse so loud I swear he must hear it too. Every step we take is one that brings me closer to unraveling completely, and I'm not sure I care about holding it together anymore. On the ride up in the elevator, I'm dizzy with desire, and I don't know if it's the thrill of an impending storm or the calm before it.

"You let me up so easily. I'm disappointed," he teases.

"Letting you *up* and letting you *in* are two different things." I lift my chin.

"You sure about that?" He moves closer, pinning me against the wall with nothing but his presence. He hasn't touched me yet, but I feel claimed all the same.

"No," I admit, my voice barely above a whisper. "I'm not sure about anything right now."

His hand comes up to cup my face, thumb brushing across my lower lip. "Then let me be sure enough for both of us."

As the elevator climbs, so does my heart rate. Five floors have never felt so endless, so *agonizing*. Each second stretches into eternity as we stand there, breathing each other's air, the tension between us a living thing.

"What happens when we reach your door?" His voice is rough but steady, laced with the kind of restraint that suggests he's holding back more than just his words.

"I think you know exactly what happens."

"I want to hear you *say* it."

The elevator stops, and the doors open to my empty hallway. The twelve steps to my apartment feel like walking a tightrope between reason and desire. And I pray reason wins before we reach my door.

I look over my shoulder at him. "Have a good night."

His eyes flash, first with surprise and then with a laugh, and his proximity sends my pulse into chaos. "You're scared."

"I'm cautious," I shoot back, trying to sound more confident than I feel as I fumble with my keys. "There's a difference." *Stay with me, reason.*

"Is there?" He covers my hand with his, steadying the trembling key. "Because this feels like fear. And I don't think you're scared of me, but rather scared of what I'll make you feel if I'm invited in."

"You are very cocky," I reply, the accusation more a tease than anything else, but he seems to know that already.

"I like to think of it as trying to get to know my fiancée better." His breath is hot against my skin, lips brushing my ear. I know how easy it would be to cave to him right now; to let all my defenses crumble and give in. But I'm not ready to lose this round. Not yet.

"Good night," I repeat, with more conviction this time. I turn the key and slip inside my apartment before my body can override the last functioning neurons in my brain.

"At least let me take you to dinner tomorrow night," he says when the door is inches from closing.

"Sounds like a plan," I agree.

"Do you work?"

"I do. But I get off at seven."

"I'll pick you up."

The thought of the hospital gossip mill churning makes me cringe. "How about I just meet you at the restaurant?"

"Not a restaurant," he counters. "My place. I'll text you the address." He leans in, so close I can almost taste him, his lips a whisper away from mine.

The brush of his mouth on mine happens so quickly I'm crushed when he pulls away. "Good night, Doc," he says with that cocky grin of his, then turns and walks backward down the hall, eyes on me the whole time.

I close the door and lean against it, my fingers rising to touch my lips. My heart thunders against my ribs, each beat a reminder that I am alive—thoroughly, wildly alive in a way I haven't felt in so long.

I need a cold shower.

CHAPTER TWELVE
Vulcan

My grip tightens on the steering wheel, turning my knuckles white as I drive toward another fire. The driver operator is out sick, leaving me to the task. The radio crackles with updates, each transmission a lifeline to the chaos unfolding. We swing around the corner, brakes screeching as we pull up at the scene. It's worse than the dispatcher described—a beast of a blaze, clawing at the skeleton of what was once a peaceful residence. Flames gnaw at the structure, windows glowing like the eyes of some ravenous creature.

"Captain, look!" One of my guys points to the upper floor where the fire is greediest, licking at the sky.

"Got it," I acknowledge.

"Hydrants spotted on the right. Let's move!" I command, though it's unnecessary. They're already in motion, swift and sure. "Vent team, you're up!" I yell, watching them gear up with axes and saws, ready to tear into the building.

"Search team, with me!"

As we assess the situation, my mind races. Where is the fire the hottest? What's the structural integrity? Who's still trapped inside?

"Cap, we gotta move fast," one of my crew says, his voice strained under the urgency.

"Right with you," I reply. We need to be in and out. "Let's save some lives," I declare, a rallying cry that sets us into action.

"Keep it tight. Watch each other's backs." We charge forward into the belly of the beast, ready to wrestle life from the jaws of destruction.

We sweep room after room, shouting for anyone still trapped inside. Then I hear it. The faintest cry coming from upstairs. It sounds like a child—fucking hell. My heart lurches as I race toward it, taking the steps two at a time. The floor groans dangerously under my weight, but I don't slow down; every second counts. I find the boy cowering under a desk, tears streaking his soot-covered face. "It's okay, I've got you," I say gently as I scoop him into my arms. His little body trembles against my chest.

Just as we turn to leave, a thunderous crack splits the air. I look up to see the ceiling giving way right above us. Without thinking, I twist my body around to shield the boy. Searing pain explodes through my shoulder as debris rains down. I stumble but stay on my feet, adrenaline flooding my system.

My shoulder screams in protest as I carry the child down the crumbling staircase, and I have to grit my teeth against the pain. All that matters is getting him to safety. Thick smoke billows around us as we make our escape. The boy clings to me, crying into my jacket.

"We're almost there, buddy. Just hold on," I tell him through labored breaths.

Suddenly, the front door appears through the haze. The cool afternoon air rushes in, and with my last ounce of strength, I lunge through it, collapsing onto the sidewalk. My crew surrounds me, helping the child from my arms.

"Captain! You all right?" Chen asks, grabbing hold of my good shoulder. I try to respond but only manage a pained grunt. The world spins as the adrenaline drains from my body. Chen's voice sounds far away, drowned out by the ringing in my ears. I blink hard, struggling to stay conscious.

I feel my mask being lifted off my face. "Cap, eyes open. Stay with us now." It's Ramirez. Her face blurs in and out of focus. I want to reassure them that I'm all right, that this is just part of the job. But I can't form the words, my tongue thick and clumsy in my mouth.

The paramedics are suddenly beside me, moving with quick efficiency as they assess my injuries. I try to tell them I'm fine, but nothing comes out. My vision blanks as they examine my shoulder and collarbone, and they move me to the back of the ambulance, where they start an IV line and monitor my vitals. I blink up at the ceiling, the fluorescent lights searing into my vision.

This is not how I saw my day ending. I want to yell at them that this is just a scrape. Nothing a hot bath and a glass of whiskey can't fix. But the words are stuck again, an unspoken protest swallowed by the sirens wailing above me. I'm aware of every bump of the ambulance, every jolt sending massive amounts of pain through me.

As the ambulance speeds toward the hospital, I start to slip from consciousness. I finally come to and catch glimpses of a few crew members running alongside the stretcher as they wheel me in. Chen. Ramirez. Harry. I want to reassure them, but the more I try, the further away they seem. Helpless, I feel myself start to slip away. Their worried faces swim in and out of my vision. Then, the world fades to black. I drift in a haze of pain and confusion.

"... *minor burns on his left arm and possible fracture of the clavicle...*"

I make out voices, but they're faint.

"... *smoke inhalation, but his O2 stats are holding steady...*"

The words come and go, disjointed. Strangers' faces peer down at me and bright lights stab into my eyes. I can't respond. Can't even flinch. I don't know how long I've been out for.

"... *he is going to need surgery. We need to move quickly.*"

It's as if I'm drowning in words, murky and slow. I feel them cutting my clothes. Or trying to. I'm still mostly in my turnout gear. You can't cut through this. The voices around me muffle, and I'm lost in a sea of darkness once more. My mind retreats, desperately reaching for anything to hold on to.

And then I feel it. A cool hand brushing my forehead.

"You're going to be okay, Vulcan. I've got you."

The voice is a beautiful melody and all I can think about is Karina. We were supposed to have dinner in a few hours. I'm looking at three for three on bailing on her. I want to laugh, but I can feel myself drifting again before I can finish the thought.

When I come to, I'm in a hospital room. The antiseptic smell hits me first, then the soft beeping of machines. My throat feels like I've swallowed shards of glass and my shoulder throbs with each heartbeat. I blink, focusing my vision on the ceiling tiles.

"Welcome back to the land of the living."

I turn my head slightly—mistake. Pain shoots through my neck and shoulder like a bolt of lightning, sharp enough to make me wince.

Karina's sitting in a chair beside my bed. Her beautiful smile has been replaced with genuine concern, her eyes soft and searching as they lock onto mine.

"How long?" I rasp. Speaking sends another wave of pain through me, but the need to know outweighs the discomfort. How long have I been in this twilight zone? How long was I out? My thoughts race ahead, trying to piece together the lost time. The fire. The kid.

"About eighteen hours," she replies, relief washing over her face as she stands. Her touch is light as she adjusts the sheet that's tangled around my arm. "You had surgery on your shoulder," she continues, and I don't miss the catch in her voice. She might be trying for a detached tone, but I can hear her concern. I want to reach out, say something to ease her worries, but the pain and meds make my movements sluggish.

Before I can collect my scattered thoughts into words, a nurse strides into the room. She and Karina speak about my vitals, and I find myself watching Karina's face as she slips back into doctor mode. Her brow furrows slightly as she listens to my stats, and I notice the dark circles under her eyes. Has she been here since I was admitted?

"Everything's looking good, Mr. Montgomery," the nurse says, adjusting the IV in my arm. "Dr. Reyes has been keeping a close eye on you."

When the nurse leaves, Karina sits back down beside me. Her hand hovers over mine for a moment before she places it gently on the bed rail.

"The boy," I manage to croak out. "Is he—"

"He's fine," she says, her eyes softening. "We treated him for smoke inhalation, but he was discharged this morning."

"Good. That's good."

The room grows silent, and then Karina clears her throat. "You gave me quite the scare."

I swallow hard, my throat burning. "Oh yeah?"

"Seeing my soon-to-be husband come into the hospital on a stretcher unconscious was not on my list of potential disasters." Her lips twitch briefly before forming into a thin line.

"With my wife being a doctor, I know I'm in good hands," I say, and Karina blushes, standing up slowly.

She touches my arm gently. "Your shoulder took quite the hit from that falling beam. You were lucky." Her gaze turns serious. "I know you see it as your duty to put yourself in harm's way, but..." She pauses. "I—your team can't lose you."

I reach for her hand, lacing our fingers together. Despite the pain, I give her one of my lopsided grins. "Hey, I'm too stubborn to go anywhere."

Even now, in this bright white room, I feel that unspoken connection between us. My heart swells at the sight of her, so beautiful even after almost a day's worth of stress. I want to tell her how much it means that she's been here, but before I can, her hospital pager beeps.

"Get some rest," she orders, a hint of playfulness lightening her tone. "You're still doped up on codeine."

She looks around quickly before leaning in, her lips brushing gently on my forehead. "I'll come check on you later. Hopefully by then your voice will be better," she says.

I watch her walk toward the door, each step graceful and confident. Her dark hair swings softly with her movements, and a pang of gratitude—and something I don't have the clarity to dissect right now—hits me as she steps out into the hallway.

I let out a weary sigh and sink back into the stiff hospital pillows. Despite my bravado with her earlier, my body aches from the beating it took during the rescue. I adjust so my weight is mostly on my uninjured arm then close my eyes, letting the medicine do its work.

The soft click of the door stirs me out of sleep. I watch through heavy lids as Karina slips back into the room. "I didn't mean to wake you. I wanted to check in before my shift ends." She leans down to inspect the IV line. I study her face, noticing that she isn't wearing makeup, and on her nose she has tiny freckles that I've never noticed before. They make her even more beautiful, if that's possible.

"You must be exhausted," I say.

She smiles wearily. "I am, but I needed to see you first."

I return her smile. "I'm all right, just a little smoke inhalation."

She nods, checking the monitor by my bed. I can tell she's in full doctor mode, assessing my condition. "Right, you forgot I've been here since they brought you in. You've had surgery to repair a scapula fracture, and you've narrowly avoided thermal injury. So, yeah. Don't even try with the 'just a little smoke inhalation.'" Her gentle fingers brush my hair back from my forehead, lingering a moment longer than necessary. "I'm about to marry a real-life Avenger." She playfully rolls her eyes.

I chuckle, ignoring the ache in my chest that has nothing to do with the fire. "I'm always ready to play the hero."

"Well, this hero needs to take better care of himself." Karina's voice is stern once more. "I don't want to see you in here again anytime soon."

"Is that your professional opinion?"

"It's my personal opinion as well. My check won't clear if you're dead," she says with a wink. "Kidding… *maybe*, but I care about you, Vulcan. More than I probably should, with how little we know each other." She bites down on her lip.

I reach for her hand, threading our fingers together. "Karina, I—"

A knock at the door interrupts the moment, and she snatches her hand back. Harry pokes his head in, eyes narrowing. "Sorry to… interrupt. But the guys are getting antsy out here. They want to make sure you're still in one piece."

I clear my throat in a bid to regain my composure. "Give me a minute."

Harry nods, shooting Karina a wink before ducking back out.

"They've been setting up camp in shifts. Causing quite the commotion with the nurses." She shakes her head, a rueful smile on her face. "I should get going. I have to be back here early in the morning. Promise me you'll take it easy."

"Cross my heart," I vow, giving her a mock salute.

Karina leans in, brushing a feather-light kiss against my forehead again. "I'll hold you to that."

I watch as she slips out of the room and sigh. It's going to take months to recover fully, months of dealing with the pain and the frustration of not being able to work at full capacity.

But knowing she'll be here, helping me heal—helping us both figure this out—makes it all bearable.

CHAPTER THIRTEEN

Karina

I leave Vulcan's hospital room and am back in front of where his crew is gathered. They've been tagging each other in and out for the last day, most of them still on active duty at the fire station. They look anxious and hopeful, like a bunch of kids outside a principal's office waiting for news they can't control but desperately want to hear.

It's nice to see, and it's clear they consider one another family. I can only imagine the thoughts that ran through their heads when he left the scene, when everything changed instantly. I know what went through my mind in the beginning, when all I could see was him lying motionless. I could barely keep it together.

I bet the gossip is already buzzing around the hospital. They probably saw me as a lunatic or a girlfriend from hell. I didn't want anybody's hands on him but mine, but I knew to step back and let my team take over. It would've been a HIPAA violation and a half had I not disclosed our… *entanglement*, I guess you could call it.

So, I had to keep myself in check, even if it was a difficult task.

The urgency, the commotion, the usual clatter of a hospital in chaos made me feel alive and terrified at the same time. It's how I've lived most of my life, but it's different with *him*. There's more at stake when it's someone you care about whose life is hanging in the balance. My professional detachment crumbled like ash as I watched the doctors swarm around him. Their efficiency was my salvation and my torment all at once.

"Hey, Dr. Reyes," Harry says, standing from his crouched position against the wall.

"He's going to be okay," I reassure them, though they likely already got this news when he was cleared from surgery. "The doctor said he just needs rest. You can see him, but don't stay too long. Thirty minutes to an hour tops." I look to Harry. Visiting hours are long over, and I was able to pull a few strings to allow this. I don't need them overstaying, and I won't be able to do something like this for them again. "And make sure he does not get out of that bed unless it's to use the bathroom. I'm sure he's going to try and act like he's fine in front of you all, but he *is* in pain—"

"You got it!" Harry says, rushing into the room. As I make my way down the hall, my phone vibrates and I pull it out to see Sarah Fletcher's name flash across the screen.

"Hello?"

"Hello, Karina, this is Sarah. Am I catching you at a bad time?"

"Not at all. I'm about to call it a night at the hospital. How may I help you?" I ask. I pray it's not for another appearance at an event. I've reached my quota for the year. One and done.

"Sorry for calling so late. I meant to call earlier, but time got away from me. Before I start rambling, I called you because Vulcan reached out to me—"

"For?" I hope he didn't do what I think he did.

"Planning your wedding, of course," she squeals. "I just knew you two were together. I saw the way you two were at the Heroes Gala, that chemistry cannot be faked. I love that for the pair of you, good job on keeping it under wraps. So, please, when can we meet to get the planning started?" She's bubbling with excitement, but my mind is reeling. Vulcan reached out to her without even discussing it with me first? I take a deep breath, trying to keep my voice steady.

"Sarah, I appreciate your enthusiasm, but I think there's been a misunderstanding. Vulcan and I haven't even set a date yet, let alone started planning the wedding." *What the hell was he thinking?*

"Oh, but he sounded so sure. He said he wanted to surprise you with some of the arrangements. You know, to take some of the stress off your shoulders. It's rare to see a man wanting to be…"

I tune her out and close my eyes, pinching the bridge of my nose. *Of course he did.* Only now, with him in the hospital, the wedding is the last thing on my mind. "It's all very thoughtful, but I'll need to get back to you."

"I completely understand, darling. You know how men can be sometimes. They just want to show their love in grand gestures. It's rather romantic, don't you think?"

I bite back a sarcastic retort. Romantic? More like presumptuous and domineering. But I can't say that to Sarah. She means well, even if her enthusiasm is misplaced.

"I suppose so. Listen, Sarah, it's been a long day and I really need to get some rest. I'll call you back at a later date."

"Of course, dear! Get some beauty sleep. We'll chat soon and start making your dream wedding a reality!"

I end the call and close my eyes, leaning back against the cool wall. With Sarah as our wedding planner, it means the media will be informed, whether we like it or not.

My body is on autopilot as I make an about-face back to Vulcan's room. I shouldn't be bothered by what he's doing, but I am. I'm a private person, and just thinking about all those people, the crowds, and the cameras? We aren't celebrities, but Sarah will make it *feel* like a celebrity wedding.

A wedding should be about the couple, not about appearances—

even *if* this marriage is literally for appearances.

I pause for a moment outside his door, taking a deep breath to calm my nerves before pushing it open. Vulcan looks up at me from the bed. His eyes widen slightly. "Karina? I thought you were heading home."

"I was on my way out when I got a very interesting phone call from Sarah Fletcher." I cross my arms, leveling him with a stern look.

"Cap, should we give you two a minute?" Harry asks.

"Just text me if you need anything, and I can stop by in the morning before I head to work." My eyes instantly move to the far right of the room, where a petite woman dressed in form-fitting workout clothes stands. Is she a firefighter? A friend of his? She wasn't in the waiting area when I first left.

"Thank you, Val, but that won't be necessary," Vulcan responds without taking his eyes off me. "You don't have to baby me."

"I'll come back later," I say through gritted teeth. Why am I feeling so annoyed? This is not like me, but her eagerness to tend to him rubs me the wrong way.

"Wait, please." He pauses, then says to his crew, "Give us the room."

They exit swiftly, leaving behind well wishes and promises to visit again tomorrow. I try not to seem too interested as *Val* leans in to hug Vulcan, but my eyes are drawn to their embrace nonetheless. She starts to adjust his sling before kissing him on his forehead. *Well, excuse the fuck out of me.* Maybe she should be the one marrying him.

When she walks past me, she gives me a warm smile that I refuse to return. The door shuts behind her, and now it's just the two of us again. "I'm sorry about that. Val means well, but she can be a bit *motherly.*"

I arch an eyebrow. "Is that what you call it? Because from where I'm standing, it looks like she was marking her territory. But by all means, if that is the case, you should make her Mrs. Montgomery."

His lips twitch, fighting back a smile. "Jealous, Karina?"

"Hardly." Heat rushes to my cheeks.

"Come here or I'm going to get out of this bed to get you."

"Stay." I approach, and he pats the space next to him on the mattress. I awkwardly sit down, leaving a good distance between us.

He takes my hand in his and gives it a gentle squeeze. "Val's my baby sister." He grins, his eyes crinkling at the corners.

"Sister?" Oh.

I was bothered by his hermanita. Get a grip, Karina.

"Yep." His thumb traces circles on the back of my hand, sending shivers up my arm.

I shake my head lightly. "Oh my gosh. I'm so sorry. I overreacted."

"Did you now?" Vulcan arches an eyebrow.

I roll my eyes, ignoring how my heart flutters at his teasing. "I wanted to talk to you about Sarah. She called about our wedding. She's a lovely woman, but I don't want the bells and whistles that come with her being our wedding planner."

"I want you to have the best. This might not be your last wedding, but it's your first, and I want you to know how much I appreciate what you're doing for me."

"I get that, I really do, but like I told you the other night: it's too much." I don't want to unload my family drama on him, but I'll have no choice if he pushes for this. My mother is like a blood-sucking leech, and if she knows I'm having such an extravagant wedding, she'll show up with her hand out.

He sighs. "Fine, small wedding it is. And it's still a no for an engagement party? I know we talked about it briefly at dinner."

"It's still a no."

He slowly nods. "Okay, it's whatever you want. Now, go home, okay?"

"Are you mad?" I ask, pulling my hand away and removing a loose thread on his blanket.

"No. Never would I be mad at you for not wanting to do something that makes you feel uncomfortable. But I want you to get some rest. Or do you want to sleep here with me? I'm a big man, but I can make room."

"That could've happened after our date, but here we are."

He groans. "Such a tease. I can't wait till I'm all healed." He dips his chin and I stand. "I'll call and let Sarah know her services are no longer needed, and we can finish this conversation in the morning. Remember, I'm not mad at you. So, don't go overthinking once you leave this room."

I nod, feeling a warmth spread through my chest at his words. Having someone who cares about what I want and think—it's a novelty. As I turn to leave, Vulcan's voice stops me. "Karina?"

I glance back over my shoulder, eyebrows raised in question. "Hm?"

He hesitates for a moment as if searching for the right words. "I know this whole situation is… unconventional, to say the least. But I want you to know that I'm here for you. And I will *always* respect your wishes."

His sincerity throws me and I have to swallow hard, trying to ignore the way my heart races at his declaration. Three years of marriage with this man might not be so bad after all.

"I—thank you, Vulcan. That means a lot."

"Anytime. Good night, Karina."

"Good night, Vulcan."

My night goes from better to worse once I get home to the familiar red light flashing on my answering machine. I really need to get rid of my home line and throw the relic away; my mother is the only one who leaves messages. I already have a stack of bills in hand that she's forwarded to my home. It shouldn't come as a shock that every time I get a bill, it's from a new place—yet it always does. I don't bother stopping and continue to the bathroom.

After showering and running through my nighttime routine, I play the first message, listening as my mother complains about her unpaid phone bill. What the hell is she doing with the money I've been sending her?

I delete the message, cutting her off mid-ramble. This is why I can't let my mother know I'm getting married or ever find out when I am married. If she finds out Vulcan is my husband *and* a station captain with a trust fund, her demands will only increase.

I abandon the task and head to my bedroom, crawling beneath the blankets and feeling the day's stress settle over me. As I shut my eyes, I think back to Vulcan's earlier remarks, and it dawns on me that this marriage might entail more than just legal documents and cohabitation. Emotions could be a part of it… complicated, unpredictable emotions.

CHAPTER FOURTEEN

Vulcan

When I wake next, it's to the sight of Valkyrie stepping into my room, her long blonde hair falling in soft waves around her face. In her hands are two steaming cups of coffee, the aroma immediately reaching my hazy senses.

"Morning, shithead," she says, her mouth wide open, yawning. Could she be any less ladylike? "Got you a cup of joe."

"Please tell me it's not any of the hospital crap." I sit up and take the cup from her. "I'd rather not stay longer than needed, and I fear that drinking their coffee will only extend my time here."

"Nah, it's from Junior's bodega." She plops down on my hospital bed.

"Thanks," I say, feeling a bit more human after my first sip. "What time are you heading to work?" She's wearing her signature yoga pants and oversized hoodie, further convincing me she owns nothing but workout clothes.

"Oh gosh, please don't get me started on my new client." She rolls her eyes.

"Then don't."

"Well, I'm going to tell you anyway." She hits my leg. "It's Marino Wilde, the gold medalist swimmer? You've probably heard of him." I haven't.

"That sounds exciting, having such a high-caliber client," I tease, knowing all about Val's roster of athletes she claims are self-entitled and needy.

She lets out an exaggerated groan. "Exciting? It's *exasperating*, more like a royal pain in my ass. This guy's ego is so inflated I'm surprised he doesn't float away during our sessions. He thinks he's God's gift to water."

"Seems like you've met your match."

"Pfft. As if. He's constantly moaning." She puts on a whiny voice. "'Oh, Doc, how can I possibly clinch gold if I can't nail my butterfly stroke?' I swear, Vully, he makes me want to shave my head and join a monastery."

"Sounds like you've got a real *prima donna* on your hands."

"Understatement of the century," she deadpans. "I'm *this* close to slapping a 'handle with care' sticker on his forehead and shipping him back to whatever chlorine-filled petri dish he crawled out of."

"Easy there, sis. You don't want to end up as the PT who sank an Olympic career."

"Please, with that ego, he'd bob right back up." She pauses, a devious look in her eye. "Actually, that gives me an idea for a new rehab exercise."

"Do I even want to know?"

"Let's just say it involves a pool noodle and a crash course in *How Not to Be a Douche 101*." She smirks and glances at her watch. "I've got about ten minutes before I need to run. How are you feeling?"

"Like shit, but if I want to get discharged sooner, I need to fake it."

"Or just get a doctor to make home visits. Like that doctor from last night. She's feisty." Val chuckles.

"What are you on about now?"

She takes a sip of her coffee. "I think she was jealous. Did you tell her who I was?"

"I did." I *don't* tell her how Karina apologized for baring her fangs—Val doesn't need the confirmation.

"So, are you two dating?" she asks.

"We are, and that's all I'm going to share for now. And I believe your ten minutes are up. You'd better get going."

"Oh, come on!" she whines, her eyes sparkling with curiosity. "You can't just drop that bomb and leave me hanging. I need details!"

I shake my head, fighting back a grin. "Nope. Doctor-patient confidentiality and all that."

"Since when did you get so coy?" She narrows her eyes at me. "Wait a minute. You *like* her, don't you?"

"You need to go. I'm sure your Olympian is waiting for you."

"So evasive!" Val's eyes widen. "Come on, spill the tea."

"I wouldn't be dating her if I didn't like her, Valkyrie."

She grins triumphantly, like she's just won an argument I didn't know we were having. "Well, duh. But this is different. You're getting all squirmy and defensive."

"I am not getting squirmy," I protest, shifting uncomfortably in my bed. Damn these hospital sheets, they make everything feel like an interrogation.

"You totally are. It's cute. My big brother, flustered as shit over his girlfriend."

"Get going. We'll talk later. I promise."

She rolls her eyes, snatching up her bag. "And don't you break that promise." She glances at her watch. "Crap, I need to get going. I'm cutting it close, and I can't leave his royal wetness waiting."

"Try not to drown in his charisma."

"I swear, dealing with him is like trying to reason with a stubborn toddler who thinks he's Michael Phelps." She lets out a deep breath. "Hey, let me know if I need to pull strings to get you home visits. There's an annoying doctor at my clinic who needs more patients."

"Let me guess, you want him out of the clinic and out of your hair?"

"You know me so well." She lets out a loud cackle. "His name is Ralph, and he won't stop asking me out. And you're going to help get him off my back!" She places her hand on her heart and bats her lashes. "See, this is why you're my favorite brother."

"I'm your only brother." I raise an eyebrow.

"Don't be a buzzkill. Do you want the in-house care or not?"

"Sounds like a plan. Thank you. And remember," I call as she heads for the door, "there are plenty of other fish in the sea."

The sound of her groan echoes down the hallway, leaving me chuckling into my coffee. I settle back into my pillow, and my phone screen lights up with a message.

> **Karina: In the cafe downstairs, would you like some coffee? Anything to eat?**

I smile, fingers flying over the screen.

> **Me: My sister just dropped off some coffee, but I can go for something to eat—a bacon, egg, and cheese on a cinnamon raisin bagel?**
>
> **Karina: You got it. See you shortly.**

I toss aside the sheets, suddenly motivated to look a bit more presentable. I shuffle into the cramped bathroom, splash cold water on my face, and attempt to tame the mess that is my hair.

When I walk back into my room, dressed in the fresh clothes Valkyrie brought me yesterday, the door opens.

"Good morning. Are you getting discharged?" Karina takes in my attire, her eyes lingering on my sling.

"I was given some pain meds. I barely feel anything so I was hoping to leave today. I prefer to be comfortable; I hate hospitals."

"Comfort is key," she agrees, stepping closer and handing me a paper bag with a greasy bottom.

A nurse walks in, clipboard in hand. "Mr. Montgomery, ma'am." She nods at us both, her eyes flickering with recognition at Karina. "Oh, Dr. Reyes, I didn't realize you would be tending to our patient."

Karina's eyes meet mine briefly. "I'm not. He's the fire captain over at Station 112 and a good friend of mine."

"It's okay to say *boyfriend*, everyone already knows about the incident in the ER a few days ago." The nurse smiles.

"What happened in the ER?" I look to Karina.

"Nothing," she rushes to say. "Let Andrea do whatever she came here to do." Karina takes a step back as the nurse gives me a rundown of my discharge process, each word sounding more like a promise of freedom. I knew Val was going to pull some strings but damn she moves quick.

When the nurse finally leaves, Karina turns to me, her brown eyes serious. I can see she's going to like things her way. Not that I have a problem with that, but she'll have to know that compromise is key in *any* relationship.

"I don't know how you managed this, but I don't think you should leave just yet." She grabs the clipboard from the bed. "Per the doctor's note, you're out of commission for twelve weeks and must leave the sling on for three."

"Two days out of commission should be fine." I take a bite of my bagel. "You look more beautiful without makeup on. I love to see your freckles."

"Thank you, but let's not change the subject here. As I was saying, it's not up for debate. It's an order for a reason and is the only way to avoid infection and further injury." She waves the paper in her hand. "You follow them as if your life depends on it. In your case, it does."

She's right, but I don't want to admit it. I won't let a little shoulder injury stop me. I have a legacy to protect. My father never let any injury, minor or serious, stop him from doing his job, and neither will I. I take another bite and nod my head slowly. The best way to avoid a scolding is to stay silent.

"Don't just nod your head. Tell me with your words that you understand what I'm telling you and that you'll take it easy." She tilts her head to the side, eyebrows raised.

"I understand. I'll try. I guess with this time off, I could organize the wedding, and meet your family—"

"No, that's not important. They're busy. Also, my brothers go to college in Ohio." Her body language tells me there's a story here, but if she doesn't want to share, I won't push it. Karina and I aren't close to where I can start poking into all her business. "Besides, I prefer it just be me, you, our witness, and the officiant. We agreed on a small wedding, remember?"

"I think our definitions of small vary slightly. Our marriage may be contractual, but we're still legally getting married. My family and the guys at the fire station won't be happy if I say *I do* without them." I would never hear the end of it.

"Umm…" She trails off, and that's when I notice how stiff she's become. "I see we want different things. I would hate for you to regret marrying me, contractual or not. I'm just not huge on family gatherings."

"If you don't want to invite your family, you don't have to. And I can invite just my sister and Harry." I know this wedding is essentially a business transaction, but I'll still need to explain things to the nosy people in my life. "I'm sure you would like someone there with you, a friend maybe?"

"Yeah." She tugs at her earlobe, glancing at the ground. Something I notice she does when she's feeling unsettled.

"Okay, then our guest list is settled." I smile, and she looks up at me with wide eyes.

"Seriously? You don't mind? It's just that having my mother there will be a lot to deal with. I know we aren't marrying for love, but when she finds out who you are and what you do... She would expect something. She always does," she rambles.

So, her mother is the problem. *Noted.*

"I understand." I reach out, grabbing her hand and easing it away from her earlobe. "You can call the shots. You're helping me, not the other way around. My happiness depends on your happiness, okay?" I gently squeeze her hand, and she lets out a deep breath.

"Sure, but you're helping me as well."

"Tomato, tomahto."

"Thank you. For understanding," she says, and I smile, feeling like a fresh page has been turned.

I let the comfortable silence wrap around us for a moment before finally voicing what's been on my mind. "What happened in the ER a few days ago?"

"Nothing."

"If she thinks I'm your boyfriend, *something* happened. Talk to me." I lean forward so we're almost touching, and a slight tremble passes through her body.

"I might have threatened to end a few careers if they didn't give you the best care possible."

I feel a slow smile spreading across my face. "My fierce little doctor," I say, and she doesn't pull away when I slide my hand to the nape of her neck. The tension between us shifts, thickens. I can't remember the last time I wanted to kiss someone this badly. "I should ask this time."

"Ask what?" she whispers.

"Can I kiss you?"

"Yes," she breathes.

I lean in, and then there's a knock on the door. Shit. Karina steps back quickly as it opens, and Harry walks in carrying a carafe of coffee. I see everyone had the same idea today.

"I suppose I should start my rounds. I'll try to see you before you're discharged. Even though I think you *should* stay." She places my file back on the bed and heads toward the door. I consider telling her I'll have a doctor visiting me back at my penthouse, but as long as I'm not at work, I think that's all she really cares about. I watch as she greets Harry and then exits.

Harry wiggles his eyebrows. "Getting cozy with the doctor, I see."

"That's my future wife you're talking about." I'd rather get it out of the way now.

"*Wife?!*" He puts down the coffee container and starts pacing in front of me. "What did I miss? Is she pregnant?"

"Why is that the first thing you think of?"

"I've only seen you interact with her once, and that was at the bar weeks ago. So, if she isn't pregnant, what is it? Don't take this the wrong way, but is she in a tough spot financially, and you are playing suga daddy?"

My blood starts to boil. "Why do you think she is using *me*? Why can't it be me using her? What if I just want to marry her before someone comes in and sweeps her off her feet. And if I ever hear you say that shit again, I will beat the shit out of you."

He raises his hand in a gesture of surrender. "Whoa. Sorry, Vul. I get it; you're serious about her. My bad. How about you start from the beginning? I can't believe you've been holding out on me. Did you two know each other before you met at the bar? Do you have some kind of kinky foreplay where you act like you don't know each other in public and then go back home to fuck like wild rabbits?"

"Seriously?" I rub my forehead with my good hand. "No, we don't have some weird arrangement. I just don't like sharing my love life with others."

"But I'm not *others*. I'm like your unofficial best friend."

"I've never been one to overshare. But now you know."

"So tell me more."

I tell Harry how we met but change the place and stretch the timeline slightly. I don't want anyone to doubt our relationship. We both signed an NDA, but this has to be believable, otherwise what's the point? Convincing Harry's easy, but I have a feeling things with Valkyrie will be a struggle. Val is more of an "I need to see it to believe it" kind of person. Karina and I will have to spend more time together before I let Val meet her officially. Because one thing Val loves to do is overanalyze every little thing. That's just how she's been since she was young. Which means I have to go the extra mile to make sure she doesn't find out the truth.

"I know I haven't been gone too long but how have things been at the station?" I ask, wanting to change the subject.

"The higher-ups sent over Lieutenant Kendall from Station 34."

I raise an eyebrow. "Kendall? That hothead from the west side? Why him?"

"They needed someone with captain experience to fill in while you're out," Harry says, dropping into the chair beside my bed. "He did say he won't be touching that paperwork on your desk."

That makes me laugh. "Of course he won't. Kendall thinks paperwork is beneath him." I shake my head. "How's the crew handling him?"

We spend the next hour catching up on station gossip. Apparently,

Ramirez finally got asked out by that dispatcher who's been pining over her for months, and Cruz has started some health kick that has everyone avoiding the kitchen when he's making his protein shakes. By the time Harry leaves, I feel more like myself. The pain meds are working well, and I'm itching to get out of this sterile room.

CHAPTER FIFTEEN

Karina

"I need a vacation as of yesterday." Cassie yawns as she walks into the break room. "Is it me, or has today been the worst? I swear, it has me reevaluating this career path. I almost got pissed on twice, and that fucking patient in room 3201 threatened to spit on me." She takes a deep breath. "She's lucky she didn't. I would have walked out of here in cuffs."

"Well, I'm glad she didn't. Did you at least—"

"You don't even have to ask. I changed rooms with Ericka," she huffs. "Today has been one for the books."

"It's about the same as any other day for me. I didn't have lunch, and crazy Josh came strolling in with his shopping cart of bags, saying he had a headache. I wanted to tell him *don't we all* and then send him right back out the ER doors." I rub my temples. Josh is our regular ER patient. He's thirty-six and unhoused, and he's harmless, but he *loves* to rattle off the latest conspiracy theories. Ninety percent of the time, there is nothing physically wrong with him, and most of the staff at St. Mary's let his and others' visits slide; we know it's mostly about these people seeking company and warm beds.

"Speaking of Josh, I heard the hospital director is looking to put an end to the homeless people faking sick to get a place to sleep for the night," Cassie says, and my heart drops.

"But the shelters in this area are at capacity," I protest.

"I know you want to be a savior to all mankind, but this is a hospital, Rina. There are patients who need our care. What happens when we start to fill up?"

"We can't turn away—"

"*Technically*, we can, but we choose not to." She's right, but winter is coming. I shudder to think about the Joshes of the city who will struggle when the temperatures drop.

"I don't know how they plan on implementing real change in a matter of months. We can't rush as doctors. One wrong move, and that could be it for us. I don't think the hospital director would put his neck on the line for us." I glance at my watch. Shit, I need to see Vulcan. "I need to check on the captain before he leaves."

"Leave? Wasn't he damn near dead yesterday? He should be here for at least a week, if not longer."

"I got a look at his file. He's hiring a private doctor to make house visits, but I think that's his way of getting back to work. He doesn't want to be confined to a bed for three months." I knew something was amiss when the nurse came in to review his discharge process. There is no way *I* would let a patient leave the hospital after what he went through, not even twenty-four hours after the incident.

"You went to see the fire captain this morning?" Cassie unwraps her brownie and stares at me. "Like, before you did your rounds?"

I nod.

"Wait, Rina, are you seeing him?"

"When you say *seeing*, do you mean—"

"You know what I mean, like seeing, kissing, fucking, touching, sucking, eating, devouring, being manhandled by the captain. Did you see his fire hose yet?" She winks. "Are we even best friends if you say yes?"

"We are best friends even *if* I say yes, but it's a no for everything except seeing and kissing. We've been enjoying each other's company lately." I don't want to lie to Cassie, but I signed all that paperwork for a reason. Vulcan wants complete discretion regarding this matter. Now I just need to figure out how to break it to her that we're getting married. "We've been talking since the Heroes Gala, and then we had dinner."

Cassie lets out a shriek of excitement, and I cover my ears. "So he *is* the guy who took you out the other night. You didn't let him fuck after Jean-Georges? Tell me all the things! Why did you keep this a secret? You know I would have supported you no matter what. Also, didn't I tell you he wanted you when we went to the bar that night? I hear older men love to take control in the bedroom. And he looks so strong and—"

"I'd rather you not go down that rabbit hole." I toss a spork at her. "But I can say, I don't think the age gap will be an issue. He and I have a lot in common." Sort of. "And we're both looking to date for marriage."

"Marriage? Wait, who are you, and where is my best friend? Are you sure you two haven't had sex yet? I mean, this sounds like a *dickmatized* answer."

I burst into laughter despite myself. "Dickmatized? Really, Cassie?" The stress of the day seems to melt away as her ridiculous terminology hits me. "I promise you, my judgment isn't clouded by anything below the belt."

"Uh-huh, sure." She takes a bite of her brownie, grinning. "But seriously, Rina, I'm happy for you. You deserve someone who treats you right. And if Captain Hottie is making you smile like that after the day we've both had, then I'm all for it."

Her enthusiasm is infectious, and I find myself grinning back. "He does make me feel... lighter, somehow. Like maybe there's more to life than just surviving these brutal shifts." I stand up. "FYI, we haven't had sex yet. I'll be back." I leave the break room before her head pops off her shoulders.

I knock once on the door before opening it and seeing a sleeping Vulcan. I tiptoe closer to his bed, watching his chest rise and fall in a steady rhythm. His eyes are shut, lashes fanning over high cheekbones that speak of a classical handsomeness not often found outside of old-world paintings. The salt-and-pepper beard gives him a rugged look that I adore.

"Vulcan," I whisper, unsure if I want to wake him. His eyelids flutter, revealing dark irises that lock onto mine.

"Karina," he rumbles. "You came back."

"Of course I did," I reply, trying to keep my tone light despite how my heart kicks at seeing him. "I told you I would."

He sits up and pats the bed next to him.

"I'd better not. I've been dealing with patients all afternoon." I take another small step back. "So, did you see the doctor yet?"

"Yeah, around one," he answers, and I look down at my watch.

"Wait, you've been discharged for two hours."

"I wanted to see you before I go." He swings his feet off the bed, stands up, and I step back once more. "Did you not want to see me?"

"I'm here, aren't I?" I'm starting to think I'm a hopeless romantic because every little thing he says and does makes my damn body react as if I'm some lovesick puppy.

He closes the distance I carved out, wrapping his arm around my waist and pulling me into his chest. "I've been thinking."

"Yeah?" I swallow hard.

"We need to be more comfortable around each other. I want you to meet my sister before the wedding, and I realize we know next to nothing about each other outside of work."

I chew on my lower lip, pondering his words. "You're right," I say, my heart pounding. "So, we go on dates."

Vulcan shakes his head and loosens his grip but doesn't let go completely. His touch is both unnerving and exhilarating. "With me on bedrest and your schedule, dates would be kind of hard, don't you think?" He doesn't wait for me to answer before he drops a bomb on me. "I think you should move in with me before the wedding."

My mouth drops open, and I'm speechless for a moment. I thought he would want his own space until we made this whole thing official. "*Before* the—?" I manage to find my voice, though it comes out higher than intended. "Vulcan, we barely know each other's favorite colors, let alone living habits."

His thumb traces along my waist through my scrubs, sending warmth radiating through my tired body. "That's exactly why we need to do this, Karina. People will see right through us if we can't even have a natural conversation about mundane things like how you take your coffee or what side of the bed you sleep on. Us living together would be like a crash course in learning each other's habits and interests..."

I feel heat creep up my neck. The bed comment shouldn't affect me this much, but something about the way his voice dropped makes my pulse quicken.

"If we want to make this believable, we should do it," he adds.

Taking a deep breath, I nod slowly, the idea settling in my stomach like a heavy stone, yet somehow fluttering like butterflies too. "Okay," I whisper. "I'll move in, but we need ground rules. This is still a business arrangement first."

Vulcan's face lights up. "Okay," he says simply. "I have an extra bedroom you can sleep in, unless"—he pauses, his voice lowering to a husk that sends a shiver down my spine—"you decide you want to share mine?"

Don't seem too eager, Rina. "Having my own space is fine. And, um, about the rent? Fifty-fifty?"

"No need," he says. "Consider it part of the arrangement. All I want is for this to run smoothly."

I nod, feeling a sense of relief and warmth toward him. It's a strange sensation, this growing trust and dependency on someone I'm entering a legally binding marriage contract with. I would normally feel my hackles raise at such an offer—I know better than anyone there's always a catch when something sounds too good to be true. Yet, here I am, about to share a home with him, rent-free.

"So, about those boundaries, what did you have in mind?"

I take a moment to think it through. "Things like privacy needs, sharing chores... maybe even guidelines about... *guests?*" I say the last word with a slight hesitance.

He nods, understanding clear in his eyes. "There will be none of that. I won't have you disrespected, even if we stay the course and keep things purely professional. And if at any point you want to change the parameters, rework some of the terms..." He trails off, his gaze holding mine with an intensity that feels like a direct challenge. "Well, I'm open to that too."

"Let's take things one step at a time," I say. "Moving in together is already a big adjustment."

He nods. "Fair enough."

And with that, I leave him to continue my rounds, wondering how to reconcile these very real feelings for who is about to be my very *fake* husband.

CHAPTER SIXTEEN

Vulcan

"You asked her to move in with you? Before the wedding?" Minji questions as she opens the folder containing more of my father's assets and properties.

"I did." I look around her office; everything has a place. This level of organized is what I strive to be, but then life happens, and organization goes right out the fucking window. "And she said yes."

"Just like that?"

I think back to a week ago at the hospital. I thought she would have told me she needed time to think it over. But then again, it's been a week, and our text messages haven't been as consistent as I would like, which tells me she could be second-guessing.

I hate that I'm out of work for another eleven weeks. I have too much time on my hands and nothing to do. My life revolves around my career; without that, I'm trying to find out who I am. That's sad, really. At almost forty, without my career, I have nothing. I'm beginning to see why my father's will is set up this way.

"Just like that," I answer, then gesture toward the file. "What do you have for me today?"

"All the assets, properties, and monies you will inherit once your marriage is finalized, and then I will show you what you'll receive once the contract has been fulfilled," Minji says, her voice all business.

"Are you still taking divorce cases?"

"Excuse me?" She looks up from the paperwork. "You can't possibly be thinking of divorce before you've even said your vows?"

"I'm not. I was—"

"No, I no longer take on divorce cases. When I got married, I promised I would—enough about me. Why do you ask?"

"Curious, that's all. When Karina and I... I would like for you to handle our divorce when this is all said and done."

In what I've come to know is her unique way, she doesn't even bat an eye. "Noted. Okay, let's review these documents."

Minji flicks through the paperwork. "Everything seems to be in order," she begins. "Karina knows what will be offered to her once the marriage is finalized, but she has requested some changes be made."

My heart skips. She doesn't seem like the type to be money-hungry, but then again, I don't really know her. "Changes? Don't you think you should have told me this before my dinner with her weeks ago?"

"Your father was my client, and that extends to you. I'll always make sure my clients are looked after. If anything, the changes are in *your* favor." Minji shuffles the papers, handing me a document. "She only asked for three hundred thousand of the million being offered."

"Are you serious?" My eyebrows lift and a small laugh escapes me. That's peanuts compared to what I was bracing myself for. It's as if she's not interested in the money at all. She told me she was seeking financial stability. Does she really think that amount will get her far in this city?

"Why would she ask for so little?"

"She is experiencing financial hardship. During discovery, it was revealed that she transfers a sizeable amount of money to her mother every month," she tells me. "She confirmed as much in our meeting and was the reason she was open to the date—"

"Speaking of," I interrupt, unable to contain my curiosity, "you told her it was a date rather than—"

"It's a *date*," Minji explains with a sly twist to her mouth, "to a wedding, where she will be the bride. I just didn't disclose that part." She waves her hand dismissively. "Anyway, Karina wants to give her mother that money in hopes she'll leave her alone for a few years, or maybe even forever. I'm sure her salary is more than enough for a comfortable life, but when you have a leech sucking you dry... I suppose it's no surprise she's found herself in a situation like this."

She sighs and it lingers in the air, mixing with my thoughts. I've always assumed anyone entering this sort of arrangement would aim for the maximum benefit. But Karina... she's different. Unpredictable. Intriguing. Someone as young as her, not wanting to take me for all I've got, is a breath of fresh air, and I'm more than happy that I decided to pick her as my wife-to-be.

Still, as I mull over this new information, it's hard not to feel a sting of guilt. Why should she have to use this marriage as a getaway vehicle from her financial troubles? A part of me wonders if there's something more I can do for her, something that might ease her burden without attaching strings or making her feel like I'm pitying her.

"It explains the humble wedding she wants," I mutter.

She should never have to feel like she's carrying the world's weight on her shoulders twenty-four-seven. She deals with enough pressure at work. Hers is, what, one of the most stressful jobs in medicine? A pang of guilt hits me again, and I wonder if I'm being selfish by even involving her in this mess.

"What a shame," Minji says. "You're right. She does seem to want distance from her mother. It's probably best, given the circumstances."

Minji hands me the folder. The papers feel weighted with more than legal jargon and inheritance details. They are a blueprint for a future I didn't anticipate wanting this much.

"You seem to care about her a lot, and I think she may care about you more than she lets on."

"Or maybe she just wants the money," I reply, but even I don't believe it. Not anymore. Especially not after what I've just learned.

"If it were only money," Minji counters, "she could have asked for millions." She taps the document again, emphasizing the low number. "She has no intention of bleeding you dry, and you know that."

"You're right. If you're confident everything's in order, we can get this finalized." I look down at my watch. "I need to get going. I have new furniture arriving today."

"Already turning *your* place into an *our* place." Minji's lips curve into a knowing smile. It wasn't a question but a statement. I nod.

"Of course. I hope it helps her feel at home," I tell her. Also, my penthouse is closer to the hospital, so that's another plus.

"Before you go," Minji adds, "let's go over the timeline."

I nod, gesturing for her to continue, and lean back in my chair. In the beginning, it felt like three years would be an eternity. Now, I'm not so sure. Maybe my perspective is shifting. Maybe living with Karina will fly by, and we'll both get what we want before going our separate ways. Or maybe it will be a complete fucking disaster. "I remember you saying I won't be able to get the full amount until the end."

"That's right. And once you tie the knot, you will receive the twenty million that is not contingent on the three-year marriage term, plus all the properties and assets that don't have that clause attached. If Karina's signature is on that certificate, it will be yours." She gives it to me straight, and I appreciate that about her. The properties and assets my father left me are more than I imagined. It's more than I'd ever need.

"Does Karina have to wait for the three hundred thousand to clear before the wedding or after?"

"The funds will be transferred within three business days of the marriage certificate being filed. Once the documents are signed by both parties, we'll need to schedule a meeting with the executor of your father's estate to oversee the process." Minji shuffles through some papers and pulls out another document. "There's also the matter of the prenuptial agreement."

I groan. "Is that really necessary? She's not asking for anything."

"It's standard procedure, particularly with assets of this magnitude," Minji says firmly. "And it actually protects both parties. Remember, your father's will stipulates that if you divorce before the three-year mark, you forfeit the remaining thirty million. A prenup ensures that your current assets remain protected regardless of what happens."

"Fine." I sigh, running a hand through my hair. "Draw it up."

Minji nods. "I'll have it ready for review by next week."

The place is pure chaos.

My penthouse hasn't been this unkempt since I moved in over two decades ago. I don't like mess, and right now that's exactly what it is. It's like a cardboard fortress. A maze of boxes in the living room, stretching into the hallway, and exploding into the guest room. The furniture delivery is supposed to make the place feel more like a home, but right now, it resembles a warehouse. I should have known better than to set up a delivery like this when my surgery's still so fresh. With my arm in a sling, there's not much I can do but stare helplessly at the growing mess.

I want to tear into the boxes and start putting things together, but even the simplest task feels overwhelming when you're down an arm. They just dropped everything off and left without so much as a second thought. I'd consider it a practical joke if I had the energy to find it funny.

Why did I assume the delivery crew would build the damn things?

Apparently, "assembly included" is a loose term these days. My pathetic attempt to push a box with my foot ends in defeat. There's no way I can handle this alone. I want Karina's transition to be seamless, and right now, it's anything but. My phone buzzes in my hand before my thoughts can run rampant even more. Valkyrie's name flashes across the screen.

"Yes, baby sister," I answer.

"Ew, you don't have to answer like that *every* time—it's annoying. Anyway, what are you doing? I need a drinking buddy tonight. Can I come over?" There's a hesitance in her voice, an uncertainty that isn't like her. Plus, she never asks, she just shows up.

"Hell, why not? I could use a drink or two," I answer as I hear a knock on my door. "Hold on, Val, someone's here." I walk over and open it, half expecting to see a delivery person who forgot one of my items. Instead, it's Valkyrie with a huge smile on her face.

"Surprise!" She lifts a bag, glass bottles clinking together. The sound is both an invitation and a threat. "I knew you were going to say yes."

Ending our call, I slip the phone into my back pocket. "And what if I had company over?" I let her inside, and my eyes stray to the boxes.

"You? Entertaining guests? Doesn't even sound right. But then again, I didn't know you were dating that doctor. And I'm here for the tea—" She stops, taking a look at my surroundings. "What's with all these boxes?"

I groan internally. The mess is almost as suffocating as the sling.

"I decided it's time to change up the place a bit. You came at the right time. I need someone to help me assemble this crap."

"No, I came here to drink. Not be Bob the Builder." She doesn't break her stride as she walks into the kitchen, fully expecting me to follow. I trail behind her, shaking my head at how easily she's dodged my recruitment attempt. I should have known better. Val's always had a knack for getting her way, especially when alcohol is involved.

She starts unpacking her arsenal of liquid comfort, lining up bottles of whiskey, vodka, and some kind of exotic liqueur with a label I can't pronounce. She turns to face me with a bottle in each hand. "So, spill it."

Leaning against the counter, I try to gather my thoughts. How do I even begin to explain the mess of feelings swirling inside me? "It's… complicated," is all I manage at first. I stare at the boxes again, hoping they'll give me a convenient out. "I can't lift anything—"

She pauses a bottle of whiskey halfway to the glass she's holding. "What the fuck are you talking about? I don't care about the boxes, and you know it." She shakes her head at my weak attempt to deflect. "Come on, big bro. Out with it." She pours a generous amount into two glasses, the amber liquid catching the light before she slides one across to me. It's a silent challenge. Drink up and dish it.

"You first. I know you came over because you have something on your mind," I say.

She groans. "It's my damn patient. You remember the swimmer, Marino, I was telling you about?" She pauses to drink and grimaces. "Well, during PT today, he kissed me. Like a full-blown make-out session in the pool."

I grip the glass in my hand tighter. "Excuse me? Do I need to go up there and break his jaw?"

"No," she rushes out.

"If you don't want me to cause physical harm, what's the problem?" I ask, taking a sip of whiskey that burns pleasantly down my throat.

"The problem is you don't make out with your patient. But that kiss made me feel things. Things I shouldn't be feeling." She sighs. "Feelings—"

"Feelings *I don't* want to hear about. Not from my baby sister," I warn her. "And if you don't want me to break his jaw, then I guess you should keep those feelings to yourself."

"He is such an egoistic asshole. But," Val continues, "there's something about him. I mean, the way he looks at me, it's like he sees right through to something deeper? That *terrifies* me." She takes another gulp of her drink, looking conflicted. "And hell, I wish I could drown him."

Val slams her glass down a little harder than necessary, making the whiskey slosh dangerously close to the rim. She's always been the impulsive type, flammable, ready to ignite at a moment's notice. I remain silent, letting her vent, knowing from experience she needs to purge these emotions before they consume her.

"You need to set boundaries," I finally say, trying to sound more like a concerned brother and less like a lecturing parent. "He's your patient. There are lines that shouldn't be crossed."

She scoffs, brushing a strand of her hair behind her ear. "Easy for you to say," she retorts. "You're not the one he's looking at like you're the last piece of dessert at a banquet."

The image she paints flickers through my mind, unwanted and strangely vivid. Makes me want to fucking puke. I push it away, focusing instead on her troubled eyes. I hate seeing her look anything but happy. "Maybe it's time to ask for a reassignment," I suggest, though knowing full well she's never backed down from a challenge.

"And let him win? No way." Her jaw sets stubbornly, and I recognize that determined twinkle in her eyes. It's the same one she had when we were kids, when she'd climb a tree just because someone said she couldn't. And then cry for me to help her get down. "I think he's flirting with me because I told him I would never *ever* date a guy like him."

I sigh. Reasoning with her when she's like this is as pointless as trying to stop a tide with a teaspoon.

"But what if you're wrong?" I question, unable to shake off a nagging concern for her well-being. Even though I'm the last person who should be giving any kind of relationship advice. "What if it's more than just flirting? What if he genuinely has feelings for you?" God, I can't believe these words are coming out of my mouth. I'd prefer if every man stayed away from her, but she's a grown woman.

She pauses, and her fiery facade slips momentarily, revealing a glimpse of vulnerability. *Shit.* "Then I'm screwed," she admits, her voice a whisper. "Because part of me might actually… feel something for him too. Yes, he is annoying as hell, but there is a soft side to him. Ugh."

Val has always been great at guarding her heart and controlling her feelings. So, this Marino guy must really be charming, and that doesn't sit well with me. I got time off from work; maybe I should visit her job. I won't be able to break his jaw—not like I can in this sling—but my presence alone should be enough to ward him off.

"So, what are you going to do?" I ask, genuinely curious about her next move.

She picks up her cup, taking a slow sip as she considers her options. Her next words come out slowly, cautiously weighed. "I'm going to play his game. If he's using charm as a tactic, I need to counter it with my own strategy. I'll keep it professional but make him understand that I'm not someone he can easily sway or intimidate."

"And what about your feelings?" I inquire. Because playing this game could end up with her getting her heart broken or, worse, losing a career she's worked so hard for.

Val meets my gaze. "I'll manage them. It's not the first time I've had to compartmentalize to overcome something difficult." She smiles weakly.

I nod, understanding her decision even if part of me wishes she would walk away from it all. But that's not Val's way and never has been. She faces challenges head-on, turning them into opportunities or conquests.

"Just promise me you'll be careful," I say, the thought of her getting hurt gnawing at me. I will break his fucking legs if she comes home crying to me.

"I promise," she insists. "Now, tell me about the doctor."

"Nothing to tell at the moment. We're doing well." I shrug and watch Val down the rest of the contents in her glass before pouring herself some vodka. She's going to throw up all over my house again. Fucking hell, I hate when she drinks clear liquor. It's like a demon comes out to play. A demon I absolutely loathe.

"*Doing well.* You had cartoon hearts projecting from your eyes, brother."

"I did not. I—"

"Yeah, yeah. Tell me more about her. She's pretty... no, she's *gorgeous.* And has a job... a good-paying job at that. So that's already a win-win in New York." Valkyrie hops on the counter, crossing her legs underneath her. "I want to know more."

"There really isn't anything to know. Well..." I trail off, rubbing the back of my neck. "I asked her to move in with me, and I think might—"

"You asked her to do *what?*" Val raises an eyebrow. "Holy shit, are you two that serious? I mean, it seemed like you guys were from the way she was caring for you at the hospital—besides her being a doctor, obviously. But I could tell there was more than that, especially when she walked back in pissed thinking I was there for you *romantically.*" She scrunches up her nose and feigns being sick. "Wait... shouldn't you propose first before wanting to play house? I mean, unless... is she pregnant? Is that why—"

This again. "No, she is *not* pregnant, and I, um, plan on proposing soon." So convincing Valkyrie doesn't seem like a big deal now. If anything, Karina showing signs of jealousy when she first saw Val made this easier for me. I pause. "Aren't you going to ask how long we've been together?"

"Uh, no, it's long enough if you're thinking about popping the question." Val hops off the counter. "Dude, you're totally whipped! I've never seen you like this before. Not even with... You know, what's-her-name from college."

"Yeah, it's different this time. Karina makes me feel like I'm actually part of something real." *Just say it, Vulcan. Get it over with.* I have to get married in less than two months. I need to get this out in the open. "If I'm being honest, I can see myself spending the rest of my life with her."

"Holy shit! You really are a *simp*! Wow, okay, when can I meet my future sister-in-law?" Val's teasing doesn't let up, and I grin at her excitement even if it means enduring a bit more of her relentless prodding. "She must be something else," Val speculates, her mind clearly whirring with possibilities. "She just waltzes into your life, claims your space, and makes you all domestic? I love her already! I can't wait to tell Mom!"

The weight of this deception sits heavy in my chest. Every lie I tell, every half-truth I construct, feels like I'm building a house of cards that will inevitably collapse. And when it does, it won't just be me who gets hurt. Val will feel betrayed. Mom will be devastated. And Karina...

Fuck. *Karina.*

What am I doing to her? She's agreeing to this arrangement out of desperation, and here I am involving my family, making them care about her, making this whole charade feel more real than it should. When this ends in three years, when we go our separate ways like we planned, what happens then? Do I tell everyone we grew apart? That we wanted different things?

"You okay?" Val's voice cuts through my spiraling thoughts. "You look like you're about to throw up."

"I'm fine, but let me tell Mom, I don't need you adding your own spin on my love life. And you can meet Karina soon, if you help me assemble this furniture." I look over my shoulder at the boxes and back to her, anticipating her reaction.

"Wait," she gasps, eyes widening. "Is this all for *her*?"

"Yes." I nod, amused at how fast she's switched gears. She's jumping off the countertop and rushing into the living room like a whirlwind that's just picked up speed.

"Where are the tools?" She's in full-on construction mode now.

"I thought you wanted to drink."

"Technically, you shouldn't be drinking since you're probably still on medication." She waves a finger at me. "Drop the cup. We can drink another time. I have a sis-in-law to meet!"

CHAPTER SEVENTEEN

Karina

I take a few days off from the hospital to move all my things to Vulcan's apartment—correction, penthouse. When I agreed to move in with him, I didn't think about all the packing I would have to do.

Vulcan kindly offered to help, but I was initially stubborn and turned him down. It's only been three weeks since his surgery and getting him involved with lifting and carting boxes is bound to end in disaster. Still, he refused to take no for an answer, and despite my protests, he insisted on coming over with movers in tow.

My doorbell rings, and I glance at the clock on my nightstand. It's already creeping up on eleven. I thought for sure he'd want to take advantage of the chance to sleep in a bit longer before heading over, but maybe his stubborn streak is stronger than I thought. I move quickly down the hall and swing open the door.

"Mom?" I suck in a breath, wishing I'd checked first. "What are you doing here?"

She pushes at the door, opening it just enough for her to walk through. Her eyes scan my living room, but I resolve not to tell her my moving plans. I want to keep this new life to myself for as long as possible.

"Now's not really a good time."

Her eyes narrow, picking up on the chaos of cardboard and packing tape—a visual onslaught that clearly reads as *change*. And change has never been something she is fond of. "Are you moving? To some fancy place, no doubt." She steps over a box marked *kitchen stuff* and perches on the edge of my sofa. "And I've been asking you for money. You tell me you're spread thin, but you have money to get a new place, clearly."

I hesitate, caught between outright denial and the truth. But lies have never sat well on my tongue. "I'm donating some things." That's the truth, sort of. "I've sent you everything I can." I bite back the nasty remark that she could get a job, but now isn't the time to start an argument. Vulcan will be here soon, and I can't let my mother see him.

She scoffs. "Donating, huh? Sure." She crosses her arms, lips pursed. "How about you donate to your mother. I shouldn't have to come find you because you've been avoiding my calls *and* your brothers'. You have a cell phone and a landline, and we haven't heard from you."

"I work over twelve hours a day at the hospital. I'm not avoiding you; I'm busy. I told you I'm *trying*. I can't give you money I don't have. I blew through my savings last year just to pay the bills at your house. A *new house* you insisted on because Miguel and Luis needed a… What was it? A game room?"

It's so frustrating. I love my brothers, but the way my mother treats me compared to them makes me sick. I'm footing the bill for their tuition, textbooks, their car insurance, and everything else one could imagine. Meanwhile, they are just coasting through life. And not once do I get a text message or call from them checking to see how I'm doing, nor even a thank-you. What hurts is that my mother has turned them into extensions of herself—takers who see me as nothing more than an ATM with legs.

Her face softens a touch as I lay bare the sacrifices I've been juggling, but it doesn't last long. The cold, money-hungry mother I've grown up with comes rushing back. "It's your duty to help your family," she spits. "You wouldn't be who you are today if it weren't for *my* sacrifices."

"Who I am today is an overworked doc—"

"I don't want to hear the dramatics, Karina. I didn't come for sob stories." My mother stands, her back straightening as she looks at me with disgust. A look I've learned to ignore.

Before I can reply, the doorbell rings again. My heart jumps to my throat—I know it's Vulcan. I throw a pleading look at my mother, silently begging her to behave and, just this once, rein in the insults and accusations.

I let Vulcan in and lead him into the living room, his presence commanding and unyielding. His shirt stretches across his broad chest, and I note with clinical frustration that he's peeled off his sling a week too early for my liking.

His eyes immediately lock onto the scene behind me, a quick survey that takes in everything—the clutter of boxes, the tension in the air, and most notably, my mother on her feet with her arms defiantly crossed, her whole demeanor confrontational.

"Karina," he says. "I thought I'd come early to help."

I can feel my mother's eyes boring into mine, her curiosity piqued. "Who's this then?" she asks sharply.

Vulcan steps closer, offering a hand that my mother doesn't take. "I'm Vulcan Montgomery," he says. "I'm a friend of Karina's."

My mother's eyes narrow slightly, her scrutinizing gaze shifting back and forth between us. "A friend, huh? You seem a little too *old* to be *friends* with my daughter."

"Friendships are built on connection, Mrs. Reyes, not on the details of our birth certificates," he explains with a respectful nod. His eyes meet mine for a moment, a silent reassurance that seems to say he's got this under control. I'm thankful that he does, but I don't need them arguing. Knowing my mother, she will take it there.

I take a deep breath. "Mom, he was just stopping by to help me with some heavy lifting," I explain hastily, hoping to steer her away from any lingering thoughts she might have about our relationship.

"Well, while he's here, maybe you can both find the time to check those missed calls from your family."

Vulcan raises an eyebrow slightly but addresses her with unwavering politeness. "Family is important," he agrees smoothly. "But today, we're focusing on helping Karina—"

"I'm not helping her with a damn thing. Karina, give me the money so I can be on my way." My mother's impatience boils over. She probably had a limit on how long she wanted to be in my presence. "I've wasted enough time here already." *Called it.*

Vulcan glances at me, a silent question in his eyes, but I shake my head slightly. "Mom," I say, keeping my voice steady despite the growing frustration. "I really can't give you more money right now. I don't have it."

Her demeanor shifts from demanding to incredulous. "You don't *have* it? You haven't sent me money in weeks. How do you expect me and your brothers to survive?" Her voice drips with anger, as if my financial struggles are a personal affront to her.

My mother never had to truly struggle. My father was the primary provider for our household. When he passed, she got his benefit checks and a nice chunk of money from the insurance company, which she spent on unnecessary things.

This is becoming too much for me now, especially with Vulcan here. I don't want him to see this.

Yet he steps forward, subtly placing himself between my mother and me. I feel a sudden rush of warmth at Vulcan's protective gesture. His broad shoulders block my mother's gaze, giving me a moment to catch my breath. "Karina has been managing her finances responsibly. She works incredibly hard saving lives every day. If she says she doesn't have extra money right now, I believe her. It's not easy making ends meet these days, especially in this economy."

My mother scoffs. "Oh, please. You're just defending her because you're friends," she snaps, the word *friends* coated with contempt.

"I'm defending her because it's the truth," he replies. "A job could help you feel less *dependent* on your daughter. Or, better yet, your sons could get jobs and help to relieve some of the pressure."

I'm a little surprised that he knows so much about my life, but I try to keep it hidden. Minji is a very thorough attorney; I'm guessing she made him aware of my background. *Fair enough.* I'm kind of relieved I won't have to take him through it from the start.

My mother's eyes flicker with shock and irritation. The nerve Vulcan has hit sparks an unexpected wrath in her eyes. "How dare you?" Her voice is full of venom. "You come into my daughter's home, a man I don't even know, and lecture me about my family?"

"I'm only stating what might help. Objectively," he adds, his tone still respectful, and it looks like he's pissing my mother off more that she can't get under his skin. He turns to look at me, his gaze softening slightly. "Karina can't be expected to shoulder everything alone."

I swallow hard, grateful for his support yet dreading the aftermath of this confrontation. My mother's gaze moves back to mine, but Vulcan shifts his body to block me from her death glare. "Is this why you've been ignoring my calls? Because this *man* told you to?"

"No, Mother," I reply quickly, moving to stand beside him. "Vulcan understands my situation because he sees how hard I work. I haven't called you back because I'm genuinely overwhelmed and don't have the money to spare."

She snorts derisively. "You've always been too soft," she mutters, shaking her head. "I thought you'd have your priorities straight by now, but clearly, you're letting others influence you."

Vulcan's jaw tightens at her words, but he maintains his composure. "Karina is one of the strongest people I know," he states. "Her decisions are her own, and if you have a problem with that, then I suggest you leave."

My mother laughs bitterly. "Of course you'd say that. You're standing here like some knight defending her honor. Where do you get off interfering in our family business?"

"Mrs. Reyes," he begins, crossing his arms over his chest, "my intention isn't to interfere but to *support* Karina, as any true friend would. She deserves that much, at least. As her mother, you should have more compassion. Especially when she tells you she is burnt out and does not have the financial means to lend out any money."

The air shifts slightly, and it's clear she's not used to being challenged in such a no-nonsense manner. "I think it's best that you leave." He gestures to the door.

My mother's lips part as if she's about to spit fire, but something in Vulcan's stance must have convinced her that he's not bluffing. "Fine." She spits out the word like it burns her tongue. "I'm leaving. But this isn't over, Karina. Remember who you're turning away." And with that, she storms past us, slamming the door behind her in a fit of anger.

We stay silent for a few seconds before he turns to face me. "Are you okay?" he asks gently.

"Yes, thanks to you." I manage a small smile, grateful beyond words but still processing everything. My mother has *never* backed down before. "I didn't expect you... to stand up to her like that."

He shrugs, but his eyes are as intense as I've ever seen them. "You shouldn't have to deal with that alone. As your husband, it'll be my job to be *your* protector."

Husband. Protector. Those words send a shiver down my spine.

I swallow hard, my heart racing. "Vulcan, I..." *I've never in my life had someone stand up for me* is on the verge of spilling out, but I shake my head to clear the thought.

"It's okay," he says softly, stepping closer. His hand reaches up to wipe away my tears. *When did I start crying?* "You don't have to say anything right now," he continues. "Just know that I'm here. For whatever you need, and I meant every word."

"Thank you, Vulcan. I didn't realize I was so alone in my corner until this moment."

"Don't worry." He smiles. "I'm not leaving you anytime soon. Would you like to sit for a bit?" he asks, gesturing to the couch. "The movers are set to arrive within the hour."

"No, it's fine. The quicker we pack, the faster I can get away from here." I move toward my bedroom, sensing his footsteps trailing behind.

If Vulcan notices the disarray, he says nothing about it. We get to work, carefully folding my clothes and placing them in the suitcase or packaging up small trinkets I hadn't decided whether to keep or just throw away.

He's silent, letting me have my space, but there is so much unspoken between us. I can almost hear the questions he doesn't ask: *Are you okay? Do you want to talk?*

I never imagined someone like Vulcan by my side in this way. Not just helping pack up my books and shoes but standing up for me without hesitating. His commitment seems genuine, and for once, the idea of leaning on someone doesn't make me want to run. Instead, it makes me want to trust him more.

"Karina." Vulcan finally breaks the silence as he zips up the nearly full suitcase. "The crew is almost finished removing everything. Do you have to turn in your keys?"

"My landlady told me to stop by next week since she's out of town."

He nods. "How about we grab a bite on the way to our place?"

I pause, processing his words. "*Your* place."

"Ours," he repeats. "I guess I'll cook for you once we get home. I don't want you to pass out on me from hunger."

"That sounds perfect," I admit, feeling the knots in my stomach ease slightly at the prospect of leaving this place behind—in three years, will I try to move back to this apartment building, or start over somewhere else?

I know this is all part of a grander plan, but I have to wonder... Where will Vulcan and I be when the contract comes to an end?

As if sensing my unspoken worries, Vulcan's hand finds mine, his grip warm and reassuring. "Hey," he says softly. "I can see those wheels turning in your head. What's going on?"

"Nothing. You just surprise me is all."

His eyes narrow slightly, and I can tell he doesn't quite believe me. But he doesn't push. "Oh, I'm full of surprises, Karina. You'll see." He tosses me a playful smirk.

We wait for the movers to clear out before I lock up and we head downstairs. The mid-afternoon air feels cooler, almost refreshing, compared to the stifling tension in my apartment. Moving feels symbolic, as if I'm gradually peeling away layers of my old life that no longer serve me.

CHAPTER EIGHTEEN
Vulcan

Karina hasn't brought up the incident at her apartment almost a week ago, and I've let it drop too. I occasionally catch a glossy look in her eyes and am reminded that she's hurting. Having a fallout with your parents is never easy, no matter who is in the wrong.

I see why she didn't want her mother to know about our upcoming nuptials. I can't blame her. It's a miracle Karina turned out to be such a kind and caring person despite her mother's influence.

A few nights ago, she came home from her shift with red and swollen eyes, and I knew something had happened. She told me that her mother had called and things had gotten heated. I could feel the hurt making her fragile, the weight of it all on her shoulders. I never pried or asked for details, knowing it's a sensitive topic for her. But fucking hell, it made me angry that her own mother could cause her so much pain.

As I walk through Central Park, trying to clear my head, I think about ways to make Karina feel better. I want her to know that she has me and that I'll always be there for her, no matter what. But as the days pass, I see her become more withdrawn, throwing herself into her work. When she's home, she holes up in her room, and I know she hasn't caught up with Cass in weeks.

The leaves crunch under my sneakers as I dodge a puddle, my breath visible in the chilly September air. I can't shake the image of Karina's exhausted face as she trudges through our front door every night. It's hard to watch someone you care about struggle and not be able to fix it.

As it is, I'm past trying to respect boundaries. I'm all in. I want to be a part of every aspect of Karina's life, even the mess she tries to shield me from. She has every right to deal with things her way, but damn it, I want to help—*need* to help.

I find a park bench and pull out my phone, deciding it's time to check in with Minji.

"Good morning, Vulcan." Her voice sounds far too bright for this early in the day. "The paperwork is ready. I have reached out to Mrs. Reyes, and she's set to arrive in an hour."

"Perfect, I'll be there shortly." I end the call and walk back home, taking in the scenery and trying to calm my nerves. Karina will either love or hate me for what I'm about to do. But I can't just stand by and watch her crumble at the hand of her toxic mother. I'm determined to find a way to fix it, to be the support she needs, even if it means playing it risky.

The air feels colder as I cross the street toward my building, my heart pounding. What if Gabriella doesn't sign the contract? What if I only make things worse? But I can't back down now. I set this plan in motion and have to see it through.

I shower quickly, the steam fogging up the bathroom mirrors, and talk myself off the ledge. It might be the wrong move, getting involved with Karina's mother again, but it's worth the gamble.

The air fills with the scents of soap and my determination as I towel off. I move quickly back into my bedroom, where I pull on a crisp white shirt, my fingers fumbling with the buttons, and slip into navy trousers. I wince as a sharp pain shoot through my shoulder, the injury protesting my rush.

I make it to Minji's office ahead of time, which gives me a few moments to prepare. I rehearse what I'm going to say, envisioning every possible scenario.

Minji offers me a cup of coffee while we wait. "I don't think I can drink anything right now," I admit.

"For the last time, Vulcan, do you need to think this through? I know you're coming from a place of care, but have you considered how Karina will react when she finds out?"

I rub the back of my neck. She's right. If this doesn't go as planned, it could cause more harm than good. But I can't stand by and watch her suffer, not when I'm in a position to help.

I shake my head. "She's been through so much already. And her mother is beyond toxic. I would have run away from home before I turned ten if she were my mother," I say with a bitter laugh. "The sooner I can do this, the sooner Karina will finally be able to enjoy the life she deserves."

Before she can respond, we hear the sound of Mrs. Reyes's heels clicking against the marble floor. Her posture is stiff as she enters the office, her expression serious. She looks genuinely surprised when her eyes land on me, but she twists her face back to its original grimace just as quickly.

Minji stands to greet her. "We appreciate you coming today, Mrs. Reyes. Please sit."

As she launches into small talk, Mrs. Reyes maintains a stoic expression, making it difficult to gauge her thoughts.

I wait until there's a lull in conversation to begin, choosing my words carefully. "This isn't just about an agreement. It's also about understanding and, hopefully, mending some of the fractures in your relationship with Karina."

"Mr. Montgomery, while I appreciate your concern, I assure you that my daughter and I have our way of handling things." She arches an eyebrow. "There is no need for you to get involved in something that does not concern you. I'm sure you understand that *friends* should stay in their place when it comes to family affairs."

"Your 'way' seems a bit condescending," I volley back, leaning forward and clasping my hands on the table. "I can assure you, your days of bullying Karina are coming to an end. As her hus—*friend*, I will not stand for it."

She purses her lips, her eyes narrowing into slits at my directness. "I see. It appears you have made *assumptions* about my intentions, Mr. Montgomery. Perhaps you're not aware of every detail. Karina owes me this much. I've dealt with my fair share of drama concerning that girl."

"It's not assumptions. I saw firsthand back at her apartment, or did you forget?" I meet her gaze steadily. "A parent's job is to love and support their child, not treat them like a financial institution."

Mrs. Reyes's composure cracks slightly, a flicker of anger flashing in her eyes. "You have no right to lecture me on parenting, Mr. Montgomery. You know nothing about our family or the sacrifices I've made."

I lean back, maintaining eye contact. "I know enough to see that your relationship with Karina is toxic. It will be fixed one way or another."

Her eyes flicker with a hint of surprise, perhaps not expecting me to confront her so openly. "Everyone sees and hears what they want to. I assure you, I'm no bully. I'm not here to change your mind, and I will not sit here and listen to you tell me how to speak to my child. Now, let's focus on the contract, shall we?" she suggests, attempting to steer the conversation back to safer waters. Before I can have the final word, Minji clears her throat, giving me a look that says *shut the hell up.*

"This contract comes with stipulations *and* a breach fee." She pauses to let it sink in. "What Mr. Montgomery is offering you is a lot of money: half a million dollars, to be precise. To receive this money, you will be required to leave Karina alone and never speak to anyone about our arrangement. If you breach this contract, you must pay a million dollars and possibly face jail time. Do you understand?"

Mrs. Reyes's face remains impassive, but her fingers twitch slightly as she leans forward, her gaze fixed on the documents before her. Will she choose her daughter or the money?

"I understand," she says after a prolonged silence. I can almost hear the excitement in her voice. "However, you must realize that my relationship with my daughter is complex. Money cannot simply erase that."

"I agree. Money isn't a solution to personal conflicts. And this is about giving her the space to heal and hopefully start anew with you on better terms." I pause. "Karina deserves peace, and I believe this could be a step toward that."

"Very well." She smiles, picking up the pen eagerly. "If this is what Karina needs... then I will sign." As her signature flows across the paper, relief washes over me, clouded only by my apprehension for Karina's reaction when she finds out.

"How soon will I get the money?" she asks, standing up.

"The funds will be transferred to your account within two business days."

"Very well." Mrs. Reyes coolly adjusts her purse on her shoulder. "I expect no delays. Oh, and Mr. Montgomery..." Her eyes move to mine. "Don't you think you're a little too old to be fucking my daughter."

It wasn't a question because she didn't stick around to hear my response. The door quickly closes behind her and I stand up.

"Let it go." Minji places her hand on my arm. "You got what you wanted, she signed the documents."

"But—"

"No buts. Just leave it alone," she repeats. "We have to hope it plays out the way you intend it to. Go home, tell Karina about it, and move forward."

I nod, but my mind is already racing. The secrecy and dealings with her mother feel like treacherous territory.

I'm cooking dinner when I hear the front door close, followed by Karina kicking off her work shoes. If she goes with chocolate milk, I'll tell her about today. If she reaches for the wine, I'll hold off because I know that means she's had a hard day.

"Mmm, something smells delicious," she says, walking over to the kitchen and taking out the gallon of milk from the fridge. It must have been a good day. "What are you cooking?" She gives me a grateful smile as I hand her the cocoa powder and a cup, sliding it across the counter toward her.

"Tonight, I'm making your favorite—chicken parmesan with a side of spaghetti aglio e olio," I say, watching her happily stir her drink.

Karina takes a sip, her eyes closing briefly in satisfaction. "*Mmm, delicioso,*" she murmurs, then her gaze shifts to me. "Guess what?"

"Good or bad?" I ask, turning my attention back to the stovetop.

"Good."

"You won the lottery," I quip.

"I wish. That would keep my mother off my back for the rest of my life." She snorts. "I have tomorrow off, which means I can stay up late tonight."

"That's great," I say, looking over at her, unsure where this conversation is going.

"It is. We can hang out. Talk more, get to know each other *better.*"

She flashes me a playful grin, and I can't help but smile back. The thought of spending an entire evening together is more appealing than she probably realizes.

"So, what's on the agenda?" I ask. I know the plan was to tell her about my meeting with her mother, but I don't want to ruin her good mood.

"I was thinking, Mr. Montgomery, that we could kick off our night with a movie marathon. And maybe… cash in that rain check," she teases, biting her lip.

I raise an eyebrow, intrigued. "You want to have sex?" She takes another sip of her chocolate milk, the corners of her lips curling slightly, then looks back down at her cup.

"I do."

I set down the spoon and move closer, drawn to her like a magnet.

"Well then," I murmur, "I think that can be arranged."

I place my hands on either side of her, caging her against the counter. Karina tilts her chin up and I lean in, my lips a breath away from hers.

"But first," I whisper, "dinner."

I pull back abruptly, smirking at her frustrated groan.

"I'm going to freshen up," she says, rising on her tiptoes to give me a quick kiss on the lips before gently pushing me away. She heads out of the kitchen, leaving me to finish cooking. As I'm bringing the plates to the dining room table, Karina saunters back in wearing nothing but a baby pink nightie that barely covers the tops of her thighs. My breath catches in my throat, and I nearly drop the plates I'm holding.

"I thought I'd get comfortable," she says, her voice honey-sweet but her eyes pure mischief.

I carefully set the plates down, my eyes never leaving her. The thin pink fabric clings to her curves, leaving little to the imagination. My cock twitches in my sweatpants, and I have to adjust myself subtly.

She slides into her chair, crossing her legs slowly. Fuck me. I force myself to sit opposite her, though every instinct tells me to forget dinner entirely. I pour us each a glass of wine, noticing my hands aren't quite steady.

"You know," I say, taking a sip to compose myself, "when I planned this dinner, I thought we'd be having a conversation."

Karina twirls pasta around her fork, a smile playing on her lips. "We are having a conversation."

"A difficult one when you're dressed like that."

She takes a bite, maintaining eye contact in a way that makes my temperature rise. "That sounds like a you problem, Vulcan."

I laugh, shaking my head. "You're impossible."

"Yet here you are, having a nice conversation."

"Here I am," I agree.

We eat in charged silence for a few minutes, the air between us thrumming with anticipation. I watch her take another sip of wine, leaving a faint pink stain on the glass from her lipstick.

"Tell me something I don't know about you," she says suddenly.

I consider the question, knowing there are still many things she doesn't know—including my meeting with her mother today. But that conversation can wait. Tonight is about us.

"I have thoroughly enjoyed watching *Grey's Anatomy*." I smile sheepishly as she bursts into laughter.

"No way! The big, tough Vulcan Montgomery watches medical dramas?" She leans forward, giving me an even better view of her cleavage. "I would have pegged you for action movies only."

"I'm a man who wants to know more about his wife's career," I say, trying to keep my eyes on her face and not her hardened nipples underneath the thin fabric. "Thought it would be a good way to learn more about what you do."

"That's..." She pauses, her expression softening. "That's actually really sweet."

I shrug, trying to play it cool. "Plus, the drama is addictive. I'm invested in Meredith and Derek."

Karina laughs again. "Oh, you poor thing. I'm not going to spoil anything for you."

"I appreciate that." I take another bite of my pasta, watching her over the rim of my glass. "Your turn. Tell me something I don't know about you."

She considers this, twirling a strand of hair around her finger. The gesture is both innocent and seductive.

"I wanted to be a ballerina when I was little," she finally says. "I took lessons for years. I still have my pointe shoes somewhere."

"I bet you were beautiful," I say softly. "I can see it—you're still graceful. Tell me more."

Her cheeks flush pink. "You're just saying that because you want to get me out of this nightie."

"Well, yes," I admit. "But that doesn't make it any less true." My eyes linger on her, taking in the way the soft fabric molds to her body, and I know I could have her right here if I let myself. The thought is half thrilling, half torturous. But she wants a movie night, and damn it, that's what she'll get. "You almost ready to start the movie?"

As much as I want her, I don't want to rush things and end up pushing her back into the arms of hesitation. She should be completely comfortable in this house, with me.

"Let's go," she suggests, standing up.

I nod and stand, reaching for the plates.

"Leave it. I'll clean up after." She places a hand on mine, stopping me. "It's only been a month since your surgery, you should be taking it easy when you can. Besides, the cook doesn't clean."

We settle into the living room, a couple of action flicks lined up for our makeshift movie marathon. While we're watching *Avengers*, our hands brush, and each accidental touch makes me want to drag her to the bedroom. The air buzzes with anticipation. She's got to know what she's doing to me. I'm hard as a fucking rock. Karina cuddles closer to me under the blanket as the credits roll. Her warmth seeps into my side, and I can smell her fruity, sweet shampoo. It's intoxicating—*she's* fucking intoxicating.

She shifts slightly, turning to face me with those deep brown eyes that seem to see right through me.

"Vulcan," she whispers, her voice a sultry melody that stirs something primal within me. "I think I'm done watching movies." Her fingers trace the tattoos on my arm, each touch sparking a fire.

I shift, cupping her face gently. "Me too." I lean in, allowing her the opportunity to pull away or change her mind. But she doesn't move back; instead, she closes the gap between us.

Our lips meet in a kiss that starts tender but quickly grows fierce and passionate. I'm aware of every little detail: the softness of her lips, the delicate scent of her skin, the way her body presses against mine as if she's trying to merge as one.

She pulls back, gasping for air, her eyes shining with desire. "I've wanted this," she breathes out, her hands roaming over my chest, feeling the muscles tense under her touch. She straddles me and her nightie scrunches up, and I see she isn't wearing panties. "Since I first saw you at the bar."

Yes.

"Sorry I've kept you waiting so long." I look down at her bare pussy. So fucking pretty.

Karina presses closer, her breath hot against my ear. "Don't be," she whispers, her lips brushing against my skin. "It's gonna be worth the wait." Her hands find their way into my hair, pulling me in for another deep kiss.

CHAPTER NINETEEN
Karina

I grind against Vulcan's lap, his large hands gripping my ass as our tongues battle for dominance. He digs his fingers into my flesh as he moans, a low rumble climbing up his throat. I move my hands down his chest, tugging on the waistband of his sweatpants, and he draws me closer until there's no space left between us. I can feel the hard lines of his muscles under my fingertips as I explore.

"Are you on birth control?"

"I—yes," I manage to stammer out, my cheeks burning.

"Good. I want no barriers between us."

My pulse skyrockets, and I can't seem to form a coherent thought.

"That's…" I swallow hard, trying to regain my composure. "That's quite brazen of you, don't you think?"

Vulcan's pupils dilate as his gaze drops to my lips. "Is it? We're about to be husband and wife, Karina. I'm just being honest about what I want."

Heat creeps up my neck at his bluntness. Something about the way he speaks—so confident, so sure—makes my stomach flutter with anticipation. I should be offended but instead, I find myself more aroused.

"But if you want protection, I have it. And we have years to do this bare."

"N-no protection."

"Are you sure?" he murmurs.

I can only nod, unable to find my voice as his eyes bore into me. My heart races and my breath comes in shallow gasps. I want him. I need him.

He lifts me effortlessly and carries me to the bedroom, laying me down on his bed, never breaking eye contact. I don't even have it in me to scold him for being careless with his injury as he towers over me, his body a work of art. Every muscle is defined, every inch of him hard and toned. His eyes are dark and hungry; his lips curled in a wicked smirk. I can see the outline of his cock through his pants, thick and ready for me.

He leans down, his breath hot against my ear. "I'm not in the mood to fuck you slowly."

"It hasn't even been a month since your surgery. Either we take it slow or you let me do the work tonight."

"No. I'll deal with the consequences later. I need this, it's all I've been thinking about," he says, his voice husky with desire. "I need to show you what every night could look like once I'm fully healed."

My breath catches in my throat, the dominance emanating off him sending shivers down my spine and pooling heat between my legs.

"But you *aren't* healed."

"Let me have this, please. I want to please you without you worrying about my shoulder." His mouth crashes back onto mine, silencing any further protest, filling every corner of my mind with nothing but the taste and feel of him. I moan into his mouth, my body arching, greedy for more contact, more of *everything*. His hands travel over me, stripping away my nightie with an urgency that makes me dizzy and sets my desire spinning out of control.

"I'll be fine," he promises, his teeth grazing the sensitive flesh at the base of my neck. My breath catches in my throat, and I gasp as his fingers skillfully find their way between my thighs, discovering just how ready I am for him. His expression changes, turns to one of awe, and then there's that wicked smirk that drives me wild.

"Fuck," he breathes, voice filled with hunger and wonderment, igniting every nerve and setting me on fire. "You're soaked."

He grimaces a bit as he rises from the bed. I decide to let him have his way tonight, but tomorrow, he's not lifting a finger. Quickly, he discards his clothes before climbing back onto the bed. His beard scratches gently against my skin as he kisses his way down my throat, leaving a trail of heat in his wake. He pauses at my chest, right above my racing heart. "I've been waiting so long for this," he whispers.

I reach for him, my fingers threading through his short hair as I pull him back up to meet my lips. "Show me," I whisper against his mouth.

Vulcan's response is immediate, his kiss deepening, devouring as if he's drawing every ounce of my confession through his lips. He breaks the kiss, just for a moment, to look into my eyes with an emotion that nearly overwhelms me. "Your body is perfection," he says as he traces the line of my jaw with tender fingers. "You're fucking perfect for me."

Vulcan's touch scorches my flesh like a branding iron, sending electric shocks straight to my core as his fingers trail a leisurely path down the valley between my heaving breasts. His hands journey lower, until they reach my quivering thighs.

He parts my legs, spreading me wide open for him. With a slow, deliberate stroke, he slides one thick finger inside me, filling me up in a way that makes my eyes roll back in my head. I gasp at the sensation, my back bowing off the bed as I eagerly thrust my hips, my body crying out for more of his touch. My pussy clenches around his finger, already desperate for release.

His thumb begins to work in slow circles around my swollen clit, adding a maddening layer of pleasure to the delicious fullness of his finger thrusting in and out. I whimper and writhe beneath him, my hands reaching out to cling to his broad shoulders as I lose myself in the sensation of his touch.

"Fuck, you feel so good." He growls against the skin of my thigh, his warm breath sending a fresh wave of shivers down my spine.

"Please," I gasp. "I need you inside me. Now."

Vulcan increases his pace and I cry out in euphoria, but his darkened eyes don't move from where his fingers work.

"Please," I say, frustrated and on the verge of tears.

But he isn't finished yet. He slides another finger inside me, stretching me wider than ever before. Fuck, no man has made me feel like this and he's only using his fingers. The sensation is almost too much to bear, but I crave it all the same. Each thrust is deeper and harder and more desperate than the last. He climbs up my body and begins to massage my breast, his thumb flicking my nipple in time with the rhythm of his thrusts. His lips leave a trail of desire down my neck, across my collarbone, until he reaches my aching nipple. He takes it into his mouth, sucking hard as his fingers continue to work me over.

I've never felt so full, so wanted, so completely consumed by pleasure. The feeling of his mouth on my breast, combined with the relentless thrusting of his fingers, is almost too much to bear. I can feel my orgasm building, my pussy clenching around his fingers as I rock my hips against him.

"Don't stop," I beg. "Please, don't stop."

"Come for me, baby," Vulcan whispers. "I want to feel you come all over my fingers."

With one final thrust, I lose control. My orgasm crashes over me like a tidal wave, consuming me entirely as I cry out his name. My pussy clenches around his fingers, milking them for all they're worth as wave after wave of pleasure rolls through me. I can feel myself pulsing and contracting around him.

Oh my fucking God.

As the waves of pleasure begin to subside, Vulcan slowly slides his fingers out of me, eliciting one final gasp of pleasure from deep in my chest as he does. He brings his fingers to his mouth and sucks them clean, his eyes never leaving mine. The sight of him tasting my arousal is almost enough to make me come again.

"Mm. Just as I thought. *Amazing.*"

Before I can respond, his mouth is on mine again. I can taste myself on his tongue, and it only fuels my desire further. His hands roam my body, caressing every curve as if committing them to memory. I reach between us—needing to feel him—and wrap my fingers around his thick, hard cock. He moans into my mouth as I stroke him, feeling him throb in my hand.

"I need you now," I whisper against his lips. "Please, Vulcan. I want to feel all of you."

"Whatever you want, it's yours, baby."

He grabs my right thigh, lifting it up and over his hip, opening me up to him. I feel the blunt head of his cock pressing against my entrance, teasing me with its hardness. My breath catches in my throat as he slowly pushes forward, stretching me inch by glorious inch.

"Oh god," I moan, my head falling back against the pillow as he fills me completely.

Vulcan moans like I'm his salvation, his eyes fluttering closed momentarily as if savoring the sensation, before he snaps them open again.

"You feel incredible," he breathes out as he begins to move. Each thrust is slow initially, allowing me to adjust to his size. My hands roam over his back, feeling the powerful muscles work beneath his skin.

The room seems to spin slightly as our rhythm builds. The sound of our breaths mingling with the soft moans that escape my lips fills the air. Vulcan's grip on my thigh tightens as he dives deeper, each thrust pushing me closer to the brink.

The fire in his eyes burns brighter with every motion, and I can't look away. His hand slides up my body to cradle my face, his thumb caressing my cheek softly. "Tell me what you need," he whispers against my lips.

"More."

Vulcan responds with a growl, his movements quickening, driving into me with a purpose. I cling to him desperately, digging my nails into his shoulders as if he's the only thing keeping me anchored to this world. It's too much and not enough all at once. I'm close, *so close*, the world narrowing down to the point of bliss that Vulcan is guiding me toward.

For a moment, I see the flash of pain in his expression, and I loosen my hold, guilt threading through the haze of passion. I need to be careful, to remember he's not invincible, that he's still healing. But he doesn't even slow down.

"I told you not to worry about it. Keep those nails digging into me if that's what you need."

I do as he says, pulling him deeper. He wants me like this, undone and unrestrained, not holding back. It sends heat spiraling through me like wildfire. He looks at me, eyes full of need and something more. Like he's daring me to let go more than I ever have before—to lose myself completely.

"What else do you want, Karina? Talk me through it, baby." He moves in and out of me slowly. "I will grant your every wish." He groans as I clench my pussy around him.

"I want you to fuck me like you hate me." I moan, and it's like a switch flips inside of him.

His eyes turn black as he presses his forehead to my temple, his lips grazing my ear. "Like I hate you?" he questions, the words vibrating against my skin, teasing out an involuntary shiver.

I nod, breathless, my voice a whisper of encouragement. "*Yes.*"

"I'd love to hate you, Karina, but just for tonight. Just here, to give you what you need." He pulls out of me and flips me onto my stomach, wrapping my hair around his right hand and yanking gently, forcing me up onto my hands and knees. His other hand grips my hip, pulling me back against him as he drives into me from behind. His pace is merciless, pushing me further toward the brink with every movement.

Fuck!

Fuck!

Fuck!

I was not ready for this—shit, it feels so good.

"You like that?" Vulcan asks, his beard scratching against my neck as he leans over me. "You like it when I fuck you hard and hate you just enough to make it feel this good?"

I can barely form words, lost in the sensations overwhelming me. "Yes," I manage to gasp out. "God, yes."

He tightens his grip on my hair, pulling my head back further. The slight pain only heightens my pleasure, scattering goose bumps all over my body. I can feel my climax building rapidly. He must sense it too, because his thrusts pick up speed.

"You're so fucking incredible," he growls. He lets go of my hair and then starts smacking my ass hard. "Aren't you?" *Smack*. "Say it, Karina." *Smack*. "Say you're incredible." Each slap resonates through my body, the pain mingling perfectly with pleasure.

"I'm incredible." I struggle to catch my breath.

"Yes, you are," he affirms, and his words of affirmation continue.

"You're not just strong and compassionate, but brave and beautiful." I think I'm going to fall in love with this man before I reach my second orgasm. Not only can he cook, he's caring, smart, protective, and the way he fucks is out of a fantasy. "Now repeat it word for word while I fuck you. And don't you stop until I tell you to."

I repeat the words, each syllable punctuated by his relentless thrusts. "I'm strong, compassionate, brave, and beautiful," I recite, the mantra blending into my moans of pleasure. His movements intensify with each word I speak as if he is engraving them into the deepest part of me.

Vulcan uses both hands to pulling me back against him with a force that pushes the breath from my lungs. With every repetition of my newfound labels, I feel a little less like the woman who was carried into this room and a little more like the goddess he sees in me.

"You're so much more than you give yourself credit for," Vulcan breathes out, slowing momentarily. He gathers my hair, wrapping it around his fist as he speaks. "I want you to believe it—not just now but always. In and outside of this bedroom. Do you understand?"

"Yes," I moan.

"Now, let me reward you." He grips my hair tighter, pulling my head back. "You deserve to be worshiped."

My heart races, hammering against my chest as if it's trying to keep rhythm with his thrusts. "Let go for me, Karina. Let it all go. Come for me, baby. Come all over my cock." And like a dam bursting under the pressure, I shatter.

As my trembling slowly subsides, the room around me starts to come into focus. The soft, golden lamplight throws shadows against the walls, and I feel more protected than I thought was possible, in someone else's space.

"You're amazing," he whispers, planting soft kisses on my shoulder.

I collapse forward onto the bed, my legs trembling, my breath coming in ragged gasps. Vulcan follows, his weight a comforting presence against my back. For a moment, we just breathe together, our bodies still joined, hearts pounding in sync.

"That was..." I trail off, unable to find words to describe what we just shared.

Vulcan chuckles softly, the rumble vibrating through me. "I know," he murmurs, nuzzling my neck. "It was all you, Karina."

Slowly, he withdraws from me, rolls to the side, and pulls me into his arms. I curl against his chest, savoring the warmth of his skin and the steady thrum of his heartbeat. His fingers trace lazy patterns along my spine.

"I never knew..." I start, struggling to articulate this newfound awareness of myself that Vulcan has ignited within me.

"You never knew how powerful you are," he finishes for me. "There's nothing you can't handle in this world."

His words are not just sweet, hollow platitudes floating in the air between two lovers; they are affirmations meant to repair the broken parts of me. It's as if he's creating a portrait of who I could be, or who I truly am but was too afraid to acknowledge.

"Now, let me finish cashing in on this rain check," he says, sitting up.

CHAPTER TWENTY
Vulcan

I'm completely consumed by the overwhelming sensation of Karina's body, my mind a haze of pure, unadulterated pleasure as I lose myself between her thighs. Thighs that are trembling against my cheeks as I worship her with my tongue, savoring every drop. God, I could lie here for hours.

My beard is soaked with her arousal. Hell, I think my entire face is covered in her arousal. We've both learned one thing about her tonight: she's a squirter, and I fucking love it.

Karina's fingers tangle in my hair, her grip tightening as she gasps, "Vulcan... oh God, yes." Her hips rock against my face, seeking the release she knows I can give her.

"You taste so good, baby," I murmur against her skin. "I can't get enough of you. I could eat you all day and night."

She whimpers in response, and I slide two fingers inside her, curling them to hit that spot that I'm sure makes her see stars.

"Please don't stop," Karina pants.

As if I would ever deny her. Not when I can feel how close she is, her inner muscles fluttering around my fingers. I suck her clit between my lips, flicking it with my tongue as I pump faster.

Karina cries out, her back arching off the bed as she comes undone. I ease her through it, my touch gentle as I coax her down from the peak of pleasure. When she tugs at my hair, I lift my head to meet her gaze, my lips glistening.

"Come here." She pulls me up for a kiss and our tongues tangle together, a dance as old as time itself. I can feel her heart racing against mine, our bodies slick with sweat.

I reach down to stroke her clit, feeling it swell beneath my fingers. I slide two fingers inside her again, relishing the way she clenches around me.

"Again?" She shudders, breaking the kiss.

"Again," I confirm. "I love the way you feel."

She moans as I move my fingers inside her. I watch her face, mesmerized by the way her lips part and her eyes flutter closed in pleasure. She's so beautiful like this, completely open and vulnerable, trusting me with her body.

"Look at me." I curl my fingers, hitting her sweet spot. Her eyes snap open, locking onto mine with a fiery passion that takes my breath away. "That's it. I want to see you."

I increase the pace of my fingers, using my thumb to circle her clit. Karina bucks against my hand, chasing her release. I can feel her getting close again. Fuck, I love how responsive she is to my touch.

With a cry that fills the room, she comes apart, her body shuddering beneath mine. I slow my movements, drawing out her pleasure. When she finally relaxes, I gently withdraw my fingers and bring them to my mouth, sucking them clean as she watches with heavy-lidded eyes.

"You're incredible." I press a kiss to her lips. "Are you tired?" I kiss her forehead.

"No. Why?"

"I'm ready to christen this *entire* penthouse," I answer, rising from the bed.

Her eyes widen and she bites her lip, considering my proposition. I can see the wheels turning in her mind, weighing exhaustion against desire. Now that I've tasted her, I want more. I need more.

"The whole penthouse, huh? That's quite ambitious, Captain," she says, but gets out of bed, slipping her hand into mine. "Where should we start?"

I pretend to consider for a moment, though I already know exactly where I want to take her next. "How about the kitchen? I've been dying to see you spread out on that island."

Karina's cheeks flush, but she nods eagerly. "After you."

As I lead her down the hallway, the cool air lifting goose bumps on my skin, we pass the living room and an idea strikes me.

"Actually," I say, tugging her toward the floor-to-ceiling windows overlooking the city, "I think I want to start here."

Karina's eyes widen as she realizes my intention. "But people might see..."

I press her up to the glass, my body flush against her back. "Let them," I murmur in her ear. "Let them all see how beautiful you are when you shatter for me." We both know there's no way anyone could actually see; we're forty floors up after all, but the way her breath catches tells me she likes the fantasy.

I trail kisses down her neck as my hands roam her body, cupping her breasts and teasing her nipples. Karina gasps, arching into my touch. Her breath fogs the glass as she presses her forehead against it.

"You're so sexy." I slide one hand down her stomach and between her legs. She's already dripping wet again, eager for more. I circle her clit as my other hand continues to caress her breasts.

Karina moans, pushing back against me. The heat of her body seeps into me, her thighs quaking as she searches for more friction. I press myself against her, letting her feel how hard I am.

"Please," she whimpers, her fingers trying to grip the glass.

I smile against her shoulder, nipping lightly. "Please what, baby?

Tell me what you want."

"I want you inside me." She turns her head to capture my lips in a searing kiss.

I don't make her wait any longer. With one smooth motion, I enter her, our groans audible in the otherwise quiet space. I start to move, setting a pace that has her gasping and clutching at the window for support.

The city lights twinkle below us, a sea of stars at our feet. Downtown Manhattan looks amazing at night, and I can even make out the tops of the trees at Central Park. But not even that can compare to the sight of Karina, flushed and beautiful, reflected in the glass. I watch her face contort with pleasure, her eyes fluttering closed as she loses herself in the sensation.

"Open your eyes," I command softly. "Look at how gorgeous you are."

She obeys, her gaze meeting mine in the reflection. I increase my pace, my fingers finding her clit again. Karina cries out, her body tense as she approaches her climax. I'm right there with her, teetering on the brink.

"Come for me, Karina," I whisper in her ear. "Let the whole city hear how good I make you feel."

She moans loudly, her body clenching around me. The sight and feel of her orgasm trigger my own, and I follow her over the edge, burying my face in her neck to muffle my groans. Shit. If she wasn't on birth control, she would be pregnant by the end of the night. I'm not letting a drop go to waste.

We stand there for a moment, panting and trembling, before I gently turn her in my arms. I kiss her deeply, pouring all my emotions into it.

"One room down." I place a kiss on her forehead. "Ready for the kitchen?"

She looks off to the side, and I follow her gaze. It's her work bag. Karina looks back at me, her cheeks flushed.

"Actually," she hedges.

Shit, does she to want to stop? I loosen my hold immediately, ready to let her take the lead.

"I have some things I want to use."

"You want to role-play?" I glance back at her work bag. "I'm not opposed, but—"

"No, I have something." She steps out of my arms and walks over to her bag. My cock goes hard again as I take in her naked, moonlit body. She squats, digs in her bag, and then stands up. Slowly she turns around and—*fuck me*. She has handcuffs in one hand and a bottle of lube in the other. "I want you to use these on me."

"Are you sure?"

She nods. I would never have thought in a million years that she had this side to her. I don't even know where to begin wondering what she's doing carrying those things around. But then again, she did ask me to fuck her like I hated her, and who am I to kink-shame?

"Question, Karina," I start. "Have you ever been dominated before?"

She bites her lip. "No. But I've... I've thought about it. *A lot*. Especially with you."

My cock twitches at her confession. The idea that she's been fantasizing about me dominating her sends a spark of heat through me. I take a step closer, my eyes locked on hers.

"A lot goes into being dominated. Are you wanting to explore the BDSM lifestyle, or..." My voice trails off, not sure if I'm pushing it.

"Well, it's more that I've imagined you taking control, using me for your pleasure. Making me beg. I want to surrender to you completely." Despite her warm chestnut complexion, I notice the redness creeping onto the tips of her ears. Discussing sex seems to make her shy, and that's something we'll need to change. By the end of the night, I'll ensure she's comfortable with herself, and by tomorrow morning, she'll confidently share every way she wants me to fuck her. She has the day off tomorrow, and I sure as hell have nowhere to be. We have all night to play.

I cross the cool hardwood floor and take the handcuffs and lube from her, watching as her eyes flare with anticipation. "Are you sure about this?" I ask again, searching her eyes for any hesitation. "Once we start, I won't stop until I've wrung every ounce of pleasure from your body. While this isn't a dominant/submissive situation, I would still feel comfortable if you had a safe word in case things become too much for you. Something you wouldn't usually say during sex."

"Stethoscope," she says without hesitation, and I have to hold back my laugh while praying she doesn't choose to use it—I don't want to scare her off before we can explore this together.

"Stethoscope it is, and you'll have to trust me," I let her know, tossing the lube onto the sofa.

"I trust you completely."

Music to my ears.

"On your knees," I command.

Karina rears back slightly, but she obeys without protest, sinking to her knees before me. I run my fingers through her hair, gripping it lightly at the base of her neck.

"Good girl," I murmur, watching as she shivers at the praise. "Now, put your hands behind your back. Press them together."

I secure the handcuffs around her wrists, not too tight but snug enough that she can't slip free. The click of the cuffs locking into place seems to echo in the room. I circle her slowly, admiring the sight of her bound and waiting.

"Remember, say the word if it becomes too much, and I'll stop immediately. Yeah?"

"Yes," she breathes

I grab a fistful of her hair, tugging gently, making her eyes meet mine. "Yes, what?"

Karina shivers, understanding dawning in her eyes. "Yes, *sir*," she corrects.

"Good girl," I praise. "Now, tell me what you want."

She swallows hard, her voice trembling slightly before she responds. "I want you to use me, to make me yours completely."

"Believe me, I fully intend to," I promise, my eyes scanning her beautiful face, flushed with desire. "When I'm finished, you'll forget even your own name, and only mine will linger in your mind. Now, let's find out how much pleasure your body can endure."

CHAPTER TWENTY-ONE

Karina

I don't know how long I've been asleep for, but I wake up to the sound of the doorbell ringing, wishing it would just stop. I try to sit up but stop when I feel Vulcan's hand on my breast—vivid images of last night play in my mind. I took Cassie's advice before leaving the hospital yesterday: stop overthinking and go for it.

Cash in that damn rain check. And be manhandled by Hephaestus himself, she'd said, then handed me a bag of goodies. She'd been calling him *Hephaestus* for weeks, a nod to the origins of his name

Remembering him telling me the morning paper is usually delivered around this time, I slowly remove Vulcan's hand and slip out of bed. I pick up his T-shirt from the floor and put it on. Exiting the bedroom, I quietly shut the door behind me and walk toward the foyer.

"Took you long enough," I hear as I open the door, and a weak smile graces my face. *Crap, it's his sister.* "Oh, uh, hi. Good morning." She takes in my appearance. Vulcan's shirt stops mid-thigh, and I'm sure my hair looks worse than a bird's nest being built.

"Good morning, come in, come in." I step aside, opening the door wide.

When I turn back around, I find her standing still at the edge of the living room. When I remember *why*, all the color drains from my face.

Last night, I learned Vulcan and I have very similar tastes in sex.

The main thing is that I like someone to dominate me, and he *loves* to dominate. In the light of day though, I internally cringe, seeing the set of handcuffs on the coffee table, along with lube. There's also the matter of the dishes from the meal he cooked still piled on the table.

I rush into the living room, gathering the mess. "I'm sorry. I wasn't expecting company. Umm. You can sit in the dining room—wait, no. The kitch—no! Sorry, can you just wait here for a bit?" She nods and pulls out her phone, distracting herself while I rush around, gathering Vulcan's silk ties and the half-empty can of whipped cream. Then, I'm in the kitchen, grabbing a trash bag and swiping everything off the countertop.

"You don't have to clean—"

"It's fine," I shout, the embarrassment evident in my voice. I fumble with the bag, tripping over my own feet as I try to shove the evidence of our escapades out of sight. She must think I'm a *freak.* When I poke my head into the hall, I see her standing in the foyer, her expression unreadable as I scurry about. The tips of her ears are pink, whether from embarrassment or suppressed amusement, I can't tell. I don't want to know. I laugh weakly. "Okay, all clear."

"Well, good morning. I'm Valkyrie, Vulcan's sister, but you can call me Val." She steps into the living room. "We didn't get a chance to meet properly that day in the hospital."

Her voice is warmer than I expected, easing some of the tension knotting my stomach. I force a smile. "I'm Karina, Vulcan's…" I hesitate for a fraction of a second. The realization that Vulcan hadn't mentioned anything about how to address our relationship status makes me pause.

"His soon-to-be wife," Val answers for me. Okay, so he's told her about our upcoming nuptials, but I'm sure he wouldn't let her know the truth behind it. One that involves her, loosely, on account it was their dad who'd sprung it on him out of nowhere. *God*, what a disaster.

She looks between both sofas, and I know what she's thinking without her saying a word.

"You can sit on the right one," I force out, wishing the earth would open up and swallow me whole, and she looks at me with a smile.

"Thanks." She plops down on the sofa. "So, *sister*, sit and tell me about yourself." The warm smile never slips from her face. "What do you do?"

"Umm, okay," I manage, choosing the armchair adjacent to the sofa she's perched on. I tuck my feet underneath me, pulling Vulcan's T-shirt down as I do. "Well, I'm a doctor, and it's a pretty intense job but, um, incredibly rewarding."

"Vulcan mentioned you're passionate about your work."

Her kindness makes me warm to her a bit more. Because whatever he's told her, she seems to like me. Or she's an excellent actress. "Yes, it is. And what about you? What do you do?" I ask, eager to shift the focus from myself.

"I'm a physical therapist," Val explains, her hands gesturing as she speaks. "Been doing it for a few years now. I love helping people get back on their feet after injuries or surgeries."

"*That* must be incredibly satisfying," I reply, finding comfort in our professions' common ground.

"It is," Val agrees, her smile softening. "So, enough formal talk. How did you and Vulcan meet? He's always kept his love life a bit of a mystery, so I was ecstatic when he told me about *you*." Her curiosity seems genuine, which makes me relax further.

I laugh softly. "I'd see him around the ER occasionally, but we really didn't connect until we met at a bar."

"Don't be offended, but you seem a bit young. Vulcan is an old fart. Does it bother you?" she asks, and I'm glad she brought it up now and not later. Better to just rip off the age-gap Band-Aid.

"It doesn't. He has this deep perspective on life that's really refreshing. The dating pool nowadays is shallow as hell. Plus, Vulcan is incredibly supportive of my career. We haven't been together that long, but whatever makes him happy, and he wants to do, I'll be there," I explain, finding myself opening up more than I thought I would. "The twelve-year gap is not that—"

"Holy shit! *Twelve*?" She makes like she's about to fall off the sofa.

"Yes." I stifle a giggle at her theatrics.

She grins back. "Well, it sounds like you two have a solid foundation, and I love that for my brother. It's about time he found someone who cares for him. Just don't break his heart, or I will have to hurt you." She laughs, but I detect a kernel of truth.

"You don't have to worry." I smile, relief washing over me as Val appears to understand and accept the dynamics of our relationship.

The conversation drifts comfortably from there. She shares stories about growing up with Vulcan—his quirks and all—and I laugh more freely than before. The woman has this way of making you feel like you've been friends for years rather than minutes. The initial awkwardness melts away, replaced by a budding sense of friendship. Her presence is disarming. She's much like her brother in that regard: intense yet deeply kind.

Just as I feel fully at ease, the bedroom door swings open and Vulcan steps out. He looks somewhat surprised as he takes us in, laughing and chattering away. I'm sure this is the last thing he anticipated when he woke up this morning.

"Eww, please! Put a shirt on." Val tosses a throw pillow at him.

He's only wearing sweatpants, and subconsciously, I lick my lips. One thing is for certain, I will never be able to get over this man—sexually, of course. *This isn't some meant-to-be romance with a happy ending, Karina*, I remind myself.

"You're in my house," Vulcan tells his sister, tossing it back. "Good morning, beautiful." He walks over to me, kissing my forehead, and my moment of unease is replaced with warmth. "Would you two like any coffee?"

"Good morning." I blush. "No coffee for me, but—"

"Green tea?" he asks. "With lemon?"

I nod. Val asks for a shot of Tequila, to which Vulcan tells her no and then huffs about the time she threw up on his favorite rug. She playfully rolls her eyes. "Fine, coffee it is then. Add five sugars, please, I don't like the black coffee you try to force on me."

I watch Vulcan enter the kitchen, moving around and preparing our drinks. His muscles flex, and I can't help but feel a flutter of excitement as my eyes trace the contours of his body.

"Babe?" He looks over his shoulder at me and gestures with his head toward the left. I know he's asking about the trash bag.

I grimace and turn my attention back to Val, still not sure how to explain the mess in the kitchen in front of our unexpected guest.

"So." Val smiles. "Next weekend, I'm throwing a party for my bestie. You should come! Bring a plus-one if you like, someone *other* than Vulcan. Girls only."

I glance up at Vulcan, looking for a sign of approval or hesitation, but he's engrossed in making our drinks. "I'd love to," I reply, already planning on how I'm going to convince Cassie to come.

Val claps her hands together, pleased. "Awesome! It's going to be laid-back, a few close friends and way too much food and drinks. Oh, and we'll be watching the newest episode of *Love Behind the Headlines*, so if you haven't watched, better get caught up. It's already fifteen episodes in."

I want to tell her I've never watched it, but the aroma of coffee fills the air as Vulcan walks over with three steaming mugs on a tray. After two weeks of living together, I can say without hesitation I love coming home. I love coming home to *him*. I never thought I would find a man who'd protect me, encourage me, and care for me the way Vulcan does.

I'm falling for him, and I'm falling hard. And that's what scares me.

Vulcan is quiet, sipping his coffee while Val chatters about party plans. I steal glances at him, each look making my heart race a little faster.

"Karina," he says softly after Val excuses herself to answer a call. My entire body tunes in to the sound of my name on his lips. "You don't have to feel forced to go to this party because she's my sister. I don't want you to—"

"I like her... she's nice, and I'll bring Cassie. I'm excited, honestly."

His expression softens, a hint of relief flickering across his features. "Okay, I'm glad," he says, sipping from his mug. "When she leaves, we can shower and go out. Let's do something today." His suggestion catches me off guard. I'm used to spending my days off on-call or catching up on sleep, not out with someone who makes my pulse race just by looking at me. "That sounds perfect."

Val walks back into the living room, her phone still pressed to her ear. "If I didn't *clear* you to swim for your meet, why would you think it's okay to go *splashing* at a friend's pool party? I'm convinced something is seriously wrong with your brain, Marino. You've got to be drinking chlorine water, because there isn't another way to explain your lack of brain cells." She lets out a frustrated breath. "I'll be there shortly." She ends the call and glances toward us. "I would love to stay and chat, but my client is a *fucking asshole* who doesn't listen to a word I say." She snatches up her crossbody bag.

Val gives me a quick hug goodbye, tells Vulcan to pass on her number, and then she's out the door.

"I swear, she's normally not this stressed," he says, a wrinkle forming between his eyes.

As he stands, I do as well. My heart skips a little as Vulcan reaches out and gently tugs me closer by the hand. His fingers lace through mine. "Shower first?"

I answer with a nod and follow him through the penthouse.

As he turns on the water, testing the temperature with an outstretched hand, I can't help but watch the muscles of his back shifting. He looks over his shoulder at me. "You can join me when you're ready."

I peel off his oversized T-shirt as he steps out of his sweatpants, then he pulls me into the steaming water. The heat from the shower envelops us, mingling with the heat of our bodies as we stand there, skin against skin. His hands roam over my body, tracing paths that leave shivers in their wake. His lips find mine in a tender kiss.

Water cascades over us as I moan into his mouth, one hand tangled in his hair while the other grips his shoulder for balance. Vulcan breaks away only to linger on my neck, pausing at the sensitive spot just below my ear. He knows exactly where to touch and how much pressure makes my knees buckle. "I've been thinking about fucking you here all morning."

Seeing what he's about to do, I place my hands on his chest, stopping him.

"Vulcan, your shoulder."

"I'll take all the pain if it means bringing you pleasure." He lifts me and he thrusts inside of me without warning. Each thrust pushes us deeper into a realm of sensation and emotion that blurs the line between physical and ethereal. I never thought sex could be like this, and I *certainly* never fathomed it being like this with a man I was marrying to fulfill a contract.

"You know what I want to hear," Vulcan breathes between kisses.

I blush as the words of affirmation last night come rushing back to me but still manage to rasp out, "I'm strong, compassionate, brave, and beautiful."

"Karina," Vulcan mumbles. "You're everything and more. Don't you ever forget. Don't let anyone tell you otherwise."

With a powerful thrust, I'm pressed against the cold tile wall. My fingers dig into his shoulders, and his lips find mine again in a kiss that feels like it could both start and end wars—passionate, desperate, claiming. His movements become more erratic, a silent plea for release.

Vulcan presses his forehead against mine, his breath hot against my face.

"Come for me," he whispers, a request that launches us both over the edge. As we slowly regain our senses, Vulcan gently sets me down. He wraps me in his arms under the warm cascade of water, kissing my forehead tenderly. "We should wash up," he says after a long moment of comfortable silence.

I nod but nestle closer to him for just another minute longer.

Who could've known Vulcan's idea of going out would be grocery shopping at Whole Foods. But here we are, wandering the aisles as he pushes the cart and I toss in items more willy-nilly than I usually would. It's surprisingly endearing seeing him examine labels and occasionally furrow his brow in concentration.

He makes a face as I add another bag of granola to the cart. "Are you going on a diet?"

"I'm trying to make healthier choices." I nudge him with my elbow.

"You can eat as much junk food as you want. I'm more than happy to help you burn the calories," he replies, winking at me. "You know, we can start a new morning workout. Today can count as day one."

"I bet." I playfully roll my eyes as we move to the organic section, where Vulcan skips over the strawberries in favor of blueberries and places them in the cart.

"Hey, strawberries are the best. Grab a container!"

"I wouldn't know." He shrugs.

"What? You're missing *out*."

"I mean, sure. If I want to die of an allergic reaction," he jokes.

I stop in my tracks, staring at him. "Wait, are you serious? You're allergic to strawberries?"

"*Dead* serious. It's tragic, really... denied one of life's allegedly sweet pleasures."

I reach for the green grapes instead, setting them in the cart. I walk farther down the section and stop, noticing Vulcan hasn't moved yet. "Everything okay?"

"Do you not want the strawberries?" he asks.

"You just said you're allergic."

"You don't have to stop eating them because of me. We just have to be more careful when you do." He adds them to the cart.

I smile, satisfied. "Extra careful."

As we navigate through the store, I find myself increasingly fascinated by him. We discuss meal plans with ease and chat about seasonings and produce. I even learned that he was on the verge of dropping out of the fire academy to become a chef.

"You seem to be getting the hang of this domestic bliss," I comment.

"I think it's growing on me—the idea of us like this." He gestures around the store and then back to the items we've combined in the cart. "Simple things. *Together*." I have to look away for a moment to compose myself. When did shopping for groceries feel like another piece of home? "Karina," he says quietly.

I look into his eyes as he tucks a loose strand of hair behind my ear. What he might regard as small acts of kindness or casual flirting, I perceive as expressions of love. Love and warmth are all I really need to be happy, and I'm once again terrified of this rise in affection I'm feeling for him.

"I just want you to feel comfortable. So, if you feel like I'm forcing—"

"No, this is fine. I just wasn't expecting to come *here*. I thought we were going to get breakfast or brunch," I admit. "But it's been nice, really."

"We can grab something to eat here. They've got a decent café out front, or I can make breakfast at home. Whatever you prefer."

"Here, please. I'm *starving*. Last night and this morning have me ready to eat a cow. *Para un viejo, el sexo contigo es una locura.*"

"Not sure what you said, but I know sex was involved." The corners of his mouth tilt up in amusement. "Come on, let's get some food in that belly."

I settle into a corner of the café as Vulcan orders us a couple of gourmet sandwiches and fresh coffee. The conversation flows freely as we sit across from each other, sipping coffee and sharing bites of our food.

"I like this," I confess during a pause in our conversation.

Vulcan reaches across the table, his fingers brushing mine. "I like it too," he agrees. "I know we started this whole thing with certain expectations and rules. But I want you to know that whatever happens, if things change... I'm here for you. Contract or not, *I've got you.*"

His words warm me more than the coffee ever could, and I pause to wonder whether he also feels this connection growing and strengthening. "Thank you. I've got you too," I whisper back, squeezing his hand. After finishing our meal, we pay for our groceries and have a debate over ice cream flavors and cereal brands. I can say with confidence Vulcan is indeed an old man. *Who still eats butter pecan ice cream?*

As he drives us back home, the groceries safely tucked in the trunk, I stare out the window and reflect on how far we've come in such a short time. Two weeks feels like months already. I can only imagine what the next three years are going to entail.

Pulling into the underground garage of the apartment building, he turns off the engine and gives me a long look.

"What's wrong?" I prod him when he hesitates.

He smiles, then leans over to kiss me softly on the lips. "I think you should decide how to organize the pantry," he says when he pulls back. "I'm shit at that stuff."

I tip my head back and laugh. "Is this your way of saying I have to put away the groceries?"

"Hey, I'm helping take them up. That should count for something," he reasons, then slips out of the car before I can needle him further.

CHAPTER TWENTY-TWO

Vulcan

Being away from work is a blessing and a curse. I miss my team and the rush of calls, but I've gotten to know Karina on a deeper, more personal level, and I wouldn't change it for the world. Things are going great, but I don't know how long it'll last. I've yet to tell Karina about the meeting I had with her mother two weeks ago, and then Minji called this morning to remind me that she needs to sign the prenup before the wedding.

I took the opportunity to let her know about the changes I wanted implemented. Changes that would set Karina up for life. After our arrangement comes to an end, I want her to get a one-time payout of five million dollars and the London property. I want her to maintain the lifestyle I'll provide for her while we're together. I don't want to give her the world and then take it away when all's said and done.

I just pray she doesn't read the gesture wrong and call off the wedding. And speaking of weddings, I still need to purchase rings. I have less than a month; my fortieth birthday is approaching faster than I would like.

"It's good to have you back, Cap," Ramirez calls out as I stride down the hall, and I dip my chin in greeting.

I step into my office to see Harry lounging on the sofa. I see he's been taking full advantage of the vacant space.

"What the hell?" He gives me a puzzled look. "Aren't you supposed to be off for another two months?"

I drop my bag by the desk, collapse in my chair, and power up my computer. "I'm only here to check up on things." Karina would kill me if she found out I was here to do anything other than desk work. I explained I had to stay on top of things since our station is still short-staffed.

"Yeah, but we do have an acting captain, remember?"

"One who doesn't like to do paperwork, and where is he? I didn't see him when I walked in."

"He was needed at his station today."

"Right, so good thing Karina let me come in for a few hours."

I had been counting on my lieutenant to be back, but his damn ankle is taking longer to heal because he doesn't know how to sit his ass down.

"The doctor has you on a tight leash," Harry observes, his tone teasing.

"Depends on which doctor you're referring to. My PT says things are going great. I see him three days a week instead of the two days every other week, thanks to Karina. She's more worried and concerned about my shoulder than I am. But it's all good, and—I'm rambling." I drag a hand down my face. "Stop me."

"I see Karina has you opening up more. It's a good look on you, Vul. So, ramble on."

I chuckle. "Wedding preparations are piling up. You know how it is. And Karina is either too busy to help or not interested, probably both, so it's on me."

"Can't say that I do know how it is, but I'll take your word for it."

"And I need to get rings." I rub my temples.

"You're serious about this? I know you said she's different, but don't you think it's a bit too fast?" Harry doesn't know the motivations behind our arrangement, so his concerns are valid.

"I care about her," I say.

"Caring about someone and loving someone are two different things. I know you aren't getting any younger, but think this through. I don't want you to make a rash decision, all because I nagged you about finding someone."

These past couple of weeks with Karina have shown me it's a lot more real than I'm even letting on with Harry. As cliché as it sounds, I can now relate to what a fucking Prince Charming goes through emotionally when they see their true love.

"I know, man. It's just—I love her," I admit. *I love Karina.*

Harry raises an eyebrow and leans back against the sofa, running a hand through his tousled hair, the corners of his mouth twitching as if trying to decide whether to laugh or interrogate me further. "That's a big word, buddy. Especially for *you.*"

"I know it sounds crazy, but when I'm with her, everything just feels... right. She feels like my other half. No, she *is* my other half. All I do is think about how I can make her life less stressful—how I can make her happy. It's crazy that I go to sleep thinking 'did I do enough throughout the day to make her happy?' Then I wake up thinking 'what can I do today to make her happy?'"

"Just be careful," he finally says. "Marriage is a huge deal, obviously, and it means *forever.*" He shudders.

I laugh. "Forever is a long time, huh? But I don't mind when it comes to her."

"It's the biggest commitment you can make. Just make sure you're both on the same page."

"I know. Don't worry, Harry. Karina and I are great. Hell, we're more than great."

"All right, I hear you. I'm just looking out for you." He chuckles, raising his hands in mock surrender. "But seriously. I've never seen you like this before. It's... different. You're different."

I nod, my mind drifting to Karina. Her smile, her laugh, the way she looks at me like I'm the only person in the world. "She's different," I say softly, then sit forward and shuffle some papers around on my desk. "So, how has work been without me?"

"Oh, you know, chaos as usual. But manageable. They've sent us some new recruits. All have potential but dive headfirst into everything without looking."

"Sounds like you've got your hands full."

"Always do." He grins. "But hey, someone's gotta keep these young guns from burning down the city before they save it."

On cue, the station alarm goes off, and Harry jumps up. I almost do the same.

"Gotta run. Duty calls!" he says, already halfway to the door.

I wave him off, settling back into my chair as the sound of sirens fades into the distance. I don't think I'll ever get used to the quiet of the firehouse, but I know better than to head out before being cleared. Instead, I will stick to my fire captain's responsibilities and bury myself in almost four weeks' worth of piled-up work.

My phone vibrates against the desk, and I check the caller, quickly sliding my finger across the screen.

"Hey," Karina greets. "Just checking in. How's your day going?"

"Confined to a desk is boring as shit, to be honest."

She laughs, a sound that makes everything seem momentarily lighter. "It's for the best. I hope you get everything done today because you won't be going back in. You still have two months of LOA," she says, as if I need reminding. "And they'll be spent away from Station 112."

"We're short-staffed."

"But not anymore. I heard from one of the nurses that they saw a few new firefighters at Riley's. So, no excuses, Vulcan. You're staying home after today, and that's final."

"Bossy much?"

"You say bossy, I say tough love."

I hum in response. She still hasn't given me a reason for why she called, and I know it wasn't to ask me about the new additions to my crew. I stay quiet until she clears her throat.

"So, I spoke to Minji today. She asked me if I would make time in my schedule to come in with you to sign another document. I thought I'd already signed everything. Do you know what this could be about?" she probes.

Shit.

Minji's feeding me to the wolves. I was planning on getting to it. "Ah, that." I shift uncomfortably in my chair. "It's—how about we discuss it tonight? I'll leave soon and cook us dinner."

"I'm working all night, sorry." She pauses. "Can you not just tell me now?"

"I'd rather not."

"We won't see much of each other this week. I'm working doubles, remember?" She's persistent, I'll give her that. I don't feel like this is a conversation to be had over the phone. But there's no way around it; she's not going to let this go until she gets some answers.

"Promise you won't get mad."

Karina sighs on the other end of the line. "Okay," she says, her tone softening. "I won't get mad. Just tell me what's going on."

I take a deep breath and slump back in my chair, tension knotting in my shoulders. "The contract... It's sort of a prenup," I begin cautiously. "It states that if—when—we go through with this marriage, and if, um, *when* it ends after three years, you will receive a payout of five million dollars and the London property."

The pause that follows feels longer than it actually is. I can almost hear her processing the information, weighing her thoughts before speaking. Karina never rushes to anger, never lets it burst out the way others might. I want to reach through the call and smooth her hair and say *none of this matters, not if hurts you*. But I can't.

A second passes and then another.

"Why would you do that?" she asks, confused, but there doesn't seem to be anger.

"Because it's fair," I explain slowly. "It's to ensure you're looked after, no matter what happens. This isn't just a marriage of convenience for me, Karina. I... I care about you. More than I thought possible in such a short time. I want you to have the world while you're with me and *after*."

"Hiciste esto porque mi mama te dijo?"

Slipping into her native tongue is something she does when either passionate or pissed about something. And right now, it's the latter.

"What was that, babe?"

"Are you doing this because of my mother? And *don't* ask me what I mean because you know *exactly* what I mean. I don't want you to pity me. I hate it when people pity me. I agreed to marry you for the three hundred thousand, nothing more. Once I get the money and give it to my mother, I'll be free and it'll all be worth it."

I rub the back of my neck, trying to loosen the sudden stiffness. "Karina," I begin, my voice firmer. "It's not pity. I respect you, and yes, I'm concerned about you and how things might be for you after the divorce." If there is one. Which I pray there isn't.

There's a brief pause, during which I hear her take a deep breath, and when she speaks again, her voice is softer. "I'm sorry. I didn't mean to imply... It's just hard for me to accept that someone might actually want to look out for me without expecting something in return."

How do I get her to see that this is about something other than transactions or deals? My feelings for her are genuine and have been growing stronger each day. Maybe she doesn't feel the same way about me. But why should she? She's younger and, like she said, only doing this for the money.

"I understand, it's fine. I should get going." I can feel myself detaching from this conversation. "I'll leave you a plate of food in the fridge, all right?"

I hang up, tossing my phone across the desk.

I know she's been through a lot, and her past has shaped her into the fiercely independent—if untrusting—woman she is today. But I also know that no matter how tough or self-reliant she appears, everyone needs someone they can lean on. Someone who genuinely cares.

I want to be that person for her. I want to be her rock.

I don't think *she* wants me to be that person.

CHAPTER TWENTY-THREE

Karina

It's rare when I get to relax in my office at the hospital, and it's rarer when Vulcan gets mad at me.

But here I am, staring at my phone after that call ended so abruptly. The tension in his voice was palpable, and I know I struck a nerve. I lean back in my chair, letting out a frustrated sigh.

Why did I react that way? Five million dollars and a property overseas? Sure, it's excessive and unnecessary, making me feel like he's trying to buy me off. Like I'm some sort of transaction. But I know Vulcan better than that now. He's not that kind of man.

I rub the bridge between my brows, feeling a headache forming. The double shift ahead of me suddenly feels even longer.

"I seriously can't believe he fucking hung up on me."

"Are you talking about the Director? I told you that man is a stickler when it comes to the misuse of the beds in the ER." Cassie walks into my office and hands me my smoothie. "But don't worry, he's too busy yelling at the nursing staff for not using the new charting system. I heard the receptionist was getting cussed out by one of our regulars because she told him he would need to wait in the waiting room to be seen. It's like the COVID days all over again—except now nobody's clapping for us."

I think about how many times the Director has reprimanded me for "resource misallocation." He's a bureaucrat with a punitive streak and the cheery sadism of a man who's never worked a real shift on the floor. A week ago, he sent out a mass email forbidding overnight stays for "non-residential" patients—his language, not mine—which is just a code for homeless people. The day after, three of my regulars showed up with frostbite and nowhere to go, so I bent the rules and gave them warm blankets and a bed in the endoscopy suite. I know he'll find out eventually. He always does. The memory of his last lecture is still sticky in my mind:

"The ER is not a halfway house, Dr. Reyes. I suggest you remember which side of the Hippocratic Oath you're on."

I'd like to think it's the side that keeps people alive, but I'm not sure he'd agree.

"No, not the Director. Vulcan," I say, gripping the Styrofoam cup a bit too tightly as I glance up at her. "Thanks for this."

Cassie sits down in the chair across from my desk. She raises an eyebrow, a silent prompt for me to spill more. I sigh, sipping my drink, the icy strawberry flavor barely registering. And I've been looking forward to this damn smoothie all day after cutting back on eating anything strawberry at home.

"Vulcan wants me to sign a document before the wedding," I continue. Everyone thinks we're getting married because we're madly in love with each other, which has already been a source of annoyance. I didn't want anyone knowing, but Harry let it slip to a nurse at he was flirting with Riley's a few weeks ago. It bothered me at first, but it means I don't have to constantly be spinning a web of lies. I mean, I already had people talking when Vulcan came through the ER that one night.

"A *prenup?*"

I shake my head, knowing my version of events is going to be an unfair representation of the situation but pressing on anyway. "Of sorts?

He wants me to get a lump sum payout and his property in London if we divorce."

She gapes at me. "Why are we mad again? Men don't typically want their wives to have *anything* if they divorce. And hell yes to the property in London. I always wanted a British man. Just look at how Tom treats Zendaya. But that's neither here nor there." She rolls her wrist, urging me on.

"That's just it." I place the smoothie on the desk, cross my legs, and run a hand through my hair. "It's not about the money or assets. I feel like he's doing it out of pity."

Cass cocks her head to the side, her eyes narrowing slightly, a clear sign she's switching into her "analyzing" mode. "Pity? He loves you. That's why he's marrying you, correct? Is there something you're not telling me?"

"Like what?"

"Like why now, out of nowhere, you're starting to have conflicted feelings? Is this some kind of arranged marriage? I mean, it's the 21st century, but anything's possible."

I blink.

I'm not good at lying, and worst of all, I don't like lying to my friends. I try to think of something, but it's too late. My hesitation has already made Cass's eyes widen.

"Wait! *Is* this an arranged marr—"

"No, it's not! Christ, Cass! I would never put myself through that. You know I wear my heart on my sleeve." At least that's not a complete lie.

"True and it's been a month—"

"Almost two months."

"Well, excuse me, *almost two months* since you two started dating. Maybe you should pump the brakes on getting married. Clearly you two aren't communicating properly."

Little does she know how much Vulcan loves to communicate. It's me who's having a problem opening up.

"We communicate just fine." I feel myself getting defensive, because Vulcan is a great man, and he's always trying when it comes to me. Always.

She lifts her right eyebrow slightly. "I know you, Rina. You're holding back. Is it cold feet?"

Even if this wasn't a contractual marriage, I wouldn't have cold feet. After our first night together, I've practically moved into his room. Everything about this marriage is becoming less of a convenience and more... more like something real. Something I'm afraid to admit I want *desperately*.

I shake my head, trying to clear my thoughts, which are becoming increasingly confusing. "It's not cold feet. It's just... complicated."

She leans forward, her eyes softening. "Babe, what's really going on? You can tell me anything, you know that."

I bite my lip, debating how much to reveal.

"It's just..." I start, then pause, searching for the right words. "Vulcan and I come from different worlds. Sometimes, I wonder if he really understands what he's getting into with me." I'm sure there were countless other women whom Minji reached out to for this.

Cass's brow furrows. "What do you mean?"

I sigh, running a hand through my hair. "He's this successful fire captain. Generationally wealthy. And I'm just... me. A doctor with mountains of student loans to repay and a family that comes looking for money more than a debt collector. What if he wakes up one day and realizes he's made a huge mistake?"

"Karina," she says firmly, reaching across the desk to grasp my hand. "You are an incredible woman and an amazing doctor. You're kind and funny. Any man would be lucky to have you. Vulcan sees that, otherwise he wouldn't be marrying you, especially so quickly. He knows you're special and wants you all to himself."

I feel tears pricking at the corners of my eyes. If only she knew the real reason behind our engagement. But even as I think it, I'm no longer so sure. The way Vulcan looks at me sometimes, the tender moments we share when no one else is watching, it feels like more than just an act. I think back to our conversation. *This isn't just a marriage of convenience for me, Karina. I... I care about you.*

"Maybe you're right," I say softly, squeezing her hand. "I just can't shake this feeling that I'm not good enough for him."

"Then that's something you two need to discuss. If you're having doubts, be honest with him."

I nod, knowing she's right. But the thought of opening up about my insecurities terrifies me. What if voicing my fears makes them real? What if it messes up this thing we've built together so far?

Just as I'm about to delve deeper into my swirling thoughts, my name is being called over the paging system. I'm needed in the ER. I bolt up from my chair, smoothie forgotten and adrenaline pumping as the reality of the hospital environment snaps back into focus.

"*Reyes, to the ER, stat!*" the voice blares again.

Cass looks up at me, sipping her smoothie. "And it's moments like this that I'm glad I'm just an RN. I'll put your smoothie in the fridge." She waves me off.

"Thank you," I say, rushing out of my office.

Hours later, my shift comes to an end. Dr. Montiel was able to come in earlier, allowing me to leave sooner than expected. I'm more than thankful I don't have to do a double tonight. I'm on autopilot as I gather my things and head outside, the cool night air brushing against my face as I feel all my problems rush back.

I've always avoided confrontation. Prefer to distract myself with work and trying to stay afloat. But it's something I know I will have to do with Vulcan. While I do appreciate what he's trying to do for me, I don't know how to accept it, having learned a long time ago nothing in this world comes without strings.

The scent of pasta wafts through the air as I open the front door, and my stomach immediately growls in response. I kick off my shoes and drop my purse onto the sofa before heading straight to the kitchen. Vulcan is standing over the stove, stirring something intently, but he doesn't greet me like he usually does. I wash my hands before I head to the fridge and grab the gallon of milk while Vulcan slides a cup and some cocoa powder toward me across the countertop.

"Thank you," I say.

I wait to hear him acknowledge me, but I'm met with silence.

I move around the kitchen preparing my drink, giving him the space he clearly needs.

Finally: "I want to apologize for earlier."

I stare at his back, willing him to turn around and speak to me, before giving up and walking out of the kitchen. When he calls my name, I pause and turn around slowly.

"Is everything okay?" he asks, a worried expression on his face.

"Everything is fine. I just need to shower before eating." *And you couldn't bother greeting me after I've been at work all day, so there's that.*

He nods, but he's not convinced. He follows me out of the kitchen, his steps hesitant.

"I really am fine, Vulcan. Just tired," I add.

He doesn't respond and when I glance over my shoulder, he's raking his fingers through his hair. "I'm going to finish cooking. Do you want wine or another glass?" He glances at the glass in my hand.

"Wine is fine."

I head straight to our bedroom, the weight of the impending conversation pressing down on me heavier with each step. The hot water from the shower does little to soothe my nerves, either. It's only a temporary escape, a brief pause before I face Vulcan and everything that comes with our arrangement.

I let the water run over me as I try to gather my thoughts, knowing he wants to talk. And it scares me how much I care about what he has to say.

I turn off the water, stepping out onto the chilly tile floor and wrapping myself in the towel. I dress quickly, wanting to look nice for him without seeming like I've tried too hard. He still sends those butterflies soaring in my stomach, like on our first date.

As I reenter the kitchen, the aroma of herbs and spices fills my senses once more. He doesn't turn around immediately as I walk in, focused on stirring the creamy sauce in the pan. But when he does, his expression softens and he offers me a small smile that warms my heart.

"Sit down. Dinner will be ready soon," he says, and I can see we're both walking on eggshells. This is new territory for me, as I finally see that it might be for him too. I obey, taking a seat at the kitchen island. The wine bottle he opened is already on the counter, alongside two glasses. I pour myself a glass to the rim and down the contents before pouring another half glass and downing that one, too. I need enough liquid courage to get through tonight's dinner.

Vulcan plates the pasta, his back still facing me, but I can see the tension in his shoulders. The wine is warming me from the inside, smoothing out the sharp edges of my nerves. I watch him, appreciating his meticulous care, even in such a mundane task. His attention to detail, the quiet pride in doing something well.

He sets a plate in front of me and we begin to eat in silence. It's delicious, but the heaviness between us makes it hard to focus on the flavors.

I muster up the courage to break the silence. "About earlier," I begin. "I won't sign the document. Your assets don't belong to me. I never wanted anything but what I told Minji."

Vulcan pauses, his fork halfway to his mouth. "I don't understand," he draws out, placing his fork down gently as he turns in his seat to look at me. "You agreed to this marriage knowing it was a business arrangement. Why refuse added protection for your future?"

I take a deep breath. "It's not about the money. I mean, yes, it *was* because of the money that I signed up for this, but for the amount *I* wanted. After the three years, I will leave with what I came with. I won't have any claim over what you've built or inherited. I don't want that." I pause, my heart racing. "I want this to be as clean and simple as possible."

Vulcan's brow furrows. "But *why?* This could secure your future, Karina."

I shake my head, pushing my plate away. The pasta suddenly feels heavy in my stomach. "Because I don't want to feel like I'm taking advantage of you. This arrangement... it's already complicated enough and adding more money will make it more so."

Also, you are making it so easy for me to fall in love with you.

He leans back, gaze darting back and forth between my eyes. "You're not like anyone I've ever met, Karina. Most people would jump at this opportunity."

"Well, not to sound cliché, but I've never been accused of being like most people." I force a smile, though it feels brittle on my face.

Vulcan's lips quirk up, a ghost of a smile. He reaches for his wineglass, taking a long sip before continuing. "It doesn't sit right with me to leave you with nothing after three years of… this."

I feel a flush creeping up my neck, partly from the wine and partly from the intensity of his gaze. "Vulcan, I—"

"Please," he interrupts. "Let me do this. Not for the reasons you might think, but because it's the right thing to do. We can negotiate the terms and make it something we're both comfortable with."

I bite my lip, considering. The wine has loosened my resolve, and his earnestness is disarming. "Okay," I concede. "But on one condition."

Vulcan raises an eyebrow, waiting.

"We revisit it after a year," I say firmly. "When we know each other better, when this isn't so… new."

He nods furiously. "Deal. I'll have Minji set the date in her calendar."

I sigh, feeling the relief instantaneously. "But don't hide things from me. I won't be as forgiving next time. Okay? So, if you have any other secret contracts that I need to sign, now is your time to come clean." I eye him suspiciously.

"Nope, nothing else," he says, looking away. *Is* he hiding something else…? His eyes meet mine again, and I see nothing but sincerity there. Still, a nagging doubt lingers in the back of my mind.

"Are you sure?" I press, leaning forward slightly. "Because I meant what I said. I don't appreciate being left in the dark."

Vulcan sighs, stroking his beard. "Karina, I promise you, there's nothing else for you to sign. I understand why you're wary, but I'm not trying to trick you."

His words should reassure me, and maybe it's the wine making me paranoid or the fact I've been forced to accept that people always have hidden agendas, but I'm still filled with tension.

Ultimately, I decide I've reached my breaking point for the day. I promise myself I'll sit with this feeling more tomorrow, when I have a clear head. "Okay."

Vulcan's shoulders relax, and he offers me a small smile.

We finish our pasta in silence, and it's even more unbearable than when we first began. All you can hear is the sound of our utensils scraping against the plate. I glance at Vulcan's nearly empty plate, waiting for him to excuse himself any minute.

"How was work?" he surprises me by asking.

"Work?"

"Yes, work. You said you had a double, but you're home early."

"Oh, right. Dr. Montiel was able to come in."

"That's fortunate." His tone is neutral as he reaches for his wineglass. "You work hard. It's important to rest."

His words, though simple, resonate deeply within me. When was the last time someone acknowledged my efforts? My mother certainly never does. I feel warmth spreading in my chest, but I quickly suppress it. *Don't get too comfortable*, I remind myself.

"Yeah, I guess," I mutter.

Vulcan sets down his glass, his gaze fixed on me. "Is everything all right? You seem... off. Are you still thinking about the agree—"

"I just..." I start. "I'm not used to this. To someone actually listening to me and considering what I want. It's... *unsettling*."

"I get it. I understand," he murmurs. "Trust takes time to build. I hope that over the next three years, I can prove to you that your voice matters here. That *you* matter."

I feel a lump forming in my throat, and I have to look away from his gaze. His words are everything I've longed to hear, but I'm terrified to believe them. What if it's all just part of the act? What if, after we make it official, things change?

"Thank you," I manage to get out, still not meeting his eye.

Vulcan nods, seemingly satisfied. I sense his eyes on me occasionally as I force myself to take a few more bites, though my appetite has vanished.

Vulcan stands and begins clearing the dishes, waving me off when I move to help him.

"You've had a long day."

I sink back into my chair. "Are you sure? I don't mind. Your shoulder still isn't healed."

"Karina, it's just dishes."

"So? You cooked dinner too."

"And I will continue to cook dinner. But… you can help with something else actually."

"What is it?" I ask.

"My mother is flying in from London two days before the wedding. She's here to see some friends, but—well, I know you don't want a huge wedding. Would it be okay if she came to the reception?" he asks, loading the dishes in the dishwasher.

Something catches in my chest, tightening around my heart. I can't speak immediately, overwhelmed by the implication. Vulcan is sacrificing so much for me, and it hits me with a force I wasn't prepared for.

My trauma is causing him to alter his life. I don't know why I thought that because I don't want my mother there, he wouldn't want his by his side either.

"Of course," I rush to say, ashamed of my selfishness. "Of course your mother should be there."

"If it makes you uncomfortable—"

"No, really," I interrupt. "I'd like to meet her." I'm surprised to find I mean it. Not everyone's mother is like mine.

"You don't have to be so agreeable, you know. I want you to be happy on our wedding day." He walks around the counter and takes both my hands in his.

"I want this." I look up at him. "I *want* to meet your mother. And I want her to be there for you."

Something shifts in his expression, a warmth that spreads across his features. For a moment, I forget this is all an arrangement, that we're two virtual strangers bound by necessity rather than love.

"Thank you," he says. "That means more than you know."

I nod, unable to form words as his thumb traces small circles on the back of my hand. And I know, when I end up heartbroken, I will have no one to blame but myself.

"She'll love you," he continues. "You're exactly the kind of woman she always hoped I'd find."

I wish I could be the woman he spent the rest of his life with, but we are on borrowed time. Three years will be here in the blink of an eye.

CHAPTER TWENTY-FOUR

Karina

Last night, Vulcan and I had sex to the point that calling out of work was my only option. And this is my first time in years calling out. I overslept, and then there were the marks all over my body on my neck, collarbone, breasts, thighs... Marks beyond the help of concealer.

Despite the soreness and bruises, I can't help but smile at the memory of our passionate night together. He actually let me do most of the work and now I get to gloat that I fucked him to sleep. Because after the third round, he was out like a light. Yet even as I savor this small victory, a thought persists: maybe he surrendered control so easily because there's something else he's keeping from me.

I know I shouldn't think this way because this man has been nothing but loving and supportive since I moved in with him. Yet my brain is still trying to find the catch, the ulterior motive. I close my eyes, willing myself to stop overthinking and just enjoy this unexpected day off.

I roll over on my side, wincing slightly at the pleasant ache between my thighs. The penthouse is quiet without Vulcan, who left this morning to visit Valkyrie at work. Something about showing his face with her new client. Maybe I can get a few more hours of shut-eye, and just as I'm about to drift back to sleep, Cassie calls. I slide my finger across the screen, bringing the phone to my ear.

"Hey, girl!" Cassie's bubbly voice chirps through the phone. "I'm outside."

"Umm, you're at Vulcan's penthouse?" I sit up, putting the phone on speaker.

"I guess so. You called out, and I called out. Which means we should hang out. It's been forever since we saw each other out of scrubs! Tell this man to let me up. Your building security is heavier than Fort Knox."

"How did you know where I was?"

"I've got your location, remember? Now tell him to let me up." The line goes dead, and I groan. This girl never fails to surprise me. With a sigh, I call down to security and give them the okay to let her up. Might as well make the most of the day.

While I wait for Cassie to arrive, I drag myself out of bed and throw on one of Vulcan's FDNY hoodies and a pair of his sweatpants. I hear the doorbell ring and shuffle over, wincing slightly with each step.

"Well, well, well," she says, bursting into the entryway and eyeing me up and down with a knowing smirk. "Someone had a good night."

I feel my cheeks flush as I close the door behind her. "Is it that obvious?"

Cassie laughs, linking her arm through mine. "Rina, you're wearing his clothes, walking like you saved a horse and rode a cowboy, and I can see at least three hickeys from here. It's more than obvious."

She drops my arm and twirls around the living room, taking in the space. "Damn, this is nice. Who would've thought Hephaestus was loaded like this? Please tell me he has an equally rich brother stashed away somewhere."

"Sorry to burst your bubble, but he only has a sister. And it's *Vulcan*."

Cassie plops down on the couch, her eyes still roaming the penthouse. "Vulcan, Hephaestus—same difference. Both hot gods, right?" She winks at me. "So, spill. Is he as good in bed as he looks?"

My face burns even hotter. "I'm not going to give you any details. When you tell your friends how good your man is in bed, things go south."

"Oh, come on! *I* don't want to sleep with him." She pouts dramatically. "I'm living vicariously through you here. At least tell me if he lives up to that firefighter fantasy."

I smile, remembering last night. "Let's just say... he definitely knows how to handle his hose."

Cassie squeals with delight, clapping her hands. "I knew it! God, I'm so jealous. Is his sister into girls? I mean, the apple shouldn't fall too far from the tree, right?"

"Cass, you're not sexually attracted to women."

"I know, but I am sexually attracted to money, and if she's anything like her older brother, I don't mind swinging that way for a night or two."

"Sorry to disappoint, but I believe she is *strictly dickly*."

Cassie sighs dramatically, standing up. "Figures. You going to give me a tour? Is Vulcan sleeping? Should I come back later?"

"No. He left to visit his sister at work this morning," I say. "But sure, I'll show you around. He shouldn't be back for a while, so we'll have it to ourselves."

I show Cassie all the different rooms and amenities. She *oohs* and *aahs* at everything, especially when we arrive at Vulcan's home gym. This is the first time I've stepped inside; I loathe anything gym related. My body does enough working out at the hospital.

"Wow," she says, running her hand over the expensive equipment. "This is nicer than any gym I've ever been to. Have you two fucked in here?"

I playfully roll my eyes. "Do you always have to make things about sex?"

"Honey, you're dating a man who looks like that, do you blame me?" Cassie grins, hopping onto one of the weight benches. "So, do you two get nasty in here?"

"Not yet."

I spin around to the doorway where Vulcan stands. My heart leaps into my throat at the sight of him. He leans against the doorframe, arms crossed over his broad chest, a smirk playing on his lips. His eyes, dark and intense, lock onto mine.

"But we can remedy that situation any time you'd like," he adds.

Cassie lets out a low whistle. "The man, the myth, the legend!" She hops off the bench. "Good to see you again. I've heard nothing but good things since you locked our girl down." She tilts her head toward me, a smirk on her face.

Vulcan's gaze flicks to her briefly before returning to me. "Is that right?"

I cut in, finally finding my voice. "I thought you were visiting Val?"

He shrugs nonchalantly, stepping into the room. "I did, but she had a last-minute client booking. So, here I am." His eyes scan over my body, still draped in his clothing. "But it looks like I'm interrupting."

"I hope that's okay?" I say, moving closer to him.

"This is your home, too. Anyone is welcome. Well, excluding any men." He flashes an easy smile, but his possessive tone sends shivers down my spine.

I let out a nervous laugh, the glint in his eyes telling me he's not entirely joking. Does he seriously think I would dare bring another man around?

Cassie clears her throat dramatically. "As much as I'd love to stay and watch you two eye-fuck each other, I think that's my cue." She winks at me. "Thanks for the tour. Vulcan, it was a pleasure. Take good care of this one, yeah?"

"Always." He nods. "But you should stay. I didn't mean to interrupt." His eyes never leave mine. "I'm sure you two have plenty to catch up on. I'll be in our room."

I bite my lip, torn between wanting Cassie to stay and craving some alone time with Vulcan.

"No, no," she says with a dismissive wave. "I've monopolized enough of her time. You two lovebirds enjoy yourselves." She gives me a quick hug and whispers in my ear, "Call me later with all the juicy details."

"Let me walk you to the door," I tell her, looping my arm through hers.

"Girl, you've got it bad," she whispers, nudging me with her elbow as we make our way down the hall. "And that man? He looks at you like he wants to devour you whole while giving you the entire world. I pray that kind of love finds me."

I shush her, but I can't help the smile tugging at my lips. We reach the door, and I pull her into a tight hug. "Thanks for coming by. I'm sorry it got cut short. You're still down for going to his sister's get-together this weekend, yeah?"

"Of course, I will never turn down free food or liquor," she says, pulling back to look me in the eye. "Now, go be with your man, you deserve a day in bed."

With a final wink, she's gone, the door clicking shut behind her. I take a deep breath before turning back to face Vulcan. He's leaning against the wall, arms crossed, watching me with a ferocity that makes me weak in the knees.

"So," he says, his voice all gravel. "Where were we?"

"I believe you were saying something about who is and isn't allowed in this penthouse?"

He pushes off the wall, stalking toward me with that predatory grace. "No man will ever touch what's mine."

My breath catches as he reaches me, his large hands coming to rest on my hips. "And am I yours, Vulcan?"

His grip tightens, pulling me flush against him. "*Every. Fucking. Inch.*" He captures my lips in a kiss and I melt into his embrace, my hands sliding up his chest to tangle in his hair. Vulcan's hands roam possessively over my curves, igniting sparks wherever they touch. I'm screwed when it comes to this man.

Physical touch and words of affirmation are what I crave, and *dio mios*, he's providing both.

We finally break apart and I look up into his smoldering eyes. "I need to eat first."

"All right," he concedes as he leads me to the kitchen, his hand on the small of my back.

"Do you think I can't cook?" I ask as he ushers me to sit down then moves to the fridge. Since I've moved in with him, he cooks *all* the time. I know he's out of work for a while still, but even when I've had a day off, he's insisted.

Vulcan chuckles. "You lived by yourself for a while, I'd be concerned if you didn't. Unless you're a takeout kind of person."

"I know the basics."

Vulcan closes the fridge door and looks at me. "It's okay, you can be honest. I can teach you."

I feel my cheeks flush hot with embarrassment. "I... I can make cereal. Bake ziti..." I mumble, avoiding his gaze. "And I'm really good at ordering takeout."

"This might be a touchy subject, but did your mother not teach you? I mean, all the Hispanic people I know have a wide range of family recipes passed down to them." He places the egg carton on the counter and begins to move toward me. As if he knows I'm going to need him for what I'm about to share.

"My mother rarely spent time with me once the twins were born. When I reached ninth grade, I had to fend for myself. Public school lunches held me over for some nights, and then, when my father didn't have to work night shifts, he cooked. But nothing really stuck. He'd promised to set aside some time, but then he passed away. So… that was the end of that."

"Are you close with any of your other relatives?"

I stare at the countertop, watching sunlight angle across the marble, and try to formulate an answer that doesn't sound like a eulogy. "My mother's family basically decided I don't exist, so we don't talk. Sometimes it felt like I was a reminder she'd rather forget. On my father's side—" I swallow, the old bitterness catching in my throat. "They're mostly in the Dominican Republic. And the few left in the States, they're scattered. Most of them moved out of the city, started families of their own, drifted." I take a breath. "There's my aunt Maria and my nana—my papá's mom. They're upstate, in a little house outside Poughkeepsie. Sometimes Aunt Maria calls, but only to check if I'm alive or to remind me of a birthday. Nana doesn't speak English, and she's hard of hearing, so our phone calls are basically me shouting 'Te quiero' three times and hanging up."

My memories of them are strange, like watching an old telenovela rerun in a language you know half the words to. I remember long car trips with my papá, the windows down, the warm, briny smell of the Hudson drifting in as he sang along to old salsa on the radio. I remember Aunt Maria's kitchen, always smelling like garlic, always a loud party even on a Tuesday morning—plastic tablecloth, mismatched coffee cups, the crust of laughter over every conversation. Nana's arms, surprisingly strong, pulling me into a rib-crushing hug that left flour on my dress and lipstick on my cheek. Those moments now feel like someone else's story.

But after my father died, it all vanished. I stopped going upstate. Aunt Maria's voicemails went from weekly to monthly, and then whenever she remembers, I guess. I think she mourned my father more than I did. Or maybe she just couldn't handle the silence he left behind. As for my nana, the last time I saw her was at the funeral. I sometimes tell myself I'll visit her, but I never do. Work and paying my mother's bills have consumed my life.

"So, you don't have any relationship with your mother's side?" he probes.

"No, my mother made sure of that." I pause, feeling the familiar knot in my chest whenever I think about this. "I've only met one cousin, and I was maybe seven or eight. When my mother visited her family, she would take the boys, and I would just go with my papa to see Nana." I shrug. "How about you? Are you close to your family? Besides Valkyrie and your mother?"

"Yes. My entire family is pretty tight-knit. Well, my mother's side of the family. My father's side cut him off when he married my mother. They felt like he was too good for her, and when she got pregnant with Valkyrie, they basically told him to choose between them or us. He chose us, obviously," he says. "It was hard on him, but he never once made us feel like we were a burden or that he regretted his choice."

"That must have been difficult for your mother."

"It was. She blamed herself for years, thinking she'd taken him away from his family. But my dad always told her that family isn't just blood, it's the people who choose to love and support you unconditionally." He glances over at me with a soft smile. "That's something I've always believed too."

His words hit me harder than I expected them to. The idea of being chosen, of someone deciding you're worth fighting for... it's foreign to me. My mother made it clear early on that I was more of an obligation than a choice.

"You're so lucky," I whisper.

Vulcan reaches out to cup my cheek. "I'm sorry. I didn't mean to bring up painful memories."

I lean into his touch, drawing comfort from his warmth. "It's okay. It was a long time ago. And now I'm starting a new life with you." If I tell him the truth—how desperate I am, how much I want this to be real—will I jinx it? There's a superstition in my bones, passed down from generations of women who warned that joy vanishes if you stare at it too long. So, I hide my longing and ignore the tight ache in my chest.

But my mind can't leave it alone. I keep replaying the last few weeks. I wonder when I started living as if there were no exit strategy. Vulcan makes everything so easy. The little rituals, like the way he always wakes before me to grind coffee. Or when he's tired, he'll flop onto the couch with his head in my lap and close his eyes and listen to me ramble on about my day. Even his affection feels like he's spent his whole life learning the choreography of gentleness just for me.

And me? I eat it up. I let him hand me towels still warm from the dryer, let him tuck my hair behind my ear when I'm reading, let him carry my bags and my burdens, bit by bit, until I hardly recognize the woman who I once was. Each day, I fall deeper into my feelings, and each day, I tell myself not to. Because this arrangement has an expiration date. I've always known this, and yet every heartbeat betrays me. It swears allegiance to this man, and it dreams of a future with Vulcan's name scrawled across it in permanent ink.

I swallow hard, blinking back the hot pressure behind my eyes. It's ridiculous, how much hope hurts. Maybe that's why I want to hoard every moment, even the silly ones. He's so good to me. So unreasonably kind and gentle and stubbornly present. I want to believe that we could be together, in a way that lasts.

Gosh, why did he have to be so kind and perfect? He makes it impossible not to hope, and hope is the most reckless thing I've ever done. I shake my head, trying to dispel these dangerous thoughts. If I let myself fall any harder, I'm not sure I'll survive the landing.

Vulcan gives me a kind of self-satisfied, lopsided grin. He leans in, lowering his voice. "Well, since we are family now, it's my duty as a responsible partner to teach you the ancient, sacred art of cooking a proper breakfast." He gestures dramatically to the kitchen, as if unveiling an altar. "You may never have learned the family recipes, but you will at least master the holy trinity of eggs, toast, and… whatever else we have in the fridge."

"Just so you know," I say, only half joking, "I once tried to fry an egg and nearly set my kitchen on fire."

"Thankfully, I'm a fire captain." He winks. "Also, don't beat yourself up that you don't know how to cook. You have other talents that make up for your culinary shortcomings, and after we eat, I'll be happy to let you showcase them." He turns to gather ingredients from the kitchen. "But for now, you need to save your energy." He shoots me a heated look over his shoulder. "You'll need it later."

My meaning behind saving her energy and Karina's were two different things. Her mind went to sex, while mine was focused on where to take her ring and dress shopping. Is she thrilled to do this? I look over at her as we walk into the jeweler's. Nope, not thrilled at all. The huffing and puffing have stopped, but the pout is still on her face.

The precious metals and the sparkle of gems encased in velvet-lined displays surround us as we walk deeper into the store. Karina's hand feels small in mine, and I can sense her tension. This isn't where she imagined picking out a wedding ring, not by a long shot. Karina doesn't like to spend money on herself, but I'm prepared to show her she's more than deserving.

"Something modest," she murmurs, pointing to a delicate band that is undoubtedly beautiful but lacks a certain... grandeur. It doesn't scream *Karina Reyes* to me.

"You need something that reflects how extraordinary you are." My gaze meets hers, willing her to understand that she's timeless, just like these upscale pieces gleaming brightly at us.

She bites her lip, her eyes flickering between the rings and my face. "Vulcan, I don't need—"

"Karina," I cut in. "I'll be damned if my wife doesn't have a ring that makes her feel as valued and cherished as she truly is. Arrangement or not," I add, lowering my voice.

The fight leaves her with a slow exhale, her shoulders relaxing. She nods, finally allowing the smile I love so much to curve her lips. "I see I'm not going to win this fight. But nothing too flashy!"

"No promises." I grin and signal the associate.

"Fine, let's take a look." She smirks.

Karina is more stubborn than she lets on, but we finally agreed on one. Two fucking hours later. It's a stunning and tasteful ring, a fitting symbol for our unconventional union. She caved and let me get the five-carat marquise diamond. We head to Galia Lahav next—the best bridal store in New York City, according to Val—and are immediately surrounded by an endless sea of white, ivory, silk, and satin. Karina disappears into the changing room with armfuls of dresses, and I take my place on the plush sofa. One after another, she emerges in a whirlwind of tulle and lace, each dress transforming her into a vision of bridal elegance.

The first is a classic A-line, lovely but not quite right. The second is mermaid-style, accentuating her hourglass frame, but it's too constrictive. The third, covered in intricate beadwork, seems almost there, but it's still missing something. Every time she steps out, her expression is one of displeasure. If given the choice, I know she would prefer to don her scrubs and white coat down the aisle instead.

"Number four," she says, and when she steps out, I'm in awe. This one's different. It's her—the flowing skirt, the fitted bodice. Karina catches my eye in the mirror, and her cheeks flush with a glow that no dress could ever replicate.

"Looks like we found the one," I rasp.

"I do like this one, but there's one more I haven't tried on." She walks back into the changing room, her steps light with an excitement that's been absent so far. Minutes tick by, and then I hear her calling out for help. The associate is off with another bride-to-be, and I can't seem to find any other available attendants.

I push off the chaise and walk to the dressing room, half expecting another round of taffeta and satin. But Karina... She's something else in this last dress. It's as if every other gown was just a prelude to this one—the finale that leaves your heart thumping. I'm rooted to the spot, breath hitching in my throat.

My God, she is perfect.

"Could you..." Her voice trails off as she turns to face me in the mirror, the ivory fabric hugging her in all the right places. "Vulcan—"

"Wow." The word barely escapes my lips. My hands are itching to touch her, but I have to keep myself in check. We're in public. I close the door behind me, locking it.

She bites her lip, the flush on her cheeks spreading. "I think it's stuck," she murmurs, reaching a bare arm around her back.

"Let me." My fingers find the delicate track of the zipper, brushing against her skin. There's an electric charge in the air, and it hits me all at once, what I feel for this woman. *I love her.* I find myself daydreaming about how to broach the topic more often than not these days. Sometimes, I wish Minji had never shown up at the station that night, and we could've started things off differently. I give my head a subtle shake and continue working at the dress, freeing the stuck zipper without snagging the delicate fabric or her skin. "There," I say. "Perfect fit."

"Vulcan..." Her eyes meet mine in the mirror, and there's that look.

"If we weren't in this bridal boutique, I'd—" I lean in close, whispering the words into her ear. "I'd have you against this mirror, showing you exactly what being mine looks like. Making you come undone on my tongue first, and then my cock."

She doubles down on that look, like she's inviting a predator in. And it's all the encouragement I need. I slide my hand under the skirt of her wedding dress, fingertips grazing the lace of her panties. A shiver runs through her, and I can feel her warmth through the thin fabric.

"Vulcan," she gasps, a warning or a plea; I can't tell which. It could be a mixture of both, and my cock hardens instantly.

"Shh," I whisper. "Just let me touch you. Just for a second. *Please.*" She doesn't say anything, and I think I may have pushed it too far. I'm about to pull my hand away when she grabs my wrist, holding me in place. Her eyes are dark with desire as she nods almost imperceptibly in the mirror.

I slide my fingers beneath the lace, finding her wet and ready. She bites back a moan as I start to stroke her, slow and teasing.

"Please," she whines, tilting her head back against my shoulder, giving in to the moment, to the rush that's always there when it's just the two of us.

"You have to promise to be quiet." She closes her eyes as my lips press against the pulse point on her neck. "Put your hands on the mirror," I tell her, and she does as I say. She's ready for me, hot and eager, trembling slightly in my arms.

I unbutton my jeans and they drop to my ankles, taking my boxers with them. I move her panties to the side and then thrust into her as deep as I can go. We stifle our moans as I stretch her completely. The mirror fogs up from her breath.

Her eyes meet mine in the reflection, wide and wild. I move slowly, painstakingly so, prolonging every sensation as I pull back and push into her again.

Karina's fingers curl against the mirror, leaving streaks as she struggles to stay quiet. I can see the tension in her shoulders and the way she's biting her lip to hold back her cries.

"That's it," I murmur in her ear, driving into her. "You're doing so well, baby. So good for me. Fuck you feel fucking amazing."

I slide one hand around to her front, finding her clit and circling it with my fingers. Karina's entire body jerks at the touch, a strangled gasp escaping her lips.

"Quiet," I remind her as I increase the pressure on her clit. "We can't get caught, remember?"

She nods frantically, pressing her forehead to the mirror. I can feel her getting there, her inner walls starting to clench around me.

"Close," she whispers, and I nod because I am too. My other hand finds hers on the mirror, fingers lacing together as I increase my pace just a fraction. The slight shift has her head falling back onto my shoulder, a silent scream of pleasure that makes my cock twitch inside her.

No doubt I'll be buying two wedding dresses today. But it doesn't matter, it's worth it. She's fucking worth it. Finally, as another couple laughs outside our door, oblivious to our escapades, Karina clamps her hand over her mouth as she comes, her body locking tight around mine. The sight of her like this pushes me over the edge too, and I follow swiftly after her into blissful oblivion.

We remain still for a moment longer as reality seeps back in— the hush of voices outside, the gentle rustle of fabric. We disentangle ourselves, and then suddenly, Karina turns around and drops to her knees.

"What are you—fuck." I groan, grabbing a handful of her hair, and my eyes roll back as Karina's mouth envelops me. She looks up at me through her lashes as she swirls her tongue around my sensitive tip. I have to bite my lip to keep from moaning too loudly.

"Karina," I whisper urgently, tugging gently on her hair. But she just hums around me, the vibrations sending goose bumps all over my body. She grips my thighs as she takes me deeper, her throat relaxing to accommodate my length.

My hips start to move of their own accord, thrusting into her willing mouth.

Just then, we hear a knock at the dressing room door. "Ms. Reyes? Is everything all right in there?"

Karina pulls off me with a soft *pop*, her lips swollen and glistening. "Si, just a moment!" she calls out, her voice only slightly breathless.

Our eyes lock and a silent conversation passes between us. Then she grins wickedly and takes me back into her mouth, doubling her efforts.

I grip her hair tighter, my knuckles turning white as I fight to stay quiet. The pressure is already building rapidly again, my release hurtling toward me like a freight train. Damn, the hold this woman has over my body needs to be studied.

"Karina," I moan. "I'm gonna—"

She doesn't pull away; instead, she takes me impossibly deeper. With a stifled groan, I come down her throat, my body shuddering with the intensity of it. She moans in delight as she drinks every drop. Karina rises gracefully, smoothing her dress and hair.

I nod, still catching my breath, and tuck myself away, straightening my clothes. "If you're going to swallow, make sure you get all of it." I reach my thumb over to wipe at the corner of her mouth before pushing it inside. Karina's eyes darken as she sucks it clean, her tongue swirling sensually. The sight makes my cock twitch with renewed interest.

"You look amazing, by the way," I say, pulling back my thumb. "Now let me leave before I get on my knees to return the favor."

Outside the room, my eyes instantly lock on the bridal associate. She smiles and shakes her head knowingly. *Maybe we weren't as quiet as I thought.*

"So, you will be getting *that* dress, correct?" she asks. *Okay then.* There is no need to speculate; she knows what happened in there.

"Yes, and the one she tried on before it."

"Perfect. Happy wife, happy life." The bubbly associate turns on her heel and walks toward the register.

Karina emerges a moment later, her cheeks flushed, radiating with spent energy and possibly a hint of embarrassment. She catches my eye and the corner of her mouth quirks up with a shy smile that has my heart doing somersaults.

"Stop looking at me like that," she says, approaching with both gowns.

"Like what?" I ask innocently, even though I can guess at what she means. I'm looking at her like she's the only woman in the world.

"Will you need this taken in, or are they the right fit?" the attendant asks once we reach the front counter.

"Could you make a slight adjustment on the first one, please? But the second one we'll take now," Karina says.

The associate nods enthusiastically. She moves around the counter with a measuring tape. Fifteen minutes later, she's gotten everything she needs. "The dress will be ready in six weeks. We'll reach out once it's ready for pickup."

"We'll need it by next week," I say, and her eyes widen.

"Oh, umm, give me one minute. Let me get my manager."

Karina turns to look at me once the associate walks away. "I'm sorry."

"For what?"

"We wouldn't be in this position if I were a little more easygoing."

"And what position is that? Because the only thing I see is that I'm going to happily spend an excessive amount of money on a dress to make my wife happy."

Before she can object, we're interrupted.

"Hello, I'm Stephanie, the boutique manager." The dark-haired woman extends her hand, and I shake it firmly. "Ashley tells me you need a rush order on the Marchesa gown?"

"That's right. We're getting married next weekend," I say, placing my hand on the small of Karina's back.

Stephanie's eyes widen slightly. "Next weekend? I see... that is quite expedited."

"Is it possible?" Karina asks, her voice tinged with hope.

I lean in slightly. "Money isn't an issue."

"Well..." Stephanie taps her nails against the counter. "We typically don't do rush alterations this extreme, but"—she looks between us, and I see her mental calculations—"I can have our head seamstress work exclusively on your gown. There will be a substantial rush fee."

"Name your price," I say without hesitation.

Karina squeezes my arm. "Vulcan, you don't have to—"

"I want to," I interrupt, placing a kiss on her forehead. "This is important to you, which makes it important to me."

The manager quotes a figure that would make most people balk—hell, it would've made me balk two months ago—but I merely nod. Karina's sharp intake of breath doesn't go unnoticed.

Stephanie smiles, clearly pleased with the sale. "We'll have the Marchesa ready by Thursday for a final fitting."

While she processes the payment, Karina leans into me, her voice a whisper. "This is insane. That rush fee alone could pay for my student loans."

"Consider it my first gift to you. You've already done plenty to fulfill your end of the bargain. Let me take it from here." I brush my lips against her temple.

"You're doing so much."

"And I'm going to a lot more," I say, signing the receipt Stephanie slides across the counter.

As we leave the boutique with the second dress carefully bagged, Karina is quiet. I wrap my arm around her shoulders, pulling her closer.

"If I had known trying on wedding dresses with you would turn out like this, I'd have taken you a long time ago. Maybe we can go shopping again another time."

Karina laughs and tucks into me as we walk down the bustling sidewalk. "Don't get any ideas," she says, but her smile betrays her amusement. "I think one steamy dressing room encounter is enough for now."

I chuckle, pulling her even closer as we navigate the crowded streets. The late afternoon sun casts long shadows between the towering skyscrapers, and a cool autumn breeze carries the scent of street vendor pretzels and roasting chestnuts.

"So, about that second dress," I begin.

"I want you to ruin me tonight in it."

A cheeky smile finds its way onto my face as I lead us towards 787 Coffee in Soho. I lean close, my lips brushing her ear. "Careful what you wish for."

"I wish upon a star that my future husband ruins me to *filth*."

Someone gasps behind us, and I glance over to catch an elderly woman looking affronted. Karina buries her face into my chest. I can't help but laugh, pulling her even closer as we quicken our pace.

"What has gotten into my sweet doctor?" I murmur into her hair, inhaling the sweet scent of her shampoo.

She lifts her head, her cheeks flushed with embarrassment. "You bring out the worst in me."

"And I love it."

We duck into the café, the warm aroma of fresh ground beans enveloping us. As we wait in line, I slip my hand under her shirt and jacket, my fingers tracing idle patterns on her lower back.

"Are you excited for this weekend?" I ask.

"Yes, and nervous."

"Nervous? Why?"

"Your sister is the female version of you," she replies.

"I assure you only I can make that pussy of yours weep."

She swats at my arm and scowls. "That's not what I mean! She's just... very charming. And intimidating."

I chuckle, understanding her concern. "She can be a bit much, but she likes you. Just be yourself."

Karina bites her lip, a habit I find utterly endearing. "I know, it's just... I want to fit in with your family."

I cup her face gently, tilting it up so our eyes meet. "Hey, she likes you plenty. If she didn't, she wouldn't have invited you for girls' night." I pause, letting my eyes roam her delicate features. "Just... don't mention that this is a contractual marriage. I never told my mother and Val about it, or about the money my dad left me."

"Do you plan on telling them soon?"

"No."

"Why not?"

"The thought of anyone looking at you differently because you're marrying me for money bothers me. It's nobody's business but ours why we're getting married. I'll tell them when the time is right."

"And when will that be?"

"I don't know. Maybe never. I don't really see us divorcing." The words come out with a sort of stubborn finality—I want her to know I mean it, that I will make it my mission every day to keep her happy, to keep the word "divorce" at bay for as long as my body draws breath. "Now, don't worry about that," I say, "and worry about how I'm going to devour you in that dress when we get back home."

She moans, the sound evaporating in the air as the espresso machines whir, and I kiss her deeply, right there in the middle of the coffee shop, not caring who's watching.

"You can't say things like that in public," she whispers as we break apart.

I smirk. "Why not? I love seeing you all flustered and needy."

"Because now that's all I'm going to think about."

"Patience, my love," I tease, even as my own body thrums with anticipation. "First, coffee. Then I'm having my way with you."

CHAPTER TWENTY-SIX

Karina

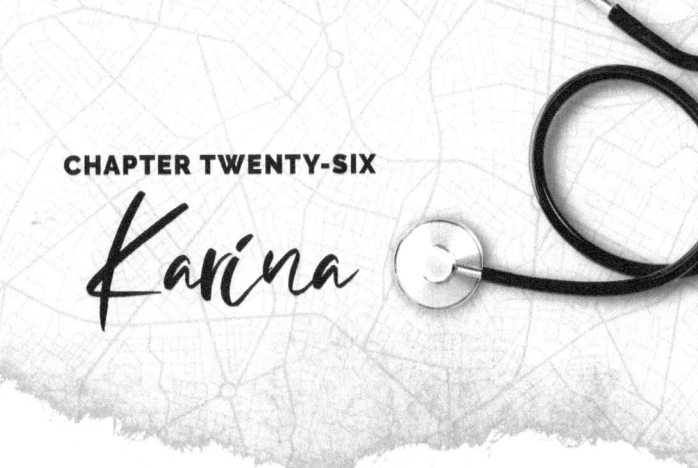

The weekend came quicker than I would have liked. Not because I don't want to go to Val's gathering, I'm just a nervous wreck. Before I left the house, Vulcan tried to put my mind at ease, and after two orgasms, it worked. Now, here I am, standing with Cassie on the steps of Val's townhouse on the Upper West Side.

I've never been part of a big friend group before. Growing up, I kept to myself, and as I got older, between college and work, I didn't have much time to be social, meaning I was usually passed over for more intimate gatherings like these. Lately, Cassie has been my most constant friend, and I'm so grateful she's here with me.

"Ready for this?" I ask her.

"Always," she replies. "But the real question is, are you? This is your first time hanging out with your future sister-in-law, right?"

"Yeah, I think I'm ready. She was nice when she came over last week." We exchange a quick smile before I press the doorbell. Moments later, the door swings open, and there stands Valkyrie, tall and radiant with her blonde hair styled in loose beach waves rather than the messy bun she wore last time I saw her. Workout clothes must be her thing too, because she's in a pastel orange Nike set today.

"Karina! And you must be Cassie." She beams, ushering us inside with the casual grace of someone who's thrown a thousand parties. "Come on in, the gang's all here. And they can't wait to meet the lady who captured my grumpy older brother's heart."

Inside, four women are chatting and laughing amongst themselves, the space buzzing with energy. Her home is just how I imagined it. The living room is a cozy collection of plush sofas and soft throws, all neutral tones with splashes of vibrant green from the lush plants scattered throughout. I'm about to comment on the beautiful decor when Val speaks.

"Everyone, this is Karina, my sister-in-law, and Cassie, her best friend," she announces, and heads turn toward us, appraising and friendly all at once.

"Let me introduce you to the ladies," she continues. "This is Naomi, my partner-in-crime since we were in diapers."

"Hey, ladies. So happy you could join us," Naomi says as she wraps her box braids into a makeshift bun atop her head.

"That's Sharon." Valkyrie points to a woman who looks up from her phone.

"Welcome, welcome," Sharon greets before looking back down at her phone, laughing at something on the screen.

"Over here we have Tasha—" Valkyrie gestures to a petite woman wearing a red denim jumpsuit and draped in gold accessories. Her style screams New York runway, yet her warm gaze softens the high-fashion aura.

"Hey, chicas! Hope you're ready to have some fun." Tasha winks.

"Last but not least, we have Kaylor," she says, tipping her head toward a woman with a playful grin who's pouring herself a glass of what looks like chilled rosé.

With introductions out of the way, the night descends into laughter, shared stories, and the kind of bonding that turns strangers into friends in the blink of an eye. I'm a little disappointed in myself for not having done more of this in my early twenties.

The clink of wineglasses punctuates the snippets of conversations humming around me. Naomi's latest hotel horror guest story, Sharon's culinary adventures, Tasha's tales from the front rows of Fashion Week, and Kaylor's endearing misadventures in dating. I'm so impressed with their chic-sounding jobs that when the focus turns to me and how I met Vulcan, I feel shier than even before. My worries are for nothing though, because by the time I finish the same story I'd given to Cassie and Valkyrie, they're eating it up.

I pop a cheese cube in my mouth as Val asks, "Are you ready for the big day?"

"I am," I reply, swallowing the richness and reaching for a gherkin. "I love him, Val." It's the first time I've said it out loud, and I quickly realize I'm no longer just trying to sell them on a story. *I love Vulcan.* It's been two months since I first met him, and already I'm head over heels. He's the first man to truly break through my defenses. The only dark spot to this situation? It's not real.

Though, based off the books he's been giving me recently, not to mention our move into the physical, it might be time to sit down and lay all our cards out on the table.

"He's been ten toes deep planning the wedding," Val tells the girls, which earns her gasps all around. I knew this was coming—it's unconventional, that's for sure. He's asked me questions here and there and sought out my opinion, but he's taken care of the bulk of it. I felt bad at first, but he assured me he needed something to occupy his time with being out of commission from the fire department.

"So, wait, Vulcan is doing this himself?" Naomi smiles. "How did you manage to get Mr. Grumpy Pants so involved?"

"He wanted a big wedding, and I was just as happy with a courthouse one. But he's allll about grand gestures," I explain, swirling the wine in my glass, watching it catch the light. "He said that if we're doing this, we're going to do it right. And honestly? Seeing him so passionate about the flowers, the menu... even the band! It's endearing." I can't help the smile that spreads across my face.

Kaylor tilts her head. "You've got a keeper, Karina. I mean, Grumpy Pants planning a wedding? That's unheard of! Shows how much he loves you."

Val shimmies her shoulders. "Do you want to hear a secret?"

I nod eagerly and sip my drink, sighing as it warms a path to my belly.

"Vulcan has been taking dance lessons," she reveals quietly.

"No way!" Tasha gasps theatrically.

"Yes! He wants to surprise Karina with a special dance at the wedding. He's been practicing every Thursday night." Valkyrie grins, then must see my concerned expression. "Don't worry about his shoulder! He's been running his dance moves by his doctor and PT."

My hands fly to my mouth as tears prick my eyes. The thought of Vulcan doing something so out of his comfort zone just to make our day special tugs at every string in my heart. "I can't believe he's doing all this," I say, more to myself than anyone else.

"He loves you." Cassie squeezes my hand, and while I appreciate the reassurance, there's so much she can't know, which makes her statement feel a little empty. "And soon enough, everyone will see just how perfect you two are for each other."

The room buzzes with excitement and curiosity. Valkyrie gives me a warm smile—she's fully on board with this new chapter of her brother's life. A new chapter that is built on a lie and a three-hundred-thousand-dollar contract. I feel bad for lying to the people we love, but if we can make this marriage last more than three years, it could all be worth it. "We'll need to celebrate properly," she declares. She raises her glass higher, initiating another round of toasts. "To Karina and Vulcan, may their journey be as adventurous and passionate as their love."

The warmth inside me grows, fueled not just by the wine but also by the genuine affection surrounding me. I never thought I'd be lucky enough to have something like this in this lifetime.

"Hey, Val, can I talk to you for a second?" I ask, pulling away from the girls.

"Sure, what's up?"

I clear my throat. "As you know, I wanted a small wedding."

She nods. "Yup, and thank you for agreeing to have our mom there."

I sip my wine. "Well, Vulcan has been doing so much for me. I know your family is tight-knit, and I want to surprise him."

"Are you about to do what I think you're about to do?"

I nod, feeling a blush tint my cheeks.

"As in our grandparents, aunts, uncles, and cousins?" Her eyes twinkles with excitement.

"Mhm. All of it. I love him, and his family is important to him. They should be there to witness this. My family won't be coming, but I want him to be happy."

"Wow." She pauses. "I don't know what to say. I mean, thank you. He's going to love this. But are you sure? Not to bring it up, but Vulcan mentioned you don't do well with big crowds."

My heart skips a beat. He covered for me, and that makes my decision to have his family there the right one. "Well, *this* big crowd will consist of his people, so it's a little different. Plus, with Vulcan around, I feel safe and protected."

"Okay, I'll reach out to everyone. Not sure how many will be able to make it since it's like, a week away, but my brother has always been the prized one in our family, so I'm sure they'll make it work." She rolls her eyes good-naturedly.

"And—"

"I'll make sure no one spills the beans," she adds.

My throat tightens with emotion. "Thank you."

"No, thank you. I'm so happy he found you. You two are made for each other. I have the best sis-in-law ever!"

Before I can respond, Naomi squeals, catching everyone's attention.

"Okay, ladies, it's time for *Love Behind the Headlines*." She grabs the remote off the table. "I really hope Max and Talia do *not* recouple. He's just stringing her along. And *she* is just going along with everything that idiot says."

"Facts!" Cassie chimes in, walking toward the sofa. "He's only telling her all those sweet nothings in case Brandy decides to recouple with Eli."

I take a seat between Cass and Val, listening to them discuss their favorite pairings on the show. I've watched fifteen minutes of one episode, so I only know Juno and Ryan. Every time I've *tried* to watch it, Vulcan has had other plans, and those plans always ended with back-to-back orgasms on the couch.

The opening credits roll and the familiar theme music plays, drawing everyone else to sing along while I sink further into the plush couch, sipping my wine and eating more cheese squares. The celebrities' complex love lives seem to parallel the ones we navigate in our relationships, and soon we're all hooked.

About thirty minutes in, I check my phone to find a text from Vulcan.

> **Vulcan: Hope you're having fun tonight. I miss you.**

My heart flutters at the sweet reminder of *my* reality waiting for me back home.

I type back a quick response, telling him about the show. His reply comes quickly, light and teasing.

> **Vulcan: Sounds like a battlefield. Save some energy for later.**

I can almost hear his deep voice, and it sends a shiver down my spine.

Just as I'm about to put my phone away, Valkyrie notices the shift in my demeanor. "Is that Vulcan?"

"He's just checking in."

"Tell him we're taking good care of you. He is so possessive." She laughs, and then her eyes are once again glued to the screen.

As the episode nears its climax, my phone buzzes again.

> **Vulcan: I just remembered you drove to Val's place. So, if you're drinking, I can get you.**

I smile and type out a quick response.

> **Me: I promise I'm fine to drive. I've switched to water.**

Setting my phone aside, I tune in as Valkyrie begins passionately debating whether Max or Andy deserves to find love after all the chaos they've caused.

When the show ends, there's a satisfied sigh among us. Naomi turns off the television and Valkyrie stands, stretching her arms wide. "All right, ladies," she announces with a grin. "How about some dessert? I've got chocolate fondue set up in the dining room." Groans of delighted anticipation fill the room as we all rise from our seats. The night is far from over, and as we move toward another round of indulgence—this time sweet and decadent—I realize how fortunate I am to have found such an open group of women.

When the evening winds down, we say our goodbyes and exchange numbers. On the drive back home to Vulcan, all I can think about is his text message. *Save some energy for later.* Pulling into our spot in the underground parking lot, I see him waiting by the elevator.

"Welcome home," he says as I step into his open arms.

"Home," I repeat, realizing that no matter where life takes us, being with him truly feels like home.

CHAPTER TWENTY-SEVEN
Vulcan

Karina called in sick today—a rare indulgence—and we've spent the morning in comfortable silence. She's curled up on the couch, her fingers tapping away at her laptop as she researches resources for the homeless patients who cycle through her ER. Meanwhile, I'm sprawled in the armchair, captivated by season three of *Grey's Anatomy*. My heart races as Derek stands at the edge of that damn ferry dock, searching for Meredith in the dark water. I still can't believe how hooked this show has me.

I steal another glance at Karina, watching the way she bites her lower lip when she's concentrating. The sight sends a familiar heat through my chest. It's becoming harder to pretend this is just an arrangement when every mundane moment with her feels like a gift I don't deserve. The more I think about it, the more I know I won't be worthy of her until I come clean about having her mother sign that contract.

The truth has been wedged in my throat for weeks now, and every day I let it remain there, it grows heavier. But if I tell her now, I know I'll lose her for sure. I watch her profile against the afternoon light streaming through the windows, her hair falling across her face as she works. How can something so simple as watching her read make my chest ache with longing?

"You're staring," she says without looking up from her screen, but I catch the small smile tugging at her lips.

"Can you blame me?" I lean forward in my chair. "My fiancée is beautiful and brilliant, and she's wearing my shirt. Sue me."

She finally looks up, her eyes meeting mine. "Your shirt is comfortable. Don't read too much into it."

But I can see the flush creeping up her neck, and I know she's fighting the same pull I am. These past weeks have blurred every line we drew in the beginning. I've never been the kind of guy to beat around the bush, but I don't want to scare her.

"I can practically hear your thoughts from over here." She closes the laptop. "What is on your mind?"

"Have you spoken to your mother lately?"

I watch as her expression shifts, the warmth in her eyes cooling slightly. "No, she'll probably reach out to me as we get closer to November."

"Why is that?"

"My brothers will be back for holiday break, and most likely they will want to buy a ton of useless things with my money." She sighs. "It's always been this way. Some months she calls me every other day, and then there are months when she eases back because she has something expensive she's gearing up to ask for my help with. Anyway, she's not big on keeping in contact with me unless she needs something."

The bitterness in her voice makes me want to pull her into my arms, but I resist. Instead, I nod, trying to find the right words. "I understand. Family can be... complicated."

Karina gives me a sad smile. "That's one way of putting it."

I take a deep breath. I need to tell her that I met with her mother, about the contract I had her sign. But when I look at Karina, so peaceful and content for once, I can't bring myself to shatter this fragile happiness we've built.

"What if..." I start, then pause, weighing my words carefully.

"What if we invited your brothers to the wedding?"

Her eyes widen. "My brothers? Why would we do that?"

"Because they're your family. And despite everything, I know you care about them."

"I care about them, yes. But what they know of me fits in a Venmo notification. Miguel and Luis only reach out when they need something. My last two birthdays, they sent wish lists instead of well wishes." She looks down at her hands, her voice softening. "I've made peace with celebrating milestones without them. Ever since Papá died... It's just better this way. Our wedding day should be filled with people who actually want to be there."

She looks at me for a long moment, and I run a hand through my hair, debating how honest I should be. I'm a fucking coward when it comes to Karina. I can't tell her. Not yet, I tell myself. Later, when I'm sure she won't walk away. I want to have this a little longer.

"Your forehead gets all crinkly when something's bothering you," she says, setting her laptop aside completely now, giving me her full attention. "What's going on in there?"

"I've been thinking about us," I say. "This whole situation—are you actually happy with how things are turning out? With me?"

She tilts her head slightly, concern flickering across her face. "Where is this coming from? Did something happen?"

I pause the show and shift in my chair, the weight of my feelings making it impossible to sit still. "Everything's fine. More than fine, actually. I just want—I don't want to say I do with you thinking I'm doing this out of obligation. Yes, at first it was the reason. But now I just want it to be real," I say finally, the words spilling out before I can stop them. "Us. This."

Karina stares at me, her eyes as wide as saucers now. She puts her laptop on the coffee table and shifts to face me fully, tucking her legs beneath her. My shirt—the old FDNY one with the faded logo—slips off one shoulder, and I fight the urge to cross the room and press my lips to that exposed sliver of skin.

"Vulcan," she says softly, "what exactly are you saying?"

I close my eyes for a moment, centering myself. I've faced burning buildings and collapsing structures, but nothing has ever terrified me like this moment. "I'm saying I don't want to marry you because of some contract. I want to marry you because I'm in love with you."

The silence that follows feels endless. I watch her face carefully, trying to read her expression.

"You don't have to say it back," I rush to add. "I just needed you to know how I feel. These weeks with you, they've been... I've never felt this way about anyone before."

She looks down, her fingers fidgeting with the hem of my shirt. "Vulcan, I—"

"It's okay," I interrupt. "I understand if you don't feel the same way. The arrangement still stands. Nothing has to change if you don't want it to."

But God, I want everything to change. I want her to be mine— truly mine. Not because of some contract or because her mother needs money, but because she chooses me the way I've chosen her.

Karina stands up suddenly, and my heart sinks. She's going to walk away, retreat to her room, put distance between us. But instead, she crosses the living room and stops directly in front of me.

"You impossible man," she whispers, and before I can respond, she's climbing onto my lap, straddling me in the armchair. Her hands cup my face, her touch so gentle it makes my chest ache. "Do you have any idea how hard I've been trying not to fall in love with you?"

My breath catches. "You have?"

She nods, her eyes shining with unshed tears. "I've been so afraid this was just an arrangement for you. That I was reading too much into every touch, every look, every moment we shared."

I slide my hands up her thighs to rest on her hips, anchoring her to me. "It started that way," I admit. "But, Karina, somewhere between our first date and this morning, you became everything to me."

A tear slips down her cheek, and I catch it with my thumb. "I love you," I say again, because now that I've finally said it, I never want to stop. "I love your brilliance, your compassion, and your strength." I slip my hand over hers, feeling her fingers tremble against my cheek. "I love your stubbornness. I love your dedication to your patients. I even love the way you hoard all the blankets at night."

Karina laughs through her tears, the sound making my heart swell. "I do not hoard blankets."

"You absolutely do," I whisper, pressing my forehead against hers.

She closes her eyes, her breath warm against my lips. For a moment, we just stay like this, suspended in a new, quiet truth. I've never been one for vulnerability—my job demands strength, control, composure—but with her, I want to tear down every wall I've ever built.

"I love you, Vulcan," she says, and I feel like my heart is about to leap from my chest. "I've been fighting it so hard because I was scared of what happens when our arrangement ends. I kept telling myself not to get attached, not to hope for more than what we agreed on."

I tighten my grip on her hips, pulling her closer. "Forget the arrangement. Forget the contract. I want forever with you, Karina. Not three years, but a lifetime."

She pulls back slightly, searching my eyes. "Are you sure? This isn't just… the heat of the moment?"

"I've never been more certain of anything," I say firmly. "I knew it the first night you stayed over. When I woke up and saw you there, everything in my life clicked into place. I want forever with you, Karina

Reyes—to have children, grow old, fight and make up, and build a messy, beautiful life that's completely ours."

I watch her eyes fill with tears again, but this time they're accompanied by the most radiant smile I've ever seen. My heart hammers against my ribs. She leans down, pressing her lips to mine in a kiss that feels like a promise.

"Yes," she whispers against my mouth. "Yes to all of it. I can't tell you how long I've been waiting for this day. To finally love you without worrying about an expiration date."

I kiss her again, sliding one hand into her hair, cradling the back of her head as if she's the most precious thing I've ever held. And she is. In this moment, I understand why people write songs and poems about love. It's the only way to capture something this overwhelming, this transcendent.

When we finally break apart, both breathless, I can't help but laugh.

"What's so funny?" Karina asks, her fingers tracing patterns on my chest.

"I can see our relationship turning out like Derek and Mer—"

"No, sir!" Her eyes widen. "Finish watching all the seasons before you make grand declarations."

I laugh and reach up to tuck a strand of hair behind her ear. "Fine, fine. But you have to admit, their chemistry is undeniable."

Karina rolls her eyes, but she's smiling. "Chemistry isn't enough when one of them keeps drowning or getting hit by plane or crashing in the woods."

"Crashes in the woods? I don't remember that episode."

"Just wait," she deadpans, settling more comfortably on my lap. Her weight against me feels right. Like she was made to fit there.

I trace my fingers along her bare thigh, marveling at how smooth her skin is. "So, does this mean our arrangement is officially... not an arrangement anymore?"

"I think it means we're doing this for real now. No contracts, no time limits."

"Good," I slide my hands under my shirt she's wearing, feeling the warmth of her skin. "Because I wasn't looking forward to letting you go after three years."

"I wasn't looking forward to leaving."

I bury my face in the crook of her neck, breathing in her scent. "You know what this means, right? We have to tell Minji to tear up that prenup."

She laughs, the sound vibrating against my lips. "Good, because I had no plans of signing it anyway."

I nip gently at her neck.

"We should probably call her today," she adds, her voice breathless as I continue my assault on her neck. "Get it taken care of before the wedding."

"Mmm," I agree, but I'm too focused on the way she's responding to my touch to think about legal documents right now. My hands slide higher and I'm gratified to discover she's not wearing a bra.

"Vulcan," she whispers, and there's something in her tone that makes me pull back to look at her.

"What is it?"

"I'm serious, let's call her today, and"—she winks at me—"then we can celebrate."

"I'll call her *after* our celebration. What did you have in mind, Dr. Reyes?"

"Well, Captain," she breathes, grinding down slightly, "I was thinking we could christen this chair. We haven't done that yet."

I growl, capturing her lips in a hungry kiss. "I like the way you think."

Her fingers tangle in my hair, tugging just enough to make me groan. "I thought you might."

When I stand, her legs wrap around my waist instinctively, and I turn to press her against the nearest wall. "I love you," I say again, because I can, because the words feel like freedom after being trapped for so long.

"I love you too," she whispers, and I swear I could live on those words alone.

CHAPTER TWENTY-EIGHT
Vulcan

Today's the big day, and I'm pacing grooves into the church floor, anxiously ensuring every detail is just as it should be. The guest list is small, just my mom, sister, and Harry, but even so, I'm determined to make it unforgettable. The air hums with anticipation as I take in the beauty of St. Patrick's Cathedral. The colors Karina chose are stunning. We settled on a dusty blue, sage green, and gray, and these simple hues have come together in an unexpectedly elegant tapestry that fills the room with calm.

Each shade mingles softly together. A testament to her quiet but vibrant presence. I smile, thinking about how little I expected this day just a few months ago, and how quickly things have changed.

Today, I am marrying the woman I have fallen deeply in love with.

"Can't believe this is really happening." I look up to see Harry walking down the aisle in his tux. "You're really getting married today."

"I really am."

"Nervous? Excited?"

"Happy. I'm so damn happy to be marrying my other half." I smile, fixing a flowerpot that is slightly askew.

"I pray this love never finds me," he jokes. "I love my women wild, free, and with no attachments. The day I fall in love to the point I'm talking marriage…? Hell probably froze over."

"And I can't wait to see that day."

"That won't—"

Loud chatter catches our attention, and I look down the aisle to see my mother walking into the church with Val. But what really has me in shock is the horde of relatives following behind her. *Oh, this is not going to go over well.*

I rush over to them, trying to keep my composure even as panic rises in my chest.

"Val, Mom, what's going on?" I whisper, watching as more relatives pour through the doors—aunts, uncles, and some cousins I haven't even seen in years.

My mother beams at me, oblivious to my distress. "Talk to your sister; she's the one who invited them." She waves me off and continues walking with my stepfather, who gives me a polite nod.

Valkyrie offers nothing more than a shrug and an easy smile.

"What did you do? Shit." I hiss, grabbing her elbow and pulling her aside. "Karina specifically wanted a small wedding. You knew that."

"And then she changed her mind. She *wanted* them to be here, Vul." Val smiles. "She loves you and knows that you might regret not having the family here one day. So, this was her surprise for you."

I search her face for any sign of deception, finding nothing but honesty. Something warm spreads through my chest at the thought of Karina going out of her way to do this. I know we talked about this no longer being a marriage of convenience but for her to do something like this…

"This doesn't sound like her at all," I say, still skeptical.
She doesn't falter. "I swear. We planned it all at our girls' night. You know I wouldn't do anything to ruin your wedding."

A wave of overwhelming emotions crashes over me, leaving me stunned. That unpredictable, endlessly fascinating woman.

"Congratulations, brother, you've found the one," she continues.

"*Valkyrie,*" I murmur, unable to find more words.

She nudges my arm. "Don't get all mushy on me. Go take your spot, and I'll check on the bride."

I head to the altar, my heart drumming against my ribs. Every step feels significant, weighted with the knowledge that today marks the start of something new despite the secret I'm holding in. The one that's slowly killing me. The goal is to tell her after tonight; which day precisely is still up in the air.

"You okay, man? You look like you've seen a ghost," Harry says, and gives me a knowing look as I take my place.

"Better than okay," I manage, straightening my tie. "She invited my entire family. Behind my back."

Harry's eyebrows shoot up. "The same woman who said, and I quote, 'I don't give a damn about centerpieces'?"

"That's the one." I smirk.

The church continues to fill with familiar faces, each one a welcome gift from my soon-to-be wife. My cousins wave enthusiastically. My uncle Leo, who taught me to fish when I was seven, gives me a thumbs-up from the third row. My mother and stepfather are up front, and I see Valkyrie's friends—now also Karina's friends—sitting in the audience. Sharon and Naomi are huddled together, whispering to one another.

Then there's Tasha, snapping pictures like she's on a mission to document every second while Kaylor watching her, grinning. I even catch Minji dabbing discreetly at her eyes with a tissue. There are a few doctors and nurses from Karina's job, and my crew from the station—my brothers and sisters in arms—are here too.

The music changes suddenly and everything else fades away.

The doors at the back creak open, and there she is.

Karina's standing there with Cassie and Valkyrie flanking her like loyal guards. My heart jumps into my throat. She's fucking breathtaking, a vision in white. The soft lace of her dress clings to her curves like it was made just for her, and I suppose it was. Her long, wavy hair is pulled away from her face in a complicated-looking twist, and her eyes are locked on mine. Her beauty could rival that of the goddess Aphrodite.

She steps forward, and with each step, my pulse quickens. It's like watching my dreams take form—except she's real. More real than anything I've ever known. My tough-as-nails facade is cracking, and damn if tears aren't welling up. Memories flood in—late-night talks, shared meals, her head resting on my shoulder as we watched the city lights from the living room window.

Today, among friends and family who have seen me through hell and back, I will marry this incredible woman. We still have plenty left to talk about, plenty for me to tell her, but all that matters is I will fight for her every day for the next 1095 days. And I'll continue fighting every day after, if she'll have me.

As Karina approaches, I offer my hand, helping her up the steps. She hands her bouquet to Cassie and turns to me.

"You invited my family," I rasp.

A faint blush colors her cheeks. "Don't make a big deal of it," she murmurs, but I can see the pleased smile tugging at her lips.

"Thank you," I say, taking her hands in mine, giving them a squeeze. "For someone who claims to hate surprises, you've certainly mastered dishing them out."

"Well," she says softly, "I figured if I'm going to be stuck with you for at least the next three years, I might as well make sure your family is here to bear witness."

As we turn to face the officiant, her fingers intertwined with mine, I whisper, "Ready?"

She looks up at me. "I've never been more ready for anything," she says, and I believe her.

The officiant, Pastor Adams, begins to speak. "Dearly beloved, we are gathered here today…" His words float around us, but I'm too caught up in Karina's eyes to pay them much heed. Her thumb lightly strokes the back of my hand, a simple gesture steadying my racing heart.

"I invite the bride and groom to exchange their vows," Pastor Adams prompts, his gentle voice pulling me back to the reality of this moment—our moment.

Karina takes a deep breath, her eyes never leaving mine, and begins. Her voice is clear and strong yet imbued with a vulnerability that only adds to her beauty.

"Vulcan Montgomery," she echoes, her words wrapping around us like a protective shroud, "you are the unexpected flame that lit up the darkness of my world. You've shown me strength in vulnerability, courage, compassion, and love in places I never thought to look."

Her expression softens even more, if that's possible. "Today, I vow to walk beside you through whatever trials may come. To support you, challenge you, and cherish the quiet strength that defines you. I promise to see you—the man beneath the shield—and to honor the sacrifices you make every day. Your love has become my beacon, guiding me through the chaos of this life."

"And so," she finishes, "I pledge to be your sanctuary, confidant, and partner in all things. Through the heat of battle and the calm of peace, I am yours. Always."

The church is utterly silent, everyone moved by her words. A lump forms in my throat as I take in every ounce of her sincerity.

I swallow hard against the tightness in my throat, giving the crowd a "Yeah, yeah" as they chuckle at my obvious display of nerves. "Karina, I've faced many fires in my life, but none burned as bright or as warm as my love for you. You're my calm amid chaos, my hope during despair."

My words flow more freely, carrying the weight of everything she has come to mean to me.

"Your spirit, your compassion—they've been my salvation. In this life of unpredictability, you have become my *constant*. And so, I vow to build a life with you that honors both the woman you are and the partnership we've forged. I vow to keep our flames of passion alive." I reach up to wipe a tear escaping down her cheek with my thumb. "I promise to be yours every single day, 'til death do us part."

The officiant nods approvingly before turning to gather the rings from Harry, who's wiping his own eyes discreetly. "Vulcan and Karina will now exchange rings as a symbol of their love and commitment."

As we slip the rings onto each other's fingers, I feel a sense of completeness.

"By the power vested in me," he declares. "I now pronounce you husband and wife. You may kiss the bride."

The room bursts into applause as I step closer to Karina, lifting her chin gently with my finger. Our kiss is the perfect seal on our vows. When we part, her eyes are gleaming and she looks genuinely happy.

At the reception hall in the Beaufort Hotel, family and friends congratulate us. All of my cousins have embraced Karina with open arms, and don't get me started on my mother, who literally announced to everyone that she's unofficially adopted her as a second daughter. Karina didn't seem to mind, but I've been keeping an eye on her, making sure she doesn't get swallowed up by my (sometimes) overbearing family.

Though, I soon find there's no real need to. Our people are showering her with love, and she is soaking it all up. I guess my words of affirmation have been working: Karina has turned into the goddess I knew she always was.

Harry approaches our table and leans over with a grin. "So, Captain, ready for the real adventure now?"

"It's been real since day one."

"Are you ready for the dance?"

"Yeah. It's been seven weeks since surgery, so Dr. Simmons said I'm good to go," I say, standing up.

"I have a surprise for you." I kiss Karina's forehead before heading to the dance floor, where the firehouse crew waits impatiently. Val drags a chair center stage, grinning mischievously, while Cassie pushes Karina into it. For weeks now, we've rehearsed this number, and leaving choreography to Harry now feels like a gamble. As "It's Raining Men" blares, our routine devolves into a hilarious spectacle of enthusiasm over skill.

Karina's eyes widen in shock and delight. I may be red-faced from embarrassment, but her sparkling excitement and clapping make it all worthwhile. The guys, committed to the bit, shake their hips and strike exaggerated poses. I spot my mother and Valkyrie doubled over in laughter, supporting each other. They are never going to let me live this down.

When the tempo shifts to a reggaeton beat, one I picked for Karina, who adores "Danza Kuduro," her mouth drops open, then blossoms into the widest smile I've seen yet. She leaps to her feet, dancing in place and laughing so hard she struggles to catch her breath. It's chaos at its best.

As the last beats fade, I breathe hard, a mix of adrenaline and sheer joy coursing through me. Karina runs to my side and kisses me, and I hear the hoots and hollers of everyone around us. "I can't believe you planned all this," she exclaims, shaking her head in shock.

"You weren't the only one with a surprise today," I say, grinning like a fool. "Did you like it?"

"I loved it. Now I wish I'd done a dance for you." She pushes onto her toes to kiss me again. We linger like that for a moment, wrapped in each other, wrapped in happiness.

"You have three years to make up for it," I murmur. "I prefer you to dance for me behind closed doors anyway."

As the night progresses, the guests begin to trickle out, offering final congratulations and embraces before they depart.

The band plays what must be their last set—slower, softer, like a sweet farewell. It's as if this moment is crafted especially for us, a melodic hum that wraps around us like a tender embrace.

"You know," I whisper as we sway gently amidst the scattered petals, "I meant every word today."

Karina rests her head against my chest. "So did I."

"Ready to get out of here?"

"More than ready," she whispers back.

I think I broke twenty traffic laws getting us home.

I carry my wife up the elevator and across the threshold into the penthouse. It's quiet and softly lit with the gentle glow of the lamps we left on. Setting her down, I pull her into a kiss, and she wraps her arms around my neck.

We don't speak as we undress each other, and I can feel the anticipation building with each piece of clothing that falls to the floor. Her hands roam over my back, while mine explore the curves of her hips and the softness of her breasts.

Karina's hardened nipples graze against my chest and the wetness between her legs almost send my eyes rolling to the back of my head as she grinds against me. My cock aches to be inside her.

With a low growl, I pick her up and carry her to bed, our lips never breaking contact. As I lay her down on the sheets, I take a moment to admire the sight of her body. She bites her lip, her eyes full of lust, as she watches me climb onto the bed and position myself between her legs.

I tease her at first, running my fingers along her inner thighs before finally reaching the wetness at their apex. She gasps as I slide two fingers inside her, her muscles clenching as I move them in and out. Karina never ceases to amaze me. Her body is always greedy for my touch.

When I know she's close to shattering, I remove my finger and slowly enter her, relishing the stretch of her around my shaft.

"Vulcan," she moans. "Your shoulder, do I—"

"Babe, I'm fine. My shoulder is fine. Nothing's going to stop me from fucking you into this mattress."

With that, I begin to thrust, hips moving in a steady rhythm. She whimpers and bucks up to meet me. I lean down to capture one of her nipples between my lips, sucking it hard as I thrust inside of her. Her pussy clenches around my cock, drawing me in further, and I can feel the tension in her body beginning to unravel.

"Fuck," she moans, arching her back and meeting my every stroke.

I pull out of her briefly before rubbing my tip on her clit, watching her eyes flare and then pushing back in, filling her to the hilt.

"Harder. Fuck me harder." Her nails are still carving half-moons into my back, and I'm sure she's broken skin. I love it when she gets this way. The headboard slams against the wall with each powerful thrust. As I feel myself getting closer, I grab on to the polished wood for leverage and plunge deeper and faster inside of her, giving her what she asked for. Her legs wrap around my waist like shackles holding us together, connecting us in a primal way.

"Fill me up," she whispers through gritted teeth. "I want all of you."

I moan, lost in the feeling of how she welcomes me with every touch and kiss. With one final thrust, I groan loudly as I explode. Our breathing slowly evens out, and our heart rates return to normal as we lie together. I can feel Karina's body still trembling from her orgasm.

"You're amazing... so fucking amazing," I whisper against her ear before gently kissing her neck, shoulders, and collarbone, nipping at her soft flesh. I pull out and roll onto my side, facing her. Our bodies press together as I wrap my arms around her waist, drumming my fingers against her heated skin.

"Now what?" Karina asks as she runs her fingers through my chest hair.

"I think it's about time for round two, and I want to hear those words spill from your lips as I fuck you like I hate you."

She bites her bottom lip and arches a brow before moving her hand south to palm my erection.

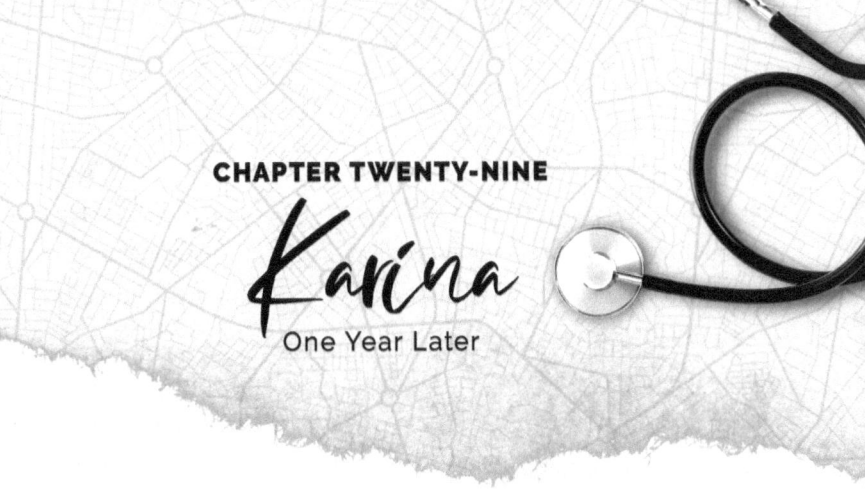

CHAPTER TWENTY-NINE

Karina

One Year Later

It's been a year since Vulcan and I exchanged vows. A year since I fell in love with a man who made me believe in fairy tales again. I trace my fingers along the wedding band on my left hand, still marveling at how natural it feels there. Some mornings I wake up and have to remind myself this isn't a dream—that Vulcan Montgomery actually chose me, loves me, wants forever with me. But love's tricky when you're married to a man whose schedule is just as hectic as your own. Vulcan's days are long, and we're like ships passing in the night.

I'm charting notes in my office when the door swings open. Dr. Stevens strides in, his face etched with a concern that mirrors the furrow of worry lines I feel carving into my forehead. What happened now?

"Karina, do you have a moment?"

"Of course," I reply, setting the patient file aside. "What's wrong?"

"It's Mr. Alvarez in 204. His vitals are falling, and I think we need to consider moving him to the ICU."

I nod, my heart beating a little faster at the news. Mr. Alvarez has been one of those patients who claw their way into your heart. He is a lovely man, always going out of his way to make everyone who walks in and out of his room smile. "Let's go take a look," I say, pulling my coat off the back of the chair.

We arrive at room 204, and I quickly consult his chart while Dr. Stevens explains our concerns to the attending nurse. As we make plans for his immediate care, my phone vibrates insistently in my pocket.

"Excuse me a moment," I murmur to Dr. Stevens, who nods as he continues to give instructions.

I step into the quiet of the hallway and answer the call. "Hey."

"Hey yourself." Vulcan's deep voice comes through, immediately soothing some tension from my shoulders. "I'm sorry to call you at work—I know you're swamped—but I just *needed* to hear your voice."

A small smile tugs at my lips despite the chaos of my day. "It's always good to hear yours, too," I admit. "Everything okay on your end?"

He sighs, and I picture him running a hand through his hair. "Yeah, all fine here. I'm just wrapping up a board meeting about fire safety protocols." I lean against the cool wall as he continues. "I miss you."

"I miss you too," I confess softly. The distance between us isn't just measured in miles, but also in moments missed, dinners left cold on tables, and morning coffees sipped alone. I miss my husband, and I hate to admit this, but our marriage is now starting to feel like one of convenience. The very thing we said we would overcome.

"We need a plan. Maybe a weekend away? Just you and me."

"That sounds perfect," I agree enthusiastically.

"Perfect. We'll go over details tonight. I'll make sure to leave work at a decent hour."

"Promise?"

"Promise." His voice is laced with that authoritative edge that never fails to reassure me.

We exchange a few more words before I hang up and head back into Mr. Alvarez's room. Dr. Stevens glances over as I step in. "Everything okay?" he asks.

"Yes, just a family call."

The rest of the day flies by in a blur of patients, paperwork, and hurried consultations. By the time I hang up my coat and gather my things to leave, the sun has long since set. I check my phone, hoping to see a message from Vulcan, but there's nothing.

My drive home is heavy with the weight of exhaustion but also with anticipation. As I walk through our front door, the house is quiet. There's also the distinct absence of herbs and spices sizzling in oil. Which means he isn't home yet.

I pull out my phone and try calling him, but it goes straight to voicemail. I send a quick text and get an instant reply. He won't be able to leave work early after all. He was asked to assist with some intradepartmental training, so I take it he's still helping the new captains at the fire station in Long Island. I let out a slow breath, feeling disappointed but not surprised.

I heat some leftovers and settle on the sofa, where I turn on the TV and watch some wilderness survival show. The melodic tones of a British narrator drones in the background, but it's difficult to focus on much after the day I've had. The promise of a weekend together, a brief escape from the relentless commotion of our lives, is the only thing keeping me from pacing the living room in frustration.

I check my phone again, hoping for a message telling me he's on his way home. The time on the TV reads 9:47 p.m. I stand to wash my dishes, and a sudden bout of irritation hits me.

This wasn't what I envisioned when we promised to support each other's careers. We're both so caught up in our duties and responsibilities that it feels like we're losing each other in the process.

My phone vibrates on the counter and I quickly dry my hands and grab it. Disappointment sets in as I glance at the screen to see Cassie's name flashing.

Our communication has been sparse over the last two months since she took a job at the children's hospital. So, this call comes at the perfect time.

"Hey, stranger. How's the flashy new job?"

She chuckles on her end. "It's been crazy but rewarding. I miss our old gang, though. How are you holding up?"

I pause, tempted to spill about my marriage struggles, but decide against it. She doesn't need that dumped on her. "Oh, you know, just living the dream. If said dream involves running on fumes and charting patient notes at three a.m. in your sleep."

"The ER life is something I don't miss." She laughs. "And how's married life? Still having mind-blowing sex a year in?"

"Vulcan's good. Actually, we're planning a weekend getaway," I say with a smile, bypassing the Cassie-level intrusive question and trying to sound more excited than skeptical. It's looking less and less like that'll happen.

"About time! You two workaholics need to make time for romance."

"Yeah, if our schedules ever decide to play nice." I snort. "Right now, they're like arguing toddlers."

"You know, if anyone can make it work, it'll be Vulcan. That man will move heaven and hell just to be with you," she says, and I bite the inside of my cheek to keep from complaining any more.

I let Cassie fill me in on her new job and crazy love life before we say our goodbyes, promising to catch up properly soon. The call managed to provide me with some hope though as I was reminded of how our love looks from the outside. *I need to have a little more faith in my husband.*

I wander over to my laptop and begin researching possible destinations for our getaway. As I scroll through charming bed-and-breakfasts and quaint small towns, images of couples strolling hand in hand as they browse farmers' markets flood my vision.

A ping from my phone drags my gaze away from a rustic inn in the Catskills.

Vulcan: I'm sorry, baby. It might be a while, don't wait up.

It's not unexpected, yet it stings a bit more tonight. I reply with a simple acknowledgment and close my laptop. I need a hot bath. A small attempt at self-care. Lately, that seems like the only care I've been getting.

I slip off my clothes and sink into the warm water, sighing in relief as the heat envelops me. Closing my eyes, I allow my mind to drift back to when Vulcan and I were inseparable. When times were good, and he was only the fire captain at Station 112. Before he started helping out another fire station all the way in Long Island.

As I soak, I can't help but think about how different things are now. Vulcan's work out in Long Island has meant a two-hour daily commute—if there isn't any traffic. But even prior to being given the promotion, our schedules have clashed for months, leaving us with little time together as a couple.

And it's not just our jobs that have caused a strain on our marriage. Lately, there's been distance between us. A lack of communication, of understanding, of intimacy.

I let out a frustrating sigh and sink deeper into the water.

I hate to admit it, but I even miss my mother's constant demands and nagging. She's reached out sporadically over the last year, but not as frequently as before. Not wanting her negativity to ruin my happiness, I've miraculously been able to dodge her calls since the wedding—a wedding she still knows nothing about. So it was strange when she texted yesterday, saying it was urgent. Which probably means she has already blown through the three hundred grand.

Even my little brothers, who hardly ever make an effort outside of birthday and holiday calls, have been more present than ever. Wanting to know how my day is going and what's new with me, sending me articles on doctors traveling abroad to help in other countries, and letting me know how they finished up at the end of every semester. All text messages have been left on read. If they had done this a year ago, I would have welcomed them with open arms, but now I'm happy with where I am in my life and I just don't want to invite that negative energy back in.

Vulcan's words of affirmation, both in and out of the bedroom, have stuck with me. I see myself as a powerful woman who no longer seeks her mother's approval. But on nights like these, when I'm alone with my thoughts, I wonder if I've made the right choices. Yes, all she wants is money, but at least I could count on her relentless calls to keep me from feeling this way. The penthouse without Vulcan is a lonely place.

A little while later, the sharp ring of my phone cuts through the tranquility. I consider ignoring it and staying wrapped in this warm embrace a bit longer, but something propels me to reach out with damp fingers and check the caller ID. *Vulcan.*

"Hey," I answer, trying to keep my voice even, not wanting him to detect the disappointment that had pooled inside me earlier.

"Hey, love." He sounds tired. "I'm really sorry about earlier. Right when I was leaving, we got a call for a three-alarm fire."

"It's okay," I tell him, though we both know it's become the norm rather than the exception.

"Listen," he continues. "I just left Long Island and am heading home now. Do you think you'll still be up? I want to spend some time with my favorite lady."

"Si." I find myself saying without hesitation. "Yes, I'll wait up."

"Thank you. I miss you."

"I miss you more," I say as I rise from the now-tepid water.

After ending the call, I quickly dry off and cover myself with a robe. Moving through our bedroom, I get dressed in a cute nightgown before heading into the living room. The minutes pass slowly as I sit on the couch, flipping absentmindedly through a health magazine.

Finally, I hear keys in the lock and snap out of my half-distracted state. Vulcan walks in, looking exhausted but undeniably relieved to be home. I stand up and toss the magazine aside. He pauses briefly at the sight of me and drops his bag, then steps forward to wrap me his arms.

"God, I missed you so much," he whispers, nuzzling into my hair. I often fall asleep before he gets home, and then there are the nights when I work double shifts at the hospital and don't see him at all.

"It's been a long day for both of us," I say softly.

He takes a step back. "You could definitely say that."

"Well, I'm happy you're home." I kiss him softly on the lips. "Let's get you relaxed. How about a bath," I suggest, slipping my hand into his and leading him toward the bathroom.

"Are you going to join me?"

"I already had one," I tell him, then let go of his hand and head toward the bathtub, turning on the faucet and adjusting the temperature. I add some Epsom salts and a few drops of lavender oil. "I can fix you something to eat while you unwind."

"The only thing I want to eat is *you*." He undresses and steps into the tub, letting out a sigh of relief.

"I'm not opposed, *but*—"

"Get in with me," he insists.

"I already—"

"I know, but I'm telling you what I want now. *Please*? I just want to hold my wife."

I relent and slip in next to him, letting him guide me onto his lap. Our bodies press against each other, and I wrap my arms around his neck.

"This is perfect," he whispers. "So, how was your day?"

"Too many emergencies, not enough time. So…" I continue. "About this weekend. What did you have in mind?"

"How about a cabin up in the mountains? It would be just the two of us, with no cell service or interruptions, just snow and firewood."

"That sounds perfect. But are you sure you can manage it?"

"Positive. I have some good news as well. I'm finally back at Station 112 for good. Which means I'll be back to cooking dinner and waiting for my favorite person to come home."

"Really?" I smile. "You aren't joking, are you?"

"Of course not. I got news before I left earlier. So, this weekend I've already made all the arrangements, and we can leave Friday afternoon," he says.

"That makes me so happy."

"Would you want to have children one day?" he suddenly asks, and I'm at a loss for words. Vulcan mentioned it once before the wedding, but with our schedules conflicting, any thoughts about having children went out the window for me. I've been diligent about taking birth control every day since because I didn't want any surprises.

"Kids?" I stutter.

"Yes." He nods slowly. "I mentioned it before, remember?"

"Well, yeah… but"—my fingers trace patterns on his chest absentmindedly—"our lives are hectic at the moment, and I don't think I'd make a great mother. We both know mine didn't set a great example."

"You'd make an amazing mother," he says, capturing my wandering hand with his and pressing it to his heart. "How many times do I have to remind you that you are nothing like her?"

I blink and whisper, "You think so?"

His eyes soften as he brushes a strand of hair from my face. "I know so. The way you care about people, how deeply you love... I've seen it firsthand, Karina." His thumb traces my cheekbone. "You're nothing like her."

"I never really allowed myself to imagine having children. It seemed... impossible."

"With our careers, it would be challenging," he acknowledges. "But not impossible. Especially now that I'll have more time at home."

I bite my lip, picturing a little girl with Vulcan's determined expression or a boy with his quiet strength. The image brings an unexpected ache of longing. I want to have his children, but I don't know if I'm ready yet.

"Would you want that?" I ask. "A family with me?"

"Mrs. Montgomery, I have told you countless times I want everything with you. We got married because we are in love. Yes, things got pretty hectic once I was assigned to help cover other fire stations, but one thing that hasn't changed is my love for you and wanting a family with you. *Unless...* you want to get divorced in two years?"

I shake my head, not wanting to entertain the thought.

"It's been a while since we talked about having children. So, it slipped my mind, but I don't want to divorce you. It will always be till death do us part."

"I love you, Karina. No need to feel pressured about this. We have a lifetime together and all the lifetimes after."

"I love you, too." I lean in to kiss him. The water ripples around us as he deepens the kiss, his hands roaming over my back. "And thank you for always being so understanding. I don't want to rush into having children only to later regret it."

"Of course. We will take it at your pace," he says, kissing my forehead. "I want you to be one hundred percent sure you're ready. But in the meantime, we can practice the art of making babies."

CHAPTER THIRTY

Vulcan

Snowflakes dance in the air as Karina and I pull up to our rented cabin nestled in the mountains just west of the Hudson. She's got this childlike wonder in her eyes, lighting up at the sight of the snow-covered trees. We cart our duffels inside and shake the snow off our boots, relieved to find it adequately heated.

"Wow, Vulcan, this place is incredible," Karina breathes, her eyes full of awe. While the place is cozy, it's got the amenities of a luxury getaway. Plush sofas, a roaring fireplace, and an entire wall of windows offering a panoramic view of the winter wonderland.

"Only the best for you," I say.

The real reason I wanted to get away was so I could come clean to Karina. Our conversation the other day where we spoke earnestly about our future—possibly bringing kids into the mix—made the weight I've been carrying on my chest feel crushing. It's overshadowed every precious moment we shared for the past year, and not a day has passed where I haven't thought to tell her.

I still remember the look on her mother's face when she signed the contract. The greed and satisfaction made my stomach turn—still does. But I did it for Karina, didn't I? To give her peace, to let her live without that toxic presence looming over her life. Her mother was a leech who never let up, always ready to tear her down, taking and taking until there was nothing left.

So, I stepped in. I *had* to step in, to be the protector, the fixer.

But what does it make me, now that I've kept it hidden?

Everyone knows the truth now except Karina. My wife—the one person who should never be kept in the dark. I still remember that night two months into our marriage when she stood in our bedroom doorway, arms crossed, eyes blazing. "Tell your family about our arrangement, or I'm sleeping in the guest room until you do." By sunset that same day, we sat in the living room on FaceTime with Val and my mother, and I told them everything. How we'd met through Minji, how the arrangement had started as a business deal, how we'd fallen in love despite ourselves.

My mother had gone silent for a long moment before bursting into tears of joy. "The beginning doesn't matter," she managed between sobs, "I see the love between you now, and that's everything." She followed this with a string of colorful expletives about my father. Val just smirked and whispered, "I had a feeling this start of it was a little too suspicious. But it worked out for both of you, and that's what matters."

But this secret about her mother? This feels different. Heavier. More dangerous to the foundation we've built"

Vulcan, come see the view from here!" Karina calls out.

I join her, slipping an arm around her waist as I look out at the endless stretch of white peaks against the clear blue sky.

"Beautiful, isn't it?" she asks, and I can only nod, my throat feeling tight. God, this is going to be harder than I imagined. "Hey, what's up?" She tilts her head back and looks up at me, and my breath catches. "You seem… distant. Are you really okay with being away from work for a weekend?" she teases.

"Work hasn't even crossed my mind. I'm just thinking about how lucky I am," I settle on, needing a little more time to think of the right words.

Later. I'll tell her later.

"I'm lucky, too," she whispers, turning slightly within the circle of my arm to face me, her hands finding their way up to my chest. "If something is bothering you, you don't have to carry it all by yourself. I'm here for you. You know that, right? I've got you."

I look down into her eyes, so full of concern for *me*, and there's that familiar tug of conflict again. On one hand, there is a deep-seated desire to protect her from everything harsh and ugly, including the reality of my arrangement with her mother. And on the other, there's this desperate need to lay it bare and obliterate any secrets between us.

But now is not the time, not when she's looking at me like I hung the moon.

"If you must know..." My voice trails off as I pretend to think long and hard.

Karina waits patiently, her gaze never wavering from mine. Her fingers gently stroke my beard as if to encourage me. *After the trip, I swear.*

I muster a smile, focusing on the beauty of the moment rather than the weight of everything left unsaid. "I'm ready to devour you all over this cabin." She gasps as I push her gently against the frost-lined window, my hands roaming over her body. I don't ever want to use sex to avoid problems, but I can't help myself.

With a low growl, I claim her mouth. My tongue explores every inch as if I'm a man starved and she is my sustenance. She moans into my mouth, her hands tangling in my hair as she pulls me closer. I trail my lips down her neck, biting and sucking at the sensitive skin, leaving marks.

"Wait." She pulls back, eyes narrowed. "You're not trying to distract me, are you?"

I take off my coat and then hers. "This is what I need right now," I confess. "To feel close to you. To forget everything else just for a moment."

Her eyes soften, understanding flickering within them.

"Then let's forget the world together." Her fingers trace patterns down my back, and I can feel her hot breath against my ear as she whispers, "I want you to fuck me hard and fast."

We race to undress, and I lift her effortlessly, her legs wrapping around my waist. I carry her toward the roaring fire, thankful for the staff I hired to set things up before we arrived. Our bodies grind against each other in anticipation. I lower her gently onto the plush rug, my hands roaming over her body as she arches her back.

I can feel her wetness against my fingers as I tease her clit, her moans growing louder with each passing moment. She grabs my cock, her hand gripping it tightly as she guides it toward her entrance. I thrust into her hard and fast, as requested, and she begins chanting my name, over and over again. I pound into her, each thrust pushing her closer to the edge.

She screams out in pleasure as she reaches her climax, her body convulsing around my cock. My own orgasm builds, my muscles tensing as I thrust deeper. "Swallow it," I command, pulling out and stroking my cock. Karina doesn't need to be told twice. She sits up, opening her mouth and taking me inside, swallowing every last drop as I find my release.

Another thing I learned about Karina: she loves the taste of my cum. She never turns down a chance to swallow, and I love that.

We lie there in the firelight, and I couldn't tell you how much time passes. When she stretches her arms overhead, her body glowing, I feel a spark of desire at the base of my spine.

"Turn around," I groan.

Karina smirks and lazily turns to face away from me on her hands and knees. I rise up and run my hands down her back, admiring the curve of her spine and the swell of her hips, my cock hardening again.

Her pussy glistens with wetness, begging to be fucked. I waste no time entering her, sliding in easily. Her warm walls gripping me feels indescribable, and I groan in pleasure as I begin to thrust.

"Mmmm. Fuck, you feel so good, baby," I moan, grabbing on to her hips and pulling her toward me as I lose myself in her. She moans and gasps, her body rocking forward and back.

I don't know how long we're in this position, but eventually Karina's arms give out, and she collapses onto her elbows, changing the angle, sucking me deeper inside. "Oh god, right there," she gasps.

I reach around to rub her clit as I continue to drive into her. Her inner walls flutter around me as she approaches another orgasm. "Come for me again, baby," I urge her as she cries out, her body giving out.

My orgasm builds once again, my muscles tensing as I wrap my form around hers. But I want more, *need* to taste her on my tongue, so I pull out of her with a low growl, reveling in her whimpers. I flip her on her back and spread her legs wide, tilting her hips up to give me better access.

I dive in, my tongue lapping at her clit. She lets out a gasp as I suckle on her sensitive clit, my hands gripping her thighs tightly. I can feel her body trembling beneath me, her hips bucking as she chases her release. I continue to tease her with my tongue, sliding it up and down her slit before dipping it inside her. Her walls clench around it, her body begging for more. I replace my tongue with a single finger, slowly pumping in and out of her as I move up to lick and suck at her clit.

She lets out a low moan, her body writhing. I increase my pace, my tongue and finger working together to take her to the brink.

"I'm close... I'm so fucking close, Vulcan," she pants.

With one final flick of my tongue, she lets out a scream as her orgasm crashes over her. I continue to lap at her pussy, savoring the salty sweetness of her release. I pull away, giving her a moment to catch her breath before I enter her.

"I fucking love you." I lean down to capture her lips, moving again, slowly at first, savoring the sensation of her. Everything about this woman reduces me to my baser instincts. Her moans fill my ears, spurring me on as I gradually pick up the pace.

Her hands drift down to where our bodies are joined. She rubs her clit, her breaths coming out in quick gasps. The sight of her pleasuring herself while I'm buried deep inside her is enough to make my control start to slip.

"Vulcan... fuck... *fuck me*."

I reach down to intercept her hand with mine, our fingers tangling together as we work to stimulate that sensitive bundle of nerves. Her inner walls quiver around me, and I know she's nearly there. With a few more purposeful thrusts, I watch her face contort with pleasure, and the tension at the base of my spine coils tighter.

And then she's there, crying out as another powerful orgasm rips through her body. The sight of her coming undone beneath me sends me over the edge and I release deep inside her, my moans mingling with hers. We collapse onto the rug, a tangle of limbs and labored breaths. After what seems like an eternity, Karina shifts under me and looks up with those eyes that seem to always be filled with care and tenderness. Just for me.

And there goes that sharp pang of guilt.

"I never thought I would be this happy." She yawns. "Ever."

"You should sleep," I tell her, smoothing a lock of hair away from her face. I fear I might fuck up this moment and tell her the truth if she doesn't.

"Mmm." She hums in agreement but doesn't close her eyes just yet. Instead, she captures my hand and kisses my knuckles. A tender act that nearly breaks me. "I love you."

Settling beside her on the rug, I pull a throw blanket over our exhausted bodies and wrap my arms around her. "I love you more."

Karina falls into a peaceful slumber, her breathing soft and steady against my chest. I gaze down at her, tracing the lines of her face with a gentle finger, longing to protect her from the harsh truths. But I know I will no longer be a protector in her eyes once I tell her, and that scares the shit out of me.

CHAPTER THIRTY-ONE

Karina

"All right, I'm up!" My voice squeaks with false bravado as I push off into the snow. But instead of gliding gracefully down the slope, my skis decide they're not on speaking terms and cross like two lovers in a spat. Jeez, this is fucking harder than I thought. I don't know why I told Vulcan I wanted to knock this off my getaway wish list. Horrible fucking idea. I'd rather be back in the cabin making babies than watching my life flash before my eyes.

"Karina, you look like a baby giraffe learning to walk." Vulcan laughs from behind me.

"Ha-ha, very funny." I try to regain some control. My arm flies out, and my hands grasp at the air as if it could save me from another inevitable tumble. *This is utter bullshit!* Skiing shouldn't be this hard. The other skiers made this look so effortless.

"Lean forward. Trust the mountain," Vulcan advises.

"Trust the mountain to *kill me*," I mumble. Yet, I take his advice, leaning forward. Now, for one glorious moment, I feel like I'm doing it right, the rush of cold air against my cheeks. Then gravity remembers its duty, and then I'm face-first in the snow again.

"Oof!" I protest, spitting out a mouthful of snow.

"Need help, snow angel?" he teases, offering me a gloved hand.

I pout but accept it, letting him pull me up. Despite my bruised ego and likely bruised everything else, I'm happy. We really needed this time away. I'm seeing another side of the man who has stolen my heart, and I pray he will never return it.

"Come on." He chuckles. "The mountain isn't done with you yet."

Somehow, between his teasing and my stubbornness, we managed to make it down the mountain—almost an hour later. Vulcan snowboards like he's part of the snow, while I look like Bambi learning to walk. But despite the tumbles, the cold, and the increasingly creative swear words I invent, I had the time of my life.

Snow clings to my boots as I kick them off by the door. The cabin is so warm when we enter that I thank the Heavens. I wasn't sure about the staff coming in and out while we were gone, but I'm thankful for it now. Vulcan is right behind me, hanging his damp coat and scarf.

The smell of soup and toasted bread wafts from the kitchen where lunch awaits. We settle at the wooden table, steaming bowls in front of us. I take my time eating before finally addressing the weight that's been pressing on me since we arrived. I know I will lose my appetite once I tell him about my mother. I swore I would never keep secrets from him, yet here I am.

I finally put the spoon down into the empty bowl.

"Vulcan," I say at the same time he says, "Karina."

We look at each other and laugh.

"Oh, you go first," I say.

"No, you go ahead."

I look at him. *Just rip the Band-Aid off.* "Well, okay... so my mother has been texting me the past few months, which I've been ignoring, but she reached out me a few days ago claiming it's urgent." My hands clasp tightly around my bowl. "She wants me to call her," I rush out.

"Do you want to talk to her?"

"I don't know," I confess, my heart thudding heavily. "Part of me does, but then... I remember everything. There's just so much hurt there. I'm the happiest I've been in a very long time. I finally have someone in my corner I trust and love. I don't want anything or anyone to mess up what we have. And I *know* my mother would find a way to. She probably wants more money."

"Karina," he says softly, reaching across the table to gently squeeze my hand. "If you want to talk to her, I'll be here. And if you don't, I'll still be here. Whatever you need. Your mother will never come between us. I won't let that happen."

"I'm scared," I admit. "Scared of opening old wounds, scared of what she might say, or worse, what she'll ask for." I've been doing so well with my finances for the past year. I have more money in my bank account than ever; Vulcan does not let me pay for *anything*. It used to bother me, but I've found it's much easier to just let it happen now.

"Hey," he says, standing up and moving around the table to me. His thumb brushes away a tear that must've escaped. "It's okay to be scared. But you're not alone. Not anymore."

"Thank God for that," I whisper, wrapping my arms around his waist. "For you."

"Always," he promises. "Come, let's go sit by the fire."

We relocate, getting comfortable on the rug, and he pulls me closer, tucking my head under his chin. He lets out a heavy sigh, and I can feel his heart beating rapidly against my ear. Something is going on with him, but I don't want to push it. I want him to tell me what it is on his own. We sit in silence for what feels like hours as I watch the fire burn behind the grate, but it's only been mere minutes. And yet, his heartbeat has not returned to normal.

He lets out another heavy sigh. "Karina, there's something I need to tell you," he begins, and I tense. He's never used a tone this serious with me before.

"What is it? You're scaring me." I sit up, my heart beating just as fast as his had been.

He lets out another deep sigh that seems to carry the weight of a thousand confessions. I'm honestly not sure if I want to hear what he has to say at this point. "Before we got married…" He trails off. Did he sleep with someone else? Did he get someone pregnant? *Come on, Vulcan, say something.* I'm trying to be patient and allow him to gather his thoughts, but I want to shake whatever it is out of him.

Fuck it.

"What happened before we got married? Did you sleep with someone else?"

"No," he quickly answers. "I would never cheat on you."

"So what is it? It can't be *that* bad, right?"

"Depends on how you look at it." He holds my gaze. "I made a deal with your mother."

"A… a *deal*?" My voice doesn't hide the tremor of confusion. I untangle myself from him, putting just enough space between us. "With my mother? Why?"

"Baby, promise you will hear me out first." Why do I *know* this isn't going to end well.

"What did you do? I'm not promising anything. Tell me. *Now.*"

"I met with your mother before the wedding and had her sign a contract to leave you alone," he says, each word setting off a bomb in my stomach. "Not for good, but long enough where you might find some space to heal."

My world stops spinning, and I almost lose the ability to breathe. "Now it all makes sense." I clutch at my throat, feeling it tighten with emotion, with anger. "How much did you give her?"

"Please don't get mad."

"We are way past that. How much money, Vulcan?!"

"Five hundred thousand."

No. Tell me this isn't happening. "Y-you gave my mother *half a million dollars?*"

"When you say it like that, it sounds bad."

"Because it fucking *is.*"

"I'm sorry."

As the words leave his lips, the room seems to tilt, disorienting me as if I have a bad case of vertigo. My breath catches in my throat, and it's like the cabin has been sucked out.

Half a million dollars. The number bounces around in my head. What the hell was he thinking? My heart thuds painfully as a wave of disbelief, anger, and utter betrayal crashes over me. It's all fucking suffocating. I'm trying to process what he just said, but the betrayal burns through every rational thought, leaving only searing anger in its wake. With each breath, my rage solidifies, a white-hot ball of disbelief gathering strength in my chest.

I can't believe this. After everything, he went behind my back to make a deal with the one person I've spent my life handling. I can barely stand this, can barely stay here, can barely *look* at him.

"How dare you?" I leap to my feet, yanking my hand from his. "You had no right!"

"Karina, listen—"

"No, *you* listen!" My voice rises an octave. "She's *my* mother, *my* family. It was never your place to interfere! I told you countless times I don't want—"

"Damn it, Karina! I did it to protect you!" His anger flares, matching mine. "I couldn't stand watching her tear you apart anymore. You're my fucking wife. *My* fucking wife, and I will *always* put you first. I will always protect you."

"You think money is *protection?* Do you think doing what you did behind my back put *me* first?" I spit the words at him. "That's your answer to everything, isn't it? Throw cash at a problem until it goes away? I should have known this was a mistake."

"A mistake? You think we're a mistake?" I can see the hurt in his eyes before he blinks it away. "Sometimes, money is the only language people understand. It's certainly the only language your *mother* understands." He stands so we're toe to toe, his frame towering over me. But I won't back down, not now.

"Then you don't understand *anything*." Tears blur my sight, but I blink them back fiercely. "This wasn't about money. This was about choices, *my* choices. And you took that away from me. I should get to choose when it comes to matters involving my mother. Not you."

"Just because she's your mother doesn't mean she has the right to make you suffer. What I don't understand is how you can be her punching bag and see nothing wrong with that." His fists clench at his sides, the muscles in his jaw twitching. "I've seen what she does to you. Dealing with her leaves you shattered. It's not fucking right, Karina. I will not allow it to go on."

"Maybe so, but it's *my* problem to deal with." My voice cracks, betraying the hurt beneath the fury. "Not yours to fix."

"Karina..." There's a plea in his voice now. "I was trying to be your... your partner in this."

"Partners don't make *unilateral decisions*!" I retort. "They *communicate*. They *trust* each other. Not whatever the fuck you did."

"Can't you see?" He pushes a hand through his hair. "I was trying to help!"

"Help I didn't ask for! What was and is going on with my mother has nothing to do with you. Nothing to fucking do with you! It's crazy because here you go again, imposing on my life. First you did it with that asset allocation and now this."

"I thought I was doing the right thing. All I wanted to do was help you, Karina."

I see the sincerity in his eyes, but I can't cave. I don't *want* to. He thinks a fucking sorry is going to fix what he did. *Bull fucking shit.*

"You think because you're older, more experienced, you know what's best. I didn't marry a man almost twice my age to be controlled."

"Whoa. Age has nothing to do with this," he counters sharply.

"Doesn't it though?" I challenge, stepping closer. "You think I can't handle my own life; that much is obvious."

"That's not what I'm saying, and you know it."

"Then maybe you should have thought about what you were really *saying* before you decided to be a *puppeteer* of my life." I push past him, needing space. "You may have signed a contract with her, but you broke an unwritten one with me."

"Karina—" he starts, but I hold up a hand to stop him.

"I gave you a chance, last year, to come clean. Told you I wasn't going to be so forgiving the next time."

He nods, but he seems to have run out of steam because he doesn't interrupt.

"And what did you say? *There's nothing else for you to sign.*" I drop my voice to mimic his. "*I'm not trying to trick you or hide anything,* you said. So, was this before or after you played sugar daddy with my mother?"

"That's not fair."

"You want to talk about fair?" My laugh is filled with sarcasm. "Fair would've been letting me handle my own shit. Fair would have been talking to me before you did whatever the fuck you did. You know what? Part of loving someone is trusting them to fight their own battles. Supporting them through it, not taking their power away. When we professed our love to one another before saying I do, you should have told me this. Now, it feels like your love for me is a lie." I ball up my fists and walk away.

"Where are you going?"

"To clear my head," I throw over my shoulder. "To remember who I am without you or a half-million-dollar contract defining me—us."

"You're not going out in this fucking weather. You want to clear your head, use the fucking bedroom." He gestures with a hand, his jaw clenched. "If you want the cabin to yourself, then *I* will leave."

I pause at the door, my hand on the knob, feeling the chill seeping in—Vulcan's right. I could barely walk back earlier without falling and needing his help. I pivot and storm down the hallway instead, forcefully pushing open the door and then slamming it shut behind me. I collapse onto the bed, burying my face in the pillow. A sob escapes me as I think about all that's happened in the span on one conversation.

I never wanted my mother to latch on to him as she does me. Vulcan giving her that much money only opened a door I don't think either of us can close now. Tears soak the pillow as I try to sort through the tangle of emotions wrestling inside of me. Anger, hurt, and betrayal, each vying for the top spot.

I hear the door creak open, sense him hesitating at the threshold. I sit up, wiping my face with the back of my hand.

"Come in."

He crosses the room in two long strides and sits beside me, the mattress dipping to accommodate his weight.

"I'm sorry," he begins, and his voice cracks slightly. "I thought I was helping. Protecting you in the only way I knew how."

"You think putting money between us is protection? How could you not trust me enough to handle my mother?"

"It's not about trust," he says firmly. "It's about seeing her hurt you over and over again. It makes me..." He pauses, searching for the right words. "It makes me *desperate*."

"But desperation shouldn't lead to decisions that drive us apart," I whisper.

He bobs his head, taking my hands in his. "I know that *now*. I just… I can't stand the thought of you being used by anyone."

"And you think money will stop my mother? Because it won't. I'm more concerned that you made it worse."

"It was a mistake," he admits. "Just… just don't leave me. I don't know what I'd do if you decided to call it quits. My love for you has never been a lie and will never be a lie. I love you so much, Karina."

"I'm not leaving you, Vulcan." I sigh, shaking my head. "I love you, but I can't ignore how this makes me feel. You might think I'm overreacting, but you lied to me. I get it; we were still getting to know each other, but you've crossed the line. You had a whole *year* to talk to me."

"I was scared of losing you."

"You would lose me by lying. I would rather you be honest and talk to me than lie. I've come such a long way from the woman I was before, and you had a huge part in that. I love how you love me, care for me, and protect me. But just stop trying to fix things for me when it comes to my mother."

"It's hard for me," he confesses. "It's what I do. I put out fires, real and metaphorical. I know I fucked up. But I did it because—"

"Because you're a control freak with a hero complex?"

"I prefer overprotective husband with good intentions, but sure, we can go with your version."

I hate that he makes me want to smile when I'm this angry. I hate even more that part of me understands why he did it, even if I want to strangle him for it. But I'm not ready to let him off the hook. Not by a long shot.

"Good intentions? The road to hell is paved with those, and you just bought a fucking highway." I huff. "I just want to be alone right now.

Can you give me some space?"

He clenches his jaw but reluctantly nods, releasing my hands and rising from the bed. He looks at me with those eyes so full of concern. "Of course. Take all the time you need, Karina." He gives me one last lingering gaze that tugs at my heartstrings before gently closing the door behind him.

I know he means well. His protective instincts make him who he is, just as my desire for independence and the ability to make my own choices are ingrained in me. I curl up tighter under the duvet, my mind racing. I battle with the urge to call Vulcan back, to feel his strong arms comfort me. But I know I need this time alone to process everything.

I replay our conversation in my head, dissecting every word and expression. The hurt in his eyes when he thought I would leave him. The tension in his shoulders when I asked him for space. I know this isn't easy for him either.

However, I have to stand my ground.

CHAPTER THIRTY-TWO

Vulcan

The wooden floorboards protest beneath the weight of my restless steps. I can't stand still. I fucked up. It's not supposed to be like this. I, Vulcan Montgomery, the man who prides himself on being able to handle explosive situations, is now scorched by the flame of regret. I'm supposed to protect, to serve, to save. Not inflict pain. Especially not to her.

I can hear her sobbing through the walls, and it's breaking my fucking heart.

I never should have given her mother money—at least not without speaking to her first. I should have never butted into her family business in the first place, but at the time, all I could think was *She's going to be my wife.* And isn't that what husbands are supposed to do? Make sure their wives are taken care of?

A shuddering breath escapes me as I turn from the window and lean back against the wall, sliding down until I'm seated, knees drawn up. I bury my face in my hands, trying to block out the sounds of her crying, but it's futile. It seeps into my very bones, a constant reminder of how I fucked it all up.

But she asked for space, and damn if I can't at least give her that, even if it feels like I'm tearing my own heart out by staying away.

I can handle pain.

I just can't handle her *in pain.*

The minutes seem to bleed into what feels like hours as I sit here. Every now and then, her whimpers and sniffles reach me. I need to do something, anything, to fix this. To make her pain go away.

I rise and make my way back to the bedroom. My hand hovers over the door handle, trembling slightly. The battle between respecting her wishes and my desperate need to make things right wages within me. With a deep, steady breath, I rap my knuckle against the wood. It's been hours since I left her looking so small on the bed. I need to know she's okay... if we are okay.

"Karina?" Silence answers back. I lean my forehead against the cool wood. "I know you asked for space, and I'm trying. God, I'm trying. But if you need me, even just to sit with you, I'm here."

Still no reply, but this time it feels different, like she's right there on the other side contemplating whether to let me in or shut me out completely. Minutes pass that feel like eternities until, finally, the sound of shuffling feet approaches from within. The door opens a crack. There she stands, eyes red and swollen from crying. Without thinking, I reach through to cup her cheek, but she flinches away. I let my hand drop, feeling the weight of her rejection. This is not good.

"I don't know if I can forgive you yet," she says, her voice hoarse. "But I'm willing to listen."

"That's all I ask. Can I come in?"

She hesitates before stepping back, and as I cross the threshold, I feel like I'm entering a different world. One where everything we are hangs by a thread. She sits on the edge of our bed. I cautiously sit next to her, as if one wrong move might scare her away.

Her next words come out slowly. "I'm hurt because you didn't trust me enough to discuss this with me. That you would go behind my back."

I move from the bed to kneel in front of her, making sure not to touch her. Not until she touches me first. "I know. And I'm so sorry,

Karina. It was stupid and insensitive of me. I thought I was protecting you. I thought..."

"You thought you were being my hero. My protector. I know."

"Yes."

Karina sighs deeply and leans forward, her elbows resting on her knees. Her eyes meet mine. "I don't need a hero. I need a husband. *My husband.* Someone who stands beside me, not in front of me. And I don't know..."

Her words hit me like a punch to the gut. I've been so caught up in trying to protect her that I've forgotten to respect her resilience. Would she want to draw the line between us? Go back to what we were when it was all legal documents and signatures in ink?

"Do you want to take a step back? Do you want to end things?"

Karina's eyes widen, a flicker of panic crossing her face. "No, *no.* That's not what I want at all."

Relief floods through me, but I hold my breath, waiting for her to continue. It seems like a but is going to follow.

She reaches out, her fingers lightly brushing my cheek. "I love you. That hasn't changed, Vulcan. I don't want to end what we have. I'm just asking for... transparency. For us to be equals."

I lean into her touch, craving her warmth after hours of distance. "I want that too. More than anything."

Karina slides off the bed, joining me on the floor. We're face-to-face now, our knees touching. "I'm going to meet with my mother when we get back to the city."

"Do you need me to go with you?" I ask, then mentally cringe. The last thing she probably wants is for me to go with her.

"I think you've done enough. I can handle it from here." She smiles, and I can already sense the shift between us. She probably doesn't know she's doing it, but she's pulling away from me. It's subtle, but it's there.

A cold realization washes over me. My actions have truly hurt her, perhaps more deeply than I had feared. I am always trying to be the fixer, yet here I am now, potentially breaking the most precious thing in my life.

"Karina," I start. "I'm going to go—"

"You don't have to leave." She places a hand on my forearm, stopping me from standing up.

"I'm going to go for a walk."

"In this weather?"

"I'm only going to walk around the cabin. If you need me, shout out the window. I won't be too far." I pat her hand as I stand up.

She nods, but it's clear from the furrow in her brow that she's overthinking.

"I just need to reflect. I don't want you to think that you are to blame for anything. My actions are what caused you pain, and I need to—"

"Vulcan, you don't need to be hard on yourself. I don't want you to do that. Will you always be this way when we get into an argument or have a disagreement?" she questions.

"I won't make the same mistake twice. You can believe me on that, if nothing else."

"You don't have to be perfect. Just be my husband." Her gaze softens. "When it comes to my family, I want us to discuss it openly. But in the end, *I* will have the final say."

I take a deep breath. "I know," I admit. "I'll be back soon."

"All right," she allows. "Just don't go too far. It's getting dark."

I've been walking for nearly an hour and still feel like shit. Will I ever do something behind Karina's back again? Hell fucking no. Just the thought of her leaving me for what I did has me fucked up. I shove my hands deep into my pockets; I should have brought my gloves. The crunch of snow beneath my boots is the only sound breaking the stillness of the forest. My breath comes out in puffs of white vapor, dissipating into the darkening sky.

I come to a small clearing and pause, looking up at the stars starting to peek through the twilight.

"I won't lose her," I mutter to myself. "I can't."

The thought of life without her is unbearable. She's my anchor, *my home*. Now I have to prove to her that our love is stronger than my mistakes. I know she told me not to be hard on myself, but I fear I'm going to lose her. She doesn't like confrontation, so what if she's just telling me what she thinks I want to hear, then turns around and asks for a divorce?

No, don't think that way. Have faith and trust your wife.

I head back to the cabin once I can no longer feel my fingers. As I approach, I see Karina standing by the window, looking for me. I push open the door, my boots leaving prints on the wooden floor. She turns, and our eyes lock in a silent conversation. "Cold enough out there?" she murmurs.

"Just a bit," I manage, my teeth chattering. I pull my layers off before moving closer to her, gauging her reaction with each step. Will she let me touch her?

She steps closer, her hand reaching out to touch my arm, instantly thawing my skin. "You're freezing."

She leads me toward the fireplace, and I go willingly.

As we sit, I let out a sigh, watching the flames dance and flicker. It eases the chill but not the unease that knots in my stomach.

Karina seems to read my mind, or perhaps she feels it too, because she shifts to face me. "Talk to me," she whispers. "Whatever conclusion you reached out there, I want to hear it."

"It's nothing."

"Are you going to shut me out now?"

"Never," I say. "I'm terrified of losing you, Karina. That's what I realized out there. The thought of you not being in my life... It's unthinkable."

"I'm not going anywhere," she says. "I've never doubted your intentions. But you lied to me, and you need to know that is something I don't want for our marriage. Lying is one thing I won't tolerate."

"I know I've messed up." I take her hands in mine. "But I want to fix it."

"You have done so much for me over the last year. Things you didn't have to do. I don't want you to change who you are," she continues. "In a way, you helped me see that my mother never truly cared for me. It's still just a bitter pill to swallow, especially since you've been holding this in for over a year now. But believe me when I tell you: I love you, Vulcan, and nothing can change that."

And it's everything I needed to hear. I just hope I can make her see I'm worthy.

CHAPTER THIRTY-THREE

Karina

I take a deep breath, the kind that's supposed to steady nerves but never really does. My hand hovers over the door handle for what feels like an eternity before I finally push it open and step out onto the curb. The familiar crunch of gravel underfoot is oddly comforting as I make my way to my mother's house, each step heavy with reluctance. I still can't believe she pocketed eight hundred thousand dollars off the back of my marriage to Vulcan.

I don't want to be here, but I need to know what the woman wants.

I raise my fist to knock, three short raps that sound too loud on the quiet street. The door swings open, and there she is.

"Karina," she says, surprised. Of course she would be; I didn't respond to her text last week—she likely assumed I wouldn't show.

"We need to talk."

She doesn't say anything but steps aside. As I walk through the threshold, I can see that the money she's taken hasn't gone to waste. Almost everything in her house looks brand-new and *expensive*. I follow my mother into the kitchen, where she's already setting out two cups on the table. Well, this is a surprise. She's never offered me anything during past visits.

"What brings you to the Bronx? Getting tired of Manhattan?" Her attempt to sound casual fails miserably.

"I know about the money. The half a million dollars from Vulcan, and the agreement that you would leave me alone for three years." I level her with a cold look. "And yet you only lasted *one*. So I'm here to find out why. *Why* didn't you tell me? How could you do this?"

She pauses, her hands frozen on the handle of the kettle. Then she turns, and her expression hardens. "You come into *my* house questioning me about something *your* friend had a hand in. Did you ask him?"

I hope Vulcan didn't tell her we were getting married. I'd prefer not to go down that road with her.

"Yes, I spoke with Vulcan. But you shouldn't have taken it in the first place. I'm your daughter. And you didn't think twice about not speaking to me for *three years*? You just took the money as if I'm nothing?"

She scoffs. "Here we go again with the dramatics, Karina. I reached out to you because I figured you wouldn't be associated with that man any longer. Little did I know he would run to you and snitch."

"Mother," I start. "Vulcan and I… we're more than friends now, but that's beside the point. What I'm upset about is that you choosing money over a relationship with me."

Her eyes widened slightly, and she clearly did not expect this twist. "*More than friends*? Karina, are you serious?" She leans against the counter, crossing her arms. "You think he cares about you? Why would you date someone old enough to be your father?"

"Now you're pushing it. Vulcan is not that much older than me." I can't believe she has me arguing about this. Classic Gabrielle Reyes behavior: distract and deflect. "He cares about me and yes, I'm serious about him." My hands clench into fists on my lap as I struggle to maintain composure. "I need you to explain to me what would possess you to manipulate us into getting almost a million dollars, collectively."

"You don't understand the pressures I was under. He *forced* me to sign, and that money—your father left me with nothing but debts, and

I—"

"Stop!" I cut her off, my voice sharp. I stand up, slamming my hand down on the table. "I know all about the debts. *I've* been helping with them since I started my residency, hell, even before that. They've long since been paid off. What I don't understand is how you could choose money over your flesh and blood."

It happens so quickly. One second she's standing by the kettle and the next she's in front of me, rearing her hand back and swinging it to connect with my face. *What just happened.* My mother has never put her hands on me—correction, she has never slapped me before ever. Growing up, did I get hit with a *chancla* or two? Yes, but slapping me... *never.*

"I did what I had to do!" Her face twists angrily. "Do you think you know everything because you went to college, and now you're saving lives? You don't know what it's like to be left with nothing!"

Tears well in my eyes, not just from the physical pain but from the raw, emotional wound that has just been sliced open between us. "You weren't left with nothing. Papá made sure you were taken care of. It was you who got a taste of a lifestyle you couldn't keep up with. A lifestyle whose bill *I* had to foot." I take a deep breath, needing to get us back on track, not letting her derail this conversation.

"Greedy? You must forget who the parent is here. Watch your mouth and tone, or you can leave my house now." She takes a step back. "I see that man has put something in your head to make you think it's okay to come in here and behave this way."

"This is about us, about you and me." I've always and will always respect my mother because isn't that what you are supposed to do? Honor thy mother and father. Right?

"Then why bring him into this?"

"You!" I exclaim. "*You* brought him into this, not me. Remember when you went behind my back and were handed half a million dollars? You signed on the dotted line, thinking he and I wouldn't be together in a year. Well, news flash. He is *my husband*, God damn it; he respects me and loves me more than you ever have."

My face snaps to the right with the force of her next blow. "Get out. Just get out of my house and never come back. You married that man without telling me? Are you even my daughter?"

I stare at her, shocked, as the tears spill over. For a moment, I'm that little girl again, desperate for her mother's love and approval.

No. I'm not her anymore. I'm a woman who's found strength in herself and in the love of a good man.

"I'm the daughter who's been trying to make you proud her whole life. The daughter who's been paying *your* bills and cleaning up *your* messes. The daughter who kept hoping that one day, just maybe, you'd love me as much as I love you. You'd love me like you love Miguel and Luis. So, Mother, when I walk out those doors now, you will never see me again. I swear to God you will never see or hear from me again."

Her face crumbles. "No, don't say that. You don't mean it."

I swipe my cheeks roughly. I refuse to cry any more tears in front of her. "I can't do this anymore. I can't keep sacrificing my happiness for someone who doesn't even appreciate me."

She clasps her hands together, pleading now. Of course she'd change her tune. Her meal ticket is about to leave her behind for good. "We can fix this—"

"No, we can't," I interrupt sharply. The finality in my voice feels like a door slamming shut. "Are you even sorry for what you did?" It's sad, how desperate I am to forgive her.

My mother has had enough with the play-acting, it would seem. "No, I'm not." She crosses her arms. "And you shouldn't want me to feel *sorry*."

"I sacrificed so much for you and the twins. There were times I'd barely have enough money left over for groceries. I can't and won't do this anymore. I have a great man, and my life has been amazing. I don't want you in my life ruining that for me. I finally know what it feels like to be loved—truly loved."

"It's just money, Karina. *Money.*" She speaks as if I'm the unreasonable one.

"It's not just money. It's about respect, trust... love. It's about putting me first. Your own daughter."

She looks at me as though she's seeing me clearly for the first time in years, and the look of pure hatred that flashes across her face chills me to the bone.

"I have to go," I say. That look alone tells me everything I need to know. I don't belong here.

"So ungrateful." Her mask of motherly concern slips away entirely. "I knew I should have told your father no when he took you in. I raised an ungrateful child who can't see past her own needs."

Every muscle in my body tightens. What is she implying...? "What did you just say?"

"You're old enough for the truth now." She smirks. "Let me put this to you very clearly: you are not my biological daughter. Your father *cheated* on me, and to add insult to injury... I was forced to raise you. Your own mother didn't want you. So, I got stuck with the burden, didn't I?" I watch her lips move, my whole world rattling with the force of an earthquake. But she's not done. "Don't give me any fucking crap about not giving me money. It's the least you can do. When I look at you, all I can see is *her*. The woman who couldn't keep her legs closed to a married man and got pregnant."

The room spins, and I grip the edge of the kitchen counter to steady myself. I struggle to breathe, my chest constricting as if I'm drowning on dry land. What is happening? What the *hell* is happening? She's lying; she has to be lying. There is no way this can be— I can't—

"How... how could you keep this from me?" I choke out.

She scoffs, rolling her eyes. "Oh, don't be so dramatic. You had a roof over your head, didn't you? Food on your plate? More than that ungrateful bitch of a mother would have given you."

Her words cut deep, each one a dagger to my heart. I want to scream, to cry, to lash out, but I'm frozen in place. My mind is reeling from the betrayal, not only from her but from my father. Because she has made me pay the price for his error for *decades*.

"All these years," I manage to say, "all the times I tried to make you proud, to earn your love..."

"Love?" She sneers. "You want to talk about love? Try raising another woman's child, a constant reminder of your husband's infidelity. *That's* love. A twisted sort of sacrifice."

I shake my head, tears streaming freely down my face. "No. That's not sacrifice. That's cruelty."

"You don't get to judge me, Karina. You've no idea what I've been through. It makes me fucking sick to my stomach looking at you."

"And you have no idea what you've put *me* through!" I retort. "I've spent my entire life feeling like I was never good enough, never worthy of your love—it all makes sense now. You used me." The realization stings. "You've just been *using* me."

"I did what I had to do to survive, and your brothers needed that money, too. You wouldn't understand."

I take a step back, my hands shaking. "You're right. I don't understand. I don't understand how you could look me in the eye every day and pretend to be my mother when you hated me so much."

She laughs a harsh, bitter sound that grates against my nerves. "Hate you? Oh, Karina, I don't hate you. I feel *nothing* for you."

"Then leave me alone," I snap. "You and your sons are dead to me. If you need money, consider finding a job. Why put yourself in a position to see the face of the woman you hate so much? You could have cut ties with me after I graduated from high school. But now you don't have to. I'll do it. You will never see me again."

"You're choosing him over your own family?"

"What *family*? You've never shown concern for my well-being. So, no, Gabriella, I'm not choosing Vulcan or anyone else over this fake family. I'm choosing myself," I correct her. "I'm choosing the life I deserve." I walk away without looking back, ignoring the urge to fix things like I always do. She is the only mother I've ever known, and to hear her spit such vitriol at me… It's like a knife twisting in my gut.

I storm out of the house, slamming the door behind me. I stumble down the steps, my vision blurred by tears. I fumble for my car keys, desperate to escape this place.

As I slide into the driver's seat, I count down from ten, over and over. I have to pull myself together.

I have to.

I have to.

My phone buzzes. It's Vulcan. For a moment, I consider ignoring it, but his name on the screen is like a lifeline.

"Karina? Are you okay? You've been gone for hours."

I take a trembling breath, trying to steady my voice. "I… I'm not okay, Vulcan. Can you… Can you come get me? I don't think I should be driving right now."

"Of course. I'll be there as fast as I can."

"Please hurry."

"I'm on my way, babe. Just stay put, all right? I'll be there soon."

I end the call and lean back in my seat, closing my eyes, years of pain and disappointment pouring out from my eyelids. I don't know how long I sit here, lost in my grief, before I hear the engine of a car.

Vulcan's out of the taxi before it's fully stopped, striding toward me with determination. Without a word, he opens my car door and pulls me into his arms. I collapse against his broad chest, inhaling his familiar scent.

"I've got you," he murmurs, his strong arms banding around me. "I've got you, Karina."

For the first time in my life, I truly believe those words.

We stand there for what feels like hours, Vulcan's steady heartbeat a comforting rhythm against my cheek. His hand strokes my hair, soothing away the tremors that rack my body, until my sobs subside into hiccups, then quiet sniffles.

"Do you want to talk about it?" he asks, still rubbing at my back.

I shake my head, not ready to relive the confrontation. Not yet. "Can we just go home?"

He nods, pressing a gentle kiss on my forehead. "Of course. Come on, I'll drive."

Vulcan helps me into the passenger seat, his tender touch bringing fresh tears to my eyes. As we pull away from my mother's house, I watch it shrink in the side mirror until it disappears. I will never step foot in there again.

The drive is quiet for the most part. Vulcan's horrible singing fills the car, and I don't think I can take another rendition of Bruno Mars's "Versace on the Floor," but it keeps me from crying. By the time we reach home, the adrenaline has faded, leaving me bone-weary.

Vulcan scoops me up and carries me inside as if I weigh nothing. He sets me on our bed, then kneels to remove my shoes.

"Vulcan." I reach for him. "I'm sorry I ruined our evening." I know he wanted to take me out for dinner tonight, but I'm nowhere near up for it.

He looks up, his eyes filled with understanding and love. "You didn't ruin a thing, love. I'm just glad you called me."

As he crawls into bed beside me, gathering me close, I allow myself to feel safe in the arms of the man I love.

CHAPTER THIRTY-FOUR

Vulcan

I remain quiet while Karina recounts what happened. I hold her close, feeling her body tremble against mine as she relays her mother's harsh words. My jaw clenches, my anger simmering beneath the surface, but I force it down. Right now, Karina needs my strength, not my rage.

"And for her to say she doesn't love or hate me... that she feels nothing for me? It was horrible." She hiccups. "I have my birth mother's eyes, and she hates it. She loathes that she had to raise the child of her husband's mistress."

I tighten my arms around her, wishing I could shield her from the pain. "Karina, listen to me. That woman may have raised you, but she doesn't define you. You are so much more than her cruel words."

I cup her face in my hands, brushing away the tears with my thumbs. Her eyes, those beautiful eyes that her mother claims to hate, are pools of vulnerability and hurt. I want to take away every ounce of pain reflected there.

"You are kind," I continue, kissing her forehead softly. "You are brilliant." Another kiss on her cheek. "You save lives every day." My lips brush against her other cheek. "And you are so, so loved."

I capture her lips with mine, pouring all the love and adoration I feel for her into that kiss. When we part, I rest my forehead against hers, our breaths mingling.

"Your real family isn't defined by blood, Karina. It's defined by love.

You're my family, and I'm yours. Always."

I feel her body relax against mine, the tension slowly ebbing away. Her fingers curl into my shirt, holding on as if I'm her lifeline. I'll be exactly that for her for as long as she needs me.

"Thank you," she whispers. "I don't know what I'd do without you, Vulcan."

I pull her tighter, if that's even possible. "You'll never have to find out, love. I'm not going anywhere."

As we lie there, tangled in each other's arms, I silently vow to spend the rest of my life showing Karina just how worthy of love she is. Her mother may have rejected her, but I'll make damn sure she never feels unwanted again.

After a few moments of silence, she speaks. "I wonder if she's alive... my biological mother."

"Do you want to find out?"

Karina's body tenses against mine, her fingers tightening in my shirt. I can feel her heartbeat quicken, a physical manifestation of the turmoil my question has stirred within her.

"I... I don't know," she says. "Part of me wants to know *why* she gave me up. But another part..."

She trails off, burying her face in my chest as I run my fingers through her hair.

"Another part is terrified," I finish for her, feeling her nod against me. "Don't force yourself to do something you don't want to do. Just take it one day at a time."

She tilts her head to look up at me, staring at me for a minute, then lets out a deep breath. I wait, giving her the time she needs to sort through her emotions.

"I think..." she starts, her voice raspy. "I think I should leave it alone. It's been twenty-eight years now, and she hasn't attempted to find me."

"I understand." I kiss her temple, then the tip of her nose. "You don't owe her anything. Your family is right here."

"Can you do me a favor?"

"Anything," I tell her.

"Can you fuck me? Can you just fuck all my worries away?"

I want to tell her sex isn't the answer. But she's hurting, and I'm not about to deny her a release. "I don't know if I can fuck your worries away for good, but I do my best to make you forget about everything outside of these four walls for a few hours." My lips melt against hers.

The kiss is hungry, desperate, a physical manifestation of our need to connect, to forget, to feel. Something I didn't think we would be able to do after our weekend getaway fiasco. Karina hasn't let me satisfy her in *days*, and it's killed me.

Her fingers tangle in my hair, pulling me closer. I can taste the salt of her tears on her lips, and it only fuels my desire to make her forget. I undress her slowly, eyes mapping each inch of skin as it's revealed.

"Vulcan," she breathes, her voice thick with need. "Please..."

I trail kisses down her neck and across her collarbone, taking my time to worship her body. Her breaths come in short bursts, her fingers digging into my shoulders as I suck on her nipples.

"I've got you."

I slide my hand between her thighs, finding her wet and ready. I stroke her slowly, building her pleasure as I continue to kiss and nip at her skin.

"More," she pleads. "I need you inside me."

She whimpers as I remove my hand to undress myself, and then I position myself between her legs, the tip of my dick teasing her. Our eyes lock as I push into her, coaxing a guttural moan from her.

"Faster," she demands, and I comply, increasing my pace.

And I realize, as I draw an orgasm out of her, and the another, that I'd move mountains if it meant keeping the blissed-out look on her face for even a moment.

I leave Karina sleeping in the bed and make my way to the kitchen. I need a moment to clear my head. I know I told her I wouldn't overstep my boundaries, but part of me wants to make this right. Make her feel better. But I'm nothing if not a fast learner, and she explicitly told me not to butt in. I'll just have to keep showering her with love and affection, letting her know I'm here for her no matter what.

I pour myself a glass of water and lean against the kitchen counter, lost in thought. I'm refilling it to bring back into the room with me when I hear the soft padding of feet behind me. I turn to see Karina standing in the doorway, drowning in one of my shirts. Her hair is tousled, and her eyes are still heavy-lidded. She looks absolutely beautiful.

"Everything okay?"

I nod, setting my glass down. "Did I wake you?"

She shakes her head and moves toward me. "I rolled over and you weren't there. I got worried."

I open my arms and she steps into them, nestling against my chest. I breathe in the scent of her hair, feeling my heart swell with love for this woman.

"I'm sorry. I just needed a moment to think."

She pulls back slightly. "About what?"

I hesitate, not wanting to bring up her troubles again when she seemed so peaceful earlier. But I also don't want to lie to her.

"About you," I admit. "About how I can be there for you without overstepping."

She sighs, resting her forehead against my chest. "You being here is enough. You don't have to fix everything."

I run my hand down her back, feeling the warmth of her skin through the thin fabric of my shirt. "I know. I just... I hate seeing you hurting."

Karina lifts her head, cupping my face in her hands. "I know you do. And I love you for it. But right now, what I need most is just this. You, holding me, loving me."

I lean down and capture her lips in a tender kiss. "That, I can definitely do."

I sweep her up into my arms, cradling her against my chest. She lets out a surprised giggle, wrapping her arms around my neck. "What are you doing?"

"Taking you back," I reply, my voice low and husky. "Where I can hold you properly."

In the comfort of the bed we've shared for over a year, I turn to my side and face my wife. "I love you," I whisper. "More than I ever thought possible."

Karina scooches over onto my pillow, her lips brushing against my jaw. "Show me," she breathes, her hands already roaming across my chest.

I don't need to be told twice. As we lose ourselves in each other, I silently vow to be her safe harbor. Whatever challenges we face, we'll face them together.

CHAPTER THIRTY-FIVE

Vulcan

It's been three weeks since the "she's not my mother" bombshell and a month since the cabin trip, and Karina has continued to let me in and drop her guard around me. We're stronger than ever, yet I hear her muffled cries when she thinks I'm asleep.

She does it *almost* every night. Just like clockwork, at three a.m., she slips out of the room and walks to the kitchen. I follow her, usually wait in the hallway and listen, but lately, I've been getting bolder and watching the woman I love break apart from the shadows.

Could I go to her? Yes.

Could I comfort her? Yes.

But she's chosen to soothe herself away from me, and I know it's because she wants to heal. I can only continue to pour all my love into her, and hopefully, these late-night crying sessions will come to an end.

"Knock, knock." I'm pulled from my thoughts and look up from the pile of paper on my desk to see Val walking into my office with a box of pizza. "You're a sight for sore eyes, big brother. But I come bearing gifts."

"You're a lifesaver," I say, pushing the folder aside and making room for the much more appealing box of cheesy goodness.

Val sets it down and plops into the chair across from me. She smiles at me, and just like that I know she wants something. "What's the catch? You don't usually grace my office with your presence just to feed me."

"Can't I visit my brother?" She leans back, shrugging nonchalantly.

"Val," I warn.

Her grin widens as she opens the box, and my stomach growls. "I just thought you'd need something to eat."

"Why are you *really* here?" I ask, taking a slice of pizza.

She takes a bite of her slice, chewing slowly before she answers. "Well, since you asked. You know my birthday is coming up soon, and I want to throw a party in your penthouse. Since Karina is leaving in a week, I thought—"

"Excuse me? Karina's leaving? *Where?*" I pause mid-bite, my heart skipping a beat.

I'm not an idiot to think I didn't play a part in this. I overstepped, and the woman I love with every fiber of my being is paying for it.

She's leaving me.

She's been planning to leave me and hasn't said a fucking word.

Val's eyes widen slightly, realizing she's just dropped a bomb on me. "Oh. I thought you knew..." She fumbles with the crust of her pizza.

"No, Val, I *didn't* know."

She sighs. "I think it's for a job opportunity, somewhere in Boston, for about three months? She, um, mentioned it in passing when we bumped into each other at the coffee shop this morning. I didn't get all the details; I assumed she'd told you."

Boston?

"I need to talk to her," I say abruptly, standing up so fast my chair screeches against the hardwood floor.

"Hey, take it easy. I'm sure there's a good explanation. Maybe it's not definite yet. But, well, can you give me a yes or no about my party?"

I'm already grabbing my coat and heading for the door. I've never visited her at the hospital, preferring to maintain the boundary between work and personal, but I don't care.

"Wait, Vully!" Val calls out. "You didn't let me finish."

"There's more?" I stop in my tracks. What the fuck?

"My party!" Val swallows a bite of her pizza.

"Yes, fine," I snap, my mind already racing ahead to what I need to say to my wife.

Val nods, seeming satisfied. "Good. And second, before you storm the hospital like a man possessed, she also mentioned she turned it down." Val smiles and I want to choke the living shit out of her. She waits a beat, clearly enjoying my sudden change of expression.

"What the hell, Val? You couldn't lead with that?" Relief floods through me so fast it makes me dizzy.

"And miss that look on your face? Not a chance." She winks, taking another bite of pizza. "Calm down and sit. Your food's getting cold."

I collapse back into my chair, wiping a hand down my face. "Jesus Christ. Don't play with me when it comes to my wife." I glare at her, but can't maintain any real irritation. "Why did she turn it down?"

"That's for her to tell you, not me." Val points her slice at me like a weapon. "Also, she didn't tell me why."

Maybe I should make an impromptu visit to her job anyway. I close the box of pizza and stand back up. "Thank you for lunch."

"Hey, where are you going with the pizza I paid for?" Val protests, but her eyes are twinkling with amusement.

"Consider it payment for nearly giving me a heart attack." I tuck the box under my arm.

"Shithead," she calls after me.

The drive to the hospital feels both too long and too short. I'm rehearsing what to say to Karina, searching for the right words—ones that won't come across accusatory or controlling. I don't want to fight.

I just want to understand why she wouldn't tell me about something so important.

I park in the visitors' lot, grab the pizza box, and head inside. The hospital's antiseptic smell hits me as soon as the automatic doors slide open.

"I'm looking for Dr. Montgomery," I tell the elderly volunteer manning the desk.

She smiles up at me. "Are you family?"

"I'm her husband." The words still feel new on my tongue, but I like the way they sound.

Her eyebrows shoot up, and I can practically see her reassessing me. "Well, isn't that nice. Take the elevator to the basement level and follow the signs to the ER."

Downstairs, the ER is exactly what I'd expect: controlled chaos. Nurses and doctors move with purpose, patients wait with varying degrees of distress, and through it all, there's a strange sense of order. I scan the area for Karina's familiar form.

A nurse notices me and approaches. "Can I help you, sir?"

"I'm looking for Dr. Montgomery."

The nurse, whose badge reads *Tanya*, gives me a curious once-over. "She's with a patient right now. You can wait in that area." She points to a small alcove with a few chairs. "I'll let her know you're here."

I nod my thanks and settle in to wait, pizza box balanced on my knees. Ten minutes later, I spot her—hair pulled back in a practical ponytail, stethoscope around her neck, focused expression on her face as she reviews something on a tablet. She hasn't seen me yet, and I take a moment to just watch her. Even in scrubs, she's the most striking woman I've ever seen.

Tanya says something to her, pointing in my direction, and Karina's head snaps up. Our eyes lock, and I see surprise and confusion flash across her face. I stand as she approaches.

"Vulcan, what are you doing here?"

I hold up my offering. "Thought we could have lunch."

"That's—thank you. I just need to finish up with a patient."

"No rush. I'll be here."

"I'll have Tanya show you to my office." She smiles, gesturing to Tanya. "Do you mind?"

Tanya nods and leads me through a maze of hallways until we reach a small office with Karina's name on the door. There are stacks of medical journals on a small table, a collection of framed certificates on the wall, and a small potted plant that's somehow surviving despite what I assume is irregular care.

"She shouldn't be too long," she says with a smile. "It's nice to finally meet you. She talks about you *a lot*."

"Good things, I hope."

"Very good things." Tanya's expression softens. "She's been working herself to the bone lately. This is a nice surprise. Lunch with her husband."

After she leaves, I set the pizza on the desk and take a seat in Karina's chair. The office feels like her; practical but with touches of warmth, like the photo frame tucked between reference books. I pick it up, surprised to see it's a picture of us from our wedding. She's laughing, head thrown back, while I'm looking at her with an expression that reveals everything I felt even then.

The door opens and Karina slips in, closing it behind her. She leans against it for a moment, studying me.

"Sorry to ambush you at work," I say, standing.

"No, it's… nice." She stops near the hand sanitizer wall dispenser. I watch her rub her hands together, the chemical scent reaching me. There's tension in her shoulders that wasn't there this morning. She glances at the pizza box. "I have about thirty minutes before I have to go over the lab results with my next patient," she says, opening the box. "Did you already eat two slices?"

"Actually, Val stopped by the station." I take my already bitten slice, buying myself time.

"Hmm." She sits on the edge of her desk, close enough that our knees almost touch. "Lunch with Val."

"Yeah, she mentioned running into you." I watch her carefully, trying to gauge her reaction. "She also mentioned something about Boston?"

Karina freezes, and it's confirmation that Val wasn't just spreading gossip. She stares at me, her expression shifting from surprise to something that looks remarkably like guilt.

"Why didn't you say anything?"

She sighs, running a palm over the end of her ponytail. "I was going to tell you. I just... I needed to think it through first."

"Think what through, exactly? Whether you want to move to a different state without discussing it with me?"

"It's not like that." She runs her hands up and down her thighs. "Massachusetts General has offered me a position on their trauma team. It's the kind of opportunity that doesn't come around twice."

"But you turned it down. Why? Did you think I would stop you from furthering your career? You know I will always support what you do."

"Are you mad that I didn't tell you, or are you mad that I'm not going?" Her eyebrows knit.

"Both," I say, then shake my head. "Neither. Hell, I don't know. I just want to understand what's going on with you. You've been so distant..."

She looks down, fidgeting with her watch. "It's complicated,

Vulcan."

"Then uncomplicate it for me." I move closer, placing my hand on the desk next to her. Not touching her, but close enough that she could reach for me if she wanted to. "Talk to me, Karina. Please."

Her eyes meet mine. "After everything with my mother, I've been questioning a lot of things. Who am I? What do *I* want?"

"And what do you want?"

"I don't know." She runs her hand through her hair again, tugging slightly at the roots in frustration. "The Boston job is incredible. The team there is doing groundbreaking work in trauma care. Part of me wanted to jump at it."

"Then why didn't you?"

She takes a deep breath. "Because it would mean leaving you. And I'm not ready to make that choice."

"Who says you have to choose?" I ask finally. "We could make it work. I could come with you, or we could do long-distance for a while."

"Just like that? You'd uproot your whole life?"

"For you? Yes. You *are* my whole life." The words come without hesitation.

"That's not the only reason I didn't take it."

What more could it be?

She stands up and walks to her closet. I watch as she rummages through her bag. She turns around, hiding whatever it is behind her back. She lets out a deep breath and places four pregnancy tests on the desk between us.

I stare at the plastic sticks, the pink plus signs unmistakable on all four. The world seems to stop spinning for a moment as realization crashes over me.

"You're pregnant," I whisper.

Karina nods, tears welling in her eyes. "I found out three days ago.

I've been trying to figure out how to tell you."

I reach for one of the tests, holding it carefully between my fingers as if it might disappear. A child. Our child. The thought fills me with so much joy.

She sinks into her chair. "I couldn't imagine starting a pregnancy in a new city, at a demanding new job, without my support system." Her voice drops lower. "Without you."

"Karina..." I move to kneel in front of her, taking her hands in mine. They're trembling slightly. "We're having a baby. How far along are you?"

"That, I don't know. Maybe two or three weeks. You made it your mission to knock me up during our cabin getaway." She quirks a brow, and I almost pass out from relief. She's teasing me; she has to be okay. *We're* okay.

A grin spreads across my face as memories of that weekend flood back. "I don't recall hearing any complaints at the time."

Karina blushes. "None whatsoever."

I cup her face in my hands, searching her eyes. "How do you feel about it? Really feel?"

She takes a deep breath. "Terrified. Excited. Overwhelmed." Her hand moves instinctively to her still-flat stomach. "I never thought I'd be here, Vulcan. After everything with my mother, I wasn't sure I'd ever want this. But with you..." Her voice breaks. "With you, I want everything."

I stand, pulling her into my arms, and breathe her in. "We're going to be parents," I whisper, the reality of it sinking deeper with each passing second.

"Are you happy?" she asks, vulnerability lacing her words. "I know we talked about it briefly, but with—"

"Happy doesn't begin to cover it." I lean back to look at her. "You've given me the greatest gift imaginable. A family of our own. Now, you need to eat." I peck her forehead. "You have only twenty minutes. Unless you want something else?" I pull my phone out and tap the delivery app. "What are you in the mood for? Sandwich from Moretti's? That Thai place you like? Name it and it's yours."

She laughs, wrapping her arms around my waist. "The cravings haven't kicked in yet."

"Doesn't matter. Whatever my pregnant wife wants, she gets," I say, and I can't stop smiling.

"You know, since day one, it's always been whatever I want, I get."

"You're not wrong." I kiss her forehead. "And I don't plan on stopping anytime soon."

She melts into me, her body relaxing against mine. "I need to call Dr. Patel. Set up a proper appointment."

"I'll clear my schedule." My hand rests over hers on her stomach. There's nothing to feel yet, but knowing our child is growing there makes my heart race.

"You don't have to—"

"I'm going to every appointment, Karina. Every single one. I want to hear the heartbeat, see the ultrasounds, hold your hand through all of it."

Her eyes glisten with unshed tears. "Val's going to lose her mind when she finds out she's going to be an aunt."

"God, she'll probably start shopping for baby workout outfits right away." I run a hand down the back of my head, chuckling. "Now, enough chitchat, you need to eat."

CHAPTER THIRTY-SIX

Karina

It's been a week since I told Vulcan I'm pregnant—a week of him spoiling me more than before. Today, the pampering has been replaced by pure chaos. The blaring of sirens cuts through our living room as Vulcan's phone rings for the third time in an hour. His face darkens as he listens, those strong shoulders tensing beneath his FDNY T-shirt.

"I have to go," he says, already grabbing his keys. "Five-alarm fire at the Westside warehouse district. Multiple buildings involved."

My heart slams against my ribs. "But you're off duty today."

"All hands on deck." He crosses the room in two strides, cupping my face between his palms, and kisses me. "I'll be safe, and I'll call when I can."

Before I can argue, he's gone, the door slamming behind him.

I pace our apartment and practice some meditative breathing I read about in a pregnancy book. The local news broadcast is showing massive plumes of black smoke billowing against the city skyline. Reporters use words like "catastrophic" and "unprecedented." And all the while, my phone buzzes with concerned texts from friends.

Three hours pass. Four. The baby and I need food, so I force myself to make a sandwich, though my stomach churns with anxiety.

When my phone finally rings, it's not Vulcan but my mother—correction, my stepmother. She's been calling me from unknown numbers since I blocked her.

I have to remind myself not to dwell on her relentless attempts to drag me back into her manipulative orbit. Now that I know the truth, it's clear she only wants me back in her life to use me. For my money. My husband's money. I turn my phone over, pressing it face down against the sofa. I don't have the mental capacity to deal with her.

My phone rings again and I pick it up, thinking it's Vulcan, but it's my aunt Maria. She has never called me before. I hope nothing happened to Nana Gia. That could be the only reason she would call. "Hello, Auntie Maria? Is everything okay? Is Nana okay?"

"I see you're answering everyone but me and your brothers," Gabriella hisses.

"I told you already: I'm through with you." I let out a sigh of annoyance.

"Is that any way to speak to your mother?"

"You are *not* my mother."

The line goes silent for a moment.

"Always so dramatic. But we both know you'll come around. Family is family, after all."

I tighten my grip on the phone, nails digging into the plastic casing. "Not this time, *Gabriella*. You said all you had to say that day. There is nothing else for us to talk about."

"There is plenty for us to talk about. Let's not forget I raised you."

"And I paid you back tenfold. Even though I wouldn't call what you did raising me. Yes, my father kept a roof over my head and food in my stomach. You, on the other hand, didn't give two shits about me once the twins were born."

"Yes, well, that may be. But we're still a family. We need to stick together."

"No, you need *me* to stick around because I'm your golden ticket," I retort. "I'm a respected doctor now. *I'm a wife.* I'm not that little girl who couldn't see through your facade. I don't need you anymore. Hell, I don't think I ever needed you once Pa passed away. I wanted a mother's love, but news flash, I never got that from you. And I'm not looking for it now."

"You always did have your father's stubborn streak," she says. "But mark my words, Karina, one day you'll see that you need me."

"I won't—"

"And you've blocked your brothers' numbers. Do you think it's fair to them that you—"

"As long as you have your claws in them, I don't want anything to do with them either. I'm protecting my peace, Gabriella. And you can let Aunt Maria know her number will be added to the block list thanks to you—"

"I should have gotten rid of you when I had the chance. You are so fucking ungrateful," she snaps.

"This conversation is over. Don't ever reach out to me again. Consider me as good as dead." I try not to raise my voice, but she is getting under my skin. I still want to respect her because she is the only mother I know, even if she doesn't see me as her daughter.

"You'll regret this."

"But if you call me again, I will make sure Vulcan sues you for breach of contract." She probably didn't know I knew about that clause.

"You wouldn't dare."

"Contact me again, and you'll leave me no choice. Have a good life, Gabriella."

The line goes dead, and my hands shake slightly from the adrenaline rush. The next time I pick up my phone, it's Vulcan.

"Hey, babe," Vulcan greets. "Everything's fine over here, the fire's under control. Are you okay? You sound strange."

"Just dealing with some stuff." I try to steady my voice, exhaling slowly. His voice shouldn't be able to reach me the way a hug can, but it does.

"Do you want to talk about it?" he asks. "I heard from my wife that I'm a great listener."

"Really? Then in that case. Yes, I think I do." I pause, needing to know he's really okay. "Are you hurt? The news said it was pretty bad. It looked bad."

"Just a few scrapes and bruises. Nothing serious," he assures me. "The building collapse wasn't as bad as it looked from the outside. We got everyone out."

The tension in my body releases all at once, leaving me weak with relief. "Thank God." I clutch my phone like it's a lifeline.

"Now, what's going on with you?" he presses gently.

I slump onto the couch, tucking my feet beneath me, and close my eyes. "We can talk when you get home."

"Oh, this must be serious. Should I stop and get you a gallon of chocolate milk?" Vulcan's teasing draws a reluctant smile from me.

"Make it two." I laugh, feeling some of the heaviness lift from my chest.

"Sounds like a plan."

Vulcan makes it home with two gallons of chocolate milk, smelling like a barbecue. I rise from the couch to meet him at the door, taking the grocery bag from his hands. There's a bandage on his forearm that makes my heart clench.

"You said just scrapes," I say, gesturing to it.

"This? It's nothing." He shrugs, following me into the kitchen. "So, what's this 'stuff' you're dealing with?"

"Shower first, and then we can talk." I put the milk into the fridge.

"How about you tell me while I take a shower?"

"Vulcan, we—"

"Come on."

I sigh, knowing he won't let this go. "Fine," I concede, following him to the bathroom.

Vulcan strips off his shirt, wincing slightly as the fabric brushes against a purple bruise blooming across his ribs.

I perch on the closed toilet lid, watching steam fill the bathroom. "Gabriella called me."

"Okay, go on." He steps into the shower, leaving the door open. I watch as water cascades down the drain, turning slightly gray from the soot washing off his body.

"She still thinks I'm being dramatic. As if *me* feeling this way is some kind of phase," I say, watching him suds up his body.

Vulcan turns to face me, soap suds sliding down his chest. I'm fighting with myself to not let my eyes drift down to his penis. "I can sue her if you want." He tilts his head to the side.

I don't answer, suddenly too distracted. Despite my best efforts, my eyes drift downward, taking in the full sight of him. Water trails down the defined muscles of his abdomen, following the dark line of hair that leads to his—

"You keep looking at me like that, you're going to get dragged in here."

"I'm allowed to look. Wife's privileges," I counter, forcing my gaze back to his face.

"You're allowed to do a lot more than look." He smirks, then his expression turns serious again. "So, what exactly do you want done. All she's going to do is add on stress you don't need."

"I know." I sigh, tipping my head back to look at the ceiling. "I just... I don't know."

"Strip and join me, for starters. Let me help you get some clarification."

I hesitate, then stand and step out of my clothes. I sidle up next to him in the shower, my skin prickling at the sudden warmth. Vulcan's eyes darken as he takes me in, his hands instantly finding my waist.

"There's my girl," he says, pulling me closer. Water streams between us as his lips find mine. I press against him, feeling the solid wall of his chest against my breasts, his growing arousal against my stomach.

"I thought you were going to give me clarification," I whisper against his mouth.

"I am." His hands slide down to cup my ass. "Clarity comes in many forms."

When he kisses me again, I forget about Gabriella, about her demands and manipulation. I forget about everything except the feel of Vulcan's hands on my skin, the taste of him on my tongue. His fingers trace the curve of my spine, making me shiver despite the hot water cascading over us.

"I love you and will protect you." His palm spreads protectively over my stomach. "Both of you."

I meet his gaze. "I just want her to leave us alone."

Vulcan nods, his forehead resting against mine. "Then that's what we'll do. I'll have Minji send her a formal cease and desist. If she contacts you again with anything other than an apology, we escalate. Just trust me with this, okay? I will make sure Gabriella will never bother you again unless you want her to."

"I trust you." And I do. I trust him with my life. "I don't want anything to do with her. I want to only focus on us and our family."

"And what you want, I will always make happen."

He spins me around, my back slamming into his chest, his hard cock pressing against the curve of my ass. I can feel every inch of him and I'm already so fucking wet. His hands slide down to the backs of my thighs, hoisting me up. My legs spread wide, and I drop my head back on his shoulder.

"Why do you always want to try the wildest positions when you're in pain?"

"Because you are the medicine I need to make it all go away. And I won't drop you."

He slides his cock inside me, stretching me. I gasp, my body clenching around him as he fills me completely.

"Fuck," he groans against my ear. "You feel so good."

Water streams down our bodies as he holds me suspended, my back against his chest.

"You're mine," he rasps into my ear, his breath hot and ragged.

He begins to move, using his powerful arms to lift me up and down on his dick. The sensation is overwhelming. The fullness, the angle, the water beating down on my hardened, sensitive nipples, and his hot breath against my neck. My body tightens around him as he fucks me harder, and he knows exactly how to get me to the brink and keep me there. My full breasts bounce with the force of his movements, and I reach a hand between my legs to circle my clit, desperate to find release.

I'm gasping for air, but it's more than that—I'm gasping for *him*. "That's it," Vulcan moans, watching me over my shoulder. "I love when you touch yourself while I fuck you." His voice alone could make me come. It's a deep, rough rumble that vibrates through my back, sending goose bumps everywhere.

My nerves are on fire, every touch electric. I work my fingers faster, matching his rhythm, feeling the buildup gather in a tight, desperate coil in my belly. My breath comes in short, ragged bursts. I can hear myself moaning louder with each thrust. Vulcan's grip on my thighs tightens, and I lose myself in the sensation. The heat, the water, his dick filling me over and over.

"My wife is strong, intelligent, so fucking sexy," he growls, his pace becoming erratic as my inner walls begin to pulse around him. "You are a force of nature. You are stronger than anyone I know. You are going to make a phenomenal mother, just like you are a phenomenal wife. Now repeat. Repeat every last word."

"I am..." I gasp as he hits a spot so deep inside me that stars explode behind my eyelids. "Strong... intelligent... sexy..." Fuck. "I am a force of nature," I continue, my voice growing stronger even as my body trembles on the edge of release. "Stronger than anyone... I'll be a phenomenal mother... phenomenal wife..."

The last word barely leaves my lips before I'm coming undone, my body convulsing around him in waves so powerful I cry out. Vulcan groans, his forehead pressing against my shoulder as he follows me over the edge, pulsing inside me as the water continues to cascade over us both.

"And don't you forget it. Don't ever forget the woman you are. When others try to make you feel less than, you remember those words and you remember that I see you. I see all of you." He finally puts me down and I quickly turn around in his arms.

I reach up to touch his face, my thumb tracing the strong line of his jaw. Water streams down his features, making him look wild and primordial, like some ancient god of fire who's chosen to take human form. His eyes are so intense, so focused on me, that I almost have to look away. Almost.

"I love you," I whisper. "I love you so fucking much."

"I love you, too," he murmurs against my hair.

We stay like that for a while, just holding each other under the shower spray until the water begins to cool. With reluctance, Vulcan reaches behind me to turn off the faucet.

"Now let me remind you again just how amazing you are." He grabs a towel from the rack and wraps it around me before taking one for himself, then he takes my hand and guides me to our bed.

God, I really do believe everyone needs a Vulcan.

CHAPTER THIRTY-SEVEN

Vulcan

Three Months Later

"I can't believe you're really retiring." Harry sighs.

I lean back in my chair, watching my best friend absorb the news I just shared. We're sitting in Riley's, the same dive bar where we've drowned our sorrows and celebrated victories for years. The irony isn't lost on me that I'm announcing the end of my career in the same spot Harry once talked me out of quitting the fire academy.

"It's time," I say, taking a swig of my beer. "Twenty years is a good run."

"But you're only forty. You could easily do another ten, maybe fifteen years." Harry shakes his head. "What's this really about? The baby?"

"Partly." Becoming a father has shifted my priorities. "But it's more than that. I want to be present, Harry. Not wondering if today's the day I don't come home. I just want to be with my wife."

"Man, who would have thought me telling you about your dream woman almost two years ago would lead to this?" He smiles. "But nonetheless, I'm happy for you."

"Two years." I shake my head. "Feels like yesterday and forever ago at the same time."

Harry raises his glass. "To retirement. And to Karina for finally getting you to slow the hell down."

I clink my bottle against his glass. "She didn't ask me to retire, you know. This was my decision."

"Just like it was your decision to buy that ridiculously expensive stroller last week."

"That stroller has an advanced suspension system and ergonomic handle heights," I protest, but laugh at myself. "Fine. I've gone soft. Happy?"

"Ecstatic." Harry grins. "Seriously though, what's the plan? You gonna be one of those stay-at-home dads who bakes organic muffins and runs a mommy blog?"

"Fuck off," I scoff. "I'm still going to help out with the department." With some of the money I was allowed to access after Karina and I got married, I've been secretly funding upgrades for Station 112. I know Harry and Mike had their suspicions when things started being replaced and actually became functional, but I kept with my story of an anonymous donor. They don't buy it, but they haven't said anything, and for that I'm grateful.

"And I'll be joining the board of directors for the Firefighters' Family Foundation," I add, running my thumb over the label of my beer bottle. "They've been pestering me for eight months now, and it feels like the right time. I can help raise money, do some consulting work, maybe even mentor some of the newer guys."

Harry nods slowly, considering this. "That actually sounds perfect for you. Still keeping a foot in the door without having to run into burning buildings."

"Exactly." I drain the last of my beer and signal the bartender for another round. "Plus, I want to be there for Karina. This pregnancy hasn't been easy on her."

"How's she doing with the morning sickness?"

"Better now that she's in the second trimester, but she's still working too damn hard." I can't help the protective edge that creeps into my voice. "I've been trying to get her to cut back her hours, but you know how she is."

Harry chuckles. "Stubborn as they come."

"That's putting it mildly." I smile, remembering how she worked through her shift yesterday despite throwing up twice. Her boss finally got her to reduce her load, focusing on consultations and training residents. I know she wants to open shelters near St. Mary's, but not while she's pregnant. I've put my foot down about that when she first asked for my opinion on it.

"Shelters?" Harry raises an eyebrow when I tell him her long-term plan. "Like homeless shelters?"

"Yes, she's been researching it for almost two years. They've been cracking down on ER bed misuse, and my wife wants to create shelters with temporary housing and medical care for those who don't need emergency treatment but have nowhere else to go."

"She sounds like you."

"She's incredible." I can't keep the pride out of my voice. "But right now, I just want her to focus on staying healthy. The rest can wait until after the baby comes."

Harry studies me for a moment. "You know, I never would have pegged you for the retiring type. You lived and breathed the job."

"I still love the work," I say, running my hand through my hair. "But my priorities have shifted. I used to think it was everything. Now I know it's just what I did, not who I am."

The bartender slides two fresh beers across the bar, and I take a long pull from mine. The familiar burn of alcohol hits my throat, but it doesn't provide the same comfort it used to. Nothing feels quite the same anymore, actually. Everything is filtered through this new lens of fatherhood and being a husband who wants to be present.

"Have you told anyone at the station yet?" Harry asks. "Or am I the only lucky one?"

"I'm planning to announce it next week, but as my best friend I thought you should be the second to know. However, I will finish out this month and then transition into the consulting role." I pause, thinking about the conversations I'll need to have. "Mike's going to lose his shit."

"Yeah, he will." Harry laughs. "But he'll understand. They all will. This is the right move for you, Vulcan."

I nod, feeling more certain about my decision with each passing day.

"And Karina? How does she really feel about it?" he adds.

"She cried when I told her," I admit. "Happy tears, though. Said she was proud of me for choosing our family."

"Damn." Harry shakes his head. "You really did find your person."

"I did." My mind drifts to Karina at home, probably curled up on the couch with one of her medical journals, unconsciously resting her hand on her growing belly. "I never thought I'd be the guy who retires early to be a family man, but here we are."

"And you're happy about it?"

"Happier than I've ever been," I say without hesitation. "For the first time in my life, I'm not just surviving day to day. I'm actually building something that matters."

I walk into the penthouse and am greeted by laughter from Karina, Cassie, and Val in the kitchen. And here I thought she was going to be home alone. For a moment, I just watch them—Karina's belly noticeably rounder beneath her sweater as she laughs with her friends. Cassie wipes down the counter, shaking her head at whatever Val just said.

"Are we having a party I wasn't invited to?" I ask, dropping my keys in the bowl by the door.

Three heads turn my way, but it's Karina's face that I focus on—the way her eyes light up when she sees me, the slight parting of her lips before they curve into a smile.

"Vully! How was your man-date with Harry?" Val asks, making kissy sounds.

"It wasn't a date," I grumble, moving toward Karina.

"Did you tell him?" Karina tilts her face up for a kiss.

I press my lips to hers, lingering a moment longer than necessary. She tastes like a combination of cream cheese and mustard. I don't even want to know what she ate; her pregnancy cravings are out of this world. "Yeah, I told him."

"And?" Her eyes search mine.

"And he's happy for me. For us." I rest my hand on her belly, feeling the firm roundness beneath my palm. Our child.

"Good." She covers my hand with hers.

"What's all this?" I gesture to the spread on the counter—what looks like the remnants of some kind of cooking experiment.

"Your wife had a craving that included two ingredients that should *not* go together." Val shudders.

"Mustard–cream cheese bagels with pickle slices and hot sauce," Cassie explains, looking both amused and horrified. "Your child has interesting taste. I bet once he gets to kindergarten, he will eat glue."

"Shut up," Karina and Val say in unison.

I laugh, moving to grab a bottle of water from the fridge. "Well, at least Karina's eating. Last week it was all dry toast and ginger ale."

"And for the record, it was delicious."

Val makes gagging noises as she reaches for her gym bag. "I'm heading out before you start describing it in more detail. Some of us still have functioning taste buds."

"You're just jealous," Karina says, popping the last bite of her bizarre creation into her mouth.

"Of morning sickness and food that would make a garbage disposal revolt? Hard pass." Val kisses Karina's cheek, then mine. "I'll see you both on Sunday for brunch?"

"We'll be there," I confirm, watching as my sister heads for the door.

Cassie finishes wiping down the counter. "I should get going, too. I have an early shift at the hospital."

"Thanks for coming over," Karina says, giving Cassie a hug. "It was nice having company while Vulcan was out."

"Anytime. You know I love spending time with you and my nephew." She gathers her purse and heads toward the door. "And congratulations again on the retirement decision. I think it's wonderful."

After they leave, the apartment feels quieter, more intimate. I watch Karina move around the kitchen, putting away the bagels. She's moving slower these days, more carefully, and I notice the way she pauses to rest her hand on the small of her back.

"Come here," I say, taking her hand and moving to the living room. We sit on the sofa, and she curls up against my side with a contented sigh. I wrap my arm around her, my hand automatically finding its way to her belly.

"How was your day really? Any more calls from blocked numbers?" Gabriella has been calling her for weeks. I suggested changing her number, but Karina refused; she's had it since high school. So, threatening a lawsuit was the next best thing.

"No, thank God. I think Minji's letter finally scared her off." She tilts her head to look up at me. "Thank you for helping me."

"There is no need to thank me. It's my job to protect you and make sure you're happy." I run my fingers through her hair, kissing her forehead. "Speaking of which, how are you feeling? Any more nausea today?"

"Just a little this morning, but nothing like last week." She shifts against me, getting more comfortable. "The doctor said it should continue to improve as I get further into the second trimester."

"Good. Valentine's Day is just a few weeks away, and I'd love to take you out. I've been thinking we should visit one of the properties my father left me."

"I thought you had to wait three years…"

"Not for the properties. I want to take you to the one in London."

Her eyes widen with excitement. "Really? Are you serious?"

"Yeah." I tuck a strand behind her ear. "Plus, I think a babymoon in London sounds perfect. We can tour the property, walk through Hyde Park, eat at those little cafés you're always talking about."

"But what if the pregnancy makes flying difficult? What if—"

I silence her with a soft kiss. "We'll talk to Dr. Larsen first, get medical clearance. If she says it's safe, we go. If not, we wait until after the baby comes."

Karina's hand moves to her belly, a gesture that's become second nature to her. "A babymoon in London," she murmurs, testing the words. "That sounds incredible."

"Then it's settled. I'll start making arrangements tomorrow." I pull her closer, breathing in the familiar scent of her shampoo. "I want to give you the world, Karina. Starting with London."

She turns in my arms, her eyes shimmering with unshed tears.

"You've already given me everything I never knew I wanted. A home, a family, love that feels safe." Her voice breaks slightly. "I used to think I'd never have this."

"Well, you do. You have me, and you have our baby, and you're never going to lose either of us." I cup her face, my thumb brushing away a tear that's escaped. "I promise you that."

She leans into my touch, and I feel that familiar surge of protectiveness, stronger now than ever. This woman, this incredible, stubborn, brilliant woman who's carrying my child—she's my entire world.

"I love you," she whispers against my palm.

"I love you too. Both of you." My hand finds her belly again, and I swear I can feel something flutter beneath my palm. "Did you feel that?"

Karina's eyes go wide. "Oh my God, yes. Was that—"

"The baby just said hello to Daddy," I say, grinning like an idiot. Our first real movement, tangible proof that our child is growing strong inside her.

And in this moment, in our home, feeling our baby move for the first time, I know with absolute certainty that picking Karina two years ago was the right choice. This—right here, right now—this is everything.

Epilogue

Seven Years Later

"Honey, you can't be serious." Karina looks down at me, my face buried between her legs.

I suck on her clit, glancing up at her and watching her eyes roll to the back of her head. I release her and kiss it. "Oh, I'm very serious," I answer, my breath hot against her sensitive skin.

She shivers, her fingers tangling in my hair. "It's the twins' birthday; we need to be out there with the rest of the family," she says, her voice trembling between words. But her body betrays her, arching toward me, seeking more. I love how she is always so greedy for my touch.

I chuckle softly, my tongue tracing a slow path that makes her gasp. "They're busy with their presents, trust me. A few more minutes won't hurt." My hands grip her thighs, holding her steady as I deepen my attention, savoring the way she trembles under my touch.

Karina's breath hitches, her fingers tightening in my hair. "You're impossible," she whispers, but there's no real frustration in her voice, only a desperate want that mirrors my own.

I take my time, teasing her with slow, purposeful strokes, drawing out every little sound she tries to suppress. Her hips shift restlessly, and when I finally slip a finger inside her, she lets out a sharp moan that she quickly muffles with her hand.

"Don't," I say, pulling back just enough to make eye contact. "I want to hear you."

"Vulcan, we are in the *pantry*. Someone is going to hear us."

The way her body clenches around my finger tells me she's far from wanting me to stop. I smirk, leaning close, my lips brushing against her inner thigh as I speak. "Let them hear." I nip her skin. "Let them know how much you're mine."

Karina's eyes flutter shut, a soft whimper escaping her lips as I slide another finger inside her, curling them just the way I know she likes.

"Vulcan, it's our sons' birthday party. Everyone here knows I'm yours. We are with family." She's trying to plead her case. "I—fuck, baby—" Her words become a breathless moan as I suck on her clit.

Her body arches off the counter, her hands scrambling to grip the shelves behind her, knocking over a jar of olives that rolls toward the edge. I catch it with my free hand and set it aside with a low laugh.

I suck on her clit faster before pulling back. "Careful, love, you don't want to get caught, remember?"

Karina groans, half in pleasure, half in exasperation. I stretch her slowly, savoring the way her breath hitches and her body trembles. Her skin is warm against my lips as I trail kisses up her round stomach. Karina is pregnant with our fourth child, and her belly is just beginning to show a soft curve.

"Vulcan," she gasps, her voice trembling. "Thalia is probably looking for us. God, don't stop—"

Karina is probably right. Thalia, our three-year-old, could be looking for us or, more likely, she's looking to make sure we aren't around so she can sneak some cake. "Lia's probably with Val," I whisper against her skin, my lips brushing the curve of her breast through the thin fabric of her dress. "And even if she isn't, my mother has eyes on her. You're mine right now, and nothing or no one will change that."

Her hands fist in my hair, tugging lightly, nails scraping gently against my scalp. I continue to finger fuck her faster than before and I can feel her getting close, her body tightening around me, her breath coming in short, uneven gasps. I press my lips just below her ear and whisper, "Come for me."

She does, with a muffled cry that she buries in the crook of my shoulder. Her body trembles as she falls apart, and I hold her through it, my fingers slowly easing their pace until she slumps against me.

"My sweet, sweet wife, you've deprived me. I wanted to hear you scream my name until your voice was raw."

She rolls her eyes but doesn't argue as she straightens up. She smooths her dress down over her hips, but I can still see the outline of her nipples pressing against the fabric, hard and begging for my mouth. She reaches for the jar of olives I'd saved from disaster earlier. "We should get back out there before they start wondering where we are."

"Yeah," I agree, though I don't move right away. Instead, I lean in to kiss her, but she pulls back quickly.

"Go," she says, pushing me toward the door with a smile. "Before they come looking for us."

I catch her hand before she can pull away entirely and press a kiss to her palm. "You owe me later, and tonight, I want you gagging on my cock until tears are streaming down your face. I want to fuck your throat so hard you can't speak for a week. And when I'm done with your mouth, I'm bending you over the bed and burying myself so deep inside you, you'll feel me for days."

I can see the way her thighs clench together, like she's already imagining it. "Come on, babe, just go." This time, it's a plea, not a command.

I smirk, giving her one last lingering look before I finally head for the door. But not before I promise myself and her that tonight, I'm going to wreck her in the best possible way.

I walk out of the pantry first, and Valkyrie walks into the kitchen carrying a sleeping Thalia. "There you two are. I was starting to think you two ran off to have s-e-x." Valkyrie's eyes bounce between Karina and me. "Here, take her. I have to go back out there and make sure my husband doesn't teach the boys bad words. Can you believe yours are already six? Time flies."

I laugh and take Thalia from Valkyrie's arms, her little head lolling against my shoulder as she mumbles incoherently in her sleep. She smells like lavender baby shampoo and the faintest hint of chocolate cake, probably from the cupcake she'd snuck earlier. As I adjust her weight against me, her tiny hands clutch my shirt.

"Wait, you didn't answer… were you two having s-e-x?" Val probes.

"You don't have to spell it out. Lia is asleep, and no, we weren't. And if we were, that's none of your business. It's my house and my wife," I respond.

"Ya nasty." Val smirks and leaves the kitchen.

Karina stands beside me, reaching for Thalia. "I can put her to bed."

"How about we both put her to bed?" I wink.

"No, because once you get me upstairs, I know I'm not coming back down."

She's right, of course. If I get her upstairs, there's no way I'm letting her slip away before I've made good on every promise I just made.

"Fine." I place a kiss against Karina's temple as she gently takes Thalia from my arms. The little one stirs slightly, her dark lashes fluttering against her cheeks before she settles back into sleep. Karina cradles her with that natural ease she has with kids, something that still surprises me, given how much of her life she's spent in the sterile chaos of an ER rather than the warmth of a home.

"Be quick." I trail my fingers down her arm. "Or I might just come up there and fuck you senseless."

Karina's cheeks flush a deep crimson, but she doesn't falter. She gives me that look—the one that's half challenge, half surrender—before turning on her heel and heading toward the stairs. I watch her go, and the sway of her hips in that dress makes my dick rock hard. My fingers twitch with the urge to follow her, but I force myself to stay put. For now.

I look through the patio door to see all our friends having a great time. Our twins, Sebastian and Nathaniel, are in the pool with their cousins and Val's husband. They're having the time of their lives, not worried in the slightest about Mommy and Daddy. My eyes move over to see Valkyrie hovering near the pool like the concerned mother hen she is.

Our friends are managing to mingle despite their kids running around. Everyone is enjoying themselves, and I don't see why I can't. I turn on my heels and make my way upstairs. My dick is begging to be buried in Karina. My appetite for Karina is and will forever be something I could never get enough of.

Karina quit her job at St. Mary's a year after the twins turned one. I retired officially from all things FDNY once Thalia was born. With the money from my inheritance and some fundraising expertise from our old friend Sarah Fletcher, Karina open two shelters and her own practice. She wanted to spend more time at home with the children, but also still give back to the community.

The sound of Karina's soft humming drifts from Thalia's room, and I pause, leaning against the door frame to watch her. She's bent over the toddler bed, smoothing the blanket over our sleeping daughter with tender care.

I can't help but think how fucking lucky I am to have her.

Karina straightens and turns, her eyes widening slightly when she sees me. "I thought I told you to wait downstairs," she whispers. "I don't know who is more hard-headed, you or the boys."

"You did," I say, gesturing for her to come here with my finger. "And you know I've never been good at following instructions."

She steps out of the room, closing the door softly behind her, and I'm on her in an instant. My hands grip her waist, pulling her flush against me. Her breath hitches as I pin her to the wall, my lips finding hers in a kiss that's all hunger.

"For a man pushing fifty, your sex drive is insatiable," she murmurs against my mouth, but she's already arching into me.

"And you love it," I slide one hand up to cup her breast through the thin fabric of her dress. Her nipple hardens under my touch, and she lets out a soft moan that goes straight to my dick.

"We have to go back downstairs," she says, but her hips are already grinding against mine.

"No one's going to miss us." I nip at her neck. "Val's got the kids, and everyone else is too busy drinking and laughing. Let me have you. Today is your special day, too. You birthed those little boys, so you deserve another push present."

"The last time you said that was on Thalia's birthday, and look. I'm pregnant."

"At least you know this push present won't get you pregnant."

She hesitates momentarily, pulling me down the hallway toward our bedroom. "Fine, make it quick and do not leave marks where the guest can see."

I don't need to be told twice. As soon as the door closes behind us, I'm on her again. Ten years ago, I never would have thought I'd be here, bound in marriage to the woman who sets my heart ablaze. All it took was one look from across Riley's and Karina Montgomery has become the keeper of my soul, mine to cherish, mine to adore forever.

Acknowledgments

First and foremost, shout to Vulcan and Karina for popping into my head two years ago—without you, there would be no book.

To Janelle—Thank you for sitting on the phone with me for over an hour as I mapped out this book and the entire series. You always listen to me ramble without rushing me off the phone, and you truly try to give input even when it doesn't make sense. Still, I appreciate you, and I can't wait to ramble some more.

To Josseline—I don't want you to cry, so *here damn*! lol

To Annmarie—You saw my manuscript in its roughest form. From typos to barely existing scenery lol, and I thank you for your keen eyes and your endless excitement about this project! Thank you for being one of the biggest cheerleaders for Vulcan and Karina.

To Britt—I can't put into words how *thankful* for you I am! You swooped in, helped polish my manuscript, and I'm not sure this final copy would be close to what it is now without you. I can't wait to work with you in the future. Now, I'm giving everyone names and making sure I have months and dates lol!

To Jas and Christie—my beta readers, thank you two for your honesty, support, and overall feedback for this book. (Especially you, Jas, because we are not slow-burning girlies, yet I wrote it and you read it lmao.)

To Edgar—Thank you for helping with translations (even though most of them didn't make the cut after editing lol.) And just being my hype man over the last several months. Also, thank you for letting me use your last name lol. YOU DA BEST!

To my Readers—whether you are new to me or have been following me since my Wattpad days (est. 2016) —thank you for continuing this journey with me. I look forward to sharing more stories about men who are down bad for their women with you.

Lastly, to my PA Bianca… Where to begin? You've truly lifted a weight off my shoulders and truly are the cheer captain for me and my books. I will never get tired of your 2 am – 6 am messages lol (I secretly love waking up to reading what you've been working on lol). You handle sooooo many things at once and truly do it with a smile on your face and never complain. I thank you so much for what you do. We're stuck together *foreva*!

About The Author

Jessica Powell writes steamy contemporary romances where magnetic alpha heroes collide with quick-witted heroines in stories brimming with humor, heat, and emotional truths. She believes in love stories where the bedroom steam fogs up your glasses and the emotional growth makes you ugly-cry into your wine. Whether penning billionaires brought to their knees by free-spirited creatives or reformed playboys disarmed by single moms, Jessica crafts diverse, character-driven escapes where happily-ever-afters demand humility as much as desire.

When not reading or writing, she spends her free time traveling, rewatching *Wiseman Grandchild* (yes, again), binge-watching Chinese short dramas, or spending way too much time playing Sims 4.

She lives for connecting with readers who crave romances as bold and nuanced as they are. Follow her on Instagram [@authorjessicapowell] or subscribe to her newsletter at [authorjessicapowell.com] for behind-the-scenes glimpses, exclusive excerpts and updates on her next novel.